Additional Acclaim for *Century's Son*

"There is no novelist in America now who writes about emotional secrets and the hoarding of private pass insight than Robert Boswell. He writes erosity of spirit about all his characters, h mal; if the word 'humane' means anything have to learn, or re-learn, its definition fro
—Charles Baxte.

"Robert Boswell is an author preoccupied with the questions of how to be good and how to have integrity, and how to sort them out when they seem mutually exclusive. The result is a novel that . . . is stunning."
—*Milwaukee Journal Sentinel*

"If Oprah hadn't curtailed her book club, she might consider this novel . . . It's a humane, plain-spoken, and insightful novel about human foibles and, ultimately, a certain kind of redemption."
—*The Boston Globe*

"Terrific . . . *Century's Son* is a novel about the secret emotional lives of families, what goes unspoken and why. Rather than invoking this theme dramatically, Boswell keeps the focus on his characters' interior lives, which he limns with elegant precision."
—*St. Louis Post-Dispatch*

"A wonderfully generous story about the singular, though bedeviling, matters of the heart."
—*Charlotte Observer*

"A luminous novel . . . The texture of this portrayal of Middle America and its discontents suggests an inspired collaboration between Anne Tyler and John Cheever. . . . Only a handful of Boswell's contemporaries have written anything better."
—*Kirkus Reviews* (starred review)

"A moving portrait of a family united and divided by a tragic loss, a subtle meditation on moral responsibility, and a slyly funny comedy of errors, *Century's Son* is a heartbreaking, ultimately exhilarating novel by one of America's finest writers."
—Tom Perrotta, author of *Election*

Also by Robert Boswell

Century's Son

Robert Boswell

PICADOR
NEW YORK

www.picadorusa.com

Picador® is a U.S. registered trademark and is used by St. Martin's Press under
license from Pan Books Limited.

For information on Picador Reading Group Guides, as well as ordering, please
contact the Trade Marketing department at St. Martin's Press.
Phone: 1-800-221-7945 extension 763
Fax: 212-677-7456
E-mail: trademarketing@stmartins.com

Library of Congress Cataloging-in-Publication Data

Boswell, Robert.
    Century's son / by Robert Boswell.
        p. cm.
    ISBN 0-312-42231-8
    1. Political science teachers—Fiction. 2. Sanitation workers—Fiction.
3. Teenage pregnancy—Fiction. 4. Russian Americans—Fiction. 5. Suicide
victims—Fiction. 6. Women teachers—Fiction. 7. Middle West—Fiction.
I. Title.

PS3552.O8126 C46 2002   200108101

First published in the United States by Alfred A. Knopf,
a division of Random House, Inc.

First Picador Edition: July 2003

P1

For my brother Terry

*The author wishes to acknowledge the following
people for their help and support:*

Terry Boswell, Antonya Nelson, Ash Green,
Charles Baxter, Kim Witherspoon, Gretchen Mazur,
Barry Mazur, Stuart Brown, Kevin McIlvoy, Alex Parsons,
Don Kurtz, Susan Nelson, Steven Schwartz,
Emily Hammond, David Schweidel, Peter Turchi,
Margaret Malamud, Leslie Coutant

Century's Son

1

Strengths and weaknesses are the same thing, the valuable and the invaluable.

—Peter Ivanovich Kamenev

It is amazing the things people throw away.

The doors leaned against a high plank fence in the narrow alley, old doors with arched windows, brass plates, and faceted glass knobs. A patina of frost made them glitter in the truck's headlights. Morgan drank the last sip of coffee from the lid of his thermos and climbed from the cab of the garbage truck. The doors had heft. Oak, he guessed, solid boards joined by a craftsman long dead. The windows showed runnels from the settling of the glass. In the predawn light, Morgan's breath eddied about the wrinkled glass, spreading over his distorted reflection like an erasure.

Morgan's partner rounded the truck to join him. "These are their front doors," Morgan said. "Why would people toss their front doors?"

Danny Ford didn't answer but began climbing the metal ladder to the roof of the garbage truck. Danny was a huge man, and the truck rocked as he climbed, creaking as if it might tumble over. Morgan was broad-shouldered himself, and tall. As he approached fifty, his body had become more dense and a fleshiness had entered his face, but he was still in good shape, and he had always been strong. Danny Ford, however, was in a different category. Just a kid, but built like a mountain.

< 3 >

Morgan gingerly lifted one of the doors and passed it up. Danny took it from him with one hand, raising it easily, holding it as one might hold a notebook, then turned and laid it gently on the roof of the truck. He wore the hard hat the city provided, and as he bent to take the second door, the hat fell off. Morgan snatched it out of the air just as Danny lifted the door from Morgan's hands. Like a circus act, Morgan thought.

"Hat," Danny called, holding the door at his side. Morgan tossed it up to him. Danny caught it with one hand, slipped it on, then placed the second door on top of the first and strapped them down with bungee cords. Despite his size and the fact that he was stoned, he maneuvered nimbly around the roof in the semidark.

Morgan's first name, weakened from disuse, had long ago fallen off, and he had never bothered to retrieve it. He was simply Morgan. Except for two semesters at a state university, he had lived all his life in Hayden, Illinois. The year was 1999, and Morgan had worked as a garbageman for almost a quarter of a century. It was not how he had planned to spend his life. Originally he had thought of the job as something to tide him over until the real terms of his future revealed themselves.

Still, despite his lengthy tenure in garbage, the things people threw away surprised him. He had hauled off refrigerators that merely needed cleaning, gas stoves cast off by people who decided to go electric, and electric stoves abandoned by those wanting gas. Appliances often bore signs that read FULLY OPERABLE or simply WORKS. Boxes of toys appeared during spring cleaning, couches bearing a single stain, lamps requiring only a new cord. He had even come across laundry—clothes that needed nothing but a wash. He marveled at the array of trash, the mass of it, the variety, the value, the bulk.

He and Danny worked the remainder of the alley. There had once been a third member to the crew, but the city had cut back in anticipation of the new trucks they had ordered. One day Morgan would work alone in an air-conditioned cab, operating a mechanical arm that would raise and empty canisters made of recycled plastic. Danny Ford would be offered something in Parks and Recrea-

< 5 >

tion, Morgan guessed, or a janitorial position. Danny had made it through his probationary period. His job was secure.

Morgan pulled the truck into the street instead of the next alley. "The glass in those doors will crack if we don't drop them off directly," he said. The doors would go to the union store, a crafts and secondhand shop that Morgan himself had set up. Profits went into a fund used for everything from sponsoring a soccer team to helping out an employee whose daughter had leukemia. A box of donuts slid down the dashboard as Morgan wheeled the truck around the corner, and Danny slouched forward to save it.

Morgan stopped in front of the house that had discarded its doors, a graceful old brick place with a shabby lawn. A fir tree obscured his view, and he had to lean low to peer beneath the limbs. The new doors were made of glass with push bars at waist level.

"Grocery-store doors," Danny said.

"This job never disappoints," Morgan replied. He shoved the idling truck into gear. Drop-offs at the union store were done on their own time, each trip costing them some clock. Their new contract gave them this flexibility. Morgan used it to work ten-hour days, four days a week. He turned onto Lincoln Street without stopping, catching the yellow portion of the traffic light. "So about my father-in-law," he said, and Danny moaned.

"Don't start your sales pitch this early," Danny said. "Makes me dread the whole day."

Morgan's father-in-law was moving in. There was going to be a reception on the day he arrived, which was a workday, and Morgan didn't think he could make it unless Danny agreed to come along in the truck. "Thought maybe you'd change your mind," Morgan said. "You really ought to meet him."

Danny Ford sank deeper into his corner, shrugging with the slightest movement of his shoulder. "What the fuck for?" Below the hacked-off sleeve of his shirt, a crude tattoo on his forearm proclaimed PUSSY in a blue scrawl that stood out against his pale skin. The boy never seemed to tan. Morgan assumed the tattoo spoke of desire and not cowardice. Danny Ford did not strike him as a coward. He had a criminal record—gang activities that had ended after he took this job. Morgan seemed to be one of the few people who could tolerate him; he had even fudged some figures to get Danny through the probationary period. Danny could do the work but was habitually stoned, chronically late, and missed a lot of Mondays. Now he snorted and knocked his head against the window, the hard hat tapping the glass. "What do *I* need with some thousand-year-old caveman?"

"He's just a hundred," Morgan said. "And my wife says he's lying about that." Zhenya Kamenev, Morgan's wife, was a college professor, a precise, exacting woman who nevertheless became a child in the presence of her father. It was the only thing about the old man's arrival that Morgan looked forward to. "She's got some ideas about him," he continued. "But why would anybody lie to make himself older?"

Danny had met Zhenya maybe once or twice. He would rarely condescend to visit Morgan's home. The men Morgan worked with—not kids like Danny, but the men he had known for decades—considered Zhenya to be his big mystery. Everyone who worked a job like this eventually had some kind of secret life. One man Morgan knew constructed elaborate birdcages. There was a Parks and Rec man who had a collection of antique pornography. Morgan had Zhenya: an attractive woman, but terrifying to most of the men he knew. Too sure of herself. Too smart and quick with her tongue. A political scientist, for Christ's sake. Why would a guy like Morgan wind up with a woman like that?

"I *do* like his deal," Danny said suddenly, shifting slightly in the corner to lean against the door. "Good story, the coulda-killed-that-prick story."

"That prick was Joseph Stalin," Morgan said. Then he added, "Lock your door if you're going to lean against it."

A response glided over Danny's face, something less than a smirk. He was a genius at the conservation of movement.

"He's famous," Morgan said. "Almost. He used to be on TV a lot, talking about one thing or another—civil rights, revolution, politics, that kind of stuff." He recalled watching baseball on television, the phone ringing, and Zhenya running in to change the channel because her father was on a political program, a panel of men

< 7 >

in suits discussing some issue or other. Morgan remembered the rush of excitement they felt when her father's face appeared on the screen, and how Zhenya settled in next to him, tucking her feet beneath the hem of her skirt. Those memories were good but distant and entirely separate from dealing with the actual Peter Ivanovich Kamenev, who was a pain in the ass.

They turned onto Illinois Avenue, which took them under Interstate 55. The intersection of Interstates 55 and 155 inscribed a Y on the city of Hayden right in the center of Illinois. "Peter's uncle was one of the main guys in the Russian Revolution," Morgan said.

"Yeah, yeah," Danny said. "I don't need another history lesson."

"He's known a bunch of famous people."

"Like who?"

"Lenin and Stalin. Freud. Franklin Roosevelt. Warren Beatty. There's a picture of him with Einstein. He marched with Martin Luther King. Did . . . *something* with Albert Schweitzer. Fished with Hemingway. Bitched about whatnot with Eldridge Cleaver. Supposedly he went with Bill Clinton to a strip show when Clinton was governor of Arkansas. You name it, he's done it."

"He fucked Madonna?"

"Okay," Morgan said, "he missed a couple of national events, but not many. He doesn't like me much. Thinks I'm wasting my life. He was a big deal in the sixties. Still is in university circles." Morgan was going to share his house with the man and wanted to find a way to like him. "He halfway respects me for the union stuff, though he seems to wish I'd shot someone or gotten shot myself."

Danny showed his teeth at that.

"What? You like the idea of my getting shot?"

He didn't answer. The smile was childish, and Morgan was reminded of the limitations of their partnership. Some days Danny said nothing at all, just grunted and glowered. Morgan suspected that Danny would be in prison if he didn't have this job.

As they headed toward the union store, light began to enter the sky and Morgan, as he often did, let his thoughts turn to his son, focusing today on the boy's skill with a bicycle. Philip could stand on the seat of a moving bike as if it were a skateboard. Morgan still took pride in his son's talents even though he had been dead almost a decade. Every day Morgan called him to mind, on his best days and his worst, when he was with his grandson, Petey, at miniature golf, or when he had stood over his own father's casket.

Philip had killed himself. Morgan tried to think of it honestly, though he wouldn't use the word "suicide." It was supposed to mean the same thing, but it seemed different.

His son had gotten into an argument with other kids while playing ball. He had been twelve years old and high-strung, a boy who often got into tiffs. One of the neighbors sent him home. It had been a warm August day. Morgan had been across town, at the dump, on his last run of the afternoon—he had calculated the time and his placement in the world a hundred times. Zhenya heard Philip storm in. She was working in her study and sent him to his room—the same thing a thousand other parents were doing that summer's day. When Morgan got home, she told him about the incident. "He's going to have to learn the hard way," she said. Morgan couldn't remember what else his wife said, all the other sentences that kept him from going immediately to the boy's room. He just remembered the one: "He's going to have to learn the hard way."

When Morgan checked on Philip, he found him at the foot of the bed. He had wrapped an electrical cord—an extension cord—around the bedpost and then around his neck. When he passed out, he hanged himself. A prank. A little acting out. He had only meant to make a show, Morgan believed, to display his rage. Every kid now and again thought how sorry his parents would be if he were dead. Philip let it go too far. Not a suicide, Morgan believed, although his son had killed himself. A prank, but Philip was gone.

And he had been right. His parents were sad and sorry, and for years it seemed they would never get better. Morgan wasn't certain he and Zhenya could have survived together if not for their daughter. She had saved them by getting pregnant. At first it had seemed like another tragedy. Emma had been ten when her brother died and only fourteen when she became pregnant. Even now Morgan did not know who the father was. But the pregnancy had given them a new focus. Nothing could make up for the loss of Philip, but at times it seemed that one disaster had countered the other, a double negative.

< 9 >

The union store wasn't yet open. Morgan parked in the alley and unlocked the gate. Danny climbed to the top of the truck to release the straps. They weren't the first to visit. A toaster oven, its chrome besmirched by a melted bread wrapper, sat on the rear stoop. The wrapper's letters were reversed, and the plastic, like the old glass in the doors, had wrinkled. HEALTH NUT, the wrapper proclaimed. Now and again it seemed to Morgan that inanimate objects tried to communicate with people. They had messages to convey. They had a need to be heard. He didn't give voice to this thought. It was not the kind of thing he could say to anybody.

Zhenya Kamenev declined to sit. She stood apart from the others, pacing near a high window on the back wall. The meeting was held in the overheated basement of a used bookstore, and the view from her window revealed only the gutter and the wheels of passing cars. Mrs. East had asked her to come. Zhenya was not a part of the group, and she had more work today than she could possibly accomplish, but Mrs. East had implied the meeting had to do with Zhenya's father. Zhenya had already consented to let Mrs. East hold a reception for him. Now she suspected ulterior motives.

The room had the stagnant, musty air of a tomb. New books had that wonderful smell, but they aged badly. Zhenya yanked at the metal latch to the window, which barely budged. It was April, and the weather had entered its annual crisis of faith, unable to commit to spring, unwilling to extend winter. The days were cool, then hot, then cold, then perfect, then freezing. Spring in the Midwest was not so much a season as a smorgasbord, an exam whose every answer was "all of the above." She tugged on the latch again and it gave. The cool air permitted her to breathe. Had she been holding her breath? It felt that way, even though she had been there too long for that to be possible.

Now that she could breathe, she rummaged through her purse for cigarettes. The store was not yet open for business, and she hoped she could get away with one. The owner of the bookstore professed to be sympathetic to the group's cause and volunteered the meeting space. Based on the number of flyers stapled to the walls,

Zhenya supposed he was sympathetic to all causes. Anyone with a slogan and a chip on her shoulder was a pal of his. She lit the cigarette and inhaled, propping her arm along the window ledge. She had quit smoking with her first pregnancy and had not begun again until she received the phone call from her father announcing his intention to move in. "You have plenty room there," he had told her, the accented syllables of his speech setting off the old combination of desire and dread that was her love for her father—and a similar feeling that was the longing for a smoke. "Old man like me is no trouble to daughter," he had said, and she had not then and did not now have the power to contradict him. She still had until Thursday afternoon to prepare for his arrival, but she didn't really know what to do except empty her study and move a bed into it. Stock the liquor cabinet. Count the silverware.

She had no idea how this meeting had anything to do with her father, and it was beginning to seem unlikely that she would find out. The agenda had been derailed by the lone man among them. He wanted the group to change its name. They called themselves "The Trees of Forest Avenue." A weird name for a protest group, Zhenya acknowledged, but no one else seemed bothered by it.

"It's confusing," the man insisted, "and the media isn't going to take us seriously with a name like that."

Zhenya used to know him well. Liam Haney lived at the opposite end of her block, and his children had played with hers. She and Morgan had a pool in the backyard and the Haney boys had loved to swim. It was possible that Liam's oldest son had gotten her daughter pregnant when the two were fourteen years old. It was the one topic that her daughter, twenty now, refused to discuss.

"I've made a list of names for us to consider," Liam Haney announced, fumbling through a decorated backpack he had evidently borrowed from one of his sons. Among felt marker curlicues on the bag were the words "Let's get *lanky*!" Was that a new euphemism for sex? For getting high? She wondered if Liam knew what it meant. He was a rumpled, graying man wearing dime-store eyeglasses with oversize lenses. He and his family had come to her son's funeral, but she had rarely spoken to him in the years since.

The women in the group waited patiently. Zhenya checked her

< 11 >

watch. The group met early to accommodate members who worked and it was not yet seven a.m. The nine women and one man were seated in chairs from an old dinette set and on a lumpy couch covered with a granular Indian tapestry. An armchair with erupting ticking went unoccupied. They perched around the edges of a queen-size rug, its Navajo design so stiff it looked computer-generated. Perhaps she would have joined their circle if not for the ugly rug, she thought. Though she didn't like the looks of the festering chair, either.

She had taken to wearing dresses again. Her dress had a scooped neck and long sleeves, a deep shade of blue like the evening sky. She was still thin at forty-nine, and though her features often looked tense, her face was even now unlined. *Mostly* unlined, anyway, she told herself. Besides teaching her classes today, she had promotion files to review, an article to referee, a half-dozen letters of recommendation to write, Ph.D. applicants to e-mail or call, and two committee meetings to attend. Teaching often seemed the smallest part of being a college professor.

Liam Haney finally found his wrinkled sheet of lined paper. He read the first name on his list: "People for the Preservation of History."

"Isn't that redundant?" Mrs. East asked. She was the group's organizer. Her house stood directly across Forest Avenue from Zhenya's, the corner houses where the street made a T at a small, badly kept park. When Zhenya's children were small, Mrs. East had baby-sat for them. She was in her late sixties now, a widow for as long as Zhenya had known her, a handsome woman of erect carriage and careful grooming. For the past several months, Mrs. East and the others had attended city council meetings, phoned elected officials, and written letters of protest to the newspaper. The city of Hayden meant to widen Forest Avenue, and the neighborhood group was determined to kill the plan. "What else can you do with history but preserve it?" Mrs. East continued. "If you don't preserve it, it can't be history. It's just the past."

Liam Haney said, "Are you suggesting that we call ourselves 'People for History'?"

Mrs. East shook her head. "Neither sounds appropriate to me."

That's because this has nothing to do with history, Zhenya thought. City officials had listened to their arguments, but Forest Avenue was undeniably the most direct route to connect downtown Hayden with the interstate highway. In theory, all that would be lost were slices of their yards and a strip through the middle of the park. But everyone knew what the expansion of the street really meant. Traffic would become a constant. Exhaust, dirt, noise, and litter would accompany the traffic. Businesses would replace homes. The area would die as a neighborhood and become a corridor of convenience stores, gas stations, and fast-food places. Such was not an historic event but a commonplace. The group's legal bids and lobbying had failed. This meeting was being held to discuss acts of civil disobedience.

But Liam Haney would not let them move on. The women commented on his suggestion politely while Mrs. East leaned in close to eye his wrinkled paper. From the look on her face, Zhenya guessed the list of names was long. She marveled at the forbearance of these women while, at the same time, something about their manner and bearing bothered her. Their expressions suggested the devout. They hunched forward over that awful rug as if it were a heavenly source of wisdom. They made her uncomfortable.

Liam Haney read the second name on his list, "The Forest Avenue Treenails." No one, including Zhenya, knew what a treenail was. "At first I thought 'Treetoppers,' " he said, "but then I realized that a treetopper is one who cuts trees, and that's what we're trying to stop." The widening of Forest Avenue would require the removal of more than fifty trees, including some that were as old as the dying century. At one time, dozens more trees had lined the avenue, but the elms became diseased and had to be taken down, and then a bad storm in the late eighties destroyed a number of the maples and hickories, mulberries and sycamores. Many of the trees on the avenue now were recent replacements, mere saplings. The giant mulberry that marked the corner of Mrs. East's yard was the grandest of those that had endured, an enormous and graceful tree whose branches extended all the way across the street to the edges of Zhenya and Morgan's front lawn, and whose shadow daily touched their doorstep.

< 13 >

The treenail, Liam Haney explained, was a wooden peg used in ships that would swell when it got wet. "Now *we* have become swollen with indignation," he said.

One of the bookstore employees, a young man with a ponytail who had just come down the stairs, asked if he could make a suggestion. Two men in the room, and they wanted to do all the talking, Zhenya thought. The young man said that it would be better to have a name that was not archaic. The store appeared to be one of those friendly, doomed businesses where the owner has a heart of gold and never fires anyone. He came early three days a week to let organizations meet in his dreadful basement. How much longer could such a place survive? The young man continued talking too long, but Zhenya appreciated him nonetheless. Organizations like this needed a few young men to cut through the civility.

What the group did not see was that their investment in the issue was based entirely on self-interest. Their arguments were sound enough, but they were ignoring the real need to connect the old downtown with the growing, vital perimeter of the city. It was a shame to remove the trees, but it would also be a shame for the city's downtown to founder. They could not separate the personal from the political. They confused their own memories of the neighborhood with the idea of history.

A few days earlier Zhenya had listened to a message left on the answering machine for Morgan. It was from Seth Woolrich, the city planner, and an old friend of Morgan's. Seth had been one of a handful of administrators who had supported Morgan and the formation of the union all those years ago. He and Morgan had remained friends for a time. Who were Morgan's friends now? He didn't seem to have any, not really. Sometimes he would bring home that awful thug he worked with, and there were plenty of people who were fond of Morgan, but none who were his actual friends.

Seth Woolrich, more than anyone else, was responsible for the plan to widen Forest Avenue. He had called to tell Morgan that he had tried to find another route, but it was impossible to justify the additional expense. The city owned a ten-foot right-of-way on either side of Forest Avenue, which limited the cost of the expansion. "Your neighbors seem to think I'm the devil," Seth had said on the tape. "I hope you don't feel that way. I'd love to have a beer with you sometime. It's been too long." Morgan had listened to the message, but as far as Zhenya knew, he hadn't returned the call.

The Trees of Forest Avenue was an awkward name, but kind of clever. "This is an official request from the Trees of Forest Avenue," they could say, as if the members of the group were emissaries of the actual trees, designated to speak for those who could not speak for themselves. A little self-righteous, but clever.

The boy with the ponytail now directed his attention to Zhenya. "There's no smoking in the store, ma'am."

She nodded, took a final puff, and pushed the burning end into the rusted window screen to extinguish it. She hated to be called *ma'am*. "I have to go, anyway," she said.

"You just got here," Mrs. East said, exasperated and perhaps a little angry. She quickly regained her composure. "Couldn't you stay another moment?" She tabled the discussion of names. "The city has drawn up a schedule for the destruction of our neighborhood. A *friend* has provided us with the itinerary."

Zhenya guessed that it was Morgan who had supplied the information. Someone in the union had probably slipped him the schedule.

"Tree removal starts a week from Friday," Mrs. East continued, "and they plan to begin with our own block." She nailed Zhenya with her gray eyes. "I don't know what you think we should do, but I can tell you what I *will* do. I have purchased a chain from the hardware store, and I am going to chain myself to the mulberry in the corner of my yard." She paused for a moment to let this image sink in, then added, "I would like to see all the trees on the block protected in the same fashion. People up and down the block chained to their history."

"What does this have to do with my father?" Zhenya asked.

Mrs. East nodded. "Since he is arriving approximately a week before the destruction, I was hoping we might get him to speak on our behalf. Just a word or two for the television station. I want to hold the reception for him, in any case. I'm of Russian descent myself, on my mother's side, and a man of his stature simply must receive a proper welcome to Hayden." She smiled briefly. "If he will

< 15 >

permit himself to be photographed standing next to the mulberry in the corner of my yard . . . and if he were to say a few words . . ."

"I'll ask him," Zhenya said. It was her exit line. She brushed past the boy with the ponytail and practically ran up the stairs. Her father would not be interested in saving the trees—the natural world had never meant much to him—but he would leap at the opportunity to put his face on local television.

Upstairs she found the bookstore owner lugging boxes of books. He called out a greeting to her, and she waved. The store was still not open, but the door to the street was unlocked. It occurred to her that the expansion of Forest Avenue would funnel traffic right to this door. Yet the owner supported the group anyway. A man of principle, she thought. She headed out the door before he could come over to chat.

At one point in her life, her father had been the most important person in the world to her, even though he had never lived with her mother after Zhenya's birth. Zhenya would soon live in the same house as her father for the first time. The cool morning air penetrated her stylish dress and chilled her. She folded her arms against the cold and hurried to the comfort of her car.

The blacktop road leading to the city landfill was a narrow two-lane with gravel shoulders that Morgan had to veer upon whenever he met another garbage truck. If the approaching driver was new, Morgan might have to pull over farther, slurring through mud in the spring, high grass in the summer, a crush of leaves in the fall, snow all winter long. But they were early to the dump this morning and met nobody on the road but a solitary farmer hunching over the wheel of an old John Deere. Morgan waved to him.

A gravel road intersected the two-lane, and the woods around it were a celebration of spring. Cedar and sumac thrived, as did sycamores and hickories, and someone long ago had planted a stretch of white pines. The pines grew too close together, the limbs of each intertwined with its brothers, none of them as tall as the garbage truck, the closeness of family retarding their growth. Some mornings Morgan would see deer grazing the weeds along the shoulders. Squirrel and chipmunk inhabited the trees. He had seen muskrat, owl, jay, crow, pheasant, hare, tortoise, and snake. Once he had spotted a coyote in the early hours, loping up the road, the arrogance in its eyes as radiant as high beams.

The landfill itself had a teardrop shape, large enough to be a boating lake if it were filled with water instead of garbage. The site, an old rock quarry, was rimmed by forest—a narrow cushion of nature between civilization and its rubbish. In Morgan's early years, the truck had to be driven down a dirt ramp to the dumping ground, but the pit was almost filled now. Bulldozers worked most afternoons to compress and flatten the surface. Morgan imagined the people of the future shaking their heads at the idea of just shoving trash into a hole and forgetting about it, the way adults now recalled riding as children without seat belts in the backseat of a car while their parents mixed themselves drinks in the front. It would be almost impossible to believe.

Engineers were planning to mound the garbage next. They called the project a "dross pyramid." Morgan didn't know how he'd feel about a mountain of garbage, but he had a deep affection for the existing dump. He knew it was nothing but a wound of rubbish, a place a better man would hate. Yet it fascinated him to a baffling and embarrassing extent. He tried not to talk about it.

The gravel road that circled the dump was flagged each afternoon by the bulldozer crew. Morgan had the yellow route today; a wire holding a yellow flag indicated where to dump his load. He wheeled the truck up the embankment that bordered the road, then he shoved the gearshift into reverse. The pitch of the engine altered with the strain. The truck was a relic. The union had opposed automated trucks because it meant smaller crews, but Morgan had known it was a losing argument. Technological progress, you couldn't fight. He had been president of the union for thirteen years, but when Philip killed himself, Morgan resigned shortly afterward. He pressed the accelerator, eyeing the passenger mirror to guide the truck's backward movement. Danny Ford unlatched his door, shifting the mirror's view. "Hold on," Morgan said, but Danny swung the door open and hopped out. Morgan braked to let him get clear

< 17 >

of the truck. The kid trotted away as if late for an appointment. He had surprising grace for one so thick through the limbs.

The truck did not want to move. Morgan shifted into first, careful not to give it too much gas. The truck rocked forward and he quickly shifted into reverse. Too much gas and the wheels would spin. It was easy to get stuck at the dump. He repeated the sequence twice more before the truck rolled through the soft dirt. He pulled the lever that caused the giant canister to rise and evacuate the trash.

He wished his father-in-law had another place to live. The old man was famous for a story about having the opportunity to assassinate Joseph Stalin—and failing to take it. He had worked the tale brilliantly, turning it into a study of ethics. Peter Ivanovich Kamenev had a gift for self-promotion, and the story even appeared in a few college textbooks, as if it were a part of history. And Peter had written a few books himself. Morgan had read one of them— part memoir and part political argument. A decent book, he supposed, although it had taken him six months to get through it.

The truck finished its evacuation with a metallic squeal. Morgan pushed the lever forward to lower the canister back into place. He shifted the truck into first and accelerated while easing off the clutch. The truck complained but moved. Once it shuddered to a stop on the gravel, Morgan climbed from the cab and looked for Danny.

They always took their a.m. break at the dump. Morgan would finish his thermos of coffee while Danny drank a tepid Pepsi. He had run off this morning without his Pepsi. Was it right to murder a man who was likely to do terrible things? That was the ethical question his father-in-law had posed successfully for decades now. Morgan filled the lid of the thermos with the last of the coffee. From the pile of garbage he had just dropped, an empty frame of glass winked at him.

Then he heard gunfire.

He instinctively ducked. Coffee splashed against his chest. Shading his eyes, he stared first across the sea of garbage and then down the road. Danny Ford stood at a distance in the gravel, waving. In his hand, he held what appeared to be a gun.

.   .   .

"Light was shining off it," Danny said, explaining how he had found the pistol. "It works," he added.

"I heard," Morgan said. He tried to imagine the thrill a kid like Danny would feel upon finding a gun. "You shouldn't have fired it. You shouldn't have even touched it." It had a black handle and silver shaft with sights at either end—a target pistol, not a Saturday Night Special. "We have to call this in." Weapons had to be reported, even BB rifles. A pistol required the police. "Guns make me edgy."

Danny volunteered a rare laugh, then raised the gun and fired again.

Morgan dropped to a crouch, arms bent protectively about his face. "Don't shoot that goddamn thing," he said, angry and embarrassed.

"Let's give it to the old guy you got coming," Danny said. "Like a gift."

"We've got to turn it over to the police."

"Cops?" Danny's features radically changed. "Are you kidding me? What for?"

"Rules." Morgan headed for the truck. "We're going to be here forever." He kept a cell phone in the glove box. "Wait here. You'll need to show them where you found it."

"You're joking, right? I don't want the police," Danny said, following. "I got trouble with getting the police."

"We have to report a gun," Morgan said. "You're not in trouble."

Danny grabbed his shoulder. He had a powerful grip. "Here," he said, spinning Morgan around. He tried to hand him the pistol. "*You* report it then. *You* found it."

"Don't give it to me. Put it down. Don't drop it! Just set it on the gravel there. *Gently.*" Morgan yanked on the door to the cab. "Just leave it there." He climbed behind the wheel. The truck had a busted two-way radio, but there was no longer a dispatcher anyway. The position had been eliminated during the last contract agreement. The battery light on the cell phone glowed dimly.

Danny slapped the fender of the truck. "We should give it to the old man," he said again. "Your whatcha-call-it, father-in-law."

< 19 >

"That's the last thing I want him to have." Morgan couldn't recall ever seeing his partner quite so animated. He showed Danny the phone. "This thing isn't charging. We've got to rig up something better."

"Fuck it, man. We can just toss the gun."

"Don't sweat it." Morgan pulled the door shut. He had been through this before. What bothered him was the time it took. They would be running late all week to make up for it, and he needed to finish early on Thursday. The reception Mrs. East had orchestrated for Zhenya's father would begin at the bus station and then continue at her house. Zhenya was nervous about her father moving in, and Morgan thought his making it to the reception would mean something to her. The phone screen lit up, but he didn't know the number of the police department. And he didn't want to dial 911—this didn't qualify as an emergency. He dialed his next-door neighbor, Roy Oberland, a city cop. Morgan had been at work for hours, but it was still early. Roy would likely be home.

He answered after a single ring. His wife had worked a late shift at the hospital, he said, and he didn't want the phone to wake her. Roy Oberland explained this as if to apologize for answering quickly.

"Got a situation here," Morgan said and described the discovery of the gun. "I don't want to be tied up with this all day."

"I'll see if I can't come out myself." The dump was within the city's jurisdiction, Roy told Morgan, but no one was specifically assigned to it. "My partner and I might as well take care of this." He estimated they could be there in thirty minutes.

"You're breaking up," Morgan said. "I think my phone is dying." He was cut off before he finished the sentence. Morgan reattached the phone to the charger even though it clearly wasn't working. He wanted to make it to the reception. His marriage had almost ended when Philip died. It limped along now. He and his wife slept in separate beds like characters out of a Doris Day movie. Zhenya claimed she slept better in her own bed, and he supposed that was true. "I'm tired of you waking me every morning," she had explained when she first suggested the change. Being a garbageman meant that he rose from bed at four. "Don't make more of this than what it is," she had added. He went along with it, lugging the mattresses around and setting up the beds. He probably slept better himself.

Suddenly, Danny picked up the pistol by the barrel and, in a whirling, windmill motion, sent it flying out over the dump. Morgan raised up in his seat to watch where it went. He slid over to the window. "Why the hell did you do that?"

Danny shook his head as he trotted around the cab. He threw open the door and leapt in. "Let's get going." Sweat striped his pale face.

"Come on," Morgan said. "I already called the police. We can't go anywhere." He smiled and shook his head as he slid out. Danny's irrational fear of the police amused Morgan. It was like seeing Zhenya with her father.

Morgan set out across the dump to retrieve the gun. In the old days, he had scoured the landfill every morning during his break, but the city's insurance carrier insisted that it was dangerous. Harvesting from the dump was illegal, and employees were prohibited from exploring. He liked having the excuse to hike into it. "Come on," he called again. "I'm not mad at you." But Danny didn't follow, and when Morgan stepped over the mangled handlebars of a tricycle, he began thinking again of his son. Almost anything could make him picture Philip. Morgan's grief was predatory and relentless, and to resist it felt like a betrayal of his boy.

Zhenya had not wanted their son's things given away or sold at the union store. She did not want to see a child on the street and wonder whether he was wearing Philip's clothing. One sleepless night, Morgan filled his Toyota with Philip's toys and clothing. He strapped the bicycle to the roof, wedged in an aluminum baseball bat and a shovel. During the drive, a cardboard box burst open and littered the back of Morgan's old Corolla with Philip's tiny metal cars. Morgan had taken it all out to the dump, dug a hole through the garbage, and buried it.

The memory made him stumble. He had tripped over the corner of a partially covered cage, a rusted wire thing built for a rabbit or ferret or guinea pig. The floor of the landfill had a million different surfaces, dozens of colors, patterns, messages. From a faded carton

< 21 >

of beer, a friendly tavern owner gestured to Morgan with a foamy stein, while leering cartoon faces eyed him from the back of a cereal box. Broken glass and flattened plastic containers, balled-up disposable diapers, splintered wood—couldn't any of this be redeemed? Tattered curtains encrusted with dirt lay gnarled beneath his feet. He imagined a processing plant that took old clothing and fabric, washed it, and fed it into a giant shredder before reweaving the materials into cord. There had to be something better to do with all this than to simply throw it in a hole.

Morgan cranked his head back to look for Danny. He could just make out his figure in the truck. The kid needed to understand that not every encounter with the police was destined to be an arrest. Morgan bent to lift a flap on a cardboard box. The odor of dead animal flew up his nostrils. It occurred to him that Danny had an incredible arm. Morgan kicked at a rusted can; it turned to dust.

He found the gun on top of a plastic door from a microwave oven, as if it had been placed there for viewing. Morgan picked up the weapon. It fit snugly in his hand, heavier than he expected. The microwave door held the single word QUASAR in the top corner.

He hiked back, armed now with the pistol.

Zhenya could not quit thinking about the meeting, even while she was teaching. Memory was a tricky business, how it prodded and interfered, shaped and sullied and weighed on one. At an earlier period in her teaching life, she might have simply recounted the meeting to her class, talked about its strange effect. She might have asked her students to help her understand what was bothering her or how it had anything to do with the history of U.S. involvement in Central America—which was what she was supposed to be explaining. She was no longer that kind of teacher. Perhaps the students had changed, too. They were certainly not helpful today, as distant as stars. Except for the occasional inept question, they left the talking entirely to her.

She taught one undergraduate class each academic year—a concession to the university's preference. Once she had overheard the head of her department explaining the policy to a job candidate.

"Even Zhenya Kamenev teaches undergraduate courses," he had said. Naturally, that had pleased her. Today's discussion was supposed to cover the United Fruit Company and the CIA in Guatemala, but she had trouble focusing her thoughts, and it became clear that many of students had not read the assignment. "Let's take a short break," she said. Over the years, she had written quizzes that rewarded those who had done the reading and punished those who had not. She did not like to give quizzes; they made her feel stingy. But she walked down the hall to her office, located the quiz on her hard drive, and directed her computer to print twenty-six copies.

A few minutes later, while her students scribbled anxiously to prove they had at least skimmed the assignment, she realized she no longer particularly enjoyed teaching. Her research was still important to her, but teaching no longer meant what it once had. Or perhaps this malaise was just a hangover from this morning's meeting.

The first student finished the quiz and placed it on her desk before resuming his seat. The neighborhood meeting had reminded her of something, had touched on an unhappy nerve. Her own politics had once been rooted in such groups. She had imagined her career as a college professor as only one branch of her life as a political scientist. She had pictured herself an activist—she and Morgan—protesting injustice and promoting change in the community and within the union. But the world had turned in an unpredictable fashion. The last protest march she attended had more people selling T-shirts commemorating the event than participants ready to make a statement.

Zhenya discovered that she could be most effective by doing her research, which was now internationally recognized. Still, it was conceivable that the meeting had aroused a latent feeling of guilt about the decision to give up one thing for the other. A few more students handed in their quizzes, and she leafed through them. They were surprisingly thorough, but the early finishers were always the best. It took longer to create plausible lies. She recalled the group meeting she had attended just one time after her son died. A support group. She had not liked the attitude of the people. Perhaps the women of Forest Avenue reminded her of that unfortunate crowd.

< 2 3 >

When the students finished the quiz, Zhenya decided to send them home. "If you don't read the material, you can't pass the course," she said. "And you won't learn a thing." She paused for dramatic effect, then said, "Now get out. Go home and read."

They fled. One student lingered to talk to her. She ran her finger over the class list. He could be Cliff, or maybe Alex. He wore a gray sweatshirt with the sleeves pushed up above his elbows, ragged denim shorts, and thongs—as if the university were on the beach in California instead of the plains of Illinois. "Mrs. Kamenev? I have a problem?" Cliff or Alex hooked his long locks behind his big ears. A quality of his speech made every sentence sound like a question. "You remember my asking if you would read this thing I've been writing for an incomplete I got last semester?" He pulled a stack of typed papers from his backpack. "I typed it like you said?"

She glanced at the name on the top sheet. "Where are you from, Cliff?"

"Virginia?"

The title of the essay was "What's Love Got to Do with It? Patriotism and Jewish Nationals in Nazi Germany." It made her cringe. The essay looked to be thirty pages long. "I'm not sure that I'm going to be much help with this," she said.

"If you could just, maybe, you know, tell me about the gross mistakes? My great-grandfather was a slaveholder, so I have a natural interest in this?"

Zhenya did not follow the reasoning but didn't want to ask. "Next week soon enough?"

He thanked her and headed for the door, flip-flops slapping the bottoms of his feet.

"It's April in Illinois," she said, and that stopped him. "Cover up a little. Protect yourself from the elements."

He stared at her a moment—thinking, presumably—then nodded and went on.

Zhenya's office had little to distinguish it from any other in the department, except for the large framed photograph of two naked people in such shadowy illumination as to turn their embrace into a geometry of crooks and bits of light—an original piece she had paid a small fortune for back when she was single. Last week a colleague had remarked on its beauty, saying that she preferred abstract to representational painting. Zhenya told her that it was not a painting but a photograph, and that the people in it were not only not abstract but naked and embracing. Her colleague had studied it another moment, and then suggested that it was insulting to women and should be removed.

Zhenya had almost responded with "You're a fool," but she held back just in time. "It's not a *Playboy* centerfold," she pointed out. "It's a work of art."

Her colleague didn't agree. Upon leaving Zhenya's office, she had started an e-mail campaign: *Should our students be forced to sit in the office of a professor in our department that has a photograph of an unclothed woman on the wall? Can this be viewed as anything but sexual harassment?* This had been her way of raising the question, and there were thirty e-mail exchanges about it before Zhenya knew what had happened. Almost everyone thought the photo should come down. Zhenya typed up a quick, careful response and sent it to everyone in her department. *The photograph in my office is tasteful and, I would argue, beautiful. It is neither explicit nor titillating; it is a work of art. In fact, when our colleague raising this stir first saw it, she thought it was an abstract painting. The photograph will remain on my wall. I will not be a party to any kind of censorship.*

In her e-mailbox now, a string of responses to this statement awaited her. She read a few. They were cautious because Zhenya was a powerful figure in the field and in their department, but most of the new faculty sided with Zhenya's colleague. *Art,* one of them argued, *has long been a tool of oppression.* The comment made Zhenya want to march across the hall and smack the man who had sent it. Instead, she wrote back, *If you wish to construct your private world so that it is utterly without art or with only the art that meets certain rigid requirements of correctness, that is your prerogative.*

A few of her colleagues defended her right to display the photograph, although they were careful to state that they would never hang such a thing in their own offices. With each e-mail she read, Zhenya felt increasingly alienated from the younger faculty, and now she would have to leave the photo up even if she grew tired of looking at it. She clicked off the screen.

< 2 5 >

The first six quizzes she graded were all by students who had read the work. She was pleasantly surprised and took a break to get coffee from the departmental office. Her mailbox was full of useless papers. She poured herself a cup of coffee and latched on to the newspaper, hurrying about. If she ran into the wrong person, she could be trapped talking for an hour. Posted beside the faculty mail slots, a flyer announced her father's upcoming lecture. She had reluctantly arranged the event after a colleague suggested it during a faculty meeting. She had understood that a talk by her father would be inevitable, but she had wanted to put it off until the fall semester. Her colleagues had thought it better not to wait, which reminded her that her father's current scam included his claim to be one hundred years old. He could not possibly be that old. There was no way to document his birth, but she had found references to his age in six separate sources (including a phone call to her mother) that put the year between 1914 and 1920. This discovery, in turn, led her to discredit an array of her father's claims. For instance, he professed to have been scolded as a boy by Leo Tolstoy in a rural train station. Tolstoy died in 1910.

This was not the only troubling revelation. She did not want to embarrass her father, but neither did she want his lies to discredit her own work. Decades ago, during a roundtable discussion on public television, her father had suggested that Lenin was not really the idealist he was made out to be, that the repression of the church and the media—and even the creation of concentration camps—had come directly from Lenin. The others on the panel dismissed her father's assertion. Zhenya had been in her first year of graduate school at the time, and she decided to look into it. She managed to support the claim with solid historical investigation. The article was published the year she was awarded her Ph.D., causing a controversy among Marxist scholars. Some wished to protect Lenin's image even at the expense of the truth.

Following the demise of the Soviet Union, hundreds of secret files were made public, including a few that showed Lenin to be very much as she and her father had described him. However, the files also made clear to Zhenya that her father could not have been present at *any* of the various meetings at which he claimed to have gathered his evidence. Figuring this out required a person expert in both the history of the Russian Revolution and the speeches and literature of her father. Zhenya suspected she was the only person who naturally fit into both categories, but the more lies she uncovered, the more she felt obliged to reveal them. Besides, his claim to be one hundred—an obvious lie—would be contested by somebody, and if she disclosed the discrepancies herself, pointing out that the new information validated her work even while her father's stories were discredited, she could remain an advocate of the truth without damaging her reputation as a scholar. It might even make her work better known and respected. She had no desire to destroy her father, only to separate truth from fiction, the real events from his exaggerations and stories. For that matter, she would be protecting him from harsher evaluations.

Bad coffee took her through the remaining quizzes. She had misjudged the class. Almost all of them had read the work. Only three students failed the quiz. Why had she been so certain they had not done the reading? They asked too few questions. There was a lifeless atmosphere to the classroom. Perhaps she had slipped more as a teacher than she liked to admit. Thinking this made her tired. Cliff of Virginia was among the three goldbricks. She examined his stack of dog-eared sheets. It appeared that Cliff was the only undergraduate in the United States who did not own a computer. He must have borrowed a manual typewriter from an octogenarian. The title of the essay called to mind Tina Turner and her abusive ex-husband, Ike. Zhenya did not want to imagine how they might appear in an essay about Jewish complicity in the holocaust.

It was the dishonesty that bothered her. Her thoughts turned again to the meeting of the Trees of Forest Avenue. Mrs. East had directed the group to focus on their personal loss without considering the needs of the community. They had not even attempted to suggest an alternate route for the thoroughfare. They never acknowledged that many of the "historic" houses on Forest Avenue were unoccupied. One hundred fifty thousand people lived in Hayden; were they all supposed to bow to the desires of the few families remaining on Forest Avenue? This self-inflicted blindness was an affront to the scientist in Zhenya. It was the very thing that had

< 27 >

damaged her marriage. Morgan could have been a national spokesperson for labor by now. He had been groomed for it, but he had simply turned his back, leaving nothing in his professional life but other people's waste. He had once been the kind of man who could fight the city government and win. Now he was the kind of man who did nothing. Their son's death had undone him. He wallowed in it. Men were inherently more sentimental than women. Women had to keep moving. Time meant more to them. For girls, maturing meant fertility, and while boys could screw around to their heart's content, girls got pregnant. The years were demarcated by ovulation and menstruation, the months alive in their bodies, time living within them, pushing them forward. Women were human calendars, while men could pretend they were still eighteen. Women were streams; men, puddles. Nostalgia was as male as football.

She pulled out her grade book and entered the quiz scores beside the students' names. At one time she had prided herself on knowing every student by name within the first two weeks of the semester. A form of vanity, although students liked being called by name. She looked over the list of students. She could conjure faces to match almost all the names. If she tried, and she decided that she would, she could learn their names by the end of the week. After picturing her students, she also pictured the face of Seth Woolrich, the city planner, whose message to her husband had been so kind and apologetic. It occurred to her to call him and reveal Mrs. East's plan. It was the logical, if extreme, thing to do. She thought of the bookstore owner and his support of the group even though it was against his personal interests. A rare kind of integrity.

She debated awhile before taking the phone book down from the shelf. After a moment she found the number she wanted. Seth Woolrich answered the phone himself.

"Good to hear from you, Zhenya." He sounded a little nervous. He had called Morgan, but Morgan's wife was returning his call.

"I attended a meeting this morning." She described the group's plan to chain themselves to the trees.

"Good God, what a circus that would be. That could wind up on the damn networks."

"I thought you'd want to know. *Some*one leaked the schedule for tree removal. You may want to move it up a bit. If you do, I'd keep it a secret."

"Jesus, yes. This actually simplifies matters for me," he said. "I have a crew right now—can you hold for a moment?" Music came over the phone. A Muzak version of an old rock-and-roll favorite. She couldn't think of the title—that "Ohio" song by Crosby, Stills, Nash, and Young. The phone line clicked. Seth Woolrich was back. "I should have anticipated some kind of nonsense like this. We're taking care of it, trust me."

"All right, then," Zhenya said.

"I really appreciate this." His voice changed. He was almost whispering. "But I can't keep myself from asking why you decided—"

"It's a matter of integrity," she said.

"Really?" He paused, and she could hear him breathing. "If you say so. I'm glad you understand. You happened to call at a very good time." He asked about the family before hanging up.

The malaise lifted. All she had to do was take some kind of action. Once the neighborhood was ruined, they would have to move, she realized. Funny how she had kept that thought from herself, but there it was, suddenly transparent. The widening of Forest Avenue would force them to relocate. It seemed obvious now. Their house would make a good coffeehouse or perhaps a shelter for abused women. She reached across her desk and pulled the cord on the window shade. It was still early, not yet noon. The light that entered the room was thin, like a threadbare gown. She rolled her chair over to bask in it.

Morgan sat in the garbage truck, watching the policewoman who sat beside him eat his donuts. "I don't do chitchat," she said to start the interview. Overweight, with coarse features, Officer Adele Wurtz heightened her unattractiveness by wearing a buzz cut—and smacking through the donut. "Give me the skinny." She was Roy Oberland's partner.

"He found a gun out in the trash," Morgan said, pointing at Danny Ford, who sat on his butt in the gravel. "That's it. I need to

< 29 >

get back to work." The sun was high, and he and Danny were hope-lessly behind.

She puffed out her cheeks when she shook her head, and that was all the clue Morgan needed. She was trying to be ugly—physically and in that other way, the way Morgan's mother had meant it. "That's ugly," she would say if she caught Morgan being selfish or unkind. Officer Adele Wurtz took another donut. "Start with you two driv-ing up to the trash yard. Anything happen out of the routine?"

We're going to be here until doomsday, Morgan thought. Another thing his mother had said. "All right," he said. "In order to back into the dumping area, I have to drive up that little slope there." He pointed to the embankment. "I let her roll up, and then I shift to reverse. That means I push the shifter down and over here. Shall I demonstrate?"

"You think you're being cute," Officer Wurtz said, "but I don't see it that way. Skip over a gear or two, will you?"

"While I was backing in, my partner hopped out and ran down the road there. Almost got me stuck." He hurried through the rest, leaving out Danny throwing the gun. "Then I called Roy, and you two evidently drove to China on your way over, 'cause we've been waiting a long time for the great honor of feeding you our donuts."

Adele made another pig face, then said, "Any of that coffee left?"

Morgan smiled. At least she had a sense of humor. "All out of joe," he said, and realized that was yet another expression of his mother's. What had made him think of her today? She had died not long after Philip. Pneumonia.

"One more question," she said. "He shoot at you, or you just a bleeding heart?"

"That's coffee," Morgan said.

"I get it," she said. "You're a slob."

Morgan laughed. "Guilty as charged."

Dismissed by Officer Wurtz, he went to join Roy Oberland. As he passed Danny Ford, he said, "She wants to see you now."

"No shit." He glared at Morgan but got to his feet and trudged to the truck.

Now there's an encounter of personalities, Morgan thought. He unbuttoned his shirt and yanked the tails out of his pants as he walked. He had already discarded his jacket and was ready now to strip down to his T-shirt. After a cold morning, the day was turning muggy.

Roy Oberland knelt beside a pile of plastic trash bags. They must have been dumped that morning before Morgan and Danny arrived. Bulldozers had worked the afternoon before and chewed up the bags with their treads. Morgan supposed he should point this out. If this was where Danny found the gun, it had not been there more than a day.

"It's a functional firearm," Roy said before Morgan could speak. "That may mean it was tossed after a crime." He rose from his squat, a short, handsome man in his thirties who had lived next door to Morgan for twelve or thirteen years. He took Morgan by the crook of the elbow. "You witness the discovery?"

"More or less. Danny wandered off. Then I heard shooting. I already told your partner all this."

Roy nodded.

"She's a damn attractive woman, Roy."

Roy had no interest in joking around. "How long has Ford been your partner?"

"Better part of a year."

"He's got a juvenile record that would make you shudder."

"I thought those records were erased when you turned eighteen."

"Expunged, not erased."

"What's the dif?"

"I'm not sure. It's just what's said."

Morgan explained that the bags had been dropped there earlier that day, but Roy didn't seem interested. "I've dealt with Ford myself," he said. "Not that *that's* a special privilege. Most any cop you meet will know Danny Ford. Major gangbanger."

"*Was.* He's a working stiff now. Really. He's all right. I've had him over to the house. Eats with a knife and fork, the whole nine yards."

"That's *not* a good idea," Roy said.

"What? Letting him have a kitchen knife?"

"Was your family there?"

"Of course they were there."

< 3 1 >

"Keep him away from Emma and Petey." He said it quickly, flatly, as if having to say it disgusted him. He knelt again, taking a ballpoint pen from the shirt pocket of his uniform and poking it through one of the bags. He made a long rip, freeing an orange peel and a flattened carton of milk. "If somebody tossed the gun, he might have thrown something else as well. There's no evidence of a body, but there could be gloves or shoes maybe, in case he left footprints at the site of the crime. That's what we're looking for."

Morgan squatted beside him. "If it were me, I wouldn't throw them out together. I'd toss the gun here, the gloves way over there."

Roy shrugged. "Still have to look."

"And if I was going to put anything whatsoever in a plastic bag, I'd start with the gun I wanted to dispose of."

Roy quit poking. "Why would Emma have anything to do with Ford?"

"Because he was a guest in our house."

"Jesus." Roy shook his head and stood. "That's a *very* bad idea."

"He's my partner. I know him. He's all right."

"He is *not* all right."

"Sure as hell wouldn't trade him for your partner."

Roy snorted at that, then nodded. "Don't get me started."

"Actually, I kind of like her," Morgan said. "Got a sense of humor, at least. For some reason, she made me think of my mother."

"No wonder you're a mess, if *she* reminds you of your mother." Roy stood and slipped the pen back into his shirt pocket. Officer Wurtz clambered out of the truck at the same moment and headed toward the police cruiser. Roy touched Morgan's shoulder. "I'm serious about Ford," he said softly. Then he added, "I'll see you later."

Morgan trotted to the truck and quickly had it moving. He gunned the engine as he shifted gears, and the donut box ricocheted across the dash. Danny grabbed it and tossed it out the window. "The fat one finished them off," he said.

"Chips and salsa," Morgan replied. "Cops and donuts."

Danny touched his hard hat, slid it down to cover his face. He held it there. Morgan honked at an oncoming truck to indicate he wanted through the gate first. Incoming trucks normally had the right-of-way, but he didn't have time for courtesy. "We're going to have to haul butt through the Heights," Morgan said. University Heights was the neighborhood near Hayden University. Most of the houses had three or four cans. The wealthier the neighborhood, the more trash they produced. "If I'd known we were going to have this delay, I never would have taken those doors."

"Yeah, you would have," Danny said into his hat.

"Maybe. I guess so."

Danny slid the hard hat back onto his head. "That guy arrested me once." He tapped his head against the window. "He had a different partner."

Morgan heard himself sigh. "What'd he arrest you for?"

"Fighting. He was a real prick."

This surprised Morgan. If any policeman was fair-minded, he guessed it would be Roy Oberland. "How so?"

"Clubbed me." Danny put his hand to his head and rubbed, as if reliving the injury. "Said some stuff." His voice grew soft. "He's going to fuck me on this."

"I know him," Morgan said. "He's done right by me in the past." It was Roy Oberland who had sent Philip in from the street the day the boy killed himself. Roy had suffered with them. Morgan could not believe Roy would be unfair. Besides, any man facing Danny in a fight would want at least a club. There was probably a way of explaining it. Morgan considered trying, but he didn't have much faith in his ability to carry it off. They reached the blacktop, and Morgan swerved upon the pavement without fully stopping.

"You wait and see," Danny said. "He don't like me." He settled into the corner, growing still. "I'm fucked."

"That's Charmander," Petey said, pointing at Japanese animation on the television screen.

Zhenya said, "Who does Charmander evolve into?" She knew just enough about the absurd rules of the program to make conversation with a five-year-old.

"Hoo, man," Petey said. "He's really powerful. Actually, I don't remember. But one of the most powerful ones you ever saw."

< 3 3 >

She had brought work home with her and intended to read files while the afternoon cartoons entertained Petey. His Montessori ended at one, and Emma had a class this semester on Mondays and Wednesdays that started before Morgan got home from his route. Zhenya typically watched Petey on these afternoons, although one of her graduate students filled in for her now and again, a young man who loved the cartoons himself. He claimed Japanese animation was art. Zhenya couldn't see it. The characters had halting movements, and little attempt was made to synchronize their mouths with their speech. In fact, their mouths didn't open at all; instead, a patch of color appeared on their cartoon faces that was meant to convey the idea of an open mouth. It was hardly art.

The files on her lap were thick and ungainly. She had agreed to be an outside reviewer on two tenure cases at other universities, and one of the two did not, in Zhenya's opinion, deserve tenure, which made the work tricky. The person in question was a young political scientist whose work was . . . *impressionistic*. The candidate claimed it was cutting-edge scholarship that turned its back on "the patriarchal demands of numerical justification." Which meant that her work had the appearance of a scientific survey but no statistical reliability or validity. Just her impressions of the situation. Unfortunately, some of the journals had become so polarized and politicized that she was able to publish the hooey. Whoever nominated Zhenya to be one of the woman's outside reviewers had to know that Zhenya would oppose the candidacy.

She could have worked herself up about the idiocy of current academic fashion, but instead she put the files down and walked over to the blinds, called by the mechanical bleating that accompanied the backward motion of heavy machinery. She peeked through the blinds and her heart dropped. An immense truck was parked in the street opposite her house, its headlights shining dimly in the afternoon light, the chrome lattice of its grille leering at her. She let go of the blinds and ran to her front door. She had not expected the city to act so quickly. She did not see how it was possible. "Not yet," she shouted as she bolted out the door. She checked her voice. "Not to*day*," she called more softly, scrutinizing the street for her neighbors. "Not this quickly."

A stout woman in a yellow reflector vest looked up at her briefly as she parsed orange cones from a tower she held in one arm. The truck's long bed had a gray telescopic pole with a human-size plastic bucket attached to the end. A human already occupied the bucket, a man in a brown corduroy shirt and yellow helmet. Headphones looped his neck. In his gloved hands he held a massive chain saw. He nodded in response to her gaze. She spoke to him. "It can't be today. It's too *obvious.*"

"Yeah, I guess so," he said. "You cut down all this shade, it'll make the whole street more obvious."

Was there any chance that could mean something? "What does that mean?"

The woman in the yellow vest responded. "Means we're just doing our job. Your complaint is with the politicians."

They had no idea what she was talking about, and Zhenya guessed they likely wouldn't understand even if she explained. What *did* she mean, anyway? Isn't this precisely what she advised Seth Woolrich to do? Flat metal plates connected to metal shafts slowly descended from the truck's body to the asphalt. Stabilizers. Zhenya knew the word for them. She knew a lot of words. Cherry picker, she thought, reticulating blades. She glanced at Mrs. East's house, and a few other words occurred to her—speciousness, rationalization, betrayal. She knew a god-awful lot of words.

The truck wheezed and hunkered down, its iron loins fully girded. There was no way this could have been avoided, she told herself, this vehicle had inevitability written all over it.

She wanted to leave, to get to her car and out of the neighborhood before Mrs. East or one of the others realized what was going on. The last thing Zhenya needed was to witness their histrionics. She walked back to her house but hesitated at the stoop. Petey would not willingly leave until his string of television shows was over. Which meant she was stuck until Morgan got home. The man in the bucket and the woman in yellow were talking. He handed her the chain saw and unbuttoned his long-sleeved shirt, revealing a wrinkled tee underneath. Before he finished stripping off his shirt, the long pole shuddered and began to rise, lifting bucket and man.

< 3 5 >

He yelled and the bucket halted its climb, rocking slightly. The telescoping pole looked like a cannon now. An erection.

The man leaned over the bucket to exchange his shirt for the chain saw. As soon as he straightened, the woman tossed him a plastic water bottle. He didn't catch it cleanly, trapping it against his chest. The sloppy catch embarrassed him, and he shouted to the operator, "Okay." The pole shuddered again. "Upsy-daisy."

What an undignified thing to say, Zhenya thought. But then these people were simply doing their jobs, as the woman in the reflective vest had said. Zhenya eyed the glinting blades of the chain saw. Where was Mrs. East? At the hairdresser? The grocery? When the pole was nearly straight, it spun around as if on a turntable, directing the man in the bucket toward the giant mulberry on the opposite side of the street. Zhenya stepped inside her door and shut it behind her.

When she was a child, her father told her that every human emotion lived in the blood—and none deserved more than one round trip. "Why you think is called *circulation*?" he asked her one day when she had gone on too long about a minor tragedy. His accent made every pronouncement seem profound. "Is just big circle. Let it go round one time only." He had shrugged and spread his hands. "One circle. Then let it go."

Outside, the chain saw ripped to life. As she knelt to retrieve the files, she paused to let regret begin its lap through her body.

2

We record history as if it were a sorrow pageant, each disaster competing with the next to wear the crown.

—Peter Ivanovich Kamenev

The boy delivering flowers dyed his hair. Streaks of black sweat ran from his forehead to his brows. A trail traversed his temple and colored his jaw. Zhenya had come to the door from her study, which she and her daughter were hastily converting into a bedroom. She wore cleaning clothes—denim shorts and a T-shirt—and happened to have a roll of paper towels in her hands. She tore one off for the delivery boy. "Wipe your face," she said.

He didn't know how to take this command and hesitated.

"Your hair is melting," she said. "You look like a character from Greek tragedy."

The boy accepted the paper towel and swiped at himself.

"Why don't you give me the flowers," she said. A dozen yellow roses wrapped in green paper. She assumed they were for her father. Mrs. East had turned his arrival into such a production that a bouquet of roses didn't surprise her. She lifted a tiny envelope from among the blooms. It bore the single word "Emma." An odd sensation rocked through Zhenya's chest. She swallowed as if to hold something down.

The delivery boy recoiled at the black smears on the paper towel. He gave his face another rub. "Did I get it all?"

He looked like a minstrel preparing for a show. "I suppose I'm

< 36 >

< 37 >

going to have to let you come in and wash up. Just so you know, I'm not alone in the house. So don't try anything."

"Like what?" he said, genuinely perplexed. The dye was beginning to puddle in his brows.

"Never mind." She pointed. "Bathroom's under the stairs." She waited until he had crossed the hall and stepped into the bathroom, then she removed the card from its miniature envelope. The roses were from someone named Sid. *Yellow is the color of change,* the note read. What was that supposed to mean? She slipped the card back into the envelope and called for her daughter. "There's something here for you."

Emma emerged from the study carrying a box filled with papers that Zhenya had decided to throw away—student essays, old syllabi, notes for lectures she no longer intended to write. Emma's face brightened at the sight of the flowers. She set the box on the floor. "For me? Really?" Then she made a frown. "Are they from Daddy?"

"No," Zhenya said, then realized her error. "He didn't tell me, anyway." The shower came on in the bathroom.

"Is somebody here?" Emma asked.

Zhenya explained, describing the boy's strange appearance. "There's no way that could have been construed as an invitation to shower." The pipes rattled and the water shut off. "Our poor towels," she said.

Emma didn't hear. She placed the roses in the box of discarded papers, then opened the envelope. "They're from Sid," she said. "That boy at the pool I told you about." Emma attended Hayden University. She was a sophomore and on the diving team, though without a scholarship. Zhenya did not remember any Sid from the pool.

The bathroom door opened. The delivery boy stepped out, drying his hair with a towel. "I borrowed shampoo," he said. Moisture discolored the collar and shoulders of his shirt. He continued to rub, peeking from beneath the towel at Emma.

"Let me get my purse." Zhenya headed for the kitchen. A shower, she guessed, was an inadequate tip.

"I can't believe he sent me flowers," Emma said, following her mother.

They stepped over the golden retriever in the kitchen doorway, who had not gotten up to investigate the doorbell and would not get up now to accommodate foot traffic. "There's a vase in the top cabinet over the sink," Zhenya advised her daughter, then grabbed her purse from the table and stepped over the dog again.

The delivery boy raked his fingers through his hair violently, as if trying to pull it off. A patch of white hair marked the left side of his scalp. He looked a dozen years older without the dye. Zhenya felt bad for making him clean up. "Here you go." She handed him a five.

He stared at the currency. "That's not enough."

He lost her sympathy. "I thought I got to decide that," she said and rummaged through her purse. She didn't like people who were insistent about tips, but she didn't want to short anyone either. She found two singles and handed them over. He was no older than Emma, but the white swath made his features sickly. It was as white as the fur on the dog's face.

He stuffed the money in his pants, then took an invoice from his shirt pocket. The yellow slip of paper was damp, and he dried it on his jeans before handing it over. "It's fifty bucks," he said. "Dozen roses are expensive."

"They aren't paid for?" Zhenya all but shrieked it.

Emma entered with the roses in a smoke-colored vase. The stems were too long, and the flowers flopped over the rim. "Aren't they beautiful?" She waved hello to the delivery boy. His head jiggled in response.

"Apparently," Zhenya began, "this Sid, this Romeo from the pool who has sent you flowers, neglected to pay for them."

"How much are they?" Emma asked.

"Fifty dollars," Zhenya said.

"Wow," Emma said, "I hardly know him."

"*He* isn't spending fifty dollars on you. He's forcing you to spend fifty dollars on yourself." Zhenya explored her purse another moment, then said, "I'm going to have to find my checkbook."

The boy nodded. "You wouldn't have a brush, would you?"

"I do," Emma said. "Upstairs." She lifted one finger from the vase to point, then handed the flowers to her mother. "Follow me."

< 39 >

"Wait a minute," Zhenya said. "You don't know this boy."

"I'm Frank," he said.

"He's Frank," Emma said. She took his hand and led him up the stairs.

"I'll be *listening*," Zhenya called out. "If there's a scream, I'm calling 911." She heard them laugh. She crossed over the golden retriever again and set the roses on the kitchen table. They looked ridiculous, leaning so far over the vase they almost fell out. She wrote a check to the florist and placed it on the table. Then she took scissors from a drawer and began snipping leaves and shortening stems. She tried to recall what Emma had told her about this Sid, but what came to her was an image of the flowers people sent when someone died, somber arrangements of lilies and gardenias. Some sent living plants, as if a person in that position might care to do some planting. Each year on the anniversary of Philip's death, she and Morgan and Emma took flowers to his grave. The entire day was filled with a sequence of minor events. It helped her confine her grieving. It permitted her to put it aside the other days of the year.

She left the roses partially pruned and shoved the trimmings into the garbage pail beneath the sink. "Get out of the doorway," she demanded of the dog. Prince rose slowly and walked to the door that opened on the side yard. Zhenya let her out.

Zhenya's father was arriving in a matter of hours, and still she had not made room for him in her house. He had been an absent and inattentive parent. There were entire years she had not seen him. Despite that, he had exerted a large influence on her life. Her mother called it idolatry. Yet part of what troubled Zhenya now was her duty to confront her father over his lies and contradictions. She didn't have to do it right off. She would make him feel at home first. She would see what it was like to live with one's father. It bothered her that Petey was growing up without his father, that she did not know who had fathered Emma's son.

She filled another box with things she intended to keep— stationery, a stapler, paper clips, computer disks. Emma came in carrying the flowers. "They look so cool this way." She had moved the uncut stems to the center where the short-stemmed flowers held them up. The arrangement had an architectural look, the kind of thing Frank Lloyd Wright might have come up with had he done hallucinogens. "No one's ever sent me flowers before."

Zhenya disagreed. "Leaky gave you flowers for the prom."

"He gave me a corsage. He didn't *send* flowers."

"He paid for them, at least."

"Sid probably doesn't have much money. What does money have to do with anything?"

"You can pick flowers, you know. You can go to the country this time of year. There are wildflowers in bloom."

"Oh, Mom, but aren't these beautiful?"

"His generosity at my expense worries me."

"I'll pay you back," Emma said.

"Forget it. They're nice. Come on." She led her daughter to the rear of the house where a disassembled bed blocked the rear door. "I should have made your father do this," she said, although there was nothing they couldn't easily lift. She grabbed the headboard for the single bed. "So who is this poor but romantic fellow?"

Emma carried the slats. "I met him yesterday at the pool."

Zhenya paused to stare at her. "Yesterday?"

She nodded. "I went in to practice and stayed late to do a few laps, and I wound up talking to this guy."

Zhenya lugged the headboard. "He's a swimmer, then."

"He wasn't in the water. He was there to interview me for the school paper over your dad coming here." She stared at the ceiling, concentrating. "He has wavy hair, and he's thin."

Zhenya wanted to ask why she called her grandfather "your dad," as if he weren't related to her. "Your grandfather hasn't arrived yet, and already he's responsible for your having a new boyfriend."

"He's not a boyfriend. I hardly know him."

"Evidently you made an impression."

"I can't believe he sent me flowers."

Zhenya held her tongue.

What the dog knew:

She knew *sit* and *stay* and *slow down* and *wait* and *shake*. She knew her name. She recognized the names of the people in the family. She knew dozens of lesser-used words and understood

< 41 >

them even in the speech of strangers. She knew pain was a thing that passed.

She knew trouble, could feel it in the air, could taste its metallic residue on her tongue. If she were the source of the trouble, she knew it was best to lower her head and look for shelter. She knew little of real hunger, but she had once known a passion for food. She did not know why that passion had gone away.

She did not know that her sex organs had been removed before they could be used, although she had long sensed an unnamable absence. She knew anger as a product of what was hers to protect. She knew that meat from a can originally came from a living creature. She knew birds ceased to be birds after she caught them. She could identify the members of her family in the dark by the smell of urine on their clothing. She knew love.

She had not forgotten Philip. Still she would catch a whiff of him or of the things that smelled of him, and she would begin to pace the halls to find him. Anymore, after a few moments, she would stop herself. For a long time she had not known to stop herself, but she knew how to learn, as well as how to grieve.

When the doorbell rang later that afternoon, Zhenya peeked through the study window: Mrs. East. She would want to go over the plans for the reception, and Zhenya did not want to hear about them. She fished a cigarette from the package in her pocket, flicked the lighter, and inhaled. Seth Woolrich had acted on Zhenya's information with such extraordinary speed that most of the trees on their block had been cut down the day she called him. It had caused an outcry on the block as well as a hubbub among the city employees, according to Morgan, but it had no doubt saved the city trouble in the long run. Mrs. East had come home from having her car tuned to discover the battle already lost, the great mulberry down and strewn all over the street while it was sawed into manageable pieces. It had taken two days to clear the debris from her old tree. No protest ever materialized, and now all the trees on Forest Avenue were gone. Zhenya felt guilty about the destruction of the trees that Mrs. East had loved. Zhenya had loved them, too. She took some consolation in that.

The widening of Forest Avenue was the right thing and inevitable anyway, Zhenya reasoned. She rubbed out her cigarette—only half smoked—against the plastic wastebasket and immediately lit another. Without the trees, she could see Mrs. East's stately old Victorian clearly from the window, as well as the lot next to it, empty now after a fire had destroyed the house that had stood there for a century. The tree crew had constructed a lean-to in the empty lot. They took their breaks in the lean-to to be out of the sun. She hoped they would leave it up after they were finished. The vacant lot annoyed her. Always what showed was that which was absent—the lost stretch of grass, the trees that had once lined the road, the house that had burned down—they drew the eye like a missing tooth.

Zhenya held that thought a moment as she crushed her second cigarette in the wastebasket, this one hardly smoked at all. The broad street would not bother her and neither would the memory of the cozy neighborhood and tree-laden lane. It was all she would have to forget that would burden her. Forgetting was the necessary act for moving forward, but it was not easy. Even when they eventually lived across town, this forgetting would weigh on her—though perhaps less strenuously. Perhaps it was possible to get some degree of relief.

Seeing Zhenya in T-shirt and shorts this late in the afternoon would only upset Mrs. East, Zhenya thought. She did not answer the bell. But Emma stuck her head into the room. "Was that the door chime?" she asked.

Zhenya put her finger to her lips, whispered, "We're not here."

"*Mom.*" Her daughter practically ran to the front door.

Zhenya sighed and pushed the door to the study shut. The idea of a reception for her father not only made her weary, it angered her. She did not care for spectacle. Her mother had taken her to see a parade just once when she was in eighth grade. Her mother hated parades, and Zhenya had found it impossible to enjoy herself. The ridiculous people walking and waving, the silly tissue-paper floats, the malevolent clowns and stomping bands, the freezing girls with bare shoulders and big skirts. She remembered the parade queen's white breath and the rhinestone crown riding on the girl's hair, the red tips of her ears, and the red paint of the sporty convertible that

< 4 3 >

carried her. The next car held Zhenya's father, who waved and chatted with the crowd just like the queen. When he saw Zhenya, he made the driver stop. Her mother declined, but Zhenya sat in the front seat, huddled before the heater's vent, studying the parade queen in the car ahead of them. Twice the girl turned around far enough to look into their car. Her gaze had bothered Zhenya. It was not the look one expected of a queen, but the nervous, flushed look of the condemned. And Zhenya understood that the queen was her father's lover.

That realization marked the beginning of a new, painful period in Zhenya's life that lasted through high school and into college. She began to wonder about each new woman she met. *Is she one? Would he be attracted to her?* It had been a tough habit to break. She shoved the mattress over the box spring and dusted her hands. It was idiocy to welcome this man back into her life, like opening one's arms to a childhood malady.

The door swung open. Emma stuck her head in again. "We're in the kitchen." She gave her head a jerk to indicate that her mother must come. "We're discussing my flowers."

Zhenya sighed and puffed at her hair.

"I hate that sigh, Mom," Emma said.

"I've been cleaning," Zhenya announced, entering the kitchen. She went directly to the refrigerator. "Beer? Wine? Gin?"

Mrs. East sat at the table with Emma and her roses. She was dressed to the hilt, a silk dress in shades of gray. She had aged well, Zhenya thought, better-looking as an old lady than she had been as a middle-aged widow.

"Are *you* going to drink a beer?" Mrs. East asked.

"Sure," Zhenya said.

"Then I'll have one. I've always liked beer, but I never seem to buy it." She patted Emma's arm. "Now tell me more about this young man."

Emma touched the rose petals gently. "It was just so sweet of him."

Zhenya cleared her throat in a telling way but said nothing. Mrs.

East discreetly slid her hand over the table and turned the check to the florist upside down.

"That idiot didn't take the check," Zhenya said.

"He's still upstairs," Emma told her.

Zhenya looked at her watch. "He's been here two hours."

"I dyed his hair. I used your Lady Clairol. I knew you wouldn't mind."

Zhenya touched her hair, as if it had been offended. "Doesn't he have a job? How can he take a two-hour break to get his hair dyed?"

"I cut it, too," Emma said. "You won't believe how good it looks."

"Here." Zhenya handed the check to Emma. "Make sure he doesn't forget." When she left the room, Zhenya said, "This kid sent flowers C.O.D."

Mrs. East made a face, but she wanted to talk about the coming afternoon. "What considerations should we make for your father? Can he manage my porch stairs?"

She had come for a commitment. Zhenya had been evasive about attending the reception. She had been tempted to skip it. Now she felt she might owe Mrs. East this much. "He won't have any trouble I can't help him through."

Mrs. East seized upon it. "And Morgan?"

"He's reliable," Zhenya said, as if describing a power tool.

"My mother was Russian," Mrs. East said. "She and her sisters used to sit in our living room and converse in Russian. Drove my father crazy, but I've always loved the sound of the language. Not pretty, like Spanish or Portuguese, but it's always sounded like home."

"I'm sorry about what happened with the trees," Zhenya said.

"It's a tragedy." Mrs. East nodded. "I don't know that I'll ever . . . Oh, I'll get over it, but the neighborhood won't. I hope Morgan doesn't think that I blame him for giving us the wrong date."

"No," Zhenya said. "You shouldn't worry about that."

"Our group just collapsed, you know. Lost all our energy. That's why your father coming is such a godsend. Gives us—me at least—something worthwhile to do."

Zhenya made a smile.

< 4 5 >

"And thank you," Mrs. East said, "for coming to that one meeting. I know how busy you are."

"Don't thank me," Zhenya said.

Emma appeared at the doorway. "Get ready."

Frank stepped in, smiling and embarrassed. Emma had cut and gelled his hair. It stood up like a sea anemone. The white spot was gone. He once again looked like a goofy kid. "Vast improvement," Zhenya admitted.

"It's a birthmark," the boy said. "That spot on my head. Had it all my life."

"Since birth, you might say," Zhenya said. Emma fetched the boy a beer.

"It's a wonder I never met your father before," Mrs. East said, stubbornly bringing the conversation back to her subject of the day. "I don't recall seeing him back when the children were little."

"He was around. Now and again. Not often."

Emma said, "Mom wasn't really raised by her dad. Her parents divorced when she was little."

"They were never actually married," Zhenya said. "Mother was ahead of her time. Still is." Her mother lived now in Vancouver with a man ten years younger than herself. Zhenya liked this fact about her mother. "My father was married several times but never to my mother." She recalled waiting at the front window of her mother's suburban house for her father to arrive, that happy anticipation over seeing him and the awful fear that he would not come. If she weren't careful, she would begin feeling it again now. Didn't people ever grow up? "He took me to the Empire State Building when I was six or so. I went with him to Atlanta one time to meet Martin Luther King. Who was out of town. I met Coretta and one of their children. Then my father left me in the car to do something, and I woke up the next morning in the backseat." The car had been parked in front of a bar, but Zhenya decided not to tell them this.

"How interesting your life was," Mrs. East said. "Children rarely understand the opportunities presented to them when they have people of some *size* in their lives."

"Everybody's big when you're little," Emma said.

"I should probably head out," Frank said. He held the beer

bottle up high to be certain that it was empty. "What time is the thingy?"

"Four," Emma answered. "It starts at the bus station, then moves to Mrs. East's house across the street."

"Catch you then." He waved as he left.

Emma waved back, then said, "Frank dropped out of college last semester to manage a band that broke up."

Zhenya said, "For delivering these flowers, that boy got a seven-dollar tip, a shower, a haircut, a dye job, a beer, and a date."

"It's not a date," Emma said. "Sid is coming."

Zhenya said, "When did you invite Sid?"

"I've only ever talked to him once."

Mrs. East said, "He sent you roses after one conversation?"

"Despite the fact he was cheated out of a haircut," Zhenya pointed out.

"Love at first sight," Mrs. East said. "How rare and wonderful." The conversation shifted to romance, and Zhenya left the kitchen. She let Prince in, then returned to the work of preparing for her father. She remembered waking in a panic in that car in Atlanta, a long strand of her own hair in her mouth. From the quality of the light, she guessed it was early morning and slipped from the car to knock on the door of the bar, the Glowing Embers. She never forgot the name. The front door was locked, and she had to walk through an alley to get to the back. On a screened porch, her father lay sleeping on a glider, naked and exposed. On a rug beside him, a naked woman was curled into a ball, also asleep. A bottle of dark liquor cast a phallic shadow over her back, which was dimpled and tan. Dinner plates littered the floor, enough for several people. A tabby chewed on fat from a remnant steak. Zhenya had looked at the scene a long time, studied it as if it meant something, then returned to the car and locked the doors.

She had the impulse to do the same thing now, lock out her father, the neighbors, delivery boys with white spots, and lame-headed kids who sent flowers without paying for them. She and Emma and Petey could be perfectly happy without them. She worked the fitted sheet over the bed. She had left out Morgan, she realized, tucking in the corners, pulling the material tight. She stuffed the pillow into its

< 4 7 >

case. A boy had sent Emma roses. A boy wished to sweep Emma off her feet. Zhenya knew that a psychologist would say she felt threatened by her daughter's sexuality or that she was jealous of her daughter's youth and attractiveness. But she did not feel threatened or jealous, and she hated that kind of generalizing. Yet she did feel odd. The roses—the possibility that Emma could fall for a boy and leave home—had touched a tender place in her. Once Emma and her son moved from the house, she would leave, too, she thought. She would leave Morgan. The idea sent a tingle rushing through her limbs.

She made herself examine the logic. Her father was moving in, and she was thinking about leaving—surely that was the real dynamic at work. But she could not dismiss that thrill, the possibility of living on her own. Pushing a file cabinet aside, she found a thick layer of dust and a card of some sort. No telling how long it had lain there. She picked it up. A baseball card. Philip had collected them. Because she declined to speak their son's name, her husband seemed to think she had forgotten their boy. But that was not true. She simply understood that to move forward meant concentrating on the next thing, not the past things. Morgan's sloppy obsession did not honor their son. It was vulgar. He could not help it, but it was unseemly. She would do nothing to make their tragedy into a display. This was the latest fashion—public grief. Making a spectacle of one's emotions. It was all over the television, and it sickened her. She crumpled the card without looking closer and tossed it in the trash.

It seemed to her that the entire house had begun to smell of roses.

Officer Roy Oberland guided the cruiser into the city lot. Hayden had an ordinance that required businesses to pave their parking lots, but the city's own was nothing but dirt with a little gravel thrown in. A badly whitewashed concrete-block building held a small office and three bays for servicing vehicles. A high chain-link fence topped with a spiral of razor wire surrounded the lot, which held, at the moment, three white pickups and a single white van. The place was an eyesore.

"We're early," Officer Adele Wurtz said. A slash of powdered sugar marked her cheek. "I used to know a joke about a girl who thought she was pregnant because her period was early."

"Where do you think we should park?" Roy asked.

"Can't remember the punch line," Adele said. "Something about being early."

"I wanted to give us time to find the right place to put ourselves." Roy guided the cruiser past the building. The gun Danny Ford claimed to have found in the city dump had been used in a shooting the night before its discovery. Gang kill. Only the victim hadn't yet died. Roy, on his own time, had been to the hospital to see him, but the young man's hold on consciousness was tenuous, and he was not capable of speech. One of the tubes that entered his arm bisected a tattoo—a gang tattoo, presumably, although white tape obscured most of it. Roy had knelt beside the bed and whispered "Danny Ford" in the man's ear, and he had flinched. Nothing else made him move. This was not admissible evidence, of course, but it was the kind of story cops liked to tell each other. Here was the defining truth of being a policeman: everyone who puts on the uniform comes to believe that he or she has better access to the truth than any court. By this measure Danny Ford was undeniably guilty. A nurse had found Roy in the room and made him leave.

The wide doors to the service bays were padlocked. He considered tapping the horn and getting someone from the office to open one, but he didn't want the commotion. "If Ford sees the car, he may take off. He could have more sense than that, but I don't want to risk it. Clean yourself up." He touched his own cheek to show her.

"That's a project beyond my capabilities," she said and slapped her face. "I like to be careless when I eat. Everybody needs one thing they're careless about, you know?"

He did not know and did not want to know. He had put in a request for a new partner, but he had been told to tough it out. If the funding came through, he would be promoted to detective in the fall. Until then he had the unpleasant job of dealing with Adele Wurtz. Now add to that Danny Ford. He drove to the far end of the building.

"You must have *one* thing you're careless about," Adele said.

< 49 >

"The greater the thing, the bigger the kick. Eating, for me, is a pretty big thing. You ever notice?"

He did not want to talk to Adele Wurtz, did not want anything she might say to touch on the most private parts of his life, especially his love for Emma. He felt something like careless in his love for Emma. Although that was not the precise word he needed. Another white truck was parked beyond the building, out of sight. Roy backed the cruiser in beside it. He was not thinking of when they had started their affair. "Careless" was inadequate to describe the onset, but it did touch on the surge of emotion he felt in her presence, and the permission he gave himself to see Petey, to love Emma. His love for them was the most precious thing he possessed. It was possible that he cherished it more because he had to keep it secret, but that was not the only source of its power. He needed a bigger word than careless, a wilder word. He needed something grand and terrible. His love for Emma cast a shadow over every other thing in his life.

Not that he didn't love his wife, but it was a different kind of love.

"Don't cut the engine," Adele said. She had the air conditioner cranked so high Roy's ears ached. He had to give her credit, though. She had filled in the one blank that had bothered him. It was clear enough that Ford had brought the gun to the dump and then pretended to find it, but why had he let Morgan see it? "Calling the cops would never enter that kid's mind," Adele had said. "Not an idea in his range of thinking. Couldn't *conceive* of it." Ford would be charged with disposing of a weapon, making him an accessory after the fact. If the victim died, he would be an accessory to murder.

"You know you shouldn't be involved in this shit," Adele said. "Neighbor of yours is a material witness. Book says take yourself out of it."

"I want to arrest Ford." He did not care what the book said. It disturbed him that Morgan had brought a criminal home and introduced him to Emma. Roy had busted Ford for possession of pot and for beating senseless a kid from a rival gang. Ford had been fifteen at the time, which meant he did a few weeks in juvenile detention. He had been a suspect in a dozen crimes since then, including a stabbing death and a drive-by. Morgan would argue that people could change. Roy knew that was true. At the same time he was certain Danny Ford had not.

The afternoon lacked the clarity of most spring afternoons. Low clouds cut off the sky, and something hung in the air—dust or pollution or some other damn thing. Adele put her hands to her face and rubbed them up and down, as if she were spreading face cream or sunblock. Another from her repertoire of gestures. She didn't seem to know how people behaved, and substituted these stupid displays like a kind of sign language for idiots. Rumor had it that she was hired only because she was a woman. Though he had to admit that was the rumor with every woman they hired. The department had a lousy history for hiring women.

"If the book says jump, I jump," she said. "Without the big blue book of procedures, I couldn't wipe my ass. Have trouble with it anyway, big as mine is. Have to go at it this way." She reached between her legs, shoved her hand underneath. It was a supremely obscene gesture. "There's that look of yours. One day I'll get a partner knows how to have some fun."

"I've heard enough about your fun," he said. She scared him. And she was a bad cop, a show-off, always flashing her gun, making a display of her big ugly body as if it were a thing to take pride in. She posed in doorways and on stairs, partly to look tough, and Roy could understand that—stare down the opponent, declare your dominance. But there was another aspect to it, a feminine insistence, as if she were a contestant in a bizarre beauty pageant. *Here it is,* her stance seemed to assert, *this year's model.*

Danny Ford also had the kind of body that made people turn and stare—and then back away. If he were a cop, everyone would want to be his partner. Roy was certain that Morgan and Ford would be in the first of the garbage trucks to return. Morgan wanted to make it to the reception for his father-in-law. All they had to do was wait another five minutes, ten tops.

"Headcase was a good partner," Adele said.

"Because he let you jack him off?"

" 'Cause once I jerked him off, I had him under my thumb. Soon as I get the goods on you, you'll be a decent partner, too."

< 5 1 >

"What if there are no goods to get?"

"Then you wouldn't be human, and I'm fairly certain you are. That's why I'll let you *do* with your neighbor, even though any fool can see you're in his pocket."

"What's that supposed to mean?"

"You're not objective about Mr. Morgan or the punk. Got no perspective."

"I've had a run-in with Ford before," Roy said, speaking too quickly. He made himself slow down. "I want to see him in the lock. It's that simple."

"You want to do for the neighborman more than any normal person would or it wouldn't be us who even went to the dump in the first place. You're obsessed." She paused, but he didn't bite. He didn't have to say another word. "So okay, you want the rope, I'll dole it out. Soon as you have your head in the noose, I'll step in and save your skinny-ass butt. You ever looked at my thumbs? Monkey thumbs. Hardly look human. Take a peek."

He swatted her hand away. "I've seen your deformities."

"You've seen a *few*." She snatched the louvered microphone from its carriage to call in their location.

Roy opened his door and stepped out into the muggy afternoon. He could see how his love for Emma would look to Adele, and how she would make it sound to others. She wouldn't understand how it began—the death of Emma's brother, the crushing guilt Roy had felt. He had been the one to send the boy inside. He had given the kid a lecture on behavior. He thought the boy needed some discipline. When he heard the ambulance, when he saw Morgan on his knees in the yard, Roy had felt a sudden spinning within himself, a whir of disbelief and fear, which was quickly replaced by the urge to defend his actions. "If you had just made him *behave*," he imagined himself saying to Morgan, and imagining it was enough. Roy understood that he could say nothing. He could not deny his part in the boy's death, and he had no one to whom he could acknowledge it.

He carried the weight of that around for years. Until one night it all changed. He had been out with a woman named Irene Simms, a dull, bitter woman who managed a fabric store. He had met her when her ex-husband came to her store and punched her in the back. She was good-looking, with bleached hair, bad skin, and a greedy, appealing manner. Roy had gone to the mall that weekend with the intention of seeing her. "You act like you've come to save me," she had said on their first date, "but you're really just out to fuck me." While they were in bed, she taunted him. "You hate me," she would say while he thrust himself inside her. After seeing her for a couple of months, he began to feel she was right. He stayed with her as a means to deny it.

They had drunk whiskey and watched a movie that night on her VCR, something with Robin Williams and Robert De Niro about people with a neurological disorder who temporarily come out of their oblivion because of a drug and then slowly sink back into it. Irene had sucked his cock during the video, which he had liked because it meant she could not talk and tell him how much he hated her. He liked Robin Williams, too, even when he wasn't being funny.

Roy hadn't wanted to spend the night. "Fine," Irene had said. "Don't bother with an excuse. What are manners anyway? Can you at least drop off the video?"

He took the movie and left. He knew she would call him later and tell him she loved him, that she was sorry for the way she talked sometimes. She would tell him that she liked to suck him off. If he handled it well, they would talk for a while until she became sleepy and would say good-bye. If he didn't manage it well, she would accuse him of something awful. One night she had charged him with being *ordinary*. "Just another user. Take what you like, and leave the rest. Like any other man. Absolutely goddamn ordinary."

He had said *no*. He might be awful, but he wasn't ordinary. He had tried that night, over the phone, to tell her about kids playing baseball in front of his house and how one boy had lost his temper. Four years had passed since the incident, but she cut him off. She misunderstood, thought he was talking about himself as a boy. "So your precious little feelings were hurt when you were twelve, and you want Mommy to feel bad for you. I'm not your mother, you motherfucker. You want to know what boys did to me when I was a girl? You don't want to know." That much was true, he didn't want

< 5 3 >

to know. He gave up, after that, trying to tell her anything, but they still dated. Two or three times a week, he slept over. But not this night.

He dropped the video into the metal box outside the store, and then he drove home. It was almost two in the morning. As he pulled into his driveway, his headlights swept over a form, a person sitting on the curb in front of the next house. He parked and climbed from the car. He couldn't tell who it was until he was almost upon her. "Emma," he said. "What are you doing?"

She didn't look up at him, just shook her head. She was in her pajamas, her bare feet in the concrete gutter, her thin arms wrapped around her knees, the short flannel pajama bottoms exposing her white thighs. He didn't, at that time, know her exact age, but she was fourteen years old. He asked her what was wrong.

"Bad dream," she said.

"Must be really bad to send you running out here in the middle of the night."

"I come out here sometimes," she said. "My room gets hot."

"It's not safe," Roy said, and he asked her to go inside so he could do the same. "I have to work tomorrow," he said. "I need sleep."

"I dreamed about Philip," she said, and the night seemed to collapse about them, leaving them alone in a pocket of darkness, the remainder of the world gone. Roy felt suddenly alert, no longer sluggish from drink and fatigue.

Her dead brother had come and yelled at her, she said. "He called me names. He called me a worker bee."

"Why would he call you that?" Roy asked.

"Because," she said, and she began to tremble. He sat and put his arm around her but did not pull her close. He felt her weight against his arm, and then against his chest as she leaned into him. She said, "He's mad at me for doing things. For being here at all. Without him. He wasn't really like that. It's just the way he is in my dreams."

Roy felt a tremor inside himself, an itching agitation in his limbs. "I sent him in," he said softly. Emma had been there. She had been one of the baseball players. She knew exactly what Roy had done, but he confessed to her as if she had not seen it all. It meant he could not gloss over anything. He had to say the worst about himself, and he did, telling her, too, about the depth of his regret. She leaned close to him while he spoke, and he breathed in the smell of her hair and skin. He had not, to that point in his life, thought of Emma as beautiful, but he recognized her beauty that night—her perfect skin and dark eyes, the crooked shape her body took huddled over the curb. The streetlight illuminated her bent legs, and when she dropped her head against his chest, he saw the white of her panties. Her pajamas had cartoon images of turtles, hundreds of them, and it was the turtles that brought him back to the world, that reminded him she was a child.

He could picture himself then, sitting on the curb with a teenager in front of his neighbor's house, the street quiet, the houses dark, the sky spackled with clouds. He kissed her chastely on the cheek, but he felt her body rise up to him in response, and desire for her rushed through him. He knew then that he had to get away and go to his house.

"Sleep now," he said, standing and offering her a hand. He waited in the street until she closed the door behind her. Then he went to his house and collapsed on the couch. When Irene called him an hour later, apologetic and weepy, he could not bear to talk to her. He said, "There's no gentle way to put this—"

"I know what *you* are," she said and hung up the phone. He did not answer it when it rang again, and then he took it off the hook. He slept in his clothes on the couch. When he left the house the next morning, she came running up to him from her car wearing a terry-cloth robe. "I've been here for hours," she said and threw her arms around him.

His first response had been to look to the house next door. No one was out. No one was watching. This response let him know what he was feeling, and it scared him.

When he didn't return Irene's embrace, she slapped him. He grabbed her arms and wrestled her still. "If I keep seeing you," he said, "I'm going to wind up hitting you some night—or some morning."

"I know *that*," she said. "All men are like *that*."

< 5 5 >

"I don't want to hit you. So I'm not going to see you anymore."

She jerked away from him, pulling her arms free. Her robe fell open, and she didn't close it. "I know what that means," she said. "And you don't."

"I'm going to work," he said and walked past her to his car.

"It means you're going to hit someone else," she called out.

He did not look at her until he had pulled the car into the street. She glared at him, her robe open; her black bra and panties seemed to him like the marks of a censor on an obscene photograph.

A few days later, a sunny Saturday afternoon, Emma knocked on his door. "Are you alone?" she asked him. She was wearing her best clothes, a ruffled blue dress and shoes with heels that made her gait wobbly. Green eye shadow the color of a parrot's feathers marked her lids, giving them a bruised look. She had a black choker around her neck.

"I'm alone," he said, but he didn't let her inside. He waited, thinking she was about to say something more. The dress was short and his eyes went to her legs. He couldn't deny that. He had been attracted to her on the curb, had felt that surge of blood, though he had not done anything but kiss her on the cheek. Now, staring at her body on his stoop, he recognized the thrill of the forbidden. He could admit that to himself, but that alone would not have made him act. How long did they stand in the doorway without speaking? His thoughts traveled the length of her body, comparing it, against his will, to Irene's.

"I liked talking to you," Emma said.

"Do you want to come inside?" he asked, and he felt a sudden panic saying it. "It's so hot out there," he added, as if to fool someone.

He brought her ice water. She sat on his couch. He sat in a chair opposite her. He had slept in gym shorts and a T-shirt, and he still wore them. The newspaper was spread out over the coffee table, the sports page, coffee rings on the box scores. Written on the coffee mug: COPS CUT IT CLOSE. Two empty beer bottles stood beneath the table. The room embarrassed him. Emma did not belong in it. "So," he said. "No more bad dreams?"

She shook her head, leaned forward to set the water on the table.

The short dress slid even farther up her thighs, and he recalled the glimpse of her panties.

"I sleep on that couch sometimes," he said. "In my clothes. I don't know why. Like I can't climb the stairs to my bedroom. Or maybe I think I won't sleep any other way."

She nodded at that, but she didn't say anything. The makeup bothered him. It was out of place, impure.

"Don't know why I decided you ought to hear that," he said.

"We were talking about my bad dreams," she said.

"No, we haven't really been talking at all," he said. "Just sitting here."

"I like your house."

"You could do me a favor," he said. "If I show you where the bathroom is, will you wash your face?"

Her fingers touched her temple and the swath of eye shadow. She laughed, and her laughter amazed him. She said, "Did I do it wrong?"

"No," he said. He almost added, *I just like your skin.* And though he didn't say it, she seemed to understand.

"Where's the bathroom?" she asked.

He listened outside the room to the running water. He didn't realize how close he was standing to the door until she opened it. She leaned against the door, looking up at him, her face scrubbed, the skin red from it. She said to him, "Is there anything else I should wash?"

He shook his head, and then he leaned over and put his lips against hers. After the kiss, he said, "You have to go home now."

"I don't want to," she said, and they kissed again. "I know some things you don't know," she said, and he understood that was true. It some deep way, it was inescapably true. But she didn't tell him what she knew until later, in bed, after they had made love. "Sudan," she whispered in his ear, "is bordered by Egypt, Libya, Chad, the Central African Republic, Zaire, Ethiopia, Uganda, Kenya, and the Red Sea." She laughed. That laugh of hers. "I'm writing a report for social studies. Did you know the Statue of Liberty was a gift from France? I didn't used to know that. Americans had to build the base. That didn't come with it, and it took longer than they thought."

< 57 >

"This is wrong," he said. "We can't do this again."

She kissed him. "I was so unhappy. That was my real secret. And now I'm not unhappy."

Later he would tell himself that was why had he done it. She needed that specific kind of attention from him. And he was in no position to doubt that need. He could not send her away as he had her brother. In time, though, that would come to sound like the kind of rationalization any child molester would offer. Instead he thought this: it had been wrong to love her, but it had also been beautiful. No matter what anyone else would think, he understood that it was a thing of beauty. Adele would only see the ugly. Everyone he knew would call it ugly. According to the laws he was sworn to uphold, he was a rapist. A child molester. But all he ever wanted was to make it right. As best he could. To care for the girl for the remainder of his life. That had to mean something, didn't it?

Emma was twenty now, and he was thirty-four. He had broken it off with her a dozen times, gone as long as a year without making love to her. He married a woman to make himself stop loving her. But he did love Emma. If he knew nothing else about himself, he knew that and he cherished it. At times it seemed to him miraculous that he could know that much.

A garbage truck entered the city lot, something plastic flapping from it, white and whipping about like a ghost. It was not Morgan's truck, not even the same kind of garbage truck. This one was longer, with a hopper in the middle, the cab flat in the front like a diesel. Two black men rode in bucket seats, chatting. They did not notice Roy, and he stepped back behind the building. Morgan and Danny Ford would be here soon. He returned to the cruiser and climbed behind the wheel. The air-conditioning felt good now.

"You know, Ford's got an address," Adele said almost immediately. "Lives with his mother. Why not let Franey and that harelip partner of his pick him up tonight?"

"We're here, aren't we?"

"I see that we're here. I just don't see *why* we're here. Why nobody but you can nail this Mr. Hulk. Personally, it's not the kind of thing I look forward to. Arresting giants."

He could not possibly explain to her his need to see Ford behind bars and away from the people he loved. He changed the subject. "Tell me this. How is it you have leverage with Louis Headkin? You were as much in the wrong as he was."

" 'Guilty' is not just a legal term," she said. "Headcase felt awful for coming all over his uniform. I didn't feel a thing. I don't give a shit who knows about it, while he would offer me money right now to deny the story. He's got his pension, his Winnebago, but he still worries about who knows what."

Roy, too, had spoken with Headkin, trying to get him to verify Adele's story in order to use it against her. But he was exactly as Adele had described—terrified of the truth even though he had nothing to lose now. "You shouldn't be a cop," Roy said.

That made her laugh. "None of us ought to be. Including you. Anyone who has the itch to do it ought to be disqualified. Everybody can see as much about me, but I'm going to be the first to have the goods on you."

The two black men who had left the garbage truck spotted the car and stared at it as they headed toward the concrete-block building. One of them waved. Roy gave them a nod. Early on in his career, he had loved driving a cruiser through town, recalling his own childhood awe of policemen, appreciating the deference shown to a patrol car by the other vehicles. It meant nothing to him now. The things that support you inevitably wear out, and you have to find new things. Except, in rare cases, there might be a thing whose power did not dissipate, and you had to recognize that or you were a fool. Some people felt that way about God. For Roy, there was Emma. He did not care what that made him. It began with a boy's death, and it was followed by the rape of a girl, but he could not any longer say that he regretted any part of it. Only that he would do what he could to take care of the people he loved. That love was the one extraordinary thing in his life.

He hated Adele Wurtz, but he had to quit working to get her fired. She would make it a point to know his every weakness. Already she understood it had to do with Morgan. He had to protect Emma and their son. He sighed and crossed his arms against the push of cold air coming from the AC. Who was he trying to fool? Emma had already endured her teenage pregnancy. Petey was

< 59 >

already growing up without a father. Only Roy Oberland had failed to pay.

"The most powerful thing you can be is despised," Adele said. Her voice surprised him. He wondered if she had been talking all the time and he had just quit hearing. Maybe he had been talking to her, too. He looked at his watch. Morgan and Ford would arrive any minute now. Adele winked at him and said, "Once you're despised, you've got nothing to lose. The world is your fucking oyster."

Morgan held the gearshift knob to stop the rattling. The day had turned fiercely hot. He glanced at his watch while waiting for the light to change. His shoulders ached and he was plagued by a deep thirst. Danny tapped his knees to a tune playing in his head. One finger of each hand moved. He had finally agreed to come to the reception, which permitted Morgan to drive directly to the bus station—the only chance he had of getting there in time. He did not know why the kid had changed his mind. Danny had been tense after the encounter with the police at the dump, but three days had passed and he seemed his old self again—gruff, quiet, and still. Morgan admired that stillness. Maybe Danny had intended to come all along. Maybe he just had not wanted to admit it.

"Do you have an extra Pepsi?" Morgan asked.

"There's one been in here a couple of days," Danny said.

"Can I have it?" The light changed, and Morgan accelerated through the intersection just as Danny bent to retrieve the can from its crumpled sack. His head banged against the dash, but he had on his hard hat. "Sorry," Morgan said.

Danny handed over the Pepsi. "I been writing a play," he said. " 'Bout a couple of garbage guys. Just thought I ought to get that out."

Morgan popped the top to the can, and bubbles erupted from it. He put his mouth over the opening. He could not imagine a more unlikely playwright than Danny Ford.

"Maybe I should put a hot Pepsi in it," Danny added, continuing to stare straight ahead. "Spray the audience."

Morgan let the foam fill his mouth, swallowed, then took a gulp.

It tasted awful, but it took away the chalky taste. "When—and *why*—did you start writing a play?"

"It's this class this pal of mine gets probation points for. He talked me into going with him. Everyone is either a gangster or has something wrong with them except me." He side-butted his hard hat against his window for punctuation. "Most of them have messed-up bodies. Like MS or a clubbed foot or paralyzed or something."

"What's your play about?"

"Hauling trash, man. The real world of garbage—only my partner's a lot better-looking than you." He made his sly laugh and slouched deeper into the corner. "Made her a halter-top babe. Used to be an exotic dancer. Had a baby she gave up for adoption—but nobody knows that, not even the audience. Couldn't find a way to work it in. But she don't dance anymore, and when her partner doesn't believe her, she does a striptease on these garbage cans till she's wearing nothing but her hard hat. That's the highlight."

"Sounds realistic, all right."

"Ask me what her name is."

"What's her name?"

"Morgan." He side-butted the window again and smiled. "Don't get ideas, man. You heard of Morgan Fairchild and shit. It can be a girl's name."

"As long as it's a meaningful portrayal."

"Fuckin' A. She's got three speeches." He held up three fingers. "One's about what an important job it is to haul garbage." With his free hand he bent his first finger. "One's about what a bitch her mother is." He bent the third finger so he was flipping the bird. "And one's about standing up for your rights and shit." He shook the finger at Morgan.

Morgan guided the truck around a corner. The Hayden bus terminal had once been housed in a brick building downtown, but traffic from the interstate to downtown was slow, and the terminal was moved to the old train station. The Hayden depot had been boarded up for almost thirty years, and there had been some brief hope that the bus company would rehab the building. Instead it erected a metal shack to the side of the old station. There was a ticket booth inside and nothing else but maybe three chairs. Most people waited

< 61 >

for the buses in their cars. A crowd—maybe forty people—milled about in the shade of the old depot. He should have known better than to think the bus would be on time. He drank what remained of the Pepsi.

"So if you see me bringing a play to read, it's 'cause I have to."

"I get it," Morgan said.

"Got no choice in the matter." Then he said, "Train station." He nodded at the old building, as if maybe Morgan hadn't noticed it. "Teacher says I should drop the nudity, but I don't know."

"You planning to produce this?"

"I was hoping my teacher would play the part. But I don't think she wants me seeing her pussy. Or any of the rest of it." He smiled, shrugged. "She could just dance around, I guess. But I got her using garbage lids like the way old-time strippers used feather things—I hate to lose that." He demonstrated by moving his hands back and forth while gyrating slightly in his seat. "Saw it on TV. Real strippers—now, anyway—they just get totally nude. Squat like this far from your nose and spread 'em. It cuts out all that wasted time."

"We made it," Morgan said. "Beat the bus."

"Me and my partners broke into the station one time. Cool place. Old and shit."

A brick building designed and constructed in the twenties, the depot had six large windows set in sloping concrete sills that were now covered with plywood, as was the arching doorway. One of the plywood sheets held a curious graffiti epithet: *That's some god shit!* The bricks themselves had been painted white, giving the building a ghostly appearance. The asphalt lot that abutted the station was in no better shape, riddled with cracks as various and complex as the lines of the rail system had once been. The lot slumped in the middle and had potholes the size of graves.

"This may wind up being a kind of play," Morgan said. "Theater of the absurd, or something like that."

"That's what the babe with MS is doing," Danny said. "She's the best writer in the class—worst walker, though." He snickered. "I get her with that one."

Mrs. East had described her plan for the reception to Morgan in excruciating detail. She had designed it to resemble one given General MacArthur in the fifties. Her husband, Colonel East, had served with MacArthur and arranged the general's stop. She had explained all of this one afternoon out in front of Morgan's house. He had been behind the wheel of his car, his window down, the engine idling, while Mrs. East leaned against the Toyota and talked through the window. A brass band had greeted MacArthur at this same train station, as well as a row of the city's dignitaries. Baton twirlers performed, fireworks exploded. A local poet wrote a poem for the occasion. Mrs. East still remembered two of the lines:

> *War, that Gulliver indisputably large,*
> *Lilliputian MacArthur its master at arms.*

The crowd had filled the lot that bordered the depot and spilled out into the street, which had been blocked off by policemen on horseback. Boys climbed to the roof of the brick station to get an unobstructed view of the general. Before leaving, MacArthur embraced Colonel East, who was not yet Mrs. East's husband. She had been seventeen, and even now, she told Morgan, she considered that hug between the two soldiers a part of her courtship with the colonel.

MacArthur would not recognize the current world, Morgan thought. He wheeled through the lot and parked by the street. Liam and Rachel Haney were helping their sons set up their instruments. The oldest Haney boy, King, had been a good friend of Philip's, but Morgan never saw the Haneys anymore. He hardly saw anyone in the neighborhood. Another friend from the past, Seth Woolrich the city planner, had called Morgan under the pretense of thanking him for the tip about the tree protest. Seth knew Morgan was opposed to the tree removal, knew that Zhenya had gone behind his back, and that was why he had called—to let Morgan know what his wife was doing. It had made Morgan angry with Seth, taking his wife's help and then ratting on her. And Zhenya? He didn't know what to think or how to feel about her. Why would she help the city destroy the neighborhood? The mystery of his wife grew wider every day. He had said nothing to her except "We'll miss those trees."

< 6 3 >

"This looks like a big deal," Danny said without a trace of enthusiasm. They climbed out of the truck and walked together toward the shade. "Band and everything."

One of the Haney boys was tugging at a cord, trying to get a gas-powered generator to start. Mrs. East had told Morgan that she had arranged for a band to perform the national anthem. This would be the Jimi Hendrix version, Morgan guessed.

A banner strung across the building read: HAYDEN WELCOMES THE CENTURY'S SON! A bit much, Morgan thought, although Peter claimed to have lived for the entire century, so it made some sense. Two folding cafeteria tables covered with crepe paper sat beneath the banner and were lined with gifts. Morgan wandered over to check them out. A realty company had prepared a framed map of the city. A dessert shop had brought a plastic bowl filled with pink punch. A neighborhood restaurant provided a decorative tray of egg rolls. Jiffy Lube had a certificate for a free oil-and-lube job with Peter Ivanovich's name written on it in large, elaborate script. The old man could redeem a warm-oil massage and take home a basket of organic fruit. Another store had sent three representatives to present a bag of chocolate coffee beans no larger than a woman's fist. Morgan recognized the mayor standing in the shade bearing a large plastic toy—the key to the city, evidently.

Two local television stations had crews waiting. The correspondents—both young women—slouched before the tables with microphones in their hands, doing sound checks, eyeing Morgan nervously. Evidently neither cared to include a garbageman in her broadcast. Except for Mrs. East, no one was formally dressed, so Morgan didn't feel all that bad about showing up in his work clothes. The woman offering the massage had on what was once known as hot pants. Morgan did not know what they were called anymore. She had nice legs. He was still thirsty.

"Wait up." It was Danny's voice, and Morgan turned to face him. He was eating an egg roll, still wearing his hard hat.

"I think those are for the dignitary," Morgan said.

Danny offered his half-shrug. "They didn't say nothing. Just watched me take it. They can't expect me to come here and not eat." He wanted to know how much longer they had to wait.

"My neighbor may know." Morgan led Danny away from the tables and toward the band, where Mrs. East seemed to be talking to one of the musicians. Poster board advertising the group had been stapled to one of the plywood sheets covering a depot window: THE ROTTING MAMMALS. Catchy name, Morgan thought. The Mammals were having trouble with their portable generator. It had a pull-cord, like a lawn mower, and they couldn't seem to get it going. Both of the drummers were already rubbing their arms and complaining. It fell to the string section to save the day. "Maybe it needs gas," said a boy with a guitar strung round his neck. He twisted off the gas cap. "Dry as a witch's tit," he said.

Mrs. East turned at this comment—to confront the young man, evidently, but something about his appearance stopped her. His T-shirt featured a naked woman riding bareback on a rocket ship, and Morgan guessed that was it. Mrs. East kept turning and addressed one of the sore-armed drummers. "Perhaps we'll have to cancel the music," she said hopefully.

"I can suck some gas out of my car," the boy replied.

Mrs. East nodded at the boy then greeted Morgan. "We're having musical difficulties," she said, rolling her eyes.

Morgan began to introduce her to Danny, but his partner had headed back to the tables. To get that big you had to eat a lot, Morgan figured. Nothing to be done about that. "Quite a gathering," he said. He waved to King Haney, who stood behind an electric keyboard of some sort.

King Haney waved back. "Good to see you, Mr. Morgan," he said politely. "This is my brother's band. I'm just sitting in."

"Glad to hear it," Morgan said. He could not look at King without thinking of Philip. He saw them for a moment, before the television playing a video game, the screen a careening square of color. His wife's car wheeled into the lot, and he let the image go. The Honda held Zhenya, Emma, and Petey. Zhenya was behind the wheel. Morgan had beaten them here. He felt a ridiculous surge of pride at that.

"Thank goodness," Mrs. East said upon seeing the car. "I was beginning to worry."

Morgan believed his wife's parking habits were neurotic at best.

< 65 >

She refused to ever park anywhere but the closest possible spot. She drove past the other parked cars right up to the depot, pulling in next to the band.

No sooner had the doors to the Honda swung open than a swell of noise went up from the crowd. The bus had appeared at the next intersection, waiting for the light to change. Peter Ivanovich claimed that he preferred riding the bus to the expense of flying, but Zhenya said he had just been casting about for them to buy him a plane ticket. She had not offered. "I would have if he couldn't afford it himself," she had said. Or if he had outright asked, Morgan thought. His wife had difficulty saying no to her father.

People hurried to the cafeteria tables, while Morgan headed in the opposite direction to the Honda. He opened the back door to get Petey. Just behind them, with a loud cough and sputtering whine, the generator ignited and the band members began frantically tuning their instruments. The bus sounded its horn as it entered the parking lot. Zhenya and Emma climbed from the car. Morgan gathered Petey up in his arms. The boy was singing a song about the gingerbread man.

"You didn't change," Zhenya said, eyeing his clothing, while Emma pointed and yelled, "There's Frank." A boy Morgan did not recognize approached, waving to her. "They fired me," he called out happily.

The Rotting Mammals' drummer began pounding on the snare. The bus's brakes squealed. The first off-key and inhumanly loud notes of "The Star-Spangled Banner" came screeching from the electric guitar of the boy in the obscene rocket shirt. Carrying Petey, Morgan began trotting away. As he passed Mrs. East, she covered her ears and said to him, "I feel rather faint." She joined them as they hurried away from the music.

Morgan saw Danny standing, arms crossed, on the far side of the tables. He looked like a statue—perfectly still and larger than life. He had another spring roll in his big hand. The bus lumbered to a stop. Morgan lifted Petey up to see. Baffled passengers pressed their faces to the bus's windows. The driver hopped out, a dark man with a graying beard. He stared uncomfortably at the crowd and smiled, then opened a compartment on the bus, revealing the luggage. He removed a single leather bag—huge, old-fashioned, and without wheels. Then he closed and locked the compartment. Evidently Peter was the only passenger getting off in Hayden.

Just as the national anthem reached the drum solo, Petey's voice rang out in Morgan's ear: "There he is!"

Peter Ivanovich Kamenev, in a dark suit and tie, walked bent over down the aisle, waving.

"It's him!" Mrs. East announced. "The great man!"

The bus driver hopped up the two stairs to help Peter exit. The drum solo ended, and the return of the guitar included a bolt of feedback, hardly distinguishable from the music. It split the air and created in its wake something like silence. The gray head of Peter Ivanovich Kamenev appeared just beyond the driver's cap. Peter gripped the driver's arm with one hand and waved with the other in broad strokes, as if painting that particular piece of the air. The generator failed, cutting off instrumental proof that the flag was still waving. "Zank you, Hayden," Peter Ivanovich called out.

Not until they reached the asphalt and the driver reentered the bus could one see that, sometime over the course of the long bus ride, the great man had wet his pants.

Zhenya stood beside the bed in the room that had been her study and helped her father change his clothes. She knelt to remove his shoes. "You could take a nap," she said. He lay prone on the bed, his knees bent over the edge. His socks were damp with urine. "You could shower and then nap."

"I nap on bus," he said sourly, "which is why this mess. Do something for father and get clothes from suitcase."

"I *am* doing something." She pulled off the second shoe and sock. His exaggerated accent made Zhenya flinch. He pronounced "this" like *zhis* and "something" like *somezing*. It galled her that she'd never had a "father," only a *fazzer*. "You have to shower, Papa, before you go anywhere."

"A little washcloth here and there, good as new," he said. "Most important, I cannot miss party for me in new hometown."

He had talked with everyone as if there was nothing unusual

< 67 >

about reeking of urine. He had sloshed from one table to the next, posing for photographs and hugging the young women. He had behaved with such ease and confidence that people had doubted their own senses. He was that kind of man, Zhenya thought. All her life she had heard her mother disparage him, but an hour with him would make her question everything. She couldn't help loving him. She couldn't help the sense of doom that accompanied his arrival. She unbuckled his belt and unclasped his pants, then began peeling them down his pale legs. She had to kneel again to work the pant legs off.

"I am thinking when I first see you at station you don't look so good," Peter Ivanovich said. "Is trouble, yes? I am sensitive to this. You have lost weight?"

The pants snagged on his white feet and she yanked harder than necessary to free them. "Losing weight is what we Americans do," she said. "It's not a bad thing."

"Yes," said Peter Ivanovich. "But most important, where is Emma and boy?"

"They were at the depot. Emma gave you a hug."

He shrugged and opened his hands. "There were so many."

"Don't say that to Emma." Zhenya gathered up his soiled clothing and pointed with one of his shoes. "For reasons unclear to me, she's very fond of you. It won't do to have her think you didn't recognize her."

"I won't say nozzing," he said. "Russians are experts at saying nozzing."

"The shirt, too." She motioned impatiently with her fingers.

"I don't piss on shirt. Is perfect still."

"The shirttails are wet."

"I tuck them in. Get pants from suitcase now and hand me jacket. Presents at bus station are very nice, but is nozzing to drink, not even cheap American wine you find everywhere."

She tossed the wet clothing just outside the door. The big suitcase was the only piece of luggage he had brought with him. The remainder of his things were being shipped. A jumble of dirty shirts bloomed when she opened the bag. "Good God," she said and shuffled through to the bottom, where she found a moderately clean shirt, socks, and underwear. "The shirt must be changed," she said, tossing the clothes onto the bed beside him. "And the underwear. I'll get you a damp cloth."

"You are like KGB," he said, remaining flat on his back to unbutton his shirt.

She grabbed the suitcase, glancing back at him to be certain he was joking. He winked at her. "You don't have bigger bed for your papa? How am I to love woman in this bed?" He grinned enormously. "You have lovely smile, daughter. I will make you show it more."

She stuffed the wet clothes into the suitcase and began dragging it to the laundry room. Everyone else had gone directly to the party, even Morgan in his filthy clothes. He felt responsible for the hoodlum he had hauled along and didn't feel he could take twenty minutes to shower. Typical Morgan behavior. Better to be dirty than be late. Better to force a thug to attend the reception. Did he really think they couldn't do without him for a few minutes? The scene at the bus station had been just ludicrous enough that Zhenya looked forward to the next gathering. She let the suitcase bump down the stairs to the basement, where she dumped a load of clothing in the washer, sticking tissues into the shoes to soak up the urine. On her way back, she ducked into the bathroom to moisten a washcloth and grab a towel.

Her father still lay on the single bed. He had unbuttoned his shirt; gray hair curled damply on his bony chest. He was attempting to slide down his underwear without lifting his hips. She tossed the cloth and towel on the bed and turned quickly.

"Must have help," he said. "Is stuck like cement."

She would be spared no indignity. The elastic band of the boxers was soaked. She pulled the shorts over his ugly genitalia, the uncircumcised penis and pink testes vibrating with each tug like a grotesque sea creature. He took a slip of paper from his shirt pocket while she disrobed him, wholly indifferent. Once she had the boxers down his chalky legs and then over his feet, she dropped the damp washcloth on top of his genitals. "Wash," she commanded. "Scrub."

"Here," he said. "See this." He held the paper between his thumb and index finger. "All the world spins on paper such as this."

< 69 >

She reached for it, but he closed his hand into a fist. "Is secret," he said, jerking the hand away, which caused the cloth to slide off. Zhenya marched out of the room and closed the door. She had seen enough of the slip of paper to know what it was—a woman's name and phone number.

"Papa," she said softly. He was utterly unchanged.

When Zhenya entered the house with her father, Mrs. East made a high-pitched tilting noise and bustled over to greet him. She seemed to hear herself making the sound and worked to turn it into a greeting. "Puh-lease do come in, you sweet man."

Her father cleaned up well, Zhenya thought. He was tall and thin in a suit and tie, his palms out, arms spreading, like an inviting tree of some sort, his rectangular face lit with pleasure. "You are wonderful woman to do this for old Russian." He embraced Mrs. East.

"It is an honor," Mrs. East began.

Zhenya didn't want to hear it and stepped past her into the living room, which was well stocked with food and freeloaders—so crowded that she could not immediately spot a bar, though almost everyone had a champagne glass. A caterer was laying out a buffet of turkey and roast beef with homemade rolls, and a line was forming, people holding their white plates with both hands like steering wheels. Chamber music came from the CD player. Her father wanted vodka but would settle for wine. Zhenya wanted good wine but would drink whatever Mrs. East wished to pretend was good. She wedged past the Haneys, hoping Liam wouldn't notice her. She was not in the mood to hear his lament about the trees. As she slipped by him, she spotted the waiter, a handsome young black man who held a tray of glasses and sweating bottles of champagne. Waiters should be tall, she thought, to stand out in a crowd.

She asked for two glasses. "One is for the guest of honor," she said. The champagne glasses were heavy and beautifully shaped. Zhenya took a moment to admire them.

"That old guy?" the waiter asked. He balanced the tray on one hand and poured.

"The one and only," she said.

He bent close to her and whispered, "Who is he, anyway?"

"My father," she said. "A tightwire man, used to be very big in the Russian circus. Could balance ten or twelve women while he walked on a wire a hundred feet in the air."

"Without a net, I bet," the waiter said.

Zhenya took a drink of the champagne, which was delicious. Mrs. East must have spent a fortune. "He always had a net. It was held up by another dozen women." The line behind the caterer grew longer, which thinned out the crowd on the floor. She saw Morgan at the head of the line looking her way, that needy gaze of his. It was idiotic of him not to go home and bathe. She pretended not to see him and turned, brushing up against the waiter.

"Sorry," she said.

"Finish that," he said. "The first one doesn't count."

She drank the remainder of the champagne. "I hope you're trying to get me drunk," she said while he filled the glass again.

"That's my job." He leaned close to her. "You smell like something."

An old man's urine, she thought, but she merely said, "Shampoo." From the opposite side of the room, Emma waved. She had Petey in one arm, his legs around her waist, and she was talking to a crowd of boys—the ex-delivery boy with the dyed hair, the thug wearing a hard hat who worked with Morgan, one of the Haney boys who played in that awful band, and some kid in an old-fashioned suit. Her daughter was a magnet for the most unattractive kind of people, but at least she was popular with them. Zhenya wondered whether one of the boys in that crowd might be Petey's father. She hated not knowing. King Haney had long been her prime suspect, but something Emma said one night had made Zhenya wonder. "King was never really *my* friend," she had said. That could mean she never had sex with him, or it could mean they slept together but didn't like each other. Unable to return her daughter's wave, Zhenya lifted one of the glasses in salute. At the same moment, she heard her father calling, "Daughter. Daughter." He was thirsty, no doubt, and couldn't think of her name.

"You are angel," Peter Ivanovich said, taking both glasses from

< 71 >

her, despite her reluctance to let the second one go. He took an immediate drink, as if the champagne were oxygen.

"One of those is mine," she said. He pivoted away, but she tapped his arm. "You took my drink, too."

"So zorry." He returned one of the glasses while turning back to face the hot-oil bimbo in microshorts, whom Mrs. East seemed to be literally pushing out the door. Zhenya raised the glass to her lips, but it was empty. Not even a drop, as if he had licked the bottom. She sighed. She could think of no way to make this kind of behavior charming, but she could not really pretend that it made her angry, either. No one had this power over her but her father. And now, for the first time in her life, they lived in the same house. Jesus, she needed a drink.

It was not much later that the action began.

Zhenya happened to be talking to her next-door neighbor, Diana Oberland, when Diana's husband, Roy, arrived. Diana had initiated the conversation. "If your father's a hundred years old, I'm a Jewish princess with a nose job," she said. Then she added, "And I'm not." She was loaded. "My dad looks older than yours, and he's barely sixty."

"He's lying about his age," Zhenya said. "I don't know why. He's always working an angle."

"I baked cookies." Diana pointed at a table crowded with dishes. "The heart-shaped ones. A Valentine recipe. My mother sends me holiday recipes."

Roy Oberland's head suddenly rose up above the throng, and both of the women turned to him. He stood near the door, in uniform, going up on tiptoes to look over the congestion of people crowded around Peter Ivanovich. Cops, like waiters, ought to be tall, Zhenya thought. The room was packed, but he began to make his way through, bobbing up every few seconds. "He's looking for me," Diana said, smiling, clearly pleased by this, her hips swiveling about as she spoke, as if the idea had sent a little charge to her pelvis. It made Zhenya think Roy must be good in bed—the most over-rated of the manly virtues, but still a nice thing when you could find it. Diana, she noted then, was an attractive woman, dark hair and eyes, slim and large-chested. Roy bobbed again to look over the crowd. He wasn't very tall, but he was handsome himself.

"Aren't you going to let him know where you are?" Zhenya asked. "He's working awfully hard to find you."

Diana smiled and shook her head. "Let him work. I want to see his face the instant he sees me. Did you know when we met I was engaged to be married? To someone else?"

"I didn't know that."

"I met Roy on a Sunday and called off the wedding on Tuesday."

"He's cute," Zhenya said, although she had lost track of him now. "I've always been fond of him." Of all the people in the neighborhood, of all their friends and acquaintances, Roy Oberland had been the most aggrieved over Philip's death. That meant something to Zhenya. And he had gone out of his way to be nice to Petey. A good neighbor, and she suspected that he was a good person.

"He wakes me up some nights crying," Diana said, and this surprised Zhenya—both the fact of it and that Diana was drunk enough to blurt it out. "In his sleep," she said and pointed at him, as if Zhenya wouldn't believe her otherwise. "It's his work. He sees bad things."

Zhenya tried to imagine the people Roy encountered daily, the criminals in their cells, the drugged-out children riding in the back of his patrol car. Violence seemed to linger in some men the way wit or tenderness did in others—waiting for the right person to bring it out. Little wonder he wept. She liked him for it.

And there he was again. He had slipped past a few more people, then went up on his toes once more, but this time he started on one side of the room and scanned systematically from right to left. Diana herself went to tiptoes as his gaze grew closer. Zhenya tried to recall ever feeling so excited about Morgan. She knew she had, but she couldn't remember the sensation.

Roy's gaze passed right over Diana. He had stared directly through her. Zhenya turned away, pretending not to have noticed, but she heard Diana sigh and her heels plop down. Then Zhenya felt a tug on her sleeve. Diana placed her thumb on Zhenya's chin and turned her head. Another police officer, a heavyset woman, had

< 73 >

entered the house. "They're here on business," Diana said. "That explains it, doesn't it?" Under her breath, she added, "It *better* be business."

"You think someone complained about the noise?" Zhenya asked, although it was hardly a loud party, and it was the middle of the afternoon.

Roy's gaze had stopped now, focused on the group near the kitchen—Emma, Petey, and the motley crowd of boys sniffing about her. He gave a hand signal to his partner, who made no effort to slide between people but began pushing them to the side—bulling her way through, Zhenya thought with malice. The kindest thing that could be said of her was that she did not need to shave.

Mrs. East touched Roy's shoulder, which made him jump, and her finger poked his cheek. She said something to him, but Zhenya couldn't hear her. She decided to move closer to the action.

"She's not my friend," Roy was saying. "She's my partner."

The policewoman gave Mrs. East a withering look. "We're on duty, ma'am."

Mrs. East showed a quiver of doubt. "Not official duty *here.*"

Morgan had crossed the room to join them. "They think they're going to arrest my partner. He was right about you, wasn't he? You've got a hard-on for Danny."

"That gun was used in a felony, Morgan," Roy said. "A man is in intensive care. We were waiting at the city lot for you to get in."

"You go to the door," Mrs. East told Roy. "I'll locate the young man in question."

Zhenya turned to look for Danny Ford. He was easy to spot—a titan in a hard hat, the only one at the party. She became aware of his size as she never had before. He was not merely big but massive. He took a step toward them. It looked as if he was going to walk right up and be arrested, but just before he reached them, he bolted. Roy yelled for him to stop. Morgan yelled something, too. Danny Ford did not try to get through the crowd at the front door but sprinted to the stairs, which made Mrs. East frantic. "The reception does not extend to the upper chambers," she called.

"Let me get him," Morgan said, but Roy put a hand against his chest.

"You wait here." Roy started up the stairs, taking them slowly. He was followed by his partner, who unholstered her gun as she climbed. "Better send your guests home," she told Mrs. East. "Just in case." She waggled the gun.

"I most certainly will not," Mrs. East said, but the room was already emptying. "I cannot believe this," she said.

Zhenya did not realize that she had begun seeking her father in the crowd, but when the caterer bumped against him and he faltered, she was close enough to catch his shoulders and steady him. She bent down to retrieve her champagne glass, which she had dropped, but an anxious foot had already kicked it out of reach. "Should I get you out of here?" she asked.

"Oh, no," he said. "Must see controversy."

She held him by the arm, moved him against the flow of people to the wall, where they edged away from the door and the crowd. He had almost fallen over, but he held a bottle of champagne in his hand. Not likely a drop spilled, either, Zhenya thought. She retrieved a glass someone had abandoned on a window ledge and used the serviette it rested upon to wipe the rim. "Pour me some of that," she said.

But her father had spotted the caterer's table. "Is turkey?" he said, heading across the room.

Not everyone was trying to escape. Morgan and Emma hadn't gone anywhere, and Emma still had the remaining dopey boys as entourage. Diana Oberland had joined them as well. From above came the sounds of a scuffle, and then Danny Ford came flying down the stairs, Roy Oberland in pursuit, the policewoman trailing him, her feet hammering the steps. "Hold it right there," she yelled. She looked like she might collapse on the stairs, or the stairs might collapse beneath her. Her pistol was drawn and she was huffing. She held it with both hands and aimed it at Morgan's partner.

Morgan threw up his hands and yelled, "Stop now! She'll shoot you."

Roy ran up to Danny Ford from behind. "Don't!" he yelled. "Wait!" He executed a wild sideways kick that caught Danny Ford in the back of the knees, making them buckle. As the behemoth fell,

< 7 5 >

Roy leapt past him, pitching his body in front of the onlookers, his hair brushing against Emma's nose, one of his outthrown arms slapping his wife's cheek, making her flinch. Emma hunched to cover Petey, whom she held in her arms, but Roy's body already shielded them both. "You fire that weapon and you're suspended," he yelled.

He had thrown himself in front of Petey, Zhenya thought, and she felt a rush of gratitude. He was, as she had suspected all along, a good man.

"Cuff him," his partner replied.

Roy moved cautiously around the body on the floor. He bent down, placing his knee on Danny Ford's spine, then pulling the man's big arms back and handcuffing them together. "You have the right to remain silent," he began.

Diana Oberland suddenly ran to the door, grazing her kneeling husband as she went past. It was a crying kind of run, a bitter swinging of the arms, an angry sway of the hips. I have never run that way, Zhenya thought. And then she thought, I should have married a policeman. Or a soldier. Or just anyone who went away at times and came safely home. A man who had a life outside the walls of the house in which he lived. A life that involved something more than garbage. She did not know what had upset Diana, but she guessed that it was seeing her husband at risk. That part of it would be hard to live with, Zhenya imagined, but at the same time she envied it. Their reunion tonight would be passionate.

An insistent tap on her shoulder finally won her attention. Her father put his mouth to her ear. "Is mustard?"

Morgan felt shaky. His arms had a tingling, hollow sensation, and his hands grew weak as they gripped the steering wheel. It could be simple fatigue. He had worked hard today to make it to the bus station on time. He had good reason to be weary. He let off the accelerator, became excessively cautious at intersections, worried that he was not quite in control. He didn't feel like himself.

The new police station was a bleak place, as ugly as any fast-food restaurant. In fact, its octagonal design reminded Morgan of a

Pizza Hut. Except it had no windows. He hated to think of Danny locked up in there. He had driven the garbage truck instead of his car. It took up a slash of parking spaces.

The front door of the police station, metal and uninviting, opened to a waiting room almost identical to the one at the office of Morgan's dentist: industrial carpet, uncomfortable chairs, even a table bearing magazines. The comparison ended there. The door leading to the next room had no knob, and in one corner a cubicle jutted out. Inside it, behind a wall of gray metal and thick glass, sat a young Japanese woman in police blues. She reminded Morgan of a parking attendant; the booth even had the required slot. Who had decided this was the way police stations should look from now on? She spoke to Morgan: "You just going to stand there?" She began chewing a fingernail.

Morgan lifted his hands before he spoke but realized he was wearing his work gloves. He must have slipped them on as he stepped from the truck. Habit. He removed the gloves and slipped them into the rear pocket of his pants.

The Japanese woman took a pair of glasses from her hair and, in her most exasperated manner, slid them over her eyes to study Morgan. As if the glasses permitted her to see what she had missed before, she realized she had a garbageman before her. "Are you here about that trash guy we just brought in?"

"Danny Ford," Morgan said, full of gratitude for the help. He couldn't think, couldn't keep on track. "This is stupid. I'm being stupid," he said. "My partner was arrested. The guy I work with."

She lifted the glasses from her eyes and placed them in their previous spot in the slight puff of her hair. Turning, she pushed against the back wall of her cubicle, and it swung open. She called to someone, then swiveled back and requested identification. Morgan removed his driver's license from his wallet and slid it through the slot. The door behind her cubicle opened, and a man leaned in close to her and spoke in her ear. She whispered something to him before pushing Morgan's license back. "We already have your statement. The arresting officers interviewed you earlier in the week, right? When the gun was found? If we need anything else from you, we'll call."

< 77 >

Morgan became aware of his own features reflected in the bullet-proof glass, and he was astonished by their disorder, the creases in his forehead and about the eyes. He had never been especially hand-some, but he could not recall ever looking quite so ugly.

"Sorry you had to come all the way down and all," the police offi-cer said.

A dry, scratchy noise came out when he tried to speak, and he cleared his throat. The woman leaned low and came up with a white tissue, which she pushed through the slot. This action bewildered Morgan, but he took it from her.

"Are you okay?" she said.

"I'm not crying," he said, patting his face with the tissue. "I'm just flustered. I'm having some kind of reaction." He thought of the great level in his father's toolshed, a board four feet across with a half-moon cut out of the middle and a little tube marked with red lines, filled with some visible liquid that would tell you what was level and what was tilted, what sat squarely in the world and what was off-kilter. Something about the slot made him think of this, something about the woman behind the glass, something about her Japanese eyes and his own eyes leaking their own visible liquid.

"Do you need a doctor or something?" she asked.

"Can I see him?" Morgan said, baffled by his tears, his voice per-fectly steady. "I'm the one who insisted we call the police. I don't know why I'm acting like this. I'd like to see him."

The young woman's hair, when she shook her head, transformed into ebony silk. The look of it startled him. "Family and legal coun-sel," she said, her right hand rising to her forehead to catch the glasses as they slid off her head, a gesture so familiar she didn't need to look at them, just swept them into her lap and began to wipe them on some slip of material—her shirt, a rag. Morgan could not see her lower half hidden beneath the metal bottom of the booth.

He turned and faced the metal door that led to the outside, the world still in sunshine, he knew, the day brilliant and calm and patiently waiting for him. In a frame of gold, hung on the wall beside the metal door, a newspaper photograph showed two officers holding hands with a boy. Morgan recalled the news story as he stepped out of the police station, blinking against the sun's piercing light. The boy had been playing in a canal and had fallen in. For some reason, he could not get out. His sister ran down a police car, and the cops freed the boy. Not heroism, exactly; being in the right place at the right time—a more important gift to have than heroism, which was only rarely called for. Being in the right place at the right time was in constant demand.

Morgan's mind maintained such an odd wash of thoughts that he could make nothing of them. Thoughts came relentlessly and in a pattern but not a logical one, more like the pattern on a carpet, like the one he had seen in Mrs. East's living room. The pattern on the rug was intricate and laborious but not logical, at least not with a logic Morgan could grasp in words. This was what it must be like to lose your mind, he thought, and then he retracted the idea and ran his hand through his thinning hair. This was what it had been like when he had lost his son. Only then the tears had been real. The sadness complete. He had fallen, he remembered, in the grass as his son was wheeled out to the ambulance. His legs had just given out.

This was not a tragedy today, he told himself, angry that his body could betray him this way. His wife's father had arrived to live with them. His partner was arrested and carted off to jail. A bad day, but not tragic. He took a breath and trudged across the lot to the garbage truck. Whatever wrong had taken place could yet be righted.

When Roy Oberland opened the door to his house, he caught the faint odor of marijuana and knew something was up. "Diana?" He found her in the kitchen, sitting at the table, smoking a joint. She didn't look up when he entered, a tall glass of ice water on the table. She had to have ice water to smoke pot. The ashes, she flicked onto the tabletop.

Roy stepped to the cupboard to retrieve a soup bowl for her ashes. He smelled something besides pot, a tang he couldn't identify. He sat beside his wife and set the bowl on the table. Because the two suitcases were shoved beneath the table, he hadn't seen them while he was standing. "What's going on?" He liked to smoke an occasional joint but saved it for special occasions. He and Diana

< 79 >

smoked two or three times a year; he and Emma, a little more often. Each occasion with either woman invariably ended in sex, so he felt he was getting mixed signals. Unless one of the bags was his. Did she have a surprise planned?

"You've got a head start on me," he said, getting up to hang his hat on a rack his father had made for them. His father taught wood shop at the local high school. The house was full of knick-knacks made by his father. "I should take off my uniform," he said. "Doesn't feel right to toke in uniform." She still didn't answer, but he could see now she was holding her breath. For a moment he imagined the smoke inside her lungs, swirling about like spirits. He felt certain that something was wrong.

"Maybe one toke in uniform won't hurt," he said, reversing himself out of anxiety. He had arrested a suspected felon after a fight while his worthless partner drew her gun in a crowded house, and he had not felt this anxious. That kind of fear he could deal with, while this kind he found paralyzing. He had to simply deny it, act as if he could detect nothing unusual. He reached for the joint. Diana jerked her hand away, striking the bowl, making it spin. She grabbed it to make it stop, then, in almost the same motion, swept it off the table. It bounced against the wall, spinning once again when it struck the floor, stubbornly refusing to break.

He spoke her name, his voice self-consciously calm, the gesture with the bowl permitting him to slip into cop mode, permitting him to think professionally rather than personally—a relief. His voice became measured. "What's going on here, Diana?"

She exhaled a long funnel of smoke. "I'm leaving you." She examined the glowing tip of the homemade cigarette. "I'm mostly already gone." She raised the joint again, but Roy touched her arm to stop her. She wrenched her arm from his and lurched from the table as if he had attacked her. "Don't touch me," she said. "And don't threaten to arrest me. I got the pot from you." She pointed at him with the burning end.

"Have you lost your mind?" Roy asked, and he lost his professional edge, could feel it fleeing his body. It shamed him that he had tried to don that particular mask. "Why would I arrest you? Why would you leave me?" He needed to change out of his uniform. He did not want to be in uniform for this conversation. "I'm going to change, all right?"

She said, "You're having an affair with Emma Morgan."

His legs felt suddenly leaden and watery at once, but he had begun unbuttoning his shirt and he continued, tugging at the tails to free them from his pants.

"Good," she said. "I was afraid you were going to deny it."

He sat and put his arm on the table, placed his head on the arm. He spoke into the crook of his arm. "I do deny it," he said.

She had begun to inhale, and his halfhearted lie caused her to cough. The coughing turned into a derisive laugh. "Your wife is not one of your stupid thugs. Your wife has known something like this was going on. But as long as she didn't know for sure, she could pretend." She took a big puff and held it, making her voice tight and strained. "She can no longer pretend."

He sighed, and when he inhaled, his lungs took in the fragrant smoke, but he didn't lift his head. He felt suddenly exhausted. Then he leapt off his chair in pain and stumbled back against the wall. He couldn't find his footing and slid down to the tile floor. Diana had burned his wrist with the joint.

"I'm leaving in fifteen minutes," she said. "You will never see me again. Doesn't that sound glorious? It's so *big.*"

He remained on the floor and leaned against the wall, holding the burned wrist to his mouth. When he spoke, he kept the arm crooked protectively before him. "Can't we talk a little? I just walked in the door."

"If there had been an earlier flight, I wouldn't be here now." She flicked what remained of the joint at him. "Oh, I know you want mercy. I've had the past few hours to figure it out. You blame yourself for her brother and *blah blah blah.* I could tell you weren't over that kid's death back when you first told me about it. You thought being good to her son would make up for what happened to her brother. But it wasn't enough. I could forgive you if that was all there was to it. If it were just *weakness.* But now you love her. I saw it this afternoon. You *love* her."

Roy picked up the joint from the floor and stared at it, as if it were

< 8 1 >

an important piece of evidence. He took a hit on it to avoid having to look at her. He held his breath and tried to be occupied with the functioning of his lungs and—he could hear it now—the beating of his heart.

"You were afraid Fat Adele was going to fire her gun, so you leapt in front of your loved ones. I had this flash of pride. Here I was finally seeing you in action, seeing you do the things that make you cry in bed at night. Can you imagine it? Your wife was there, thinking, It's not another woman. It's having to chase muggers and bullies and bastards. While your wife's heart is bursting with love, *you* spot the other woman and the rest of the room vanishes. The other woman is all you see. You throw yourself in front of *her.* Your wife is standing not three feet away, but you don't know she's on the planet." She drank the last of the water from her glass, then poured the ice out onto the table. It slid slowly across the expanse of wood and fell into the chair opposite her. "There isn't a room in this house with a level floor," she said, then stared at the glass in her hand. Roy thought she might hurl it at him, but she set it on the table. "I've called my parents. I'm going to Phoenix to stay with them." She looked at her watch. "A cab is picking me up. You have four to six minutes left with your wife."

Roy went to one knee, then stood up to throw the joint into the sink. He didn't want to lie to her, but he didn't want her to leave him—although a thousand times he had dreamed of just that. Diana would leave and he would be free to love Emma, to raise their son in his own house. Now that it was happening, he could see only that this woman who had loved him now thought ill of him, this woman whom he loved now wished to be free of him. Two wine bottles were upended in the sink. That was the smell.

"I bought that wine for a special night," she said. "I didn't want you drinking it with *her.*" From outside came the sound of a car horn. She said, "He's early."

"I don't want you to go." That much was true. He had spoken the truth.

She dusted ash from her skirt. "It's all downhill for you. You think Emma is going to love you? She's a child. And she isn't even pretty. Your wife is prettier, but she is no longer yours." She pulled the suitcases from beneath the table and carried them out of the kitchen.

He heard her stomping down the hall. He thought to call to her, but he didn't. He had witnessed so many domestic scenes, it embarrassed him to be involved in one, and that kept him from calling her name. The front door opened and never closed. The suitcases thumped down the steps. He eased himself to the floor, then lay flat on the tile. He felt exposed and humiliated, as if there really had been a cop present to see it all. He touched his shirt, released the final buttons from their holes. He heard the closing of a trunk, a car door.

They had been married four years. They should have had children, he thought, beginning the guilty list of things they should have done. The list would occupy him through much of the night, would permit him to worry over things he could no longer address. It was a survival technique, this fretting. It would keep him from taking action on the one thing he could affect—his actual wife driving away in an actual taxi, flying away in an airplane in the very air that engulfed his house. He could act to save his marriage, but instead he focused on the things he should have done long ago. None of these things would involve Emma. He had made love to her when she was a child, but he wouldn't count it in the tally of his mistakes. He could not imagine his life without her.

He lay on his back and let the world outside spin.

The party had not fatigued Peter Ivanovich but invigorated him. He wanted to sit in the sun with a drink in his hand and talk about the reception. Everything about it had pleased him—the flattery and witless adulation, the dimpled legs of the hot-oil woman and the absurd drama of the arrest, the marvelous champagne whose eruptions on his tongue had been nothing less than carnal. He had meant to steal a bottle and one of the glasses, too, so perfectly contoured— transparent flute with its great round mouth, single leg, and circular base, which also struck him as erotic. The connections between the

< 83 >

pleasures of liquor and the pleasures of sex ran deep. The sun on his skin was another sensual pleasure, and he would have it all today.

He led them—daughter, granddaughter, and great-grandson—out onto the pool deck, where they assembled about a covered patio table. Once it had been the habit of the family to gather there. The children would swim while the adults talked. Peter had enjoyed visiting his daughter back then. A high plank fence surrounded the pool and deck, providing privacy and defining the space—separating it from the neighbor's yard and from their own shabby lawn and concrete drive. A tree on the policeman's side of the fence furnished morning shade. Peter had written a chapter of one of his books in that shade, what? Fifteen years ago? Above the tree, the peak of the neighbor's roof showed, as well as the top half of a second-story window. Sunlight would bounce off that window in the late afternoon and illuminate a rectangle of pool water. The rectangle would slide slowly across the water as the sun plunged in the sky. Eventually the lighted box would climb out onto the deck and creep up the fence, making its geometry on the planks opposite the house, like the light of a projector being readied for slides.

But the slides this family would have, no one could bear to examine.

It bothered him that he had not recognized Emma at the bus station. She was the reason he had come to live here. He had no place else to go, of course, but still, Emma was the deciding factor. They were correspondents. She wrote to him or called him whenever he was in one place long enough to supply her with a number. He worried that he had put his hand on her butt. He had been caught up in the festive opportunity of the event—one woman after another lining up for him. She would forgive him his error, if she noticed at all, and so he had to forgive himself, didn't he? In her letters, Emma always talked about her parents, but it was Emma herself who needed him. And he wanted, at long last, to be someplace where he might be needed. What is it about old age that demands not care but the desire to be of some use? He should have written her back more often. He had meant to, and she seemed to understand that. If he could have written her in Russian, he would have sent her dozens of letters. He had never learned to think in English. That, according to someone—a teacher, a fellow immigrant, a former wife, he couldn't remember—was the key to really acclimating to a language. He had only just begun trying to write his papers in English. Thinking in it seemed out of the question.

The pool he sat beside was twelve feet deep and impossible to heat, covered now with a black pad of some sort. One of the tales Emma had written to him involved the pool. Years ago her parents had arranged to have it made more shallow by a process that began with a layer of sand followed by a coat of concrete. But Emma and her brother objected. Philip told their parents that Emma secretly wanted to become a diver. "For the high dive," the boy had said, "you need deep water." That she wanted to become a diver was news to Emma, yet she declared it was true. More than anything, she wanted to be a diver. She had been eight, and it was what her big brother wanted her to say. *Why did you and your brother want the pool to remain deep and cold?* Peter asked in a letter. Emma wrote back, *We didn't like for things to change. Something inside us resisted.*

Her parents decided to demonstrate that they listened to their children, and they didn't mind saving the expense of making the pool more shallow. *Money was always an issue while Philip was alive—and never an issue afterward.* Emma's father built a diving platform for her, which obliged her to hurl herself into the cold water. Upon her graduation from middle school, he arranged for her to attend a new high school at the edge of town that had a beautiful pool and a diving team. *I didn't want to leave my friends, but I couldn't tell my parents that.* She could tell only her grandfather. Should he have told her mother? Had Emma been asking him to step in? He hadn't considered it at the time. Perhaps he had never quite given Emma his full attention. Until now. Now he would focus on her to the exclusion of everything else. Except his own work. And the occasional entertainment, of course. But Emma would be the main thing.

I'm pregnant, she wrote during her freshman year of high school. *I'm not going to tell my parents yet. Mother will want me to abort.* Peter had been in Europe and did not receive this letter until he returned. By then Morgan was taking her to some kind of classes about how

< 85 >

to have a baby—some idiotic American fad. Peter had spent most of his life in the United States, but he still discovered things that appalled him.

After the baby was born, Emma resumed diving, and now she was on the college team. Her brother, who had determined this path for her on a whim, was long dead. His death had ended the family's gathering on the deck. A selfish boy, Peter thought. But it had not seemed right to sit out there without him while the leaves of the neighbor's tree shook with the same rustling they had always made and that parcel of light executed its daily route across the water, oblivious to the boy's disappearance. Peter was determined to change this, to reclaim at least this artificial body of water from the clutches of the dead child. The rest—the marriage, the possibility of happiness—likely could not be redeemed.

Peter Ivanovich angled his head up at the sun. He and Zhenya sat on lawn chairs and drank gin—a good liquor to follow champagne. Emma drank a diet soft drink, giving sips to Petey, who crawled about the deck at their feet, building a house of plastic bricks, describing the construction as he went, advising the grown-ups that there would be no roof because the giraffe was the tallest animal and it was his birthday party. The boy bored Peter. All children bored him. Until they reached a certain age, he hadn't much use for them. He suspected every man felt this way, and at one time the women had simply accepted this fact. Now it was heresy even to suggest it.

Emma slipped down to the deck to hear the details of her son's story. What patience the girl had. Zhenya was content to watch from a distance. Each year she became more like her father, Peter noted with pleasure. She, too, had left the reception exhilarated. It was written on her face. A farce was revealed to be a farce, and that sort of justice delighted father and daughter both. It had especially pleased her that it was Morgan's partner who was apprehended. It meant something in the unspoken battle she and Morgan waged. It proved something, vindicated an argument she could not articulate but held close to her heart. She and her husband were the kind of people who thrived on battles they never acknowledged. They had been this way for years now.

For Peter, the competition between the allure of the past and the demands of the present made his physical life more complex than those of the people around him—less imperative but more complex. He lived on the inside, which permitted him to do whatever he wanted on the outside—play the fool, pinch a bottom, speak his mind; none of it affected the world inside him. He had begun, a few years ago, returning to Russia in his mind, powerful episodes that eventually led him to book a flight to the new Russia and seek out his old haunts: the family house in St. Petersburg, the Moscow streets he had walked as a young man, the farmhouse where his father died of a stroke. But the trip had proved disappointing. Russia had not modernized and most of the places he recalled still stood, but they did not look the same. Houses, people, even the trees he remembered were slightly different—in some way fantastically dull. Nothing was as vivid as his memories from childhood, when one's sensibility is most acute and the world is both its largest and most small. It made him aware of a mistake in his philosophy. In his eagerness to disown materialism, he had turned against things, against the material world, and it was this world he longed for now, the world of objects. His most powerful memory was of collecting leaves on the way home from some forgotten event, leaves that fit a certain way in his palm, a dusty smoothness to them, a quality of perfection that led him to show them to his mother, little wings weighted with the perfection of being exactly what they were. To his mother they were just leaves, of course, but she was sufficiently in tune with her child to look at them with wonder. This memory of his mother's compassion moved Peter, but it was the feel of the leaves that possessed him, transported him.

Things were less real now, but he gravitated to them more than ever. Some days everything was laden with its predecessors. White sheets clinging to his legs would take him back to his adolescence, young Tatyana naked on the mattress beside him, her long hair tickling his thighs. A white porcelain toilet would transport him to a urinal—a trough, really—almost too high for him to reach in the St. Petersburg train terminal, his father standing beside him, encouraging him, taking his turn immediately after. What abundance lay in every moment once the insistence of the immediate slackened. A

< 8 7 >

slice of packaged white bread suddenly became cake in a china dish, the fingers of a young woman breaking off a piece, the spongy pastry floating in her fingers up to her mouth, which was painted the stinging red of fire ants, and then to her white teeth, the middle two slightly overlapping, as if out of modesty.

Other days the present remained stubbornly present, a grayness to it that he recognized as the failing of his eyes. If the day was interesting and varied enough, he might study the complex net of motivations and misunderstandings that lay beneath the immediate actions of the people around him, but even this would bore him after awhile. What did it matter, really? Memory burned so brightly that the good days were lit by it. On the gray days, he would seek out things that would bring it on—a lovely girl, the heft of a champagne glass, a moment of grace.

While Peter Ivanovich was mulling this over, his daughter shifted in the plastic chair beside him. "I'm not entirely certain that Mrs. East was satisfied with her party," she said slyly.

"What good is party where is no arrest?" Peter said. Then he pinched his facial features and spoke in a high-pitched, incredulous voice. "You're not here on official business, are you, young man?"

Zhenya burst out laughing. What a fine laugh she had. They reviewed the party, tittering their way through it, a narrative similar to the one Petey was telling—foolish people at a foolish gathering behaving foolishly. Petey said, "The police are under arresting him now." He waved a plastic animal to indicate the one being read his rights.

Emma said, "That's Roy's job. He didn't want to arrest Danny, but he had to."

"Roy threw himself in front of Petey," Zhenya said. "Did you notice that?"

"No," Peter Ivanovich said. "Is genuine champion, this policeman?"

"He's a good person, I think," Zhenya said, nodding in agreement with herself like a child.

So, that it was their neighbor who made the arrest added to his daughter's appreciation of the spectacle. That made sense, Peter thought. It fit within a pattern of justice and coincidence that

Zhenya held dear. Peter knew the policeman's part in Philip's death. Such details did not escape him. His mind was accustomed to fitting together disparate elements, finding patterns. In fact, he knew things his daughter and son-in-law probably did not. Things Emma had withheld from them. He took a self-congratulatory drink of gin. He wished they had martini glasses. Like the champagne glasses, they contributed to the sensuality of an experience. "Party does not go to upper quarters!" Peter Ivanovich cried, and Zhenya hooted again.

The back door swung open. Morgan's gloves flapped in his back pocket as he scuffed across the deck. Peter gestured to him to join them, but the sight of her husband seemed to dampen his daughter's spirits. Peter screwed up his face and offered Morgan his impersonation of prim astonishment, but Morgan didn't seem to get it. He fell into a chair, and even his exhaustion annoyed his wife.

"Oh, come on," she said. "It was hysterical."

"The reception?" Morgan asked.

Peter Ivanovich made another effort. "Yes, dear, you wonderful man, you."

Zhenya's laughter toppled over the edge of mere pleasure, becoming a dark, vindictive thing. So be it, Peter Ivanovich thought. One had to find gratification wherever one could. Any marriage that had endured so much could not be a simple, erect structure. The beauty of such a union was in its ugliness. If one could not laugh at the puckered, lopsided, sneering countenance of one's own marriage, the only alternatives were divorce or blindness. This was his gift, he thought, to see what others could not see. He threw back his head and laughed with his daughter. To see it and name it and roar with laughter. Morgan refused to laugh—the one unforgivable sin. Instead he sighed self-righteously. The wife was elated and the husband, defeated. That was the story of their life together. She was a prominent political scientist, and he, nothing but a hauler of rubbish, a slinger of crap.

The trashman said, "They wouldn't let me see Danny."

"What's going to happen to him?" Emma asked, fingering her son's plastic wall of bricks.

Morgan shook his head. "I don't know."

< 89 >

"What could you have done, anyway?" Zhenya asked. "You couldn't have done a goddamn thing." She took a swallow of her drink, a sliver of ice remaining between her lips. Peter watched intently. He loved this debacle of human emotions as much as he had loved the party. What a glorious day!

"I was thinking," Morgan said. "I was thinking we could put up the bail."

Zhenya spat the ice cube into her glass. "Have you lost your mind?"

"I can't stand the thought of him in a cell."

"You're *not* thinking. You don't *think*." She glared; her arm flinched as if she wanted to slap him. *I'd like to slap some sense into you,* Zhenya's mother used to say to Peter Ivanovich. He recalled the anger in her voice with pleasure. Had she ever actually slapped him? A time or two. Peter approved of the slaps. Small acts of violence made life richer. He himself turned the world into a riskier place for his daughter. He needed to show her that was a good thing. But his arrival did not explain everything. This state of mind of hers, this condition of excited ecstatic swings—where had it come from? What did it mean? Always, since the boy's death, they had been a troubled pair, but now their trouble had turned a new corner.

His daughter calmed herself with the drink, the ice. She said, "There won't even be a decision about bail for a while. Can't the union help with this kind of thing? If you were still in charge, you could make it happen in a heartbeat." Peter watched anger shoot up within her again, coloring her temples, but she held it down, swallowed it back. What effort she expended! He was impressed. Then she said to her husband, "There's more gin, if you're interested." This, she offered to him in her calmest voice.

"Maybe in a minute." Morgan didn't look at her, the stoic hero among the vulgar drunkards—the stoic hero stinking of garbage. What a pair they were. Each certain of the other's failings. She, at least, could think about it honestly. Semihonestly. Peter finished his gin, shook the ice, and said, "Is more?"

"Would you at least take a fucking shower?" Zhenya said.

Morgan's eyes flitted to Petey, disapproving of his wife's language. Then he simply stared at the black pad that covered the pool.

He said nothing, did not move, a big stone zero in filthy clothes, a monument to waste. Peter in this moment despised the man as his daughter did. Her anger embarrassed her, but she would redirect all the blame onto her husband. *He is always doing this kind of thing,* Peter could hear her say, her husband acting in a manner designed to cast her in a bad light. They were both fools, he realized, and suddenly he was tired of looking at them. They didn't have the sense to divorce. Or the courage. They were cowards. He said, "Emma, you must dive for us. I was remembering how you dive. So beautiful, like ballerina of air."

"Not a good idea." Morgan explained that the black pad worked as a solar heater, but it was too early in the spring, even on a day as hot as this one, for it to have heated a pool as deep as theirs.

As always, he missed the point entirely.

"Why don't you let Emma speak for herself?" Zhenya said.

Emma looked up at them and shrugged. "I'll try it if you want."

"You'll freeze," Morgan said.

"She's an adult," Zhenya said. "With a child. She can make her own decisions."

"What does having a child have to do with the temperature of the pool?"

Zhenya glared at him for a moment and then laughed. To Emma, she said, "Your father's developed an aversion to water. Doesn't even want *you* to get wet. We'll never get him to actually bathe."

"Cold water is good for circulation." Peter Ivanovich winked at Morgan. Couldn't he at least interpret a wink? It was one of the oldest human gestures. Cavemen winked at their women, and their women winked back. "Is always cold in Russia," he said. "Let her swim."

"She can do what she wants, obviously," Morgan said.

"Obviously," Zhenya said.

Morgan shook his head and stood. "I suppose I'd better go shower."

"Call a camera crew," Zhenya said, but no one laughed. Peter could have, but he didn't. "Let the dog out," she called to her husband's retreating form. Peter understood that he would have to see them separately or they would wear him out.

< 91 >

"I'll wait till you're back," Emma called to her father, "it'll be fun. I'm sorry about Danny." The back door swung open and shut. She turned to her mother. "You were being mean."

"I was just teasing," Zhenya said. "He used to have a sense of humor."

"You asked me to tell you when you were being mean to him."

"I did no such thing."

"Did you say is more gin?" Peter Ivanovich asked.

Zhenya touched Peter's hand. She seemed about to apologize for the tension and harsh words, but he would not permit it. Morgan was gone, time for fun. He tightened up his face. "Now see here!" he said, and she began laughing once more. Elation returned to her, and he understood that her state of mind stemmed from all of it— his arrival, the arrest of Morgan's partner, Morgan's stench at the reception, how he had wandered through the crowd of nicely dressed people in his stinking clothes accompanied by his hoodlum partner, and how someone official, someone with whom she and Morgan had a history of the most intimate sort, how that person had shown that such behavior could not be tolerated, that such behavior was an offense.

Yes, Peter Ivanovich thought. These people were like puppets on a paper stage, every gesture had to be broad or it would be invisible. He threw his head back so far it might have seemed about to pop off, and he let rip a long, furious cackle.

The dog orbited about the selected patch of ground, the spot designated by instinct and reason as the correct repository for her feces. She took comfort in this ritual, her movements and methods second nature to her. This part of the yard and not the spot that was once the garden where Zhenya had grown flowers, and not the long green by the wall, where the boy had liked to play catch. Never mind that the boy had been gone ten of the dog's thirteen years. To defecate in the boy's space would have been obscene.

The circling, when it began, freed her of the pain in her legs, erased the neural messages and substituted the blind pleasure of ritual, the unthinking obedience to habit. It was instinct that had

taught her this dance, but it had long ago passed into habit, and as
with any habit, one took the most comfort from it in the midst of
the foreign. And the dog stubbornly believed her misery was foreign; she could not conceive of it as her new home. Was this a
blessing or simply the misconception that marked her as a dumb
animal? It could be a mark of faith. Did it matter that her faith
was rooted in experience rather than in the spirit?

Her bowels operated smoothly and without pain. So far it was
only her legs that hurt her. She took pleasure in the evacuation of
her bowels and in the pleasing odor. Shit was not an ugly thing for
a dog. It was what it was—the remnant of that which has fed us,
all that is left after the necessary has been removed. No dog's shit
smelled quite like another. It was, like the timbre of a voice, a
defining marker, and so it contained history, even as it signified
health or illness. Her shit smelled fine—another sign that the
pain would pass. That order would be restored. She stepped away
from it, although she sensed that elemental pull, that desire found
in dogs and humans alike to roll in it. She had been trained
against that instinct, and she respected the training above the
longing. She was a good dog.

Peter Ivanovich studied Emma as she stepped out of the house
wearing a one-piece swimsuit. Not a lovely girl, but young and athletic. And her mind was interesting, full of strange turns. If her
brother had not killed himself, she would likely be a happy, dull,
tedious American child, exactly like a hundred million others. And
then this plainness in her face and body would be a catastrophe
because she would have nothing else to offer. Philip's death had
been good for her. Peter could see this, admit it into his thoughts.
The truth is not always a pleasant thing, but life had to be examined
honestly. Morgan, his thinning hair wet from the shower, could
never admit to such a thought. He wrestled now with the pool cover
despite his belief that his daughter should not swim. He was not a
stupid man, but he was absurd. He was the kind of man who could
not hold a grudge against the people he loved, and he was too shallow to see this as a failing. The shower had made him feel better,
so he would be thinking that his wife had not been cruel when

< 93 >

she cursed his odor—no, she had known all along it was what he needed.

It was during this interim of quiet that Emma crossed the deck in her bathing suit and Peter recognized what it was that this girl possessed. What he had seen when she stepped out of the house was a plain girl with plain features, nothing crooked or deformed but nothing pretty, either. But that changed while he watched her walk. As she approached the diving platform, he identified something else. She did not see herself as plain. He could tell by the manner of her walk, by the way she shook her hair off her face, the way her eyes looked out over the deck and the people and the water in the pool, as if she had as much right as anyone to be looking at that deck and those people and that container of blue water. This attitude did something to her. It changed her, made her attractive. In a certain way, beautiful. Not in her features but in her bearing. Not in the shape of her body but in her body's movement. She didn't have beautiful eyes, but what her eyes saw was made beautiful by her gaze, and one couldn't help but attribute that beauty to the one whose look had made it so. Her loveliness was created by the reflection of the world around her, a world that had been ordinary until she stepped into it. He had not seen this at the bus station, but then he had not recognized her. He identified it now, and it led him to concentrate on her every movement.

She stepped onto the chrome ladder of the high dive, her knees bending, the long muscles in her thighs pursing, her bare feet arched and extended. Peter Ivanovich let his glass slip from his hand and fall into his lap. He grabbed it quickly and brushed the ice away. He watched her climb the ladder, and the others noticed the quality of his attention, which caused them to look and then look again at the climbing girl. Peter wanted to point to the sway of her hair, the swing of her hips as she elevated herself step by step. Up on top, she strode to the edge of the platform and turned—a virtual pirouette—and when she edged out to the end and rose to the balls of her feet, her arms rising simultaneously, a gasp escaped from Peter and his old heart beat wildly.

The others noticed this and did not notice it. His excitement directed their attention to Emma on a heightened wave of stimulation, and they studied her with the same elevated sense of anticipation.

Emma leapt backward into the sunlit air, while Peter's heart executed a similar leap, bounding up into his throat as Emma's legs lifted, toes pointed to the reach of her arms, her hands an extension of her arms, her fingers an extension of her hands. Peter felt his own body rise, weightless, inches above the lawn chair, as Emma executed a flip, tumbling through the air, righting herself at the last instant, her body perfectly perpendicular to the water as she entered it, the water moving to accommodate her, practically without a splash, as if the body had slithered into the pool, as if she had made the waters part. Tears filled his eyes, while a rush of sensation inflated his chest, sending waves of heat throughout his body. "Marvelous," he said, unaware he had spoken in Russian.

The others saw it, too. Morgan felt he had witnessed perfection, and what was more, his wife seemed to feel the same. Zhenya believed it was the first time she had ever seen Emma not as her daughter attempting to dive but as a genuine diver. My daughter has mastered this, she thought. Petey clapped and yelled for his mom. Even the dog took notice. Prince planted her good legs on the concrete and rose from her curl, watching for Emma's head to emerge from beneath the water. Immersion worried the dog.

For Peter Ivanovich, the dive brought the vividness of memory into the afternoon, and he loved it. It called to mind his young mother sweeping through the house, her layered skirts moving like the tides. It returned to him the early days of sex, the exertion and the leap of the body, first into nothingness and then into pleasure.

Emma shook water from her hair, shivering as she crossed the deck to climb the tower again. On the platform, she wiped water from her eyebrows, then paced to the edge, hesitated, poised at the brink, and dived again.

Zhenya put her hand on Morgan's arm. She spoke softly, modulating the surprise in her voice. "She's become so good at this."

"Yes," he said cautiously. "She's really wonderful." He could not hide his pleasure. "She has a competition coming up. This is good practice." He said this as if to justify his joy.

The diving held them captive. It seemed to erase the troubles of

< 9 5 >

the day, return order to the chaos. Every moment she spent suspended above the water seemed outside of time—permanent in some way—as if their real lives were the distraction, while this momentary flight made up their actual existence. They were encouraged by it. They were reassured. It did not matter that in a few minutes the sun would sink below the trees, that they would rise from their chairs and dwindle back into their artificially lit rooms, that the buoyant hope would slip away. For the moment, they were happy.

High above them, in the next house, standing on his bed in the upstairs bedroom, Roy Oberland wept for his departed wife and watched his beloved fall repeatedly and effortlessly from a high place he had to strain to see, to a site somewhere below, out of his vision, a place where her body would stop its fall—her destination, his blind spot.

3

Vulgarity is an expression of stupidity, coarseness, or freedom.

—Peter Ivanovich Kamenev

They met in a little turquoise room, a cubicle barely larger than a phone booth with a clear plastic window between them. Danny was sitting in the chair and smiling when Morgan entered. His body spilled over the chair, his shoulders almost as wide as the cubicle walls. He wore a neon orange jumpsuit, and it suited him.

"Nice duds," Morgan said. Danny's expression remained frozen in that minimal smile of his. "Your clothes," Morgan explained. "They look good on you."

"They gave me these," Danny said. "No charge."

"It's good to see you're styling." Morgan paused then, unsure where to go with the conversation. Danny clearly wasn't going to help, not that he ever did. Morgan felt guilty for the time that had passed, now almost two weeks, but he had run into one problem after another. First Danny had not put Morgan's name on his visitors' list. Then Danny's family and lawyer requested that he be kept clear of any "friends." "I work with him," Morgan had tried to explain. "I'm not in any gang." Finally, the prosecuting attorney asked to depose Morgan before he had a chance to talk to Danny. That had been the final stumbling block, and all Morgan had to do was show his face to the prosecutor. "You're his *partner?*" the young man said and laughed. He did not look to be much older than

< 96 >

< 97 >

Danny and had so much gel in his hair it resembled a helmet. "I'm sorry," he said. "We had the wrong impression."

The tiny room smelled of new plastic, like Petey's plastic bricks. Family members had to hate this transparent box, Morgan thought. So close and yet so separate. A virtual visit. "I tried to see you earlier," he said at last.

"I know," Danny said, giving the slightest of nods. "Why?"

Morgan shifted and wagged his head. "To see what was going on. See how you're doing."

"Not much going on in here." His face was brightly lit, and the smile grew, seemed huge. Just a normal smile, really, but Morgan was unaccustomed to expression on his partner's face. "They arrested me," he said. "How else can I be?"

"You have a lawyer?"

"They gave me one. She's a woman."

"What does she say?"

Danny just stared and smiled.

"About the charges against you," Morgan said.

"Yeah, yeah. She says my problem is I'm guilty."

"Your lawyer said that?"

"I'm not supposed to tell nobody." Danny's smile altered at this revelation but was no less impressive. "Keep your mouth shut, okay?"

"Guilty of finding a gun that had been used in a crime?"

Danny looked up at the ceiling. Several of his teeth were capped in gold. What a lot of work it was to raise a child, Morgan thought. Gold was the least of it. "These guys I know shot some other guys up, and they asked me to get rid of the gun since I go to the dump every day. How's the dump, anyway?"

"It's all right," Morgan said. "The same."

"Good."

Morgan waited, but the boy appeared to be finished. Morgan didn't know what to do with this information, how to process it. All right, he thought, he's guilty of something but not much. Loyalty, he's guilty of loyalty.

Danny said, "The first ones they gave me didn't fit. Too little." He pinched the material of the jumpsuit. "Then I got these."

"Did your friends tell you the gun had been used in a crime?"

Danny shook his head. "No. They just said they shot up some guys."

"You shouldn't have taken the gun," Morgan said, as much to himself as to Danny, "but isn't there a deal you can cut?"

Danny shook his head. "Not without telling on the others."

He really was a child, Morgan thought, and he didn't want to be a tattletale. Panic began to swirl inside him. He took a long breath to suppress it. "They *shot* people. All you did was hide— fail to hide—the gun. Why should you go to prison while they go free?"

"If I'm lucky, I won't have to go to prison." He leaned back in his chair, but his head struck the wall behind him. "Duh," he said and rubbed his head.

"You need your hard hat."

"I miss it. And my shades. I got a plan. You wanna hear?"

"I'm not sure you should tell me."

"I can't tell nobody." He made his quick laugh, as if it were a joke. Then he shook his head and looked around before leaning in close to the plastic window. His breath fogged the plastic. "My mom got her breast cut off today," he said, and he was no longer smiling. "She don't like me anymore. But I feel bad being in jail while she's in surgery."

"Can I do anything for your mother?"

"She's got a doctor. Her sister is in town for, I don't know, bandaging and shit." He leaned back, grew still again. Then he said, "My bail is kind of high, but what do you think?"

"I'm working on the union board—the one that handles the discretionary fund. They meet day after tomorrow."

"Yeah, yeah," Danny said. "Just, how it is, what plan I've got depends on making bail. I didn't think it would be so hard. My family has had it with me. They think I'm . . . You know that I was getting into working, right?"

Morgan nodded.

"They think I was putting the con on them. They think it's so easy, you know, having a job. Just doing it every day, like they do.

< 99 >

But now is different from when they started going into work. If there was some way to tell my mom, I would. But it takes some kind of talking I don't know about."

It was the longest speech Morgan had ever heard Danny give. It surprised him and seemed to surprise Danny, too. They were quiet for a while. Morgan wiped sweat from his forehead. A tap on the plastic box turned his head. A guard pointed to his watch, then raised two fingers.

"That means two minutes left," Danny said. "There's a lot of stuff to learn in here. Like a raised hand means *Shut the fuck up*. And you got to wear flip-flops in the shower because of athlete's foot. And you don't *ever* take long showers."

"Why's that?"

"People get pissed." Danny made a face, shook his head. "I got some pals working on bail, but they're not showing up around here so much."

"I miss you," Morgan said. "They've given me lunkheads to fill in."

"I like working. Didn't really know it till this. I sort of did, but not really. Been writing on my play. Plenty of time for it. Added a whole new act. Set in jail. Jenna visited me."

"Your teacher?"

He shook his head. It barely qualified as a twitch. "The MS babe. Wheeled right in here. Says even jails have to be accessible. Can't discriminate against a gangster in a wheelchair." He leaned close again, whispered, "If she could walk a little better, I'd go for her bony ass."

Morgan said, "Why didn't you just hide the gun in the dump? Why did you fire it? Why did you show it to me?"

Danny settled back in the chair, presented his slight shrug. "Thought it might be cool to give to the old guy, you know, who was coming to live with you. In case there was somebody else he ought to kill." He rocked his head a little, maybe thinking, as Morgan was, at what little foolishness it took to ruin a life. "Ah, fuck," Danny said. "Truth is, I'm like you, man." His head twitched again at the thought. "I don't like to waste nothing."

The coffee shop, Whole Latte Love, took up the ground floor of a building that had once been a bank. In the room that had been the vault, one could purchase cards for every occasion, including, Zhenya was surprised to find, sexual encounters. On the front of one card, a line drawing of a cute, conservative college girl was captioned:

> *I've been looking for a boy who does the little things that make all the difference.*

On the inside, the girl was grinning, naked, and spread-eagle in bed, a boy's head buried between her legs.

> *Like eating me all night long!*

Zhenya had never seen such a thing before, although it reminded her of the tacky postcards she used to find in highway gas stations on trips with her mother, cartoon drawings of farmers' daughters or sexy housewives paired with stupid puns and innuendo. But those postcards were designed for men, while this product was clearly aimed at women. Was this feminism—a woman claiming her sexual pleasure—or familiar exploitation with an unfamiliar pitch? She couldn't immediately decide, and as soon as she could make herself quit looking at the cards, she wouldn't care. It was her opinion that academics too often got hung up on little cultural tics at the expense of recognizing large political movements. Besides, she remembered loving to sneak peeks at those tacky postcards whenever her mother was in the ladies' room.

Her mother had spent many years as a professional graduate student, coming close to degrees in three different areas at three different universities before becoming a proofreader and then a technical writer for a computer manufacturer, then a small-time publisher and then an editor for a major house, then, of all things, a career counselor. She was defensive about the counseling. "If I'd had someone

< 1 0 1 >

like me to advise me," her mother had said the last time they spoke, "I wouldn't have such a checkered employment history."

"Checkered employment history" had to be language she had picked up from her job. It didn't sound like her. "But you had someone *exactly* like you to advise you," Zhenya pointed out. When her mother didn't follow, Zhenya said, "I'm talking about you yourself."

"Oh, *her.* I never listened to *her.* Unfortunately. No. Instead I listened to men like your father."

"Don't start. I'm sharing my house with him, and I don't need—"

"I bear no ill will toward your father. Well, some, but not the great load of it that he deserves. In any case, I *do* listen to my own counsel now."

"That so?" Zhenya said. "Then why do you have this crummy counseling job?"

"Ha, ha," her mother said and then changed the subject.

Zhenya pulled another card from the rack. A voluptuously drawn woman in a short skirt was sprawled seductively over a couch.

What are the three special words a woman needs to hear from a man before she hops into his bed?

On the inside, the same woman, same position on the couch, only naked now and smirking.

Condoms, condoms, condoms! Don't forget next time!

Zhenya put the card back in the display. Roy Oberland was meeting her in another five minutes. She hadn't expected him to give up his lunch hour for her, but she wasn't about to turn him down. She needed information, and he was the obvious source. Morgan's partner was in jail, and it was wearing on Morgan. He felt responsible— a stupid, childish response, but that was Morgan. He was trying to get the union to use their fund to pay for Danny Ford's bail, but if the decision-making board turned him down, he planned to use the family's savings. He hadn't said anything about it since the afternoon of the arrest, but Zhenya knew him well enough. She did not want Danny Ford to have a penny of their money. But she also wanted to be fair. Half of their savings was Morgan's, after all.

He planned to attend the next board meeting. She didn't understand the mechanics of getting the issue on the agenda, but she could certainly see the irony. Morgan had founded the union store and created the discretionary fund while he was president of the union. But now that he needed help, he had no power in the union at all. Long ago Zhenya had pleaded with him not to resign. But he wouldn't listen to her. How could she help but think of this as just deserts?

She had met Morgan when the union was new and preparing to strike, and he had proposed marriage to her just as the strike was beginning. She had felt all along that she was in love with a union organizer who just happened to be a garbageman—never the other way around. When they were first a couple, she would teach during the day and then join Morgan in the afternoon on a picket line. Afterward, they would go to his apartment and make love. Once she had run to the ringing phone naked, Morgan trailing after to pull her back to his bed, and the voice on the other end had said, "You are going to fucking die if this goes on any longer," followed by the click of the receiver. Immediately Morgan's warm body embraced hers, his hands on her breasts, his erection pressing against the small of her back. She had raised her leg, putting her foot on the chair by the phone, and then leaned forward to let him enter her from behind while they stood. "That was a threat," she told him. He responded by sliding his hands beneath her thighs and lifting her off the ground. She threw her arms back and gripped his shoulders, keeping him inside her, leaning forward like a figurehead on a ship. He carried her in this fashion the short distance to the bed. Sex had never before had such power, such *wholeness*. From the day she met Morgan to the day the union contract was signed amounted to little more than three months, but it was the most intense and thrilling period of her life. They married almost immediately after the strike ended.

She stepped out of the old vault to return to her table. Her current life was so distant from that former one, it hardly seemed she

< 1 0 3 >

could be the same person. As for Morgan, he most certainly was not the same person.

Zhenya seated herself and glanced at the doorway just as Roy Oberland, in full blue uniform, stepped into it. He removed his policeman's hat and his sunglasses, dropping the glasses into the hat, which he tucked beneath his arm. He began scanning the room, just as he had done at the reception, but this time he was looking for Zhenya, and she experienced a crooked little thrill in her chest. When he spotted her and smiled, she felt herself blush. Good God, she thought, every day a new way to be a fool.

Roy's partner, the large gunslinging woman, entered behind him. She did not bother with a hat and kept her sunglasses on. Happily, she took a table at the opposite end of the café. "Do I need to get in line?" Roy asked as he approached.

It took Zhenya a moment to figure out what he meant. "No, there's a waitress," she said. "That cashier sells the cards and calendars and things. You should see some of the cards."

"I've never been here before." He seated himself opposite her.

They exchanged pleasantries, and Zhenya passed him one of the paper menus. She knew he didn't have a long lunch break and would need to get his order in quickly. The waitress, a dark-haired girl in a short striped skirt, wasted no time attending them. Attending *him*, anyway. She ignored Zhenya except to shoot glances from the corners of her eyes, as if to say *What could* he *be doing with* her?

Or maybe Zhenya imagined that. She chastised herself for it. Van Morrison came on over the speakers, that soulful, tedious voice of his, wonderful and repugnant at the same time. "When the leaves come falling down," he sang, and Zhenya heard both the cloying sentimentality and the genuine lamentation. A lot of artists were like that, not either/or but good and bad simultaneously. She thought then about her daughter's diving. It had become their regular afternoon pastime. They gathered to watch her, Zhenya and her father and Morgan and Petey, their conversation finding a specific kind of rhythm, dictated by the silences surrounding the dives and the accolades that followed. They would sit talking until Emma reached the top of the platform, then they would make themselves still, concentrating, holding their collective breath. Emma's knees would flex, her arms would rise, and she would leap into the water. It was the best time of every day.

"She would like something, too," Roy said.

The waitress had almost left without taking Zhenya's order. So much for Zhenya's imagination. "Double espresso," Zhenya said. "No sugar. Nothing to eat." To Roy, she added, "I rarely eat lunch anymore."

"Dieting?" the waitress asked.

Zhenya stifled a glare. "We're a little pressed for time," she said and showed her a brittle smile.

"You wanted to talk to me," Roy said, leaning back in the chair. "About Morgan's partner?"

"That's right," Zhenya said. He smelled of something pleasant and familiar that she couldn't quite name. The waitress still lingered by the table, which made Zhenya hesitate a second. Then she said, "I need to know whatever you can tell me about Danny Ford."

The waitress had a run in her stocking that drew one's eye to her thighs, and she bent at the waist, ostensibly to wipe the adjoining table but obviously to catch Roy's attention. His eyes slid casually, almost laconically, over the perfect saddle of the waitress's bottom, while his mouth opened and shaped the words.

"He's a killer."

Without prevarication or equivocation. Without a preamble about poverty or bad influences. No legal dodges. No pretense about what was conjecture and what was the truth. No undercutting it with a smile or heightened tone, and no melodrama in his voice or in the construction of the sentence. "He's a killer." Danny Ford was a killer.

Roy crossed his legs then and Zhenya recognized what she was smelling—shoe polish. "Well," she said. "That sounds definitive."

"The guy's going to die," Roy said. "The man shot with the gun Ford pretended to find at the dump. He's on life support. A gang-banger himself. In fact, he's almost as bad as Ford. Anyway, the doctors say there's no real chance of recovery."

"Danny shot him?"

"No. Maybe. I'm not sure," Roy said. "Maybe Ford was just disposing of the weapon for his friends. But that makes him an

< 1 0 5 >

accessory after the fact." He waved his hands as if to erase what he had just said. "If that were all he had done, it wouldn't matter that much whether we nail him. But he's got a long history of violence. The worst kind of violence." He described the first time that he had arrested Ford and mentioned the crimes for which Ford had been a suspect. Then he said, "I've got no reason to lie about this."

"I know," Zhenya said. "I believe you."

The waitress appeared with his coffee. "I'll have your sandwich in a minute," she said to Roy. "And the espresso." She glanced at Zhenya. "Haven't forgotten about you." Before leaving, she picked a piece of lint off Roy's shirt, flicked it onto the floor, and patted the spot on his shoulder. "Now you're perfect again," she said.

"You always get this kind of attention?" Zhenya asked.

"My wife left me," Roy said. "I've been meaning to tell you. And Morgan."

The non sequitur threw her, and she didn't know what to say.

"Tired of being married to a cop," he added. "There's more to it than that, but . . ." He rocked his head and lifted his hand to his hair, perhaps to touch his hat, which lay on the table. "I'm doing okay, though." He nodded for a moment, then said, "That waitress means nothing to me whatsoever."

"Of course," Zhenya said.

"I'm sorry," he said. "I saw Morgan in the yard the other day, but I didn't say anything about Diana leaving. It's hard to talk about."

"Really, it's okay. It's fine. I don't even know what you're apologizing for."

"It's good that we've split up, but it's hard."

"Of course it is."

He took a drink of his coffee. She still didn't have hers. In a few moments, the waitress appeared again, conveying his sandwich and a salad for Zhenya. "I didn't order this," Zhenya said. The waitress reluctantly turned her attention from Roy. From the look on her face, she was about to say something personal, and Zhenya was afraid to hear it. *Are you always this much trouble?* Or worse: *Are you his mother?*

"Never mind," Zhenya said. "This looks good."

"Thank you," the waitress said. "We make them in advance." She bent over the adjoining table again, in case they hadn't noticed her butt earlier, before sauntering away.

Roy missed it entirely this time, staring at the plate as if he were about to say a prayer. When he raised his head, he looked Zhenya right in the eyes. "He's a killer," he said again. Then he took the sandwich in hand and smiled.

"No dogs in the park," the woman said. She was in uniform—black shorts and a T-shirt bearing the city logo and the words PARKS AND RECREATION. At one time Morgan would have known her name, but now there were dozens of city employees he had never even met. Emma normally came to Petey's T-ball games with Morgan, but she had a date with a boy named Sid. "We're going slumming," she had told Morgan. "He knows five restaurants that give away leftovers if you know how to ask."

"Do you need some money?" Morgan had asked.

Emma had shaken her head. "It's Sid's idea of an adventure."

Having failed to get Zhenya to accompany him, he had come with Prince. "Take the dog," his wife had suggested, and he had acquiesced. At the last minute Peter Ivanovich had decided to come, too. "Must see T-ball," the old man had said. "Need subject for new essay."

"We'd be going to watch Petey play," Morgan said.

"Of course. Most important, always combine work vis pleasure."

"It's only bleachers," Morgan said. "It's uncomfortable."

"Am ready for national pastime."

There had been no way to dissuade him. He could not really be one hundred. No one that old would be willing to sit on a bench for two hours to watch T-ball. He might be as young as seventy, Morgan guessed. He could pass for sixty-five.

Petey spotted his teammates and Morgan let him run ahead. "No dogs in a park?" Morgan said. "What's the point of a park if it doesn't allow dogs and kids?"

"Kids are welcome," she said, watching Petey trot away. "Dogs are not. It's not that kind of a park."

< 1 0 7 >

"What's this?" Peter Ivanovich had caught up with him. He placed his hands on Morgan's back, patting him, moving up to his shoulders. "I can't have dog?"

"No sir," the woman answered.

The old man's presumption irritated Morgan. The dog was not his, and Morgan didn't need the help.

"How you expect old man to get round visout dog?" Peter asked.

Morgan turned to stare at him. The woman did the same.

Peter Ivanovich took hold of the leash in Morgan's hand. "Is Seeing Eye dog."

"Give me a break," the woman said. "You're not blind. I watched you walk over here."

Peter shrugged. "Not now, but later will be."

"I beg your pardon," she said.

"Will ball contest persist into dark? Yes? I cannot see in dark. Must have dog."

She turned to Morgan. "Is he legally blind? Really?"

"Only in dark," Peter Ivanovich insisted, waving his big, open hands.

"Well," said Morgan. He was having fun now. "He often seems that way to me."

"In dark, am blind," Peter Ivanovich said. "Is fact."

The woman pointed to Prince. "This dog is on a leash. Not one of those contraptions."

Peter Ivanovich said, "What is name?"

She told him.

"Okay, most important for me to know. Morgan, put dog back in car. But you, Cheryl Allen, know now if I fall visout dog after contest, I sue city, yes, but I sue Cheryl Allen, too. This decision, you make. You are responsible."

The pleasure Morgan had taken in the escapade abruptly ended. He did not exactly hate the old man, but he hated having him around. Daily Morgan found him awake, making a mess in the kitchen in his soiled silk pajamas, smoking a cigarette, buttering his toast before sticking it in the toaster. Morgan hadn't realized how much he valued early-morning solitude until he began waking to this windbag. Every aspect of life in the United States was inferior to life in Russia, down to the types of feathers used in pillows.

The woman glared at them now. "Christ. Fine. Take your dog in." She muttered something more that Morgan could not make out, but it had the sharp sibilants of the obscene. Morgan let Peter and the dog go on. To the woman, he apologized. "He's lying, of course. I should have put the dog in the car when I had the chance."

"Forget it," she said. "Clean up after him."

"Her."

"Both of them." She eyed Morgan and added, "I feel sorry for you."

Morgan shrugged. "My wife's father. He had the chance to change the world one time, but he let it slip by."

"We should all get down on our knees and thank God." Then she motioned to the next group of people. "No glass containers," she said.

As Morgan saw it, what distinguished T-ball from most competitive sports was that the players didn't know the rules. The lone umpire—this evening a black kid with an opal earring—rigorously enforced them, but the players, ranging in age from four to six, were unencumbered by any sense of what should be done. If a runner forgot to run to first and was thrown out while celebrating his hit, he would still be giving high fives as he trotted over to his pals in the dugout. Having no idea why he couldn't stay on first, he didn't care. When a player hit a home run, he was only a little more excited than when he grounded out to first. The kids all looked to their coaches with the same expression, whether they had struck out or hit safely—*Did I do good?*

The only occasion for unhappiness on the field was in the uncommon event of a runner being tagged out. The kids cried if tagged, boys and girls both, the worst players and the best, as if the rudeness of the act demanded it. The one rule they unilaterally grasped was that the ball was in play until the pitcher held it in his or her glove and stood within the chalk circle around the pitcher's rubber. Even when a runner was passing right in front of them, in easy tagging

< 109 >

range, most players would throw the ball to the pitcher—or at least in the general direction of the pitcher. Throws were much the same as hits, virtually all were grounders and involved much chasing of and occasional fighting for the ball, while runners either hurried around the diamond or celebrated at one of the bases. Many throws were off by as much as forty degrees. Fielders routinely stopped grounders with their feet. Coaches preferred first-base dugouts because runners rounding third occasionally forgot themselves and ran into the dugout instead of to home plate.

Morgan had chosen the Dolphins for Petey over the union-sponsored team. The coaches on the union team were macho and cutthroat. The Dolphins' coaches were women—secretaries in the engineering school of the university—and they were nice to the kids. Morgan thought one of them was sexy, a healthy, robust woman with a big voice, big chest, and a bowler's voluptuous build. She and her partner never yelled anything but encouragement, and every child got to play in every game. Their record was 0 and 14.

This night the opposing coaches had beards, sunglasses, and attitudes. They yelled, "Move your butt," and wore cleats and full-length regulation uniforms. Petey's team had matching T-shirts. His coaches had painted their lips and fingernails to match the shirts. The sexy coach had silver hoops in her ears and leopard-spot sunglasses.

"We're in trouble," Morgan said to Peter. He described T-ball play, emphasizing the two redeeming rules: no more than ten batters could come to the plate in any inning, and no game could exceed two hours in duration. "They seem longer," Morgan said, "but the umpire watches the clock like a hawk."

Peter revealed that he had been friends with Jackie Robinson. "Great man, very brave, but no good vis money." He shook his head. "Too many relatives." He had also known Josh Gibson and attended Negro League games. He went to one game with none other than Babe Ruth, who had disguised himself with a hat and phony mustache. "But people in audience recognize *me*!" Peter said, acting astonished, but Morgan understood this was the point of the story. The old man could put himself in the middle of anything. Morgan liked to watch CNN in the morning while he drank his coffee, but his father-in-law now watched with him, commenting on everything the newscaster said, as if he were personally involved in every newsworthy subject. It was maddening. He was still talking. "Once they are talking to me, they recognize the Babe Ruth also. We have to leave because is such crowd round us." He went on to describe how he fought for integration in major-league baseball. "Black people are better athletes. Why is controversy? People think if we say blacks is better athletes, then we imply whites is smarter. Stupid. Who can jump higher? Get tape and measure. What is smart person? This, no one knows."

Morgan nodded but was no longer paying attention. He thought of the orange jumpsuit issued to Danny Ford. What had he expected? The black and white horizontal stripes of cartoon cons? He felt a specific tightness in his gut. He had learned to recognize it—the onset of anxiety. He had begun having debilitating fits of it, but why here? Why at a ball game? He dug into his pocket and removed a plastic bottle. His doctor had prescribed a drug to help him relax. He swallowed a tiny pill without water. Danny likely had little or no choice about getting rid of the gun. Gangs were like that, Morgan knew from television. He, on the other hand, easily could have let the episode go. He could have *listened* to Danny and left the gun far out in the landfill where Danny had thrown it.

A girl with a long ponytail opened the game by grounding to the left side of the pitcher's circle. Base hit. Anything hit to the left side of the infield required a throw and was therefore a hit.

"Intelligence is mystery." Peter had not lost the thread of his monologue. "Only thing we know is good family will have books. Make children read. Is why Jews and Russians have advantage in intelligence race. They are close intellectual families."

Morgan wanted to point out that Peter had played almost no part in the raising of Zhenya but didn't want to give him an opening. His stomach tightened, and his heart seemed to flutter. When he was a young man, his mind and body had never been in conflict like this. It seemed terribly unfair.

"Lenin was anti-Semite," Peter continued. "You know this? Stalin, too, but goes visout saying. History records acts and deeds,

< 1 1 1 >

but most important, it does not record attitude of Lenin. Why? Do you want to know why?"

A pinch runner was sent in for the girl with the ponytail, who needed to pee. Base running often excited the bladder. Petey was playing right center and, for the moment, paying attention to the game. That would change as the game progressed.

"This night is like something else we do," Peter said. "One night long ago I visit, we spend evening in small coalition game."

"What are you talking about?" Morgan asked.

"Angels, they were—this I know—and Sun Devils. Angels and Devils is why I remember. I and you and Zhenya and little Emma. Philip is playing pitcher."

Morgan remembered. He could see his son on the mound. He made himself imagine one pitch, then another. He held the image long enough to see just how his son kicked his leg upon delivery of the ball, the way his head turned but his eyes remained focused on the plate. That was enough. He was here to watch Petey. "Little League," he said, "not . . . whatever you called it."

"English is stupid language. Fifty years I speak English and still it makes me a fool."

Morgan didn't swing at that one, though it was the kind of lob he could knock out of the park. The pill must already be working. Anxiety felt to him exactly like the onset of terror. He took another deep breath and called out encouragement to the Dolphins.

The dog watched the children. One of hers was out among the scatter in the big yard. With hats on and in identical uniforms, she could not, at this distance, say which of the little ones it was. This made her apprehensive. Like all dogs, she hated hats.

Another of hers sat above her and rested his hand on her head. She had the urge to whimper and also the urge not to whimper, as she knew it was not good behavior. The pain in her rear legs had not diminished. She raised her head as a white ball bounced across the yard, and she felt the urge to chase after it—this urge, a type of memory—but she also felt the prohibition against chasing after it. She might look to the one above her to be sure, but the pain in her legs was answer enough. Memory, though, once it had been wakened, coursed through her. She thought for a moment that the other one, Philip, was out there with these boys. Though she did not like hats, it was the fact of them that permitted her to think this. She had the fleeting, heightened sense that both of her boys were out there chasing the ball. Why else would she have been brought here to this strange yard—no other dog in sight— and if that were true and since the ball had been thrown again, then they must expect her to play with them after all. What else would make sense?

She rose to her feet, a pain like needles stabbing the bones, and she took steps to slip through the gate into the yard. The big one with her—Morgan—jumped up and took hold of her collar. He spoke gently, as he almost always did, with some humor in his voice but with concern, too. He pulled her back. She settled again on the ground. She dropped her head to her paws. When the children ran in, she lifted her nose to each. They touched her, petted her, recoiled from her. Her boy put his glove on her head and talked to her—sweet music of his voice, sweet music of his laughter, sweet music that again called on memory, and she twisted her head back and forth to look for the other, but he had long ago forsaken her.

How was it possible that a child could simply disappear? Daily this question, in one form or another, occurred to her. She made no progress on an answer.

She settled her head onto her paws again. The sadness passed. She was out, after all, with people she loved. Despite the pain, she now felt contented. She closed her eyes and tumbled into sleep, the white ball appearing in her dream, passed from one child who loved her and who was hers to the next child who loved her and who was hers. Her legs did not ache in the dream. She ran from child to child effortlessly.

"Where does it hurt, girl?" Morgan scratched Prince behind the ear as he spoke. She had tried to run onto the field, and her movement suggested she was in pain. How had he failed to notice this before?

< 1 1 3 >

From behind him came a familiar voice that made him cringe. "Catcher, in this kind of game, is the most boring position," the man said, indicating, Morgan guessed, that his grandchild was behind the plate. "I only played sandlot ball, and it usually ended in fights," he went on. His cap proclaimed GRANDDAD OF THE YEAR and sat at an unfortunate angle, suggesting some kind of cranial cave-in. He came to every game. For a while he was quiet, but something would set him off and he would offer commentary on every play thereafter.

A grounder escaped the outstretched glove of the shortstop.

"He has to learn to bend over."

The coach bent down in the batter's box to tie the shoe of the batter.

"If she'd just leave the boy alone, he'd be fine. She can't keep her nose out of it."

"Sir," said Peter Ivanovich. "Your voice is like cheese grater." He turned to Morgan. "Is what I mean, cheese grater?"

Morgan nodded. "I think so."

Granddad of the Year replied, "Can't eat cheese. On my no-no list. Is there anything more worthless than an HMO doctor? Don't want to spend a dime, just saying what all I can't do. You can't eat cheese, he says. You can't have wine nor liquor of any kind. You can't have a woman nor excitement of any kind. You can't get in a hot tub. You can't stay up late."

"You can't shut up," Peter Ivanovich interjected, but the man responded to Peter's attention rather then his words and kept up his list until an errant throw bounced against the fence and the sing of metal stopped him.

Petey stepped up to the plate. The coach put the ball on the plastic tee, then removed it while she told the batter in the on-deck circle to quit tapping his bat alternately on his helmet and then his athletic cup. Petey already had three hits and five runs batted in. It was the fourth inning. None of his hits had reached so far as the pitcher's circle, but they had all been to the left side of the infield. There were no errors in T-ball.

His first swing was high, well above the ball, and the metal bat swung around and hit his helmet, which made him smile and act goofy for his friends.

"This one here," Granddad of the Year said, "don't take it serious."

Peter Ivanovich stood and faced him. "This is *my* boy!" he said. "You dare not blemish him vis your libel!"

Granddad of the Year, for once, shut up, and Morgan, for once, appreciated his father-in-law.

Peter sat again. "I hate America," he said. Petey took another swing and clobbered the tee a hand's length beneath the ball. Strike two. "In any ozzer country, you would have stopped such a man yourself."

Morgan coughed out a laugh. The old man had been insulting him all along. "You've lived here long enough to know our customs," he said. "Adjust." He could have been giving the same advice to Petey, who indeed adjusted his swing and hit the ball. It bounded past the pitcher and between the second baseman and shortstop, which meant it would likely be a home run. "Good hit, buddy," Morgan yelled. "Keep running."

Peter Ivanovich cheered as well. "Go like wind, young man."

Petey settled for a triple. He would have made it home if he had not decided to slide into second and then again into third. His teammates cheered this heartily, and every other runner in the inning slid into every base.

Out in right field again, Petey flipped up the bill of his cap, then flipped it down. He pulled his pant legs up high, above his knees, and began a stomping kind of dance, as if he were wading through deep water. He appeared to be talking to his glove. It might have been talking back. The game was nearing the two-hour cutoff mark, and only the pitcher continued to pay attention. During this final inning Morgan happened to see Roy Oberland across the field, sitting alone among the opponents' fans. Morgan had not seen much of him since Diana left. He was lonely, no doubt. Which led Morgan to think again of Danny Ford in a jail cell. Morgan did not blame Roy for the arrest. Morgan could have left the gun out in the dump where Danny threw it. No one would have thought a gun could be thrown that distance. It never would have been found. But Morgan had thought he had a duty to perform, and Roy had thought the same thing.

< 115 >

The batter hit the ball hard, but the momentum of the swing sent the bat flying. She was called out for throwing the bat, which ended the inning. It was too near the two-hour mark to start another. Game over. Morgan trotted onto the field to link hands with other Dolphin parents and raise them over their heads to form a human tunnel for the players to funnel through. The Dolphins ran jubilantly to their bench, where the coaches broke out the snacks and drinks to celebrate having been drubbed.

Petey grabbed a drink, then slipped his free hand into Morgan's grip. Peter Ivanovich held Prince's leash. He winked at Morgan and began walking forward in a faltering style, intentionally bumping into people. "Sorry, blind man coming," he said, his elbow landing against the ribs of Granddad of the Year. "Excuse blind man," he said and then fell forward, his outreached hand finding a young woman's butt. "Sorry, sir," he said.

"It's all right," the girl replied. A young, attractive mother, she held hands with one of Petey's teammates.

"Ah, madam, double apology. Would you help blind man please to gate? I leave contraption for dog at home. I get by in daytime. But night is bad for old Russian."

She coupled her arm with his.

"You are," said Peter Ivanovich, "I am guessing now, but you are beautiful, yes?"

He would have it both ways, Morgan thought, and he would get away with it. Prince, he noted, was limping. He had not been paying attention. He was letting things slide. Always, it seemed, he focused on the wrong thing.

"Is Grandpa blind?" Petey asked.

"Yes and no," said Morgan. "You walloped the ball, buddy."

"I got a Gatorade." He held up the orange drink. Then he said, "Did we win?"

The team had been edged by the score of 37 to 21. "Yes and no," Morgan said. The boy was happy with that. Morgan felt the uneasy movement of fatigue—or something like it—trundle through him. Was the pill wearing off? What is fear once it has been reduced pharmacologically? Something like fatigue. Morgan held tight to Petey's hand.

.   .   .

As soon as the T-ball crowd left the house, Zhenya climbed into her Honda, a white, immaculate car she had purchased a year earlier, and took off. The Honda had a CD player, and she listened to music she never brought into the house—Dar Williams and Penelope Houston, Ani DiFranco and Mary Lou Lord—clever young women who wrote complicated lyrics about sex and fame and how hopeless and compelling it was to love a man . . . or another woman. The lyrics were frank, unsentimental, and without the obnoxious boasting or tackiness of those cards she had seen at the coffeehouse.

Right after her lunch with Roy, she had driven across town to the bank, where she withdrew all their savings. The teller cut her a check without asking a single question. She and Morgan had established the account so that either of them could get money at any time—only one signature was required—but Zhenya had prepared a story to explain the withdrawal. Her neighborhood, after all, was about to die. The widening of Forest Avenue would see to that. It was time to move. Surveyors had marked their lawn with tiny blue flags and yellow string, and then a small tractor with a blade had cut a deep swath where the new sidewalk and gutter were poured—all this before the old sidewalk and gutter were removed. It made for a strange look, the two walks and gutters lining the pavement, parallel paths on either side of the black avenue—the wide view and the narrow running side by side, the future and the past.

But the teller had shown no curiosity. He examined her driver's license for a fraction of a second, and then he instructed his computer to issue a check in her name. Danny Ford had no right to their savings. Any sane person would agree with that. Zhenya had taken the check across the street and opened a new account at another bank. In her name only. She would add Morgan's name after Danny Ford was in prison.

Since then she had been unable to think of anything but moving out and living on her own. She slowed the Honda for a traffic light and unfolded the newspaper, which lay on the passenger seat. In the ad, the condos appeared to be painted the white of clouds. Of

< 1 1 7 >

course, it was premature to be shopping for a new place to live. Her father, after all, had moved into the house just last month, but she had been thinking about it obsessively all day, and it had been circling the perimeter of her thoughts since the idea first occurred to her—once Emma and Petey moved out, she would leave, too.

Or perhaps even before they left. Emma was an adult, after all. If it weren't for her father's arrival, Zhenya might move out now. Just the thought of it made her happy and held at a distance the restlessness that too often threatened to shut down her world. Looking at the condos would make leaving that much more real, and that was what she needed—to believe it was a real possibility.

If their marriage had taken its normal course, she and Morgan would probably already be divorced. She felt cheated of the tension that would have grown between them. They were such different people, especially in their intellectual lives, and the pressure to widen that gap would have been powerful had circumstances not interfered. She wished she could have dealt with that pressure. She would liked to have succumbed to it or overcome it. She would know then who she was and what their marriage meant. But Philip's death had made it all a trivial matter.

The condos were at the very edge of town. Two stories high. Built side by side, sharing walls, set off one from another by their varying distance from the street. Each had a concrete driveway and garage, and each was genuinely the white of clouds. They would be out of her imaginary price range, but such was the advantage of imaginary shopping. No place was off-limits. She parked beside a sign that read OPEN HOUSE.

She had calculated the finances of a move. The house on Forest Avenue had a ridiculously low mortgage. The neighborhood had been in decline well before they moved in. Morgan could easily afford it. She had put down half the cost of her new Honda, and the remaining payments were low. Morgan's Toyota was paid for. It was also more than twenty years old. She had tried to get him to trade it in ages ago. He hung on to things. His car was not her problem. As long as Emma attended Hayden University, she paid no tuition, one of the perks of Zhenya's long tenancy there. With half of their savings as a down payment, she could afford to purchase a fairly nice place. She did not want to rent. The plans she had were permanent, and she needed to make that permanence as tangible as possible.

She shut off the car and climbed out into the heat. New grass, some variety she didn't recognize, sprouted in sparse patches through a layer of mulch, a grass of thicker blades than she was accustomed to seeing, and more green. A single sapling stood before each of the linked condos—willows—with trunks narrower than her wrists.

Inside, sitting behind a card table covered with real estate literature, was a girl with a clipboard who looked to Zhenya to be barely a teenager. One of the uncomfortable things she had noticed about middle age was her inability to gauge the ages of others, especially men and women in their twenties. This person had to be in her mid-twenties to be a real estate agent, but she looked like a child. Zhenya cleared her throat and said, "Hi, I'm here to look at the condo."

The girl behind the table looked up and smiled. "My mom went to get my brother from his piano lesson. She'll be back in a minute."

"How old are you?" Zhenya asked.

"Twelve and a half."

"Thank God," said Zhenya. "Can I just stroll around?"

The girl nodded. She pulled the lid off a Tupperware container that held grapes and Oreos.

It was not a beautiful place, but it was appealing nonetheless. The smell of new carpet and the blank invitation of the walls, like unpainted canvases, seemed to promise a new and unfettered life. It was the kind of place that much of her life Zhenya had hated, but at this moment it struck her as wonderful. The kitchen gleamed, its lights hidden away somewhere in the high ceiling. A square room, likely called "the den" in the literature, would make a cozy study. The stairs, too, were carpeted. She knelt to examine the pile, gray-blue, plush and strong—good quality—and that smell. She loved that smell.

Upstairs were *three* bedrooms—what had she been thinking? And a huge bath, a closet in the master bedroom where one could get lost. The place was far larger than what she needed and she was not ready to make the move, but she loved looking at it, imagining her life inside these walls where no human had slept, in a kitchen

< 1 1 9 >

where no one had cooked or eaten, in a living room where no sitcom or ball game had ever been broadcast, where no animal had ever shed or shat, where no muddy feet had ever trod. Unless the little girl below grew panicked about her mother's absence, the new owner of this condo would live in a place where no human had ever cried.

Zhenya decided where she would put the bed. It would get morning sunlight, which she liked, as she was always awake at dawn anyway. She would not even need curtains. A field abutted the back—no one but the cornstalks to see her naked. If she ever shared the bed with a man, and she had to imagine she would, he might not like to be awakened so early. She would promise him curtains. It would become a little routine between them. He would want to know whether he had earned his curtains yet, and she would tell him he had more work to do. She could almost see the glint in his eye as they spoke, although she could not see the eye itself or the person to whom it belonged.

She and Morgan rarely had sex. He went through periods where he could not come. As did she, but if she was at fault, she could tell him to get it over with, while he would plod on endlessly, rubbing her raw, before rolling off in a huff of sweat and self-recrimination, as if his failing were somehow a moral one. Sometimes it did feel like more than a physical failing, as if he were commenting on their marriage, or on her desirability, as if this were the one way he could let her know what he really thought of her, through the violence of that pointless thrusting and the reluctance to find any release from it.

During one period of their marriage, they had talked about their problems in bed. He felt he was under pressure to get it right because they rarely had sex. She told him if he could get it right, they could have sex more often. She believed the words when she spoke them, but when he had no trouble coming, she became tense, feeling he would want her more often, that he would make demands she did not want to meet.

This had all happened in the past several years. Before that there had been little annoyances or occasional gaffes, but once upon a time she had enjoyed fucking Morgan and he had enjoyed fucking her.

He claimed he still did. Sometimes, rarely, she would feel that warmth and sweetness swell her breasts, and she would desire him still. It made her ashamed, but it was true.

More often, she had sex by herself. She used a vibrator, usually in the early mornings after he had left on his garbage run. She adamantly refused to picture Morgan, but she felt uncomfortable thinking of anyone else she knew. Sometimes she would recall a boy from high school or college, the night she had sex in the back of a moving van with a poet she had only just met, the weekend she pretended to visit a girlfriend but stayed instead in a motel with a boy whose sideburns reached his jaw. But something about this seemed pathetic to her. She was approaching menopause and recalling nights from her teens.

She had tried to come without picturing anyone, concentrating on the sensation, the movement of the vibrator against her. But she had to have at least the mental image of another person. It did not have to be Morgan, did not even have to be a man, but there had to be someone. If she did not imagine someone, did not call to mind some memory or fabricate some kind of story, the sensations that should arouse her would merely irritate. She wondered if this was the real reason why Morgan sometimes could not come, that she had ceased to be a person for him. But then all he would have to do was picture someone else while he was inside her. Couldn't he at least manage that? She knew he couldn't. He wouldn't let himself be untrue, especially not like that, not while he was touching her flesh. She could almost love him for that, she could almost hate him for it.

Suddenly Zhenya became concerned for the girl downstairs. She did not know why. The girl was eating grapes, which was one of the most common choke foods. But she was twelve years old—well beyond the worry age for choking. Still, she was alone down there, and it wouldn't hurt to look in on her. Zhenya slipped back down the stairs. The card table was abandoned, but the girl appeared immediately in the kitchen doorway, drinking from a cup of water as she walked.

"Just checking on you," Zhenya said.

The girl lowered the cup a millimeter from her mouth. "On me?"

Zhenya shrugged. "Thought you might be . . . I don't know."

< 1 2 1 >

The girl nodded and returned to her chair. "It's okay," she said with resignation. "You're a mom, right?"

"Guilty," Zhenya said. She pointed up the stairs. "I'll be up here if you need me." The girl rolled her eyes. Zhenya shook her head at herself as she climbed the stairs.

From the window of the master bedroom, she could see the rows the corn made, the young stalks so orderly and uniform she could hardly believe they were living things. The sky seemed a different shade of blue out here, lighter, more friendly. It was really Morgan who needed to move, but he hadn't budged in years. A breeze passed over the field, causing the stalks to genuflect in a kind of pattern, their green leaves lifting and falling, as if in response to her attention.

She had decided today that she would have to expose her father, reveal his lies. It would take something like that to show Morgan she was serious. If his partner was a criminal, he would get none of their money, and if her father was a liar, it was her obligation to divulge the truth. She would not play favorites. Good for the goose, good for the gander. Hadn't she revealed the dishonesty of the Forest Street women? Even though it was against her private interest. If she would not let sentimentality push Morgan into throwing away money on a criminal, then she must not let the same kind of sentimentality keep her from unmasking her father.

Roy had said that the young man shot with Danny Ford's weapon was going to die. That he was on life support. Zhenya tried to imagine the silence of a coma, but she had read that the comatose could hear, they just could not respond. Not silence, then, but distance, separation. She found this easier to imagine.

Coming down the condo's stairs once again, Zhenya paused before a window on the landing. Beyond the willow sapling and the freshly paved street was a farmhouse with two giant sycamores in the lawn. Their limbs were in full bud but did not yet disguise the shapes of the limbs. They were beautiful trees. She didn't know how she had missed them before. High in the branches of one, a crow sat restfully, almost contemplatively. Then the bird turned its black beak to stare at Zhenya. She could feel its eyes focus on her before it lifted its wings, dropped into the air, and floated away.

She sat on the carpet and leaned against the wall, staring at the elongated rectangle of sunlight on the stairs. She pulled her bag from her shoulder. When the bag collapsed, the essay by Cliff of Virginia slid out.

"Christ," she said. She'd had the manuscript in her satchel for almost a month. She picked it up. It began with an anecdote:

> An uncle of mine in Sacramento has a medical condition that encourages his blood to clot and form hard knots beneath the skin. These have to be removed, but they are not life-threatening. When he felt such a knot in the sac of his testicles, he did not worry. The surgeon who diagnosed the problem, however, said that the knot was almost certainly a tumor. My uncle disagreed and explained about his condition. The surgeon said, "You're in denial." He told my uncle they would schedule the surgery quickly, and he suggested that my uncle put his life in order. Even with the surgery, the doctor said my uncle did not have long to live.
>
> The knot turned out to be a clot of blood, and my uncle is fine. I think this story raises many interesting questions, but the one I wish to pursue is this: Was my uncle in denial? If he'd had a tumor, we would all agree that he was. But he did not have a tumor, and so we may be inclined to say that he was not in denial, despite the fact that he had no control over what was going on inside his body.

The essay then switched gears to talk about the Jews who could not believe what was going on even when all the evidence seemed clear. They believed the Nazi persecution to be something other than the fatal cancer it turned out to be. How, then, should these Jews be judged?

Zhenya read the essay straight through. It had some problems, particularly with transitions, and the title was ridiculous, but Cliff had thought about his subject, and in the process he had touched on something meaningful about the way people make decisions, and how those decisions are evaluated by others. She got up from the landing. The sun had set, and the sycamores were lit from below by

< 123 >

a porch light. It did not seem possible that the trees could be more beautiful in the dusk, but they were. She recalled why she had once loved teaching, seeing the way students could grab hold of ideas, witnessing their ability to change over the course of a single semester. How could she have lost track of that? She had been focusing too much on her own work, perhaps, and let herself slip into a rut, using the same texts and lectures over and over. The shadows of the sycamores crossed the street and sidewalk and lay among the new grass in the condominium's yard. She imagined reading here, in this spot, every day. It was Morgan who needed to move, she thought again. But couldn't she do that much for him? she wondered. Was it still possible that she could find a way to redeem their marriage?

In this moment, all her thoughts flip-flopped.

Zhenya descended the carpeted stairs. The mother of the twelve-year-old had returned. She smiled at Zhenya; she was a woman with heft to her body and handsome lines in her face, a woman with friendly, intelligent eyes and slightly crooked teeth. She said, "Did Annelle give you a stat sheet?"

Zhenya replied that Annelle—a strange and lovely take on such a familiar name—had not. The slip of paper gave all of the particulars, including the price. Zhenya took a pen from the card table and jotted down a figure ten thousand dollars less than the one on the sheet. "Would this be acceptable?"

Annelle's mother pursed her lips, then shook her head. "Split the difference?"

Zhenya nodded. "But I have to talk to my husband and daughter. I guess, for that matter, I should show it to my father, too. He's living with us now." She wanted them all here with her. It was no coincidence that she had been drawn to such a large apartment. Which meant she still loved Morgan after all—didn't it? She felt a rush of emotion spread from her chest to her limbs. Of course she loved Morgan. It was a love she could only just bear, but that made it no less real.

Her eyes teared and she looked away from Annelle's mother. "And it has to be *this* apartment," she said. "I want to be directly across from those trees."

The woman nodded. She seemed not at all astonished, as if she, too, knew what a steal this place was, what an oasis, what a site of sanity.

From the foot of his bed, Roy could see a dark sky striated with clouds. Emma's bare feet lay next to his head. They had a slight sour odor. She didn't wear socks. If he ever tried that, his feet would send off toxic fumes, but she was twenty years old and her body didn't seem capable of real stench. She lay on her stomach, the soles of her feet wrinkling. Every other part of her body was damp from sweat, but the soles were dry. The house was cooled by window units that worked efficiently only downstairs. He couldn't get the bedroom to cool off. Sweat pocked his face. Trails of it ran over Emma's legs, pooled in the slight crease between buttock and thigh. Sex with Emma answered an urgency in him that sex with his wife had not, but now he could think of nothing to say to her and nothing to do but make love again. In an hour, she would dress and return home to sleep. The wide expanse of that hour lay before them like a great plain they had to cross.

She shook his leg. "You know what Petey said today?" She took hold of his big toe. "He said, 'Air makes you breathe.' " She used the toe to wag his foot. "He told me without the wind, we'd all suffocate."

"Did he use that word, 'suffocate'?"

"No. I forget." She put her mouth to his big toe and bit the nail. "Be still," she said through her teeth. She chewed the nail from one side to the next, then opened her mouth to display the crescent of toenail on her tongue.

"You're a nut." He smiled because she expected him to, but he hadn't liked it. He could tell her that. It would give them something to talk about, but he didn't want to criticize. He didn't feel confident anymore in how she would take it or whether she would simply get up and leave. Always he had been the adult and she the teenager. Then he was the married man and she the mistress. Now he didn't know who he was to her. While he had gone to see Petey's ball game, she had been on a date with a boy. Such dates had never bothered him in the past. She'd told the boy that she had to be home early, and

< 1 2 5 >

then she had used her key to slip into Roy's house. She had been waiting for him when he returned from the game. The late date was always the real one. In the past he would have laughed at the secrets Emma was keeping from the boy. Now he worried.

She spat the toenail onto the floor. "You don't even have a wastebasket."

Roy pretended to examine his bedroom. Rectangles of dust mottled the wall. One night he had tried to name what had been in each spot—a framed photograph of Diana's parents, a wedding picture, a little painting they had found in a secondhand store. Those were the ones he could remember. The erasures that remained taunted him. How was it that he did not know what they were? How could there have been so many?

Diana had demanded almost everything, and he had agreed without argument. Movers packed it up and hauled it off. Roy had watched them, marking the few things he was permitted to keep. They are the moving men, he had thought, and I am the staying man.

"I'll get around to furniture," he said, "and—I don't know, paintings? Pictures?" Morgan and Zhenya had art in their house. He didn't want Emma disappointed in his taste. He put his hand on her damp calf. She was not a shapely woman. Not yet a woman, really, even now, six years into their love affair. She had beautiful skin, though, lightly tanned, freckles on her pale breasts. And he loved the details of her face, the slant of her nose and curve of her brows. Her nostrils, shaped like teardrops.

"You know what I think is a funny expression?" Emma said. "When people say, 'You're a tough nut to crack.' "

"Is that so?" Roy said. "What's got you thinking about that?"

"You called me a nut, didn't you?" She leaned in close to his feet and put her cheek against his ankles. "Tell me again," she said, "about Diana leaving."

"Why do you like to hear about it so much?"

"I don't. It's awful. But I want to hear it once more."

He took his time with the telling. It gave him something to say, and she liked the details, the dope smoking, the ice on the table, Diana's exact words. Roy wanted to believe she liked hearing it because she was glad his wife was gone. He was ready to marry her. He had already asked. "Not *now*," she had said. "I would have before, but I can't right now. My dad is a mess right now." He had been a mess, she said, since Danny Ford was jailed. It had sounded like an accusation. In a dream, Emma answered Roy's every question with *I would have before*. It made him feel like such a coward. "From what I hear," he said to finish the story of his wife's departure, "she's over it already. Her sister made a point of telling me that Diana's dating some guy with a midengine Porsche."

Emma nodded, as if that matched her expectation, her head braced by her hand. He studied the slight tucks in her neck, the sweaty arrows of hair on her shoulders. Emma lifted one of her feet and with a toe touched the short bristles of his hair. She said, "Do you ever see her around here?"

"What do you mean?"

"You walk by an open doorway and out of the corner of your eye you think you see her, but if you look again she isn't there. Or you spot her in the mirror, just a glimpse, like she was looking over your shoulder."

"No," Roy said. Drops of perspiration hid in her brows. "That hasn't happened."

"Maybe you aren't paying attention." She gave him a particular smile, part pucker and part smirk. It could mean that she was joking. Or it could mean something else. She said, "I *do* love you." She swept her toes across his lips, then leaned down and put her mouth on the arch of his foot. He flinched. Emma had recently begun biting. She pulled back. "Did you think I was going to bite?" She put her mouth there again and bit him, which made him jump. "You were right." She checked her watch. The watch was all she was wearing. From the look on her face, he could see that no time had passed.

"How about this one," Emma said, " 'Don't pass the buck.' How'd that catch on?" She was working to keep the conversation going and to keep it light. He followed this logic to its conclusion— she didn't want him to propose again. She was right to think he might. Sex with her did something to him, and marriage would give them a topic, something he could talk about without feeling lost. He

< 1 2 7 >

could describe how their life together would work. How he would drive Petey to kindergarten every morning come the fall. The local elementary school had a bad reputation, but there was a magnet school near the police station that was supposed to be good, and Roy could drop him off. He and Emma would take an evening course together at the university. The department encouraged psychology and sociology classes. He would cook for her two or three nights a week. He made especially good stuffed bell peppers. They would dance together openly at bars—as soon as she turned twenty-one. That had been what she said the last time. "Ask me again when I'm legal tender." That wouldn't come to pass for months, and he didn't feel he had months. He was the one who was cut free, but it seemed that she was the one who might suddenly fall for another. Was that logical? Could his wife's leaving him encourage Emma to love another man? It wasn't logical, but he had felt secure with her as long as he was married to Diana. Now he was adrift.

He hated thinking about the present. It was the future—their future—that interested him. He could talk about that with her all day, but it was the one thing she asked him not to bring up. They should have more children, he thought. If she wanted to get out of the neighborhood, Roy was willing to move anywhere within the city limits. He had to live in the city for his job. When he made detective, he would be out of the blue uniform and away from Adele Wurtz. He would wear a suit and come home to Emma and Petey. A thousand details of their future life tumbled through his head, but not one thing about the present.

"I bet you start seeing her here," Emma said.

Roy shook his head. "I won't."

"Did I tell you that I'm diving in a meet?"

Of course she had told him. She ran her hand over his legs to his cock, which was flaccid and sticky. He didn't know whether he could get hard again this quickly, but he was willing to try. She merely gave it a shake, then wiped her fingers against his skin.

"You told me about it," he said. "I'm looking forward to it."

"Why do they suddenly like it so much?" she asked. "They used to watch me sometimes, but it's different now." The diving was for her father. She had explained this to Roy. He needed her to dive.

"They're all serious about it," she said. "But especially my dad. As if it made a difference somehow. As if it meant something."

"You've gotten really good."

"Maybe," she said. "I'm a little better than I was a couple of years ago."

"You don't see it, but others can," he said. "It's changed. You're suddenly . . . really good." He didn't say that he had stood on this very bed to catch a glimpse of her. That was a topic he could talk about, but it sounded pathetic.

"If you say so." She raised her legs up high, then threw them down to the mattress, levering up her torso. Then she spun about to sit on her knees. She began to beat his chest as if it were a drum, hammering out a tune. "Here's a riddle," she said, still playing the tune on his chest. "What's blue and cloudy? Endlessly blue?"

"The sky," he said.

"Right," she said and quit beating him, "and your disposition. Lately, anyway. You're just like my dad. He broods."

"I'm not brooding. I get dreamy after making love. It's hard to talk. I'm happy."

"I know," she said. "So is he, that's the sad part."

Roy didn't like to be compared to her father. "I'm not like Morgan." He started to say, "I haven't lost a child," but that wouldn't be entirely true. He hadn't suffered as Morgan and Zhenya had, but if he hadn't felt a terrible loss, he and Emma would never have become lovers. He sat up and kissed her. "I feel like we've always been lovers," he said, "and always will be."

" 'Pillow talk.' Who came up with that one, do you think? Pillow talk."

She wouldn't let him talk in clichés. That used to be something he appreciated about her. "You want to smoke a joint or something?" he asked.

"Tell me one more time," she said. "I want to watch you this time."

"Why do you want to hear it over and over? She's gone." Then something else occurred to him. "She could see that I loved you and not her." This was why she loved the story. That had to be it. "When

< 129 >

Adele drew her gun, I jumped in front of you without thinking. Diana knew that was the real test."

Emma shook her head from side to side, but said, "Yeah. And then she just left. She was so . . ."

"Certain," Roy said.

"Strong," Emma said.

This will pass, Roy thought. This was just that letdown period that followed sex. "Hey," he said, "where'd they come up with this: 'This will pass.' "

"That's easy." Emma threw her arms into the air, stretching, her back arching, her small breasts all but disappearing, the freckles on her chest growing wide. "They began saying it about bad weather, and now it applies to everything," she said. "Every every every-thing." She quit stretching and leaned against him, her hands on his shoulders, pushing him back against the bed. "There *is* something that would make him happy."

"Who? Your dad? I thought you said he is happy."

"No, he's miserable. It's just that he knows how to be miserable. That makes me afraid, you know? He's not even fighting it. I'm talking about a different kind of happy."

"What would make him happy?"

"I should have gone with him to Petey's game."

"I was there," Roy said. "He seemed fine."

"Did he see you?"

"No."

"I should have gone," Emma said.

"What would make your father happy?"

"If you could get Danny Ford out of jail. The charges dropped or whatever."

Roy made a face before he could think not to. "I can't do that."

She raised a knee, straddled him, her hands still on his shoulders. "I just said *if.*"

"And then you'd marry me?" He knew he shouldn't say it, but he felt compelled to.

She leaned harder against his shoulders, swaying a little, her breasts following the motion of her body. He loved that movement of her breasts. "I *guess*," she said, and Roy felt a rush of elation. Then she said, "I don't really expect you to."

"No," he said. "It's not possible."

"He didn't shoot anybody, did he?"

"Probably he just got rid of the gun. But a man was killed. That makes Ford a part of it." Roy had the urge to detail Ford's criminal record, as he had for Emma's mother, but he checked himself. He was not a cop today. He was not the voice of reason. "Marry me anyway," he said. Then he added, "Warts and all."

"There's one," she said. "Who on earth thought that was clever?" She let go of him and stood up on the bed, her ankles against either side of his hips. She shuffled up the bed until she could plant her toes in his armpits. He gazed up her thin legs and thighs. "We left the pool lights on," she said. "You can see the diving platform from here."

"Yeah," he said. "I watch you."

"I know." She put her hands on the insides of her thighs. "What do you see?" She pulled against the skin, and the folds of her vagina parted. "What do you see?" she said again, staring out the window. She thrust down against the bed to make it shake and demanded, "What do you see?"

Roy didn't know what she was asking. About watching her dive? She pulled harder, and the folds of skin spread wider. "I see . . . something I like." His voice quavered, and he understood that he was afraid.

Emma closed her eyes. Her hands slipped from her thighs, and she shifted her weight to one foot, placing the other on his chest. She pressed against him hard enough that he thought she was going to stand atop him. "I've got to shower," she said, removing the foot and crossing over him. She stepped down from the bed and tiptoed to the bathroom, treading softly, as if there might be someone in the house who was asleep.

Peter Ivanovich seated himself in the folding chair, turning it away from the flimsy table to watch his daughter and Morgan and the real estate woman moving about the kitchen in the ugly, empty condo-

< 131 >

minium. They had already seen the damn kitchen. It had chromium strips on the appliances, and the lights suspended from the ceiling shone on them to make them sparkle. Was there a more obvious trick? Verbal flattery *could* be more obvious, but charming words were easy to resist. The finesse required of the great flatterers was like what one sees in the strokes of a great painter—a light hand and subtle touch that, through years of practice, one can manage without much conscious thought. *Point the lights at the chrome* did not qualify. How difficult was it to make bits of light waver before the eyes of the easily beguiled?

The more important question was this: what has prepared the observer to be deceived? This question was especially relevant when the person in question was intelligent and well educated. A college professor, no less. Not that there wasn't a plethora of college professors who were fools, but Peter had never counted his daughter among them. Television, of course, offered almost nothing but the pleasure of blatant deception, and anyone enamored of television would likely think this place an absolute palace. Television was a medium of surfaces, and that was all this place had to offer, the walls nothing but cardboard masks in place of real walls, the carpet a mask for the concrete beneath it, the blue fabric new but cheap, the kind of carpet that made a beard on the rubber soles of one's shoes. He raised his foot to check. His shoe was clean. All right, a higher grade carpet than he had guessed, but it was still nothing but a disguise covering the artificial rock beneath it. The carpet was soft on the surface but hard just beneath, and the ankles, knees, and hips recognized it. Wood floors, such as the ones in the house on Forest Avenue, seemed harder on the surface, but with their deep pliancy they cushioned the exchanges in the delicate human joints, and in doing so made all the difference. In this measure, it helped to be old, to have knees that were quick to complain and eyes too bleary to be impressed by shiny superficialities. Did his daughter lack the inner mechanism, the sophistication of sensibility, the common god-damn sense, to recognize the nasty soulless quality of this painted shed? She had not grown up affixed to television (according to her mother), so what was the reason? What impasse in her life was she facing now that robbed her of this essential perspective?

They had to come here immediately after sitting for two hours on bleachers to watch children play ball. Petey was permitted to sleep in the car and Emma was out who knew where, but he had to sit here and suffer. Wouldn't this place still be standing tomorrow? And now, after spending an hour wandering through it, the rooms utterly interchangeable and devoid of life, they were back in the kitchen. And it was all mere appeasement. Morgan had no intention of moving here. He had been so shocked and pleased that his wife wanted to go somewhere with him, do something together, that he did not wish to spoil it by acting the realist. Women, at times, had to be mollified, but Morgan dealt with her from such a position of weakness that he became the contemptible one, even though it was he who was seeing clearly. Such a place as this was inimical to his very nature. Here was the question he should ask her: where would I put my work clothes? Where could pants that reek of garbage be placed? Would you mind, dear wife, if putrid flakes of ancient, rotting lettuce littered your immaculate shack? Would you ask me, kind lady, to undress and hose off in the garage?

There was something to be said for a new building—the plumbing and lighting were more likely to function—but this place had no character. Sterile and boxy rooms, cliché decorative touches, generic faddish fixtures. Tear away those paper walls and reveal the bars behind them!

"Look at this stove," his daughter was saying. "It's never been used."

Morgan obediently knelt to look inside the oven. "It's electric."

Peter sighed noisily. Morgan, from his knees, glanced his way, but Zhenya didn't seem to hear. What a queer person she had turned out to be. *She's a swimmer,* Emma had told him one night. They had been sitting at the kitchen table drinking cognac—an odd preference for a girl so young, but he was happy to drink it with her. The conversation turned to her parents, as it almost always did with Emma. *A swimmer swims. No time to do anything but kick your legs, swing your arms, and keep moving forward. Otherwise, she's convinced she'll drown.* Emma's father, she added, was a floater. *He just lies there, trying to keep his head above water, wondering whether he's in the deep end yet.* She laughed at that, but then she added, *He's in the deep*

< 1 3 3 >

now. And sinking. But all he knows to do is hold still. When she got up from the table to go to bed, Peter asked, "What about you? What is Emma?" *I'm a diver, of course,* she had said and then left Peter alone in the kitchen to ponder the meaning of it.

He sighed again, even more dramatically, and when Morgan looked his way this time, Peter motioned for him to come over. "Your old man wants you," Morgan said. How Peter hated that terminology. He was her *father,* not her old man.

"Not her, *you,*" Peter said.

Morgan acted as if he'd been told to stick his head in a noose. He could not show Zhenya his impatience, so he directed it at another. Peter did not care. Today he and Morgan were allies, like it or not. Morgan came over and bent down, as Peter directed. Peter cupped his hand over his mouth and whispered, "Go to bathroom. Piss on floor. Make big mess. She sees that and comes to senses."

"That's your recommendation?"

Peter nodded. "I am tired of this," he said, no longer whispering.

Morgan bent closer, put his mouth to Peter's ear, and whispered, "Too bad." He straightened and strolled back to the kitchen.

So he wants to play the big man. What an idiotic pair they were. Zhenya wished for a place with no history whatsoever, but that condition would last no more than a moment. It was over already. And Morgan wanted some kind of intimacy with his wife—regardless of the expense. Didn't he see what this would cost him? Unless he was actually willing to move to this closet, at some point he would have to say no. Better to do it immediately. This coddling was a mistake, raising her expectations. Make her see her blindness! Punch a hole through the pasteboard mask!

At last they were leaving the kitchen. Peter pushed against the table to get up, but the thing almost toppled over, and he fell back into the chair. Here, he thought, another metaphor for this place. Set this card table beside the oak table in their real house, cover each with a cloth—they would look the same on the surface, but only a fool would think them of equal value.

Morgan offered his hand, and Peter accepted it. He would help Morgan stand, too. He would say to Morgan's wife what Morgan could not say. "This table," he began, but Morgan cut him off, turning his back to Peter and calling to the real estate woman. "Yes?" she replied. "Another question?" She, too, seemed weary.

"Is there a pool?" Morgan asked, and even before the woman could answer, darkness entered Zhenya's face. Peter could see her searching for a way to hide it, but she could find none, lifting her head in dismay to observe her husband.

"A swimming pool?" the woman said. "There's one just a couple of blocks down Montana, across from that big Target. Several lanes, rarely crowded. Are you a swimmer?"

"Is floater," Peter said, but they did not understand him. He followed the others out the door. He had underestimated his son-in-law. Morgan had come up with the better tactic—point out, with apparent regret, the one fatal flaw. And do so by asking an innocent question. Now Morgan could commiserate with his wife over their near miss. Very impressive work. But on the sidewalk, Zhenya took Morgan's arm to keep him from the car. "Once Forest Avenue is full of traffic, we won't want to live in that house. That's the simple truth. Do you think we'll want to sit in exhaust fumes to watch Emma dive?"

"You think it'll be that bad?"

"Yes, it's that bad," she said. "And look." She pointed across the dark street at the farmhouse and the big sycamores in the yard. She had already made them stare at the trees from the inside. "Imagine looking at those trees every day."

"Our street used to be lined with trees more or less like those—"

"But they're gone. Forever. That's the truth of the situation. We have to face the truth and move on."

Morgan shifted his gaze from the trees to his wife, and there was something different in his countenance now, some new resolution. He said, "Do you really want to talk about the *truth* concerning those trees?"

Zhenya turned away from him to face the sycamores, but he took her by the shoulders. Peter had never seen his son-in-law act with such decisiveness. Morgan looked her in the eye. "I'm talking about *our* trees. The trees of Forest Avenue. Do you want to talk truthfully about *them*?"

< 1 3 5 >

Zhenya did not answer, searching her husband's face for a moment, then seeking out the neighbor's trees again.

Like Peter, the real estate woman was taking this all in. She looked to him for help, but he did not want to ease this tension. Perhaps she did not either. Likely she was feeling the dollars sliding out of her pocket, but she enjoyed this drama nonetheless. It was possible that in this domestic scene she found some compensation for the loss of a sale. The Realtor could not know what was at the heart of it—and Peter did not know himself what Morgan meant by the "truth" of trees—but in the woman demanding that the man consider the future, in the man taking the woman by the shoulders and demanding that she examine the past, in the severity of his aspect and the desperate quality of hers, this couple jabbed a hole in one of the masks worn by their marriage. Who could behold such an event and not be moved by it?

Peter and the real estate woman waited silently for the final turn. Would they embrace and weep? Would she slap and curse him? What did it matter? Melodrama follows drama as a rainbow follows rain, making a show after the real thing has already transpired. It is the rain itself that matters.

Finally, Zhenya shrugged off Morgan's hands and headed for the car.

By the time Morgan carried Petey inside and up the stairs, changed the sleeping boy into his pajamas, and tucked him in his bed, Zhenya had gone to bed herself. She often read before sleep, but the room was dark. She was angry with him. Morgan gathered up Petey's dirty clothes and went down the stairs. The old man, who had fallen asleep on the drive home, now sat at the kitchen table having a drink. Emma sat with him. Her date with Sid had been fun, she had told him, and now she had her books spread over the table. She and her grandfather were talking, and Morgan didn't want to interrupt. For that matter, he didn't want to be with anyone. Which meant he was more upset than he had been willing to admit to himself. He had enjoyed looking at the condo, right up until the end when he had to tell Zhenya it was foolish. He shouldn't have brought up the trees. He could have been kinder.

He went down the hall, opened the door to the cellar, and descended the steps. He tossed Petey's T-ball shirt, along with the pants and socks he had played in, on top of the laundry basket, which was full. Morgan opened the lid to the washer and emptied the basket into it. Might as well do the wash. At one time, the cellar floor had been nothing but dirt. Morgan and a few friends from work had poured the cement themselves in order to put in the washer and dryer. Philip had helped. Emma had been too small. The floor's amateur surface was rough, cracked, and uneven, but Morgan still took pride in it. The children had written their names in it. Once the washer started, he climbed the stairs and went outside, across the pool deck, and out to their driveway, where he climbed into his old Toyota and drove off. He knew where he had to go.

In the months following Philip's death, Morgan had been visited nightly in his dreams by his son. Morgan would see him and understand that the boy had not died. He would be seized by joy. Then he would see that his son was trapped. He might be up to his knees in mud or up to his waist in garbage, trapped in a box with slick sides, or in a sack that clung tenaciously to his ribs. In every dream, Philip would reach out for his father, and Morgan would see that he could easily free him. But something would intervene. A heavy flapping of wings would divert Morgan's attention for only a moment, but in that moment his son would disappear. A bus would pass between them, and Morgan would kneel to peer beneath the vehicle and keep an eye on him, but once the bus was gone, his son was gone, too.

The dreams had tortured Morgan, and he decided to drive to the cemetery one day after work to tend to Philip's grave and perhaps even talk to the mound as he had seen people do in movies. But upon reaching the cemetery parking lot, he hesitated. A burial was taking place, and he still wore his work clothes. The next afternoon he showered and changed before leaving the house. The wind was blowing. Leaves were torn from their limbs. They filled the air with their fluttering, and this kept Morgan in his car. He drove out seven

< 1 3 7 >

times. The last time he opened the car door and swiveled in his seat to put a foot on the parking lot. He examined his shoe on the pavement and thought, That's progress. Driving home, he understood he could not face the grave alone.

He wanted Zhenya to come, but she had emptied the house of Philip's belongings and immersed herself in her work. She insisted they move on, and that determination seemed the only thing holding her together. He could not ask her to give it up. Emma would have come, but Morgan didn't want to look to her for strength. She had been ten years old.

He began, instead, working every day to imagine his son. He made himself remember the graceful way his son tossed a ball, the barbaric way he held a fork, how he rolled his eyes, how he threw fits, how he slept with his knees raised. Eventually the nightmares ended.

Months passed. Now and again he thought about his failure at the cemetery. Over dinner one evening, he suggested they visit Philip's grave on the anniversary of his death.

"I don't care to," Zhenya said. "You should, if you want. But I don't care to."

Emma volunteered to go.

"It's too deliberate," Zhenya said. "It's too . . ." It seemed maudlin and phony to her, Morgan understood. But on the day in question, Zhenya joined them. She acted as if she was doing it to please him, but it was the anniversary of their son's death and no feat of will could block out his memory on this particular day. She had to give herself something to do, a definite course of action to guide her through the hours.

This began their annual ritual, and the first rite of August 12 became their gathering in the morning, each helping the other with the selection of clothing or the ironing. They did not sit down to breakfast but snacked, snatching fruit from the counter, sliding bread into the toaster, dashing in and out of the kitchen, encouraging a sense of bustle and urgency as if it were the morning of a wedding. They dressed in their best clothes, what other families would call their "Sunday clothes," formal and conservative and not new. August 12 would not be an excuse for the purchase of clothing.

Each procured flowers in advance and had them at the ready in the refrigerator. Morgan brought calla lilies. Zhenya selected whatever caught her eye in the florist's cool bin. Emma, that first year, had cut a single rose from Mrs. East's garden. At the grave site she announced that next year she would bring two. In each year that followed, she cut an additional sentimental rose for her dead brother.

The Toyota would be clean. They would comment on the beauty of the flowers and the prospects presented by the weather. One might dust lint from the shoulder of another, pass a hairbrush, offer a mirror for last-minute corrections. They would remark on the cleanliness of the car. "We should keep it this way all the time," Zhenya would say. Landmarks denoted their progress—a billboard advertising a hot spring, the old ice plant, the turnoff to the dump, Kerr's Family Diner, Luther's Auto, a field of corn, the carcass of a school bus, and then the cemetery.

Despite his fears, Morgan stepped easily from the car that first year. The suit he wore gave him strength, the haircut he had gotten the day before, the polish on his shoes, the wax on the hood of his aging car, and the presence of his wife and daughter. He stepped from the vehicle as if the act meant nothing, as if they were parked by an ice cream parlor.

The narrow path, marked by concrete stones, demanded that they walk single file. They might talk, but it would not be a steady conversation—an observation about the manicure of the grass or the health of the great trees that dotted the burial ground.

They had trouble, that first year, finding the grave. The layout of the parking lot had been altered shortly after Philip's burial, which disoriented them. Morgan and Zhenya disagreed about which way to turn. No one wished to ask the groundskeeper for directions. They wandered about the graveyard, singly and together, letting themselves roam far beyond the logical area to look for the grave.

Emma eventually located it. "I walked right by it," Zhenya said. "I just didn't see it." She didn't, even then, look at it closely. They did nothing for a few awkward moments, uncertain what was required of them. Emma put her rose at the base of the stone. Zhenya had no flowers that first year because she had not thought she was coming. In the future, she would not let herself be caught

< 1 3 9 >

empty-handed. She took the bouquet of calla lilies from Morgan and put them on the swell of ground alongside Emma's rose. They did not reminisce. After another moment, they made their way back to the car.

In the years to come, wandering about the graveyard became part of what they did. It kept them on the grounds but away from the marker and its abbreviated mound. Then they would lay their flowers on the grass and leave.

They ate at the same highway café every year. Emma picked it on the first anniversary because it was nearby and because they had eaten there once with Philip and he had liked it. Emma, even at the age of eleven, knew not to explain this. Neither a fashionable café nor one that had the appeal of nostalgia, Kerr's Family Diner was housed in a modest brick building with dirty windows and cloth curtains. The food was not especially good or bad, which recommended it. A sumptuous meal would be wrong, and it would be wrong, too, to eat fast food or at some greasy dive. The food was just right, and Zhenya, inevitably, would bring up the Goldilocks story. They might find themselves becoming happy—as if what? As if Philip were with them? That was the kind of question that could not be asked without ruining everything.

At home they would do almost nothing. Emma might have located the Scrabble board the night before. Morgan might have purchased a book of crossword puzzles too difficult for him to do alone. Zhenya would have rented a few videos, old movies with happy endings. They would remain in their good clothes. In the late afternoon, they moved to the kitchen to prepare the evening meal, something simple, fried chicken or turkey with gravy. A few people would join them for dinner, people who knew that it was the anniversary and knew not to bring it up. The china and scant crystal made their only appearances of the year, along with cloth napkins and the linen tablecloth. If the air conditioner was working, they would light candles.

The strangest rite, the one least like them—and the one that most made the day seem separate and special—began after dinner. It had come about by accident. When Morgan's parents were alive, Morgan and Zhenya and Emma had driven to their house bringing gifts—a bottle of bourbon, homemade bread, cookies. After Morgan's parents were gone, he found other things for them to do. The year Roy Oberland married Diana, they traipsed over and helped paint their bedroom. Another year they set up floodlights and worked to rebuild the awning over the union store. No other day of the year would they consider doing such things together.

Zhenya would not let the day become foolishly rigid. They had to avoid formalizing the meanings of things. Morgan once suggested they spend each anniversary evening working at the soup kitchen, but Zhenya believed that was exactly the kind of thing they could not do. She explained this to him, how the soup kitchen would, before long, become routine. It would supplant with false meaning the real point of the anniversary.

The final part of the day was spent again at home. They might finish their game of Scrabble or watch a movie they had never gotten around to seeing in the afternoon. Zhenya and Emma often simply read—mother on the couch, daughter in the easy chair—while Morgan sat on the floor with his book of crosswords, interrupting their novels now and then to search their minds for words.

The annual ritual of their loss involved no mention of the dead.

For Zhenya, the day gave her six stages to concentrate on, each with its little demands, each leading promptly to the next. She needed such a day, a day to formally acknowledge that Philip was gone without burying herself in grief, one wherein she knew exactly what she was supposed to do. Outwardly she paid homage, but at the same time, she had help keeping her sorrow at bay.

But for Morgan, the day did nothing. That first time, he had wondered whether he would break down. He steeled himself to face the grave. When they couldn't find it, he understood that the place had no power for him. He didn't know his way around the graveyard and neither had Philip. When they finally discovered the grave site and Morgan witnessed the rectangle of marble that held his son's name, he remained unmoved. He made himself see his son every day, and this stone had no weight next to those images. He could tell that it was good for Zhenya, and the day might mean something to Emma as well. He didn't mind it most of the time.

One year, though, he became upset with himself for feeling noth-

< 1 4 1 >

ing. That same night he had a nightmare about Philip trapped in a car. After work the next day Morgan drove to the cemetery by himself and visited the grave again. He felt nothing but a hot breeze. The following day he went once more, but the nightmares continued. On the third day, driving home from the cemetery in the early evening, preoccupied with his thoughts, he turned automatically onto the road that led to the dump, the daily route he took in the garbage truck. He hadn't realized what he was doing until he was almost to the gravel road. He sat in the idling car a few moments and then decided to continue. He left his car at the gate, let himself in, and wandered along the road that bordered the landfill.

Here, he discovered, he could grieve for his son. He walked among the ruined and discarded things, the clutter that someone had finally cleared, the waste and wrappings, the busted furniture, burned fabrics, broken mirrors, clothing worn thin as onion paper—the daily excrement of human habitation. Why did he find release here? Why did he feel close to his dead son in this place he visited almost everyday?

Philip had come with him in the garbage truck a few times, had ridden with him out to the dump, but Morgan had no specific memory of those trips. It was true that many of the boy's possessions were here—the toys and clothing that Zhenya would not let Morgan give away. His son's things were here, intact, but his son was in the cemetery in a concrete box, his twelve-year-old body, what remained of it, now without life for nearly as long as it had possessed it.

The rites of the anniversary of Philip's death didn't help Morgan. He couldn't go to the cemetery and feel close to his son. But at the dump, he could. At the dump, he could think of Philip and bear his thoughts. He didn't know why.

After returning home from viewing the condo, Morgan drove his old car out to the dump. He sat on the hood, which was warm from the drive, and he breathed in the night air. He just breathed.

4

If history is not personal, it is not history.

—Peter Ivanovich Kamenev

Morgan stood inside one of the bays of the service building at the city lot, waiting for the Parks and Rec men to begin arriving in their white pickups. Because each branch of city service had a representative on the union board, and because the representatives were not elected but passed around—everyone forced to do a term eventually—Guy Scott happened to be a member. He wasn't the type who would have run for office, and he certainly wasn't the type who would have been elected. Guy had once been Morgan's good friend. They had not hung out together since Morgan married Zhenya. Guy had dated several of Zhenya's students, and she didn't like him.

Morgan drank a ginger ale from the vending machine and counted the trucks. Fewer than half were in. Even working a ten-hour day, Morgan finished earlier than other city workers, one advantage of rising every morning to darkness. He had already showered, leaving a note to say he would miss the diving today.

He scanned each of the arriving trucks for Guy. He and Guy had played city-league basketball on the same team. They had gone fishing with Morgan's dad and toured bars to drink and look for women. Morgan had given up or lost all of these activities. Their friendship would have ended anyway, he guessed.

< 142 >

< 143 >

Guy's truck was among the last to pull in. Morgan walked to the end of the building, waited for Guy to punch his time card, then caught him on his way out. "I need you to sponsor Danny Ford," he said.

"Hey," Guy said. "You still alive?" He rubbed his eyes as if he couldn't believe what he saw. He had aged about the eyes and in the fullness of his face.

"Hanging on," Morgan said.

"I'm going to retire in March." Guy resumed walking and Morgan followed. "Can you believe it? Retirement at fifty-one. I owe that to you. Mr. Gung Ho Union Man when the rest of us had our thumbs up our asses. How many years you got left?"

"I don't know. A few. You hear about Danny Ford?"

"This is mine." Guy patted the roof of a new American car. "Caught disposing of a weapon on city property. Came up the last meeting. He did it, didn't he?"

"Is that our job now? To be judge and jury? I thought our job was to help each other get a fair shake. Danny needs bail money."

Guy took only a second to decide. "I'll sponsor it. Sure." He opened the car door. "You must know the meeting's tonight. I wasn't going. More G.D. meetings than you can shake your stick at. But I can make it. You come, too. Lean on a few people and it'll pass. Hit the old-timers who remember what all you did. We owe you, like I said. Want to get a beer?"

Morgan hesitated.

"Invite Zhenya to come, too," Guy said and laughed. "I'm calling Vinnie." He pointed to the car's interior. "Got a phone in the car. Vinnie likes to keep up. Hazard of marrying a younger woman. You'll like her. You can call yours and get permission once we're at the bar. Harder for her to say no then." Guy smiled wide, his mouth open more at one end than the other. "Hop in. We'll drink our supper, then hit the meeting."

Morgan couldn't see a reason not to join him, but he felt a little panicked about it. He fingered the prescription bottle in his pocket. "I don't know if I can. Seems like there's something I ought to be doing."

"You *ought* to get in the car. It's new. Call home and make sure you haven't forgotten anything. What, people knocking your door down?"

Vinnie chose the bar and gave Guy instructions while he drove. "Okay," he said into the phone, "I'm on Barrett Street heading—one direction or another. I made a right." He said "Uh-huh" a few times, then began reading the street signs. They were in a shabby part of town near the tracks. Suddenly he veered left. "I caught it," he said. "Barely."

The name of the bar was scrawled in Day-Glo green on black-ened windows: THE LUCK. The building had once been a neighbor-hood grocery store. Morgan had worked this route in the eighties. The area had been decent back then—working-class bungalows and brick apartment buildings, lots of people on the street. There weren't any neighborhoods like that anymore. A hand-lettered poster on the door of The Luck advertised Grease and No-Grease Burg-ers, Chicken Fajitas, Guacamole Tacos, seven-dollar pitchers, and live music after nine from a band called Michelle Gets Her Feet Wet.

"This used to be an interesting neighborhood," Morgan said. "I always kind of liked it."

The narrow street now held a mix of industrial metal sheds and boarded-up houses with overgrown lawns. An empty lot littered with broken glass served as the bar's parking lot. It was adjacent to a place called Tires Anonymous—a high fence surrounding a little white building with black smears on the walls and mounds of old automobile tires everywhere. Morgan tried to recall what the build-ing had been all those years before. A hardware store, maybe.

The Luck was larger than it looked from the outside. The bare concrete floor held twenty or so tables. In the middle of the room, a freestanding metal bar formed a square rimmed by bar stools. Within the square, a small fry kitchen was situated beneath a huge exhaust fan. A bartender in a white T-shirt leaned lazily against a beer spigot. Among the scatter of tables were folding tables, picnic tables, kitchen tables, and lawn furniture. In the way back, an alu-

< 145 >

minum stage covered the entire wall, floor, and ceiling—the remnants of a walk-in cooler. A drum set and tall speakers sat among black cables on the stage.

"Looks like a construction site," Morgan said, thinking of all the places where he had picked up garbage and yet never stepped inside the doors.

"What's the deal with you and Ford, anyway?" Guy guided him to a table not far from the bar. None of the people they passed looked to be of legal drinking age. Morgan wondered if Danny Ford frequented this place. It seemed like his kind of bar. Guy chose a picnic table. His being a Parks and Rec man meant he ate lunch on a picnic table five days a week.

Morgan sat opposite him. "I'd fit in better if I hadn't gone home and showered."

"Vinnie loves places like this," Guy said. "Been trying to get me here all month. We had our one-year anniversary in April, and she decided the thing to do was buy a case of champagne and fuck like bunnies."

A waitress wearing nothing but a leotard stepped up to take their order. Morgan wondered if this meant there would be strippers. Guy ordered vegetarian burgers for himself and Vinnie. Morgan got the regular burger. "Two No-Grease, one Grease," she said. "And a pitcher." It sounded like a foreign language.

"If Ford did this, he'll do time, am I right?" Guy said.

"He's got a juvenile record, but I'm not sure that can legally count against him," Morgan said. "So I don't know. He might get some kind of probation. I'd like to believe that, anyway."

"What I'm saying is, what's to keep him from running if we bail him out? You know people are going to ask that—or be thinking it, even if they don't ask."

"He might run, but that's a different issue."

Guy only stared at him. "I don't get it. Why should we help a kid run from the law? And get stuck paying the bail?"

Morgan had an answer, but he didn't know whether he could put it into words. The waitress arrived with their pitcher, which gave him a little time to think. He was almost certain that Danny would jump bail, but their job was to assume the best of their people.

"Beer from a tap is better than from a bottle," Guy said at the end of a long drink. "You don't want to talk, fuck it. I'm retiring come March, like I said, and everybody knows I've got no judgment. What do I care? It's not like this is going to bankrupt the fund. It's not, is it? Hey, see that doll at the door?"

A tiny woman in a yellow tank top and bell-bottom jeans stood in the sunlight. The bartender yelled for her to shut the door. Guy called her name. "We're gonna need another pitcher," he said to Morgan. "And no more shoptalk, what do you say?"

Vinnie's hair was bleached the white of stationery, which made Morgan think she might be a secretary. Her hair was shorter than his own but much more fashionably cut. She was cute, maybe thirty years old. He wondered what was she doing with Guy.

Guy and his wife kissed on the lips, then he introduced her to Morgan.

"I hear about you all the time," she said. "You're his good *and* bad role model."

"How's that?" he asked.

"She's what John Wayne would call a firebrand," Guy said. "Which means she likes to put me on the spot. You got any secrets, don't tell Vinnie. Had to teach her who John Wayne was. Never heard of him. You believe that? Greatest film actor of all time."

"He's changing the subject," she said. "He's 'bout as subtle as a stomach pump. The good role model is you at work. I know more about you and Guy twenty years ago than I do about my brother's wife and family—who are a friggin' mess." She took a drink from Guy's glass and then Morgan's. "The bad—are you ready for the bad?"

"I'm not sure," Morgan said.

"I left lipstick on your cup. Do you mind? Some people act like a little lipstick on a glass is the end of the planet." She gave Guy a meaningful look. "My lips are clean, I assure you." A slyness came into her eyes. "Although it's true you don't know where they've been. When I was a waitress we used to say, 'Loose lips, big tips.' "

She had a deep voice for such a small person, and she drank as much beer as either of them. When she hollered for another pitcher, it came quickly.

< 1 4 7 >

.   .   .

Halfway through their burgers and well into their third pitcher, Vinnie began a story. "I had a job in a canning factory in Oregon and quit. It was ruining my hands—the Scarlett O'Hara complex. Then I moved to Denver, but I didn't like it there and neither did this girl I worked with, who also worked at the Pussy Cat Lounge, but I didn't. So we were on our way to Washington—the capital, not the state—and we got hungry just outside Hayden. I buy salads at McDonald's, but I won't eat inside. Hate those plastic chairs. She eats anything, my girlfriend. Big Mac and fries three times a day and weighs ninety-five pounds. You know the type—if you didn't love her, you'd gouge her eyes out. We got directions to a park. You know Young Park?"

Morgan told her he did. He understood the nature of the story. She was answering the question everyone who met them would want to know: how did *she* wind up with *him?* Morgan was accustomed to such curiosity. He and Zhenya often had to explain the same thing; college professor and garbageman weren't a natural match. As it happened, Guy had been with Morgan when he first met Zhenya.

"Guy was working Young Park that week," Vinnie went on, "or my life would be a whole different story. He was feeding tree limbs into this machine that gobbles them up."

"It's a mulcher," Guy said.

Vinnie didn't pause. "It was noisy, and he came over to ask if I'd like him to quit while I ate, saying he would if he could eat with me. He had a sack lunch. Tuna-fish sandwich, chips, and a thermos of iced tea. He gave me his tea. I remember every crumb in his sack, but I can't recall a word we said to each other. My girlfriend left after awhile and sat in the car. Guy didn't even notice she was gone. Finally I got my suitcase out and told her to go ahead to D.C. I spent that night and the rest of the week on his couch. Then I moved into his bedroom. And I still can't recall a single word of the conversation that changed my life, and—here's the ka-boom—neither can he."

Morgan didn't know what to say. "Sounds like he used hypnosis."

"I've thought about that," she said. Their marriage seemed as much a mystery to her as it did to Morgan. "He's got some tricks up his sleeve. I'm twenty-nine, if you're wondering. Never once dated an older man. Still haven't. Moved in without dating him, and then we got married. Is this a date?"

"Sure, it's a date. We date all the time," Guy said. To Morgan, he added, "We'll get that little bastard out of jail." The beer had taken its toll on Guy.

"He's not so little," Morgan said.

When Vinnie got up to go to the women's room, Guy leaned close. "I remember what we said that day at the park, but I pretend I can't. She's got to block it out. Her life turned completely around on that conversation, and no bit of talk can live up to that." He shrugged. "She's like a gift from some kind of god, you know? You think there's some kind of a god?" Guy shook his head and touched the corners of his eyes. He was smashed.

Morgan met Zhenya in 1976, the year of the Bicentennial, the same year Hayden city employees organized their union. It had been a cold spring day after a long warm spell—long enough that women had begun wearing short skirts, men had gone to the barber for summer cuts, and farmers had been out thrusting their plows into the frozen ground. Morgan remembered stopping on the drive to the Dawning Building to look at the limbs of an oak. Ice lined the street side of the tree. Beneath the ice, new buds showed, and he thought, Even the trees were fooled into thinking spring had arrived. He considered this as he returned to his car, how every living thing was a sucker for good news.

Two elevated highways converged in Hayden, and the Dawning Building was situated in the triangle of asphalt where the freeways met. It had been built in 1899 and was named for the dawning of a new century. A great lawn had surrounded it and forest had surrounded the lawn. By 1976 concrete bunkers enclosed a triangular asphalt lot, which a local school district rented to park their yellow buses. Morgan drove to the far end of the lot to protect his Corolla, which was new. Above him, where the two highways merged, cars stalled by an accident beaded the guard rail.

< 1 4 9 >

Morgan walked through a narrow corridor created by the tall buses. At his feet, a mimeographed school newspaper bore the headline BIG LOSING EFFORT FRIDAY NIGHT. He wiped frost from the paper, crumpled it, and shoved it into his coat pocket. Because he worked for the city, he took litter personally.

The exterior of the Dawning Building was so traditional as to be a commonplace—blond brick, faux columns, a brief cascade of stairs. Guy Scott waited for Morgan on the stairs, smoking a cigarette and shivering in his thin jacket. He had grown a mustache to cultivate a likeness to Burt Reynolds. "I thought we could ride the bus for free," he said. "What's the point of all this so-called solidarity if we can't ride the bus for free?"

"What's wrong with your car?" Morgan asked.

"I can't afford to drive it." Guy dropped his burning butt to the stair and twisted his shoe over it.

Morgan had just been elevated from the position of sergeant at arms to that of president of the local union. He had been elected to sergeant at arms for his youth and physique; the other had just dropped into his lap. When the mayor pledged to bust the union, the elected president suggested the union back down. AFL-CIO advisers from Chicago suggested, in turn, that he resign. He took their recommendation and the vice president followed suit. Morgan became the pick for his willingness to accept the job.

"Free bus fare is not on our list of demands," Morgan said.

"I just assumed we'd pro bono each other with stuff like that," Guy said. He had not wanted to come to the lecture because the Dawning Building was home to the Fraternal Order of the Moose. Even now he was reluctant to enter. He had applied to become a Moose and been blackballed. "Same thing happened with the Elks," he had said. "Counting my love life, I've been shunned by all the major mammals."

Morgan had come alone to the first lecture two weeks earlier. The union sponsored the series, and Morgan felt obliged to show. He had written a column about it in the union newsletter. The inaugural speaker, an elderly historian with a slide projector, had lectured on "The True Story of the Missouri Compromise." No one else in the union had come. Neither Missouri nor compromise interested them. A lecture on compromise just as they were discussing a strike had made some of them suspicious.

This second lecture had the title "Violence and Ethics," and the speaker had an exotic name: Zhenya Kamenev.

"You're shivering," Morgan said, giving Guy a little shove to get him moving.

While the Dawning Building's exterior was ordinary, the interior was like no other place on earth. Polychromatic tile imported from Istanbul lined the walls top to bottom, a span of twenty feet, and the ceiling of the rectangular hall had a shallow dome, like a blister, in its center. At the far end, an alcove held a stage and podium. Above the alcove hung the mammoth head of a moose. Traditional and reserved on the outside; wild and unwieldy on the inside. A lot of the Midwest was like that, Morgan thought. Christmas lights strung between the moose's antlers blinked in rapid succession. Tacky, he acknowledged, and utterly incoherent. But it was a remarkable incoherence. He considered broaching the subject with Guy, but there was no way to go about it. Some things lost their significance as soon as you tried to explain them.

They selected folding chairs in a middle row and seated themselves. The front rows had filled, and more people were arriving, which surprised and pleased Morgan. He leaned back to stare at the shallow dome. It was ringed with tiles in shades of blue, growing darker as they reached the top, a design that made the dome seem deeper than it really was. From the very center hung a long chain that had once held a chandelier and now tethered a round lamp advertising Hamm's Beer. The lamp displayed a waterfall that by some trick of light seemed to be moving, the water continually falling.

"Used to come here with my old man," Guy said, tilting back in his chair to mirror Morgan. "One time he had me sit in the kitchen and promise not to come out. I knew something was up."

"Your father's a Moose?"

Guy nodded. "That's why the rejection felt personal. Anyway, a woman wearing a bathrobe comes in arguing with these guys who've constructed a plywood cake she's supposed to pop out of. The men

< 1 5 1 >

who built the thing aren't carpenters, but, well, *Moose*. They've just hammered it together, not thinking about all those nails poking through."

"You're kidding me," Morgan said.

"So I slip from the kitchen when I hear the fanfare. She jumps bare naked out of the cake, and when she turns around, she has scratches down her back and thighs, long red marks that begin to bleed while she struts around. Someone gets cotton balls and rubbing alcohol, and that becomes a way for them to touch her. She's moaning from the stinging, all these Moose rubbing their cotton balls over her."

"Unbelievable," Morgan said.

"It's true," Guy said. "Later that year she substituted in my American history class. Better teacher than stripper, the truth be known."

"My dad never went in for stuff like that," Morgan said and began counting the people in the audience. He did not know it yet, but the lecture series was a union ploy. A later speaker would present a sympathetic description of labor history, and the timing of his appearance—shortly after the strike was scheduled to begin— would permit him to address the strike directly. The remainder of the series was merely meant to legitimize his speech. While Morgan counted heads, another city employee dropped into the seat beside him, Skip Deitz, the former president of the union and a fellow trashman. He liked Morgan and had nominated him to be sergeant at arms.

"Didn't expect to see you here," Morgan said.

Skip raised up a moment and nervously studied the hall. "Here for a reason." One of his eyes was a lighter shade of green than the other. "You don't know what you're getting into, son," he said softly, settling again into his seat. "Nobody's more for the union than me, but we need to keep it local." He eyed Guy. "This is confidential, of course."

"Hey, Skip," Guy said. "You've got something on your face."

"They're tough boys," Skip said, wiping away a trace of shaving cream from his jaw, "and they deal off the bottom of the deck."

Warnings like this made Morgan weary. He was more interested in Skip shaving before coming over. Was he going to see a woman after the lecture?

"Striking right off," Skip continued, "that just isn't the way to go about it."

"If you really want to talk, we can do it after the lecture," Morgan said. "It ought to start any minute." He turned, as much to avoid Skip's gaze as to look for the evening's speaker, but Zhenya had just entered the hall and Morgan studied her. He thought she might be with the union—from the library, maybe. She had the look of books about her. She did not wear hose, he noted as she walked, despite the weather. He also noted that her legs were lovely. She strode up the aisle with confidence, as if the chairs were parting in her wake. A commanding woman and good-looking. He folded his arms and took a final peek at the dome and the tiles' illusion of depth. He needed a commanding presence himself. Maybe that accounted for his immediate attraction to Zhenya Kamenev. She provided a model. The lamp hanging from the blister in the ceiling read *From the Land of Sky Blue Waters.*

Zhenya had a different take on the story. She would start with her department head. He had given her directions to the Dawning Building. "It's where the interstates merge," he said. "Right in their *crotch.*" He liked using the word with her. One of those men who thought being crude equaled flirting. She attended the first lecture to see what to expect. The scant crowd and dismal speaker might have discouraged her if not for the weird, compelling anarchy of the room. Kitsch at its best. On such a scale that it demanded respect— like Mount Rushmore or Disneyland. Even the moose-head-in-mosque motif contributed. The sheer enormity of the head made it seem a reasonable icon for worship, the span of its antlers great enough to inspire awe. Reverence was impossible, but it had a kind of grandeur. The niche with the podium was on the north wall, she noted, which meant it faced not Mecca but Chicago. Was there any better direction for midwestern faithful to kneel?

To avoid addressing an empty hall, she manufactured a crowd by

< 153 >

posting announcements around her building, talking to students about her subject, describing the strange beauty of the Dawning Building to anyone who would listen, and announcing that there would be food and beer afterward. Her department head wanted to know whether she'd had trouble finding the building. "Right where you said it was," she told him, "in the very perineum." He left her alone after that.

She had been in her second semester at Hayden University, the youngest Ph.D. in the institution and among the youngest in the country. Her colleagues had dubbed her *Queenie*. "They never let me play in any reindeer games," she told her mother by phone. Several of the men were interested in seducing her, but none liked the attention she got from the university administration. She might have slept with one of them anyway, but they were all married and as dull as spoons. The sudden change in the weather, coming on the one night she had something planned, annoyed her, but it did not stop her from wearing the dress she had chosen. Her social life was a zero, but she still dressed well.

She was the same age as most of her graduate students, but she firmly believed in the prohibition against sleeping with them—even though she had slept with teachers in high school, as an undergraduate, as a master's candidate, and while getting her Ph.D. Her mother—and every other amateur psychologist in her acquaintance— told her she was seeking substitutes for her aged and absent father, upon whom, after all, much of her professional work was based. Her grad school peers had a nastier assessment, suggesting that her quick rise to the top had come from "fertilizing the right beds," as one rival put it.

Zhenya kept the many failed trysts with men her own age secret from her mother. The last one had taken place during her first month in Hayden. She met an English professor at a gallery and went home with him the same night. He suggested they write a paper together about political and economic influences on certain novels, and he seemed to want their personal relationship to take the same form: a collaboration on his terms and his turf. Since fleeing him six months ago, she had slept with exactly no one.

On the way to the Dawning Building to give the lecture, she

made a wrong turn and arrived a few minutes late. She walked immediately to the podium. Several rows of people waited in folding chairs, proving an axiom about graduate students: offer food and they will come. She took a moment to scan the crowd. Her father had taught her this, to let the audience consider her before she spoke. She also used the time to check out the gathering. It was easy enough to spot the only men who were not her students. Of them, Morgan stood out—well put together, modestly handsome, the broad face and wide eyes she associated with the Midwest. Corn-fed, she thought. "I'm Zhenya Kamenev," she said, slipping into her academic persona, a comfortable role that demanded of her very little beyond intellectual rigor, and she had that to spare.

At the age of twenty-six, she did not have a lecture suitable for a general audience. She borrowed her father's story about Stalin. She emphasized different things in the telling but raised the same question: was it ethical to assassinate a man you knew to be a despot? She did not supply an answer. Upon finishing, she accepted the applause of the audience and invited them to her apartment for pizza and beer. "Let's do Q and A there," she said, which provoked a round of cheers.

Morgan scribbled down the directions. Guy immediately agreed to come along. "Don't you have questions for her?" Morgan asked Skip.

"Yeah," he said. "I got one. Why don't she learn to speak plain English?" The slight difference in the colors of his eyes made him seem edgy, as if his mood was always about to change. "Those Chicago boys are just like this Stalin character," he said. "They don't take no for an answer."

"I'm doing all right," Morgan said. "I can handle them."

"Like hell you can." Skip shook his head violently. He almost spat.

Morgan sighed. "What are you advising me to do?"

"Get sick," Skip said. "I got a friend's a doctor who would write you up with something. There won't be a strike without you to put a shoulder to it."

< 1 5 5 >

"I'm not afraid of the strike," Morgan said.

"You *ought* to be." Skip looked around again as he stood. "If I didn't tell you that straight, I wouldn't sleep at night." He patted Morgan's shoulder, gave him a long stare, and walked away.

"Skip's full of crap," Morgan said to Guy at the drive-through liquor window.

"We all are." Guy had no interest in the strike or the lecture. He had counted sixteen young women in the crowd. "I love college girls, but it's hard to meet them."

"You think they were her students?"

Guy cradled the beer they had purchased and nodded. "This is like a godsend." While Morgan drove, Guy explained his theory of meeting women at a party. "Early on, they cluster." He described women leaning against walls, situated around a coffee table, or standing in the middle of a room, their heads tilted, hips jutting— every part of them at some kind of angle. "Find the cluster with the most beautiful woman in it and approach that group. You have to have some kind of gift. Doesn't matter what. A Budweiser, a joint, maybe just a *specific* compliment— something about her earlobes or the material of her sweater."

"You've given this a lot of thought," Morgan said.

"It's foolproof. Mostly. Now, this is crucial. You give the gift *not* to the most beautiful girl but to the runner-up. No matter how educated or sophisticated she might be, a woman in a group with a really beautiful gal is going to appreciate being singled out. She has to be good-looking, too, so she can have that competition thing going on."

"That's an awful complicated way to go about meeting somebody," Morgan said. "What if the one you like is only third or fourth best-looking?"

"You don't mess with the formula." Guy shook his head forcefully. "Once she goes for you, you lead her away from the others. Now all of them will be interested in you—especially the beautiful one. She needs to reassert herself as the most desirable. She doesn't know that, of course. She just thinks, 'That boy who went after so-and-so is sort of interesting. I wonder what he sees in *her*.'" Guy tapped out a tune on the beer cans. "What do you think?"

"To tell the truth," Morgan said, "it kind of turns my stomach."

"Aw, come on, it's a lonely old world out there."

"I hate to think the sole reason we're attracted to each other is to be the top dog in our little . . ."

"Cluster."

"Cluster. It diminishes the whole romance thing, doesn't it?"

"You're assuming these girls wouldn't be naturally attracted to us anyway. We're good-looking, well-meaning, happy-go-lucky, come-what-may kind of guys. And we're employed. And we have our own cars." He patted the dash. "Yours is even new."

"I *am* fond of this car," Morgan admitted, "but I don't expect a girl to go for me over it."

"Of course not," Guy said. "Only if all other things are equal, you know?"

One of Zhenya's students answered their knock and invited them in. "You *were* at the lecture, right?"

Morgan assured her they were. Guy tapped him on the shoulder. "Watch," he said. Without a moment's hesitation, he headed across the room, passing by three young women sitting on a couch. One of them, a redhead, was a beauty, but the others were also pretty. As he walked by, he was suddenly arrested by the astonishing loveliness of a dark-haired woman sitting beside the redhead. He froze. He gaped. His legs might have wobbled. The women looked up at him. He stammered slightly, his eyes never straying from her, as if the redhead and the remainder of the party had ceased to exist. Then he smiled, and in smiling he won her over. He offered her a beer, which she accepted, and sat on the floor—literally at her feet—to engage her in conversation. In a little while they left the room together.

It impressed Morgan, and he was happy for Guy, though a little worried for the rest of humanity.

The apartment had an austere quality he admired. The living room held only a couch, a director's chair, and a rectangular carpet—all black, as was the wall hanging, a huge photograph with just a shred of light revealing a formation of human limbs. The black rug attracted lint, but he liked the decor.

Zhenya entered the living room just then, drink in hand. Mor-

< 157 >

gan had no way to know that she had come to engage him in conversation. Before she could start anything, Morgan asked when she planned to begin the Q and A.

"Oh," she said. "Now, I guess."

The discussion that followed astonished Morgan. It became clear they all thought that Zhenya's father should have killed Stalin. During a lull in the talk, he raised his hand and asked whether his intuition was accurate. A graduate student spoke before Zhenya could respond. "Stalin was responsible for more deaths than Hitler. How else *can* you think?"

"You can think he was right not to kill him," Morgan said, "or you can think nothing he did was going to be right." He looked to Zhenya. "How's it a question of ethics if it's obvious to everybody what he ought to have done?"

Just that quickly she was ready to write him off. She had no interest in stupid men. But maybe she could teach this one. He might be a mathematician, brilliant in his field but unaccustomed to this kind of problem. Perhaps she had not been clear about her father's certainty of Stalin's malevolence. "It's an ethical paradox," she said, "because it presents a situation wherein the taking of a person's life is the only ethical response."

"I don't see it that way." Having said this, Morgan was ready to leave.

"On one side of the scale, we have a single life," Zhenya said. "What's on the other side?" She began listing the figures, those who died in forced labor, the political assassinations, ethnic exterminations, the mass starvation of peasants. It quieted the room.

Morgan said, "So all those people would have lived if your father had shot Stalin?"

"There's no way to know for certain," she said. "But it's likely that—"

"How likely?"

"How do you expect me to answer that?"

"It seems to me if you're going to kill a man, you need to see his hands right around somebody's throat. Otherwise, you're speculating."

"I've written myself that several of the Bolsheviks were as ruth-less as Stalin. And it's true that he had surrounded himself with vio-lent types. But there *were* moderate men who would have handled the position more humanely."

"What's that old saying about power and corruption?" Morgan asked.

She thought he was being coy, but he really couldn't remember it. A graduate student called it out: *Power corrupts. Absolute power cor-rupts absolutely.*

"That's it," Morgan said. "How can you know the next guy will be any better?"

"If you pursue that reasoning," Zhenya said, "you'll never change anything."

Then Morgan did something that astounded her. He agreed. "I guess that's true," he said. He was considering the problem, she understood, trying to get at the truth, *thinking.* He said, "I guess I just took the wrong tack. I thought the tragedy was that he'd done the right thing, not taking a person's life, which made him feel responsible for what that person did afterwards." No one leapt in, so he continued. "I've been doing this union business, and I'm fighting with some of the organizers because I don't like the way they use war metaphors. You know what I mean?"

Zhenya nodded. A union organizer, so much better than a mathematician.

"Like they say we have a 'plan of attack,' or we need to figure out where we want the next 'battle' to take place. Seems to me it's a mis-take to talk like you're in a war unless you're really in one. Your dad was a kid back then, wasn't he? A lot of young guys tend to get self-important. If they're real soldiers in a real war, that's one thing, but in day-to-day life a kid may often think the world would be a better place if he could just waste some boss or stepfather or teacher. There's a lot of tyrants out there." Morgan looked at his watch. "I've got to go. I didn't mean to hog the questions." But he cocked his head then, as if dealt a new thought. "What about his children?"

Zhenya said, "Whose children?"

"Stalin's children," Morgan said. A titter ran through the students.

< 159 >

"They'd have been fatherless rather than millions of children made fatherless or themselves butchered." Her tone softened, but she would not condescend to him. "You're right to suggest, as I think you are, that part of our certainty comes from hindsight, but that's why in the lecture I detailed my father's own conviction that Stalin was monstrous."

Morgan nodded. "I don't know if I could be certain enough about anything to kill a child's parent. *Your* father's life would've been different, too. Whether he got away with it or not. Which means you wouldn't have been born. And none of us would be here."

A student changed the subject—to save him embarrassment, Zhenya understood, but he was not embarrassed. He was trying to worry out an answer. She was not swayed by his argument, but she liked the effort. He left the party before the end of the Q and A, but one of the students told her that Morgan and his friend worked for the city.

She was not yet in love with Morgan—not enough had transpired between them to let her think it was love—but she found herself thinking about him. "Strapping" was the word she chose to describe his body as she lay in bed considering his physique, preferring it to "muscular" or "brawny." She smoked a cigarette, lounging in her pajamas, an open book facedown beside her. A *robust* body, she revised. She was not yet in love with Morgan, but more had happened than she could understand or acknowledge.

The next day she dropped in on union headquarters—a renovated garage—and volunteered to edit a press release. After reading her revision, Morgan asked her to do the next one herself. She wrote nine drafts before letting him see it. Later, at a union meeting over which Morgan presided, she felt a secret glee when he used her language. And he looked in her direction, she was almost certain, more often than could be accounted for by chance.

Skip Deitz objected to the strike plan, saying Morgan had become a pawn of "labor gangsters." Morgan responded forcefully, "I'm nobody's pawn and you *know* it." The applause that followed drowned out the remaining objections. A few people stood while they clapped, and then everyone stood, including Zhenya. At long last, she felt she was a genuine participant in a political event, rather than an observer or analyst. She called her father that very night, waking him in a distant time zone to tell him about it.

The romance of Zhenya and Morgan became inseparable from the preparations for the strike, all speculation and anticipation at first, and then, with surprising quickness, everything became serious. Morgan appeared on the local news announcing the union's intentions. He looked good on television and spoke clearly, even making a joke about the similarity between garbage work and politics. One station began a segment called "Strike Watch." A divided screen showed Morgan's photo beside the mayor's, while a voice-over read the city's stiff statements and Zhenya's clever rebuttals. But the impact of the debate was negligible compared to the effect of those photos—one man was young, athletic, vital; the other had wrinkled cheeks, bloodshot eyes, an untrustworthy purse about the lips. How could anyone doubt who would triumph?

Zhenya invited Morgan to her apartment for supper. They exchanged a kiss at her doorstep. The next night, during a strategy session in a crowded room, Morgan reached beneath the table to squeeze her hand. Afterwards, he spent an hour with a union lawyer, locked in the only private space they could find—the bathroom—analyzing the parts of the previous discussion that were "unsatisfactory." When Morgan emerged to find Zhenya lingering in the room, he rushed to her and put his arms around her. They drove to a truckstop café, claimed a booth, and talked until four a.m. when he had to leave for work.

The first time Morgan and Zhenya made love—on the couch against the back wall of union headquarters—the phone rang all through their lovemaking. Morgan had become a celebrity. NPR ran a piece on him, calling him "thoughtful" and "a commanding presence." His photo appeared on the cover of the AFL-CIO newsletter. A fellow worker was quoted in the story: "Some men can grow to suit whatever job they take on."

Morgan himself could not distinguish between his rising confidence as a union leader and his growing love for Zhenya Kamenev; one seemed the product of the other. The night before the strike was scheduled to begin, he asked her to marry him. She had not anticipated this, but she did not hesitate. "Yes," she said, "I want you,

< 161 >

too." They embraced, and Zhenya felt the awe that lovers often feel for their own boldness. She recalled how, only a few weeks earlier, she had been utterly alone in the Midwest.

Four weeks into the strike, Morgan and Zhenya were on the picket line at city hall when a messenger came to remind Morgan of a meeting about to start without him. The work shift had just finished inside the building. Men and women who had broken ranks—the scabs—crowded the interior by the door, getting up their courage to cross the picket line and go home. Anyone crossing the line could look forward to being bumped and jostled and to hearing some of the worst language imaginable, but there had been no violence. "No rough stuff," Morgan called as he left. He himself never used any foul language. He was just no good at it. "You're a pawn," he would shout, echoing the charge that Skip had leveled against him, as if it were the worst thing he could imagine saying. Zhenya didn't mind joining the others in yelling a few obscenities. It felt liberating.

As they were pulling into the street in Morgan's Toyota, a woman ducked out of the building and ran through the picket line, her arms held high to protect her head. She darted right out into the street. Morgan slammed the brakes hard and the car skidded slightly, but he managed to stop without hitting her. The woman froze in the crosswalk, her arms raised and crossed. Morgan knew her, of course. Her name was Lillie Brown, and she was a filing clerk. He revved the engine to make her move.

That night, a pounding on Morgan's door woke them. An assistant district attorney and three armed policemen showed him an arrest warrant. Morgan was charged with the attempted murder of Lillie Brown. "You've got to be kidding," he said as they hand-cuffed him. "This is going to backfire," he warned the attorney. They hauled him off.

He spent two nights in jail. Union lawyers from Chicago arrived within hours of his arrest, and by the next day they had found twenty witnesses ready to testify as to what had really happened, including the man who had crossed the picket line right behind Lillie Brown. "I don't believe in unions," he was quoted as saying, "but as Christ is my savior, I will not lie." Charges were dropped. In a newspaper interview, Lillie Brown claimed she had been pressured into making the accusation.

In less than a week, the city met all union demands and the strike was over.

Morgan appeared on national television shaking hands with the mayor. The very next day, Zhenya and Morgan announced their engagement, then canceled their plans later in the week and eloped. Within a few months Zhenya was pregnant. They found a nice house on a tree-lined street with a swimming pool in the back and a big yard to one side, and it cost them almost nothing because it was in the old part of town. "We felt like we were charmed," Zhenya used to say. Their son was born healthy and beautiful. Morgan ran unopposed and was elected to a second term as president of the union. The photo in the newspaper showed him smiling, one arm around his wife, the other holding their baby. Zhenya's dissertation was published. The reviewers called her work "provocative" and "ingeniously researched." She was given early promotion by the university, and she became pregnant again. This time, as if scripted, they had a girl, also healthy, also beautiful. Morgan gave a speech at a labor conference and served as an elector at the Democratic National Convention. *The Nation* did a brief piece on him. Their children started school. Zhenya was awarded tenure and soon promoted to full professor. She earned a commendation from an organization of women scholars.

It seemed to them that they had found a route through life that permitted them everything—to observe and create and love, and to make a difference. They knew they were lucky, but they felt they deserved it, that their love made them worthy, and that neither their love nor their luck would ever end.

But it did end. When Philip killed himself, movement ceased. Everything that had come before had to be reevaluated, even the night they met. There were times when Morgan believed Zhenya's anger with him dated all the way back to that first night. She seemed to believe now that he had been right all along, that he had instinctively known what she had obscured with her intellect.

He had understood from the beginning that one life could mean the world, and for this, she could not forgive him.

< 1 6 3 >

.   .   .

The board met in a back room of the union store. Morgan was surprised to find the store open. It seemed later than it really was. The young woman in charge knitted behind the counter. Morgan didn't know her. Though he often came to the store to drop things off, he had not been inside for a long time. There was a lot more furniture than he expected, kitchen chairs, a long orange couch, a brilliant orange easy chair that didn't match the couch, a row of wooden ladder-back chairs that someone had pieced back together, and a dirty orange ottoman. The lesson seemed to be *Don't buy orange furniture.* Homemade shelves covered one wall of the store with books. A saxophone and a slightly bent clarinet hung on fishing line from the ceiling, and three racks of clothing made a triangle in the center of the room. Every flat surface had a lamp on it. Somebody must have finally repaired all the ones they had collected over the years. The oak doors Morgan had saved leaned against a wall. They had been refinished, the wood light and lustrous. Beautiful doors, and the asking price was only one hundred dollars.

"Everybody thinks about buying those," the young woman said. "But they're a funny size. How are you, Morgan?"

"I'm fine," he said, no idea who she was. Her eyes were set wide apart, which gave her a vehicular look.

Guy had disappeared into the back, and Vinnie took Morgan's arm to lead him there. "You can shop later," she said. "We're running behind."

The six representatives sat around a table that Morgan himself had salvaged. Guy suggested they start with the Ford matter because he needed to get home. He made no effort to pretend sobriety. Two of the board members sighed as soon as he opened his mouth. Morgan suspected this was not the first time Guy had shown up loaded. The remaining three—two men Morgan didn't know and a woman who was a fellow sanitation worker—seemed happy for the diversion. One of the men looked tipsy himself.

After some haggling, the board entertained Guy's motion to put up the money to bail Danny Ford out of jail. Bail was set at fifty thousand dollars, but the bondsman only needed ten percent.

"We shouldn't ought to let one of our own rot in the pen," Guy said. "No matter what the hell goddamn thing he's done."

Morgan and Vinnie sat behind Guy on mismatched kitchen stools that made them several inches higher than the board members. The stools felt precarious, and Morgan leaned against the wall to steady himself. Discarded paintings that one person or another had mistaken for art crowded the walls. Morgan faced a nude done by a painter lacking full mastery of foreshortening. The model lay across a bed, her feet seeming to grow out of her pelvis. The painting made him dizzy.

The chair of the committee—a woman exasperated with Guy—decided to direct a question to Morgan, but first she made a speech about his tenure as union president. "Two men stepped down before Mr. Morgan said, 'The buck stops here.' " She pounded her fist on the table for emphasis. "I can tell you, without Mr. Morgan we wouldn't have a union." She went on to credit him for the creation of the union store and the subsequent fund they were now deciding how to spend.

He couldn't have asked for a better introduction, yet his first instinct was to contradict her. He had merely stumbled into the position of president and had taken it on because he was too naïve to know better. Beyond that, all he did was remain firm with the city, which was what the AFL-CIO advisers directed him to do. He understood, though, that now was not the time to correct history. He needed whatever leverage he could get. He wished he hadn't drunk so much beer.

"The idea of the discretionary fund," he said, "from the very beginning, was to help members who get into tight spots. If any one of us in here was suddenly arrested, the board would gladly bail us out. We'd be assumed innocent until proven otherwise. Danny Ford should get the same shake. He's not a bad kid. Maybe he *was* trouble for a good long while, but the city made the decision to hire him, and this job has been responsible for turning him around." He stared at them a moment, unsure how coherent he had been. They didn't look convinced, but they didn't seem embarrassed for him. "I've been drinking," he said. "I imagine that's obvious. I've been

< 1 6 5 >

upset about this. You can't let a kid down like this. People make mistakes. Lives can be ruined. All he did—if he did anything—was to try and stay loyal to some people who used to be his friends. That's not so bad. Maybe—what do we know—maybe he didn't have much choice in the matter. A lot of the worst things that happen, you don't have any choice over."

"That's absolutely correct," Guy said. "Hear, hear."

Morgan had talked too long. He could see it in their faces. "Look, if it were up to me, I'd put up the bail myself. My wife wants to wait and see what you have to say." The chairwoman squinted then. He shouldn't have brought that up. Now he needed to explain, but there was no explanation. "Maybe she doesn't trust my judgment on this one. Maybe she *doesn't* want to because I *do* want to. I don't know." Something inside him began to crumble. "We lost a child. Long time ago. Some of you know that. Marriages usually break up after something like that." He took a breath and looked up from their solemn faces to the painting. Maybe the artist intended for the nude to be deformed, he thought. If she was a deformed woman, did that make it a good painting? He felt the painting shift back and forth under his gaze, from a bad painting of a beautiful woman to a good painting of an unusual body.

"In any case," he said, looking away from the painting, "he's, well, Danny's not a perfect worker, but he's good in a lot of ways. He's not even my friend. Not really." He saw the sanitation worker glance at another board member, that telling glance. Morgan understood he was making a fool of himself. "I don't know how to talk about him. But we can't just . . ." He shook his head. "I've said enough." He slid off the stool and stood. Vinnie had hold of his arm. He hadn't realized she was holding on to him.

"C'mon," she said softly. Her eyes were glossy and red. She led him out of the room. In the part of her bleached hair, Morgan saw golden roots.

He said, "Are you all right?"

She nodded. "Let's get a drink. We'll wait for Guy in the car. Then we'll get us a drink. Here." She handed him a tissue from her purse.

Morgan wiped his eyes. "I'm not really crying. My eyes have just started to leak."

She nodded again. "Pollen," she said. "Dust. Sadness. Everything that grows on trees."

"Look at these." He directed her to the doors. They made him happy. "Can you believe someone threw away something so beautiful?" He pulled out his wallet. Nine dollars. "Hold them for me," he said to the woman with the wide-set eyes. "I want them."

She accepted his money gratefully. "They're yours," she said.

"They're mine," he said.

Outside, the world had turned gray and heavy, and Morgan felt ashamed.

The call startled her. "Adriana? Is Peter Ivanovich." He did not need to introduce himself. His voice was his signature.

Mrs. East gathered her wits quickly and said, "How nice to hear from you, Mr. Kamenev."

"Please you must call me Peter, please. We are full-grown man and woman, yes?"

"Well, yes." Though the admission was obvious, it worried her.

"But most important. Please, would you like to go vis me to lecture at university?"

It took her a moment to say, "I think I would be delighted."

"Good. You can drive, yes? Am no good on Hayden streets. All run wrong way for old Russian. You forgive Peter Ivanovich this?"

"Why, certainly."

"I am seeing you then Wednesday at seven, if you don't mind to pick me up. After lecture we can have drink and discuss."

"Wednesday? You mean tomorrow?"

"Is Tuesday already? I am not giving enough vorning to you."

It took her a few seconds to turn "vorning" into "warning." "Nonsense," Mrs. East said. "My calendar is not that busy." She immediately regretted that remark. "A lecture sounds interesting. Who is speaking?"

"Me," Peter Ivanovich said. "Is not so long, don't worry. I make short and sweet."

< 1 6 7 >

. . .

Mrs. East brought her Lincoln Towne car to a stop at Morgan and Zhenya's house. Peter Ivanovich immediately opened the front door and waved to her. He stepped from the house pulling a red wagon loaded with cardboard boxes. She climbed carefully from her car into the street. She wore a dress she had purchased earlier in the day, and she preferred that he first see it on her while she was standing. She'd had her hair cut as well, a new style, shorter and more contemporary. "Are we carrying some packages?"

"Books," Peter Ivanovich said. "These books I write long time ago and sell after lecture. Is inconvenience? I leave them here."

"No, of course not."

He navigated the wagon over the new sidewalk and curb and then over the old sidewalk and curb, but she had to help him lift the first box into the trunk. It must have strained him, as he let her lift the other two by herself. Peter Ivanovich picked up one end of the wagon. It surprised her that they were taking it, too. The trunk, fortunately, was enormous.

His cologne had an unfamiliar fragrance, more bracing than enticing. Within the confines of her car, it made her eyes water.

"This is car like I remember loving," he said. "You and I remember great cars of past. Room to live in great cars." He patted her thigh. "You remember," he said, a statement, not a question. "Cannot go to lecture in tiny Oriental car."

She turned the ignition and set the car into motion. "I've never felt safe in small cars," she said. "Or comfortable."

"Is room for all human business in car like this," he said.

She let that one go.

At Peter Ivanovich's insistence, Mrs. East parked in a handicap space. She had never done such a thing before, but he was, after all, both the guest of honor and a man of advanced years. The parking lot was crowded. The semester was still under way, but she doubted that there were enough night classes to account for the cars. They were here to see Mr. Kamenev. She felt a peculiar swell of pride. She recognized it from long ago—her husband decorating his men, her husband-to-be sharing a platform with General MacArthur. She helped Peter Ivanovich get the wagon out of the trunk. He did not attempt to help her unload the boxes—saving his energy, she imagined. He let her pull the wagon to the lecture hall as well. She was happy to do it. If one went about things the proper way, one could perform any duty with dignity. Except oral sex. She felt herself color at the thought.

A bearded fellow with a colorful tie met them at the door to the auditorium. He was effusive in his thanks to Peter Ivanovich for agreeing to give the lecture. "Please to introduce Adriana East," Peter said, then to her added, "This man's name I don't know."

He taught in the political science department with Zhenya, Mrs. East discovered, and he volunteered to take the wagon from her.

The hall seated three hundred people, and it was full. Students with notebooks sat on the stairs that led to the stage. She hoped they had thought to reserve seats. She had no need to worry. A table with two chairs was positioned at the base of the stage. Peter Ivanovich took her arm and led her to this special area. The seats were metal folding chairs and not comfortable, but she didn't care. If he didn't mind, how could she? They faced the audience, as if the two of them—Mrs. East as well as Peter Ivanovich—were the attractions. She felt flushed and happy. A crowd of people gathered about the table to shake Peter's hand and introduce themselves. She turned her chair to be certain that she could see the podium on the raised stage, but she did so without turning her back on the audience. She understood the etiquette of public behavior.

The man who had taken the wagon from her now lugged two of the boxes down the stairs. A woman followed, carrying the third box. They set them on the table and lifted out the books, which they stacked in front of Mrs. East. Peter Ivanovich turned to her. He put a hand on the first pile of books. "I forget change, so just ten dollars for paperbacks. Twenty for hard ones. We give them deal." He winked at her. "This chair is bad for old Russian back." He got up and headed for a seat in the front row, while a line of people formed before her at the table.

< 169 >

"Will he sign them?" an elderly and distinguished-looking man asked. "I assume he will?" He had his wallet out.

Mrs. East stared dumbly at the man for a moment, then turned to look for Peter. She even called his name. He had his back to her, surrounded by admirers. She colored again, deeply this time, and considered leaving. She could stand and nonchalantly climb the stairs. The man before her opened his wallet and strummed the currency within.

Mrs. East spoke through clenched teeth. "It's ten dollars." She tried to keep her voice out of the lower registers, to act as if she had known all along her role for the evening was not romantic but retail. She found an envelope in her purse and used the back to tally sales. If she had a task to perform, she would do it correctly.

"Which of these books do you recommend?" a young woman asked. "Which would be the best to start with?"

"I haven't read a word of them," she replied. "And I don't plan to start anytime in the future. I shall *never* read these books. Not one of them."

"Then I'll take the paperback," the woman said and produced a ten-dollar bill. She looked over her shoulder at Peter Ivanovich, then leaned close and whispered, "He's in my history book. Can you imagine? It's like meeting Abraham Lincoln or John Kennedy."

"Take your book and move it," replied Mrs. East.

When we talk about the class system in Tsarist Russia, the novelist is interested in the privilege of the nobility and the deprivation of the peasants. He may weave a good story, but as an examination of class, he touches only on the surface features. The economist will provide statistics to depict the complex strata of wealth and poverty, but these numbers merely articulate a skeletal design. Combine the work of the novelist, the economist, the historian, the sociologist, the anthropologist, and the political scientist and one may divine the trunk and limbs, the square head and knotted hair, the humped back and prerevolutionary arches of that beast we call social class. Studying this body of knowledge is useful, but do not think yourself an expert. You understand it no better than you would a man about whom you know the measurements of his torso, the color of his eyes, the rate of his heartbeat, the capacity of his lungs. Class in Tsarist Russia was not merely an economic system or a social scheme. It was not just a cultural network or a political device. Class in Tsarist Russia was a state of being.

Peter Ivanovich's new lecture took a centennial perspective on the Russian Revolution. He argued that it took something as severe as revolution to alter the mind-set of the Russian people. In effect, he argued that the revolution was a success, despite the terrible price it exacted. He believed the lecture would generate controversy and put him in demand once again, on campuses all around the country. The talk shows would want him. He would regain his slipping status and make a bundle of money. His booking agent was putting together a brochure. The lecture was almost ready. He needed a little help on the final section from a native speaker, and then a push from that ignorant Cyclops television. He was to be interviewed by a CBS correspondent—Jane . . . Who-Doo, he couldn't remember her name—and if he impressed her, which he would, she would sign him on to appear on a special weeklong program to air during the final week of the twentieth century. How could they refuse a man one hundred years old who had witnessed every moment of the century and been present at many of the most significant events?

Of course, he was not really that old and had not actually been in attendance at some of the events he claimed to have witnessed, but no record of his birth existed. And who knew more of such historical acts than Peter Ivanovich Kamenev? A white lie was often needed to get things started. He wanted to test out his new lecture at Hayden University, but the professor who organized the reading—a phlegmatic rustic with body odor—requested the ethics lecture instead. Louis Armstrong had once told Peter that he had come to hate "Hello, Dolly!" but could not escape playing it. That conversation had taken place thirty years earlier, backstage on the Merv Griffin set. When it had been his turn to talk, Peter Ivanovich had told a joke.

Peter Ivanovich: "What is Russian words for 'electric blanket'?"
Merv Griffin: "I don't know."
Peter Ivanovich: "Here, Rover."
Merv Griffin had chuckled his way to a commercial, then Louis

< 1 7 1 >

Armstrong joined them, singing "Hello, Dolly!" playing a few notes on his horn, the audience singing along.

Peter did not need note cards for the ethics lecture. He had given it so many times that his lines were memorized, his theatrics choreographed; even the dramatic pauses were practiced. "When do I see you without a performance?" a woman had once asked him. Who was that? How long ago did it take place? He could not remember, although it seemed to him that she was pregnant when she asked. "When am I privy to unguarded moments?" she had demanded. They had been in bed. He could not recall her face, but he could remember the light in the room. She had liked candles.

"I don't see guards here," he had said.

"You're performing," she insisted.

"Sooner or later, the magician becomes his tricks," he told her. She had accepted that, as he guessed she would. It was a line he had used in an article for *Esquire*.

Peter stared out at the great crowd and winked. He reminded himself that the name of the place was Hayden University. He would slip that in somewhere. The locals liked to be acknowledged. He repeated to himself the new line that he had decided to stick somewhere in the story: *Violence is the poor man's lawyer.* He let the room grow quiet, and then he let the quiet grow into something else—a tension. He nodded at them, squinted, waited.

"You are wondering," he said to the crowd, "if this old man has lost it. Is he just going stand there all night?" The crowd laughed, the tension dissipated, and he smiled. He had them in the palm of his hand.

Despite the ignominy of her position, Mrs. East found herself enthralled by the lecture. When she was preparing the reception for him, she had found out a few things, but she was still unprepared for the magnitude of his knowledge. To think that her escort had known such historic figures—it was amazing. His speaking style mixed self-deprecating humor with moments of great emotion. His own historic guilt he accepted willingly. It was impossible to think of him as anything but magnanimous.

The applause was loud and long. Some people stood. One of the people in the story he told was named Zhenya, which solved the mystery of his daughter's name. A microphone was carried down the stairs and positioned next to the table. A line formed behind the mike. People had questions for the great man. "What do you think Gorbachev's place in history will be?" one man asked.

"Is best dressed leader of all time," Peter Ivanovich replied, and the crowd laughed. He answered most questions with anecdotes. He spoke a little about the new lecture he was writing. At his age, Mrs. East thought, he was still at work. Even when the questions were foolish—one girl had asked if he'd known anyone on the *Titanic*—he answered with humor and intelligence. "I don't know any people on *Titanic*," he said, "but many of sharks who swam in water, I know very well." Mrs. East could not help but reconsider the resolve she had made before the lecture began, to leave as soon as she had finished selling the books, to let him find his own way home. Perhaps he had simply forgotten to mention that he needed some help, she thought, knowing it was a lie but intent on living with it.

He talked about being rebuked as a boy by Tolstoy. He revealed that he had been asked to leave a lecture hall by none other than Sigmund Freud. He told a little story about the vanity of Carl Jung, who kept a mirror in his coat to check his hair, and another story about the cat that Marilyn Monroe tossed from a moving car. He spoke at length about visits to the White House with Richard Nixon before the president's historic trips to China and the Soviet Union. He admitted to an amorous affair with Marlene Dietrich. He had danced with Ginger Rogers. He suspected from their first encounter that Errol Flynn was homosexual. He had secretly consulted with the Warren Commission and read the full report before LBJ had it edited. "Ask Gerald Ford. He and I are only people left who know whole story." He added that he had written the truth about the assassination, notarized it, and put it in a safe-deposit box. "After death, I have last word. If I am talking now, death is coming sooner."

Another round of applause followed the final answer and then the line shifted from the microphone to Mrs. East's desk. Peter

< 173 >

Ivanovich took the seat beside her and signed his books, chatting with everyone—especially the young women. He was brazen, which permitted her to get over her awe of him. She forgave him. It was so much preferable to forgive than to be forgiven. It was really he who was at a disadvantage now.

She sold books for three quarters of an hour, and Peter Ivanovich signed them. "You must be tired," she said as they stood after the last straggler had finally departed.

He shook his head. "Russian bear," he said, tapping his chest. "Ready now for drink and lady bear."

"You seem more interested in the cubs," she said, proud of the rejoinder.

He slipped his bony hands into his trousers pockets. "Is natural. A few years ago, one cub or anozzer would want to come home to Russian den. Now not so much. We have drink, yes?" He pulled his pocket inside out, then took the wad of bills from her, tucked it in the pocket lining, and stuffed it back down. "I know of good bar in downtown. Emma takes me there. Beer so beautiful like golden hair, and best vodka from mozzer country."

"It was rude of you to pretend we were out together on a social engagement and then seat me here to sell your books." There, she had said it.

"I am crude man who does what he likes," he said. "Mostly job and sex. Have you seen all these writings about reality of sex after the menopause? I am rude man, but I can find entertainment in most any evening." He smiled at her, and she could see no reason not to have a drink with him. "Now we go," he said, "but most important, where is wagon?"

Some of the people in the bar had been at the lecture. Many of them wanted to shake his hand. "Intellectual endeavor makes for thirst," Peter Ivanovich said in explanation of the crowd. The first stranger to introduce himself was a biologist. "Science is busy, very prominent," Peter Ivanovich said approvingly. "If you insist, drinks is good for us. Have you met Adriana East?" he asked. "She is Hayden native. Vodka for me, and . . ."

Mrs. East ordered cognac.

"Emma likes cognac," he said. "Most delicious."

When the biologist left, she corrected Peter Ivanovich. "I've lived in Hayden most of my adult life, but I'm not a native."

"I like that word," he said. "*Native. Na-teev.* Please to let me use on beautiful woman such as yourself."

The second person to introduce himself to Peter, a college student, did not offer to buy drinks, but Peter Ivanovich willfully misunderstood. "What timing," he said, "just as I am finishing vodka, admirer comes to buy anozzer. This is Adriana East, my neighbor and close associate. Drinks cognac."

"Is that what we are?" Mrs. East asked once the gentleman left to order drinks. "Associates?"

He shrugged. "Is just words."

He introduced her next to a group of people of Russian descent. "And this woman vis me is Adriana East. Have you ever heard a name so lovely?"

"It's been so long since anyone called me Adriana," Mrs. East said. "I rather like hearing it."

"We must let them buy us drinks, my dear," he said, although the college student hadn't yet returned with his offerings. "Is Russian custom. Make them feel at home."

One of the university officials he had met at the lecture was there. Peter Ivanovich evidently could not recall his name or title, but he hugged the man who came bearing champagne. "You must join us," he said. "This beautiful woman is Adriana East, newest girlfriend of old Russian."

Soon the table was crowded with tumblers of vodka, snifters of cognac, champagne in an iced bucket, and tall glasses of dark beer. Mrs. East had not had so much to drink in decades. The university dignitary—a dean—was tanked as well. "I sat with your daughter," he said to Peter Ivanovich. "Is she coming here?"

Peter Ivanovich shrugged dramatically. "Who's to know? She is liberated woman, goes where she pleases. Does what she pleases. Good girl to her papa but vis funny tastes."

"I like her," the dean said. "She's a damn intelligent woman."

"Russian girls is best. And French. Adriana East is half Russian,

< 175 >

half French. You have met Adriana?" he asked, although he had introduced her to the dean himself, and they had been drinking together for most of an hour.

"I really am half Russian," she said. "How did you know?"

"You drink like Russian," he said. He poured the last of the dean's champagne into his own glass. "Is magnificent woman, yes?" he said to the dean. "Must have more champagne to celebrate beauty." He turned back to her. "She is like butterfly in cocoon." He crooked a finger at her. "Come out of there. Time to spread wings and fly." He leaned in close. "You act like old woman," he said softly, "but you are not so old as you think." He ran his hand along her knee and up under her dress.

Mrs. East meant to feel scandalized, but she failed.

She did not think she should drive. Her insides were performing a pleasurable swirl, and Peter's hand on her rump radiated warmth. Besides, she could not find the car in the parking lot. It was a large car and a small lot, but none of the vehicles looked quite right. The dean of arts and sciences, who had come out to see them off, offered his cell phone. Adriana called a cab. She had not ridden in a taxi in years, not since she and Colonel East were in New York, staying at the Plaza. They had just left a theater after seeing a play, and a beautiful woman asked Colonel East if she could share a cab with them. Colonel East not only assented, he picked up the fare. He had been so impressed with her that it would have made Adriana angry, but she had been quite certain that the woman was a man wearing a dress. She could tell by his hands and the fluffy boa that hid his Adam's apple.

She told Peter Ivanovich about that night while they rested against the bumper of a car, waiting for the taxi. When she finished the anecdote, she realized it had no point. It was just a memory. "I don't know why I thought that needed telling," she said.

"Is good story. One time I make same mistake, but when I discover truth, is too late to change what already happened in car." He shrugged.

"In the car?"

"I am driving, and she is eager to get started. What am I to think when I discover is man who has done this? It felt like woman doing to me. I say to him, 'Thank you very much, but I am going home now visout you.'"

"That must have been awkward," she said, recalling dimly some bit of awkwardness with a waiter at a party. It had happened years ago, only it hadn't been at a party, and the young man hadn't been a waiter. It took a moment to remember. She had been at a grocery store, and a man who had flirted with her the night before bagged her groceries and carried them to her car. No, she thought with a sudden pang of regret, *she* had flirted with *him* after having a little much to drink. He had been handsome and funny, and he had acted as if she were the only person alive. Forty years had passed since that day in the grocery, and still it made her color. She had tipped him a quarter for carrying her bags. She shook her head at that regrettable quarter. What had she been thinking?

The cab pulled up before the curb. During the brief period she had been sitting on the bumper, her legs had become unsteady. She straightened up and walked as carefully as she could, while Peter careered happily from one parked car to another. In the cab, he dropped his head into her lap. He was saying something about Louis Armstrong. "Sit up now," Adriana commanded. "This is a new dress."

"I enjoyed your lecture," the cabbie said.

Peter Ivanovich raised his head at that. "I have even cabdrivers at lecture?" He leaned forward to talk, as if suddenly sober again.

The cabbie was a graduate student in history. "I didn't get a T.A., so I drive this. More money but bad hours."

"You must buy us drink," Peter said.

"What I don't get," he said, "is why people continue to believe in government even though they always turn out bad. Where we headed?"

Adriana gave him her address.

"You are smart boy," Peter Ivanovich said, his hand on Mrs. East's knee. "But anarchy is ugly way to live."

"My husband was a colonel," Mrs. East said, apropos of very little.

< 1 7 7 >

"Very good," said Peter Ivanovich. "She doesn't drive for reason of inebriation. Russians always drive. Many wrecks in Russia. Cars here and there. Big mess." He leaned into her and kissed her on the lips. It was as she remembered. How had she gone so long without kissing a man? "Anarchy," Peter continued, "is bad for country but good for individual person, like me. My life—"

"No one at the wheel," Adriana said.

Peter Ivanovich clapped his hands and shouted. "Exactly so! Which is why always big mess and big freedom where I am."

The cabbie turned onto Forest Avenue, and Peter's head fell again into her lap. The taxi stopped in front of her house.

"You cannot be charging us?" Peter Ivanovich said.

"Uh," the cabbie said, "yeah, I have to."

"After lecture? After you carry famous Russian and lover of famous Russian, you want money?"

"It's only four dollars and twenty cents," he said.

Mrs. East gave him a ten. "It was a most pleasant trip," she said, climbing from the car and falling immediately to her hands in her plush grass. She looked up and saw two sidewalks, two gutters. My God, it has come to this, she thought. Then she recalled the road-work and began to laugh.

Peter Ivanovich said, "Not here in grass. Bedroom." He offered his hand, and she almost pulled him off his feet. "Most important, first hearty nightcap. Good for lubrication."

"My goodness, yes," said Mrs. East. "A little bite of cognac."

They linked arms and strode unsteadily to her porch. "You get drinks," Peter Ivanovich said as she opened the door. "Where is bed?"

"Upstairs," Mrs. East replied. She guided him across her living room to the base of the stairs.

"Get bottle first," he said. "Then climb this mountain vis me."

When she returned with the bottle, he took her hand and they began the ascent. Halfway up, he sat and pulled her down beside him. The kissing started there. They moved up the remainder of the stairs without standing or breaking their embrace, pushing their butts up one step and then another. At the landing, Mrs. East stood and helped Peter Ivanovich up beside her. They linked arms again and moved down the hallway like a single, clumsy entity, bursting through her bedroom door, spinning once, and landing on her bed. The cognac slipped out of her hand and bounded across the bed to the other side, hitting the floor loudly.

She had the wherewithal to get up, fetch the bottle, shut the door, and latch it. She knew there was no one else in the house, but she had forgotten to lock the front door. This would have to do. Facing him, her dress open, brassiere unsnapped and sitting loosely across her bosom, she said, "You're only with me because none of those children at the lecture wanted to go to bed with you."

He smiled. His pants were undone and revealed a swatch of white thigh. He still had his shoes on. "Of course," he said. "So? We are starting family here, you and I? I don't think so. We are this man and that woman, this man's lips and that woman's tongue, this penis and that twat. Is bad thing? Is better being alone?"

This speech moved her to tears—drunken tears, but tears nonetheless. She went to him without stumbling or dropping the liquor.

As if to compensate for the widening of Forest Avenue, the city installed streetlights designed to look like gas lamps from the turn of the century. These went up while the old sidewalk buckled beneath the blade of a Caterpillar. Out with the old, in with the pretend old, Morgan thought. This occurred to him one night when the clouds made a low white ceiling that reflected back the lights of the city, making the night both dark and lighted.

Mrs. East also witnessed the oddly illuminated night. Colonel East, now twenty-four years in the ground, had called such brilliance in the midst of darkness "doglight." Curious, the things one remembers. If he were alive, she would ask him to explain the source of the name. He had been the type of man who supplied explanations for virtually everything. If a subject stumped him, he became angry. Adriana had tried not to ask of him anything he could not give. Often he simply made things up, and she had to accept something she knew to be false in order to be loyal. That period of her life was long past, but she still held loyalty more dear than honesty. Doglight might mean something altogether different, but for

< 1 7 9 >

her it would refer to that strange transparent darkness. Perhaps dogs could always see that well in the dark. She supplied her own invented logic to support her husband's invented facts.

In doglight, the new lamps of Forest Avenue illuminated nothing. In fact, each seemed to create a penumbra of darkness about its faintly green globe. Up and down the street, the lamps pocked the landscape with darkness. Peter Ivanovich witnessed this, too, and made a note of it in the spiral notebook he kept by his bed. He played with the idea on paper, combining it with others. Eventually he wrote, *Ideology is the light that creates the darkness.* That morning, in the wee hours while the others slept, he offered the aphorism to Morgan, and later that day he asked Adriana East what she thought of it. Her reaction to it was bound up in her thoughts of her husband. She sat beside him thinking, This ridiculous man has access to something like wisdom. Wisdom was qualitatively different from invented facts. It did not matter that the pretend facts had come from a refined, dignified man, while the wisdom came from a clowning drunk. "You intrigue me," she told Peter. "You're such an odd . . ." She paused, letting the tumblers in her head spin. "Such an odd *buffalo* of a man."

Peter liked that. He said, "Before nineteenth century, most wars is religious wars. In twentieth century, ideology is the religion. And wars is ideological wars." When she did not immediately react, he said, "Is just buffalo man talking."

Morgan's response to his aphorism did not please him.

"I don't get it," Morgan said.

Peter tried to explain, how seeing by a single light could blind one to much of the world, but Morgan only shrugged. "You say that as if we had a choice how we see." He had been filling a thermos with coffee while he spoke. "One light is all most of us ever get."

Peter did not argue. He nodded, pursed his lips, and let the man go off to work, the odd light gone by this time, and only the familiar darkness awaiting him.

5

Mystery is the truth, history the lie.

—Peter Ivanovich Kamenev

Every time he told the story, he described the beauty of the night, the brooding darkness of the winter sky—a darkness he would always associate with Russia—and the sullen drifts of snow that linked the stoops and walks and covered the gutters, a snow that memory had blanched and which grew whiter each year, a brilliant white, as if the mounds had covered lamps radiating light.

The snow couldn't really have been so pure. Automobiles shared the streets with horse-drawn carts and carriages. Soot and exhaust tainted the snow. Boots and hooves trampled it. And the day had been warm, causing melt to fill the ruts in the streets and splash against the old snow, whose knolls would have been scarred and pitted and slashed with mud. When the sun set, the air cooled so quickly that cracks grew in windowpanes and streets became plated with ice as black as the tires that trespassed against it.

But memory insisted on sclerotic, rolling hills of fresh-fallen snow, shimmering in the light of an opalescent moon.

Had there been such a moon, the sky wouldn't have been so dark. Not that much of it could have been visible to young Peter Ivanovich Kamenev, whose first name was actually Petrov and would not be anglicized until he reached the United States, and whose last name was never Kamenev, which he would adopt after fleeing the Soviet Union. He navigated the narrow streets lined with the ancient

< 1 8 0 >

< 181 >

buildings of Moscow in a borrowed car with a powerful heater and a young woman's bare thigh, as white and radiant as the imaginary snow, across his lap, one of her stockings wrapped like a noose around his neck, her drunken husband splayed across the backseat, muttering insensibly into the dark leather. Peter Ivanovich's hand caressed the soft flesh of the woman's thigh, a single finger slipping beneath the satin panties to touch the coarse hair, which in memory was the black of a bear's tongue. This was a memory of his imagination. He recalled her dark pubis as he pictured it, forgetting that he never removed her underwear, forgetting that his desire for her was never consummated, forgetting that she existed for him as that particular woman only that one long-ago night.

When he first told the story in the United States, he didn't mention the woman at all, her milky thigh across his lap, the faint aroma of sweat from the stocking circling his neck, the even fainter smell of her sex riding the currents of the artificially heated air, swirling in his lungs like the very smoke of being. He had merely stated the facts, that he had been asked by his uncle (who was not actually his uncle, but Peter saw no reason to go into that) to drive some guests to their home. The uncle was really the father of a friend. Peter Ivanovich had become a regular visitor at their house, staying a month or two at a time. The couple he was driving home had come for a dinner party—Maxim Gorky and Grigory Zinoviev had been among the guests—and then their automobile refused to start. Even when he later began telling a more complete version of the story, Peter Ivanovich would omit the sweet, nasty things the woman whispered in his ear—not out of timidity or decorum, but because he could no longer distinguish her actual words from the talk of movie stars leaning one into another on the diaphanous screen, memory diluted by the vicarious and ersatz passions of actors. Nothing destroyed your credibility like repeating a line from the cinema as if it were your own.

The husband roused himself from the car's rear seat in order to vomit, throwing open the door at the last moment, a rush of cold air infiltrating the car's warm cabin, his head draping over the portal, the sheen of ice covering the road sliding just beneath his face. His sudden movement startled Peter, and the dark car responded, an obedient lurch followed by a skid across the narrow street. The woman scrambled to retrieve her stocking from Peter's neck. Her husband's vomit froze as it fell, leaving a crooked trail across the ice like an exclamation, a statement of the body's rage.

The automobile, an elegant old model no longer manufactured anywhere in the world, had doors that opened in opposite directions, like the double doors to a ballroom. When the car at last halted, sliding the final few feet to the center of the road, the rear door canted against its restraint, then swung forward against the husband's skull, making a soft thud, as if his head were composed wholly of meat. At the same moment a revolver slid from beneath the front seat and thumped against Peter's heels. He didn't examine it, but placed it back beneath the seat. The car belonged to his mentor, Comrade Lev Kamenev, a revolutionary hero, an important man in the government. He would have many enemies. The hidden revolver was no surprise.

Peter couldn't remember what year this drive took place, but he guessed that it was 1932. It had to be after 1927, as Comrade Kamenev had returned from Rome, where Stalin had exiled him with petty work as punishment for a disagreement. It couldn't have been later than 1932 because Stalin's wife, Nadya, was still alive. She would kill herself that fall. Peter Ivanovich had not yet dropped his real last name and added that of his mentor. That didn't happen until he reached the United States, and he would tell no one his real surname, not even his wives or children.

The husband in the backseat did not rise from the floorboard or push the car door away from his head. Peter studied the inert body, then looked to the man's frantic wife, whose feet touched his pants pocket, her legs bent, thigh exposed, the stocking gone from his neck and slithering up past her knee.

He pushed her leg away, opened the door, and stepped outside carefully, holding the door's plush handle, the cold air causing his eyes to water, his ears to burn. He reached back for his hat and pulled it over his head, tucking in his ears, then put on his gloves before bending to lift the husband's head by the back of his collar. The resistance he felt was more than mere weight. Peter knelt. The man's tongue, blackened by the road's ice, was stuck to it now, frozen in place.

< 1 8 3 >

Peter Ivanovich cuffed the man. Grabbing him again by the collar, Peter jerked him up, the tearing of lingual flesh audible to the man's wife, who gasped and clambered into the backseat, the bottom triangle of her husband's tongue aflame with blood, bordered in black, the tip of his nose raw as well.

Peter climbed behind the wheel once again and let the heater warm his gloved hands. "Is he all right?" he asked, trying to keep bitterness from his tone.

"He's mutilated," she said, cradling his head. "How do you bandage a tongue?"

Peter merely shrugged, put the car into gear, and inched along the ice, driving directly now to the apartment of this couple, whose names he recalled but never used when he told this story. In fact, it was only after he had lived in the United States more than a decade that he began to include the woman and her inebriate husband as elements of the tale, understanding by that time that Americans liked to be entertained while they were instructed, that they enjoyed titillation if they could pretend it was part of something larger. He lugged the husband out of the car and to the apartment, the wife trailing, worried, as if the naked thigh she had presented Peter had torn out her husband's tongue.

Peter Ivanovich carried the man to his bed, where the woman treated her husband's wound. "He was a big man," Peter would tell his audience, "and I was winded, so naturally I rested myself on the divan." He then would raise his Slavic brows and pause, the silence salacious, the audience rooting for the young Peter Ivanovich to bed the injured man's wife. In the story as he told it—and he told this story in the U.S. for decades—the woman woke him by crawling onto the divan, wearing only her stockings and the elaborate apparatus that striped her buttocks and held the stockings in place. This did not happen, but it was not exactly a lie.

He had tried to make love to the woman that night, kissing her ear when she turned from him, his hand feeling her thigh as she pulled away to show him the door. However, he had once been awakened by a woman joining him on a divan. She had been clothed not in stockings but a silk polka-dotted scarf from Paris, and she hadn't been the wife of an acquaintance but the daughter of a friend.

He had not meant to confuse the two nights, but once he had told the story, he didn't think he should retract it. Besides, it made for a better tale. After awhile, he lost track of what had really happened, the story gaining its own currency, surpassing that of memory's. The friend's daughter, Elena Oblovna, was the only casualty, his memory of her lost to him, her own feminine thighs, which were not pale but tan, her breath, which smelled of mint, her scarf, which she knotted around his genitals, and her deep pleasure in the illicit. She was disappeared from his memory.

During his absence, the interior of the automobile had chilled and frost framed the windshield, but the engine turned over on the first try. In his memory, it began again to snow, although the sky, in his recollection, was cloudless and black like the leather upholstery to which he put his nose, inhaling a remnant odor of the woman's fragrant sex. While bent over the car seat, he realized he was more drunk than he had thought. But the snow was beautiful that night, lilting down from above like the notes of a symphony. Peter saw the snow as God's benediction, a vision that disturbed him, as he did not believe in God.

He began the serpentine drive that would return him to his bed, moving slowly along the empty streets of Moscow in the hush of snow. For several blocks, he encountered no traffic, as if all of Russia were sleeping except for him. Snow falling in the hollows of light carved by the automobile's headlamps had such grace that he felt a drunken, expansive forgiveness for the woman who had not made love to him, and even for the husband whose tongue had been lacerated.

Ahead, a dark limousine rested at an odd angle, its front end nosing a snowbank. Peter lifted his foot from the gas pedal. He might have to stop and did not want to repeat the slide of the elegant car. A man in uniform emerged from the driver's seat. He took a step into the street, slipped, and fell into the path of Peter's car.

Peter braked. The car shimmied to a stop without sliding into the snow or running over the fallen man. The uniformed man stood, but he couldn't find purchase on the slick street and began performing a kind of dance to remain vertical, a shilly-shally of the feet, a burlesque that ended in another, harder fall.

< 1 8 5 >

A second man climbed from the limousine. In contrast to the first, he strolled over the slick ice as if he were walking on the beach. He helped the fallen man to his feet. In Peter's memory, he watched the men approach for a long while, the automobile's headlamps like spotlights, rounding the darkness about their beams, the men colored with shadow and light. But he had almost run over the first man. They couldn't have walked far. Headlights, he had noted a thousand times since, spread a diffuse light forward, not the lighted cones that decorate the covers of pulp novels.

Peter Ivanovich lowered his window.

"Comrade," the surefooted man said, "what are you doing out in this weather?"

"I took some people home," Peter Ivanovich said, his throat constricting at the question. "Their car wouldn't start."

The man who had fallen spoke into the other man's ear. "That's Kamenev's boy."

What he meant by that, Peter wasn't sure, but he didn't like it and didn't include it in any version of the story. Still, more than sixty years later, whenever he described the men coming to the car, he would hear that coarse whisper. Why this bit of speech haunted him, he did not know. Why he refused to include it in any edition of the tale, he couldn't say. But he understood that it was important. It sank into his chest like a knife, and everything that followed owed something to it.

The surefooted man said, "You have the opportunity to be of service to your country." He said, "We must take your car."

Peter said, "It isn't my car."

The rear door to the limousine opened. A stout man climbed out. Something flashed inside the compartment, light ricocheting off a polished surface, a woman's hand, a bare arm, a sliver of face draped with auburn hair. The man shut the door quickly, but Peter concentrated on the woman, even after she became invisible behind the darkened window. He knew her. Her name was Zhenya, and she was married to the brother of Joseph Stalin's wife. A beautiful woman, as Stalin's wife was not.

The third man spoke harsh words to the other two. Peter began to believe his life was in danger. Mysterious deaths had become

commonplace and so not really mysterious. He reached beneath the
seat and slipped the revolver into his hand, then tucked it beneath
his coat. It made a cold, hard lump against his abdomen. The voices
suddenly hushed. The road went silent, except for a whisper of wind
wrinkling the snow as it fell.

The third man approached, stepping with care to the passenger
door. Peter finally glimpsed his face. It was the face that peopled
a hundred thousand banners, the face that loomed behind every
unasked question, the most loved and feared face in the country,
the face responsible for a thousand deaths—and even then, in 1932,
if it was 1932, the others, men like Lev Kamenev and Grigory Zinoviev, knew that this face would be responsible for another thousand
deaths, and maybe ten thousand deaths.

"Stalin," young Peter Ivanovich said aloud in the solitude of the
car.

Soon enough they would understand the magnitude of their mis-
calculation. Ten thousand would be a figure used to permit room for
error—plus or minus another ten thousand dead. Stalin's fellow
revolutionaries were not naïve men, were hardly pure by this time,
had never in any case been angels, but none imagined that millions
would die by Stalin's order. They lacked sufficient imagination.

In the memory of Peter Ivanovich, Joseph Stalin (whose real
name was Iosif Vissarionovich Djugashvili) appeared in the passenger window bareheaded, his face flushed with drink and sex, a rectangular peasant's face, dark hair unparted and standing on end,
thick brows humped in the middle, cheeks ballooning in smile, the
jowls firm, the long nose cantilevered over the famous thick, frowning mustache. A meticulously groomed man, Joseph Stalin, whom
Lev Kamenev called Koba, a term of endearment for a man he
feared and by this time despised. Stalin said nothing, framed in the
window, smiling, coming to some kind of understanding as he stared
at Peter Ivanovich.

Peter knew the woman he had glimpsed in the limousine—
Zhenya—more intimately. This fact he told no one, not back then
when he had been a handsome boy, and not in all the years since. He
had held her slender legs in his palms. He had taken her toes
between his lips and parted them with his tongue. He had torn her

< 1 8 7 >

dress and left a bite mark on the round rise of her ass, for which she had slapped him.

Stalin opened the door, letting in a rush of cold air. "Peter," he said, and Peter Ivanovich felt a numbing electrical charge in his limbs. "It is Peter, is it not?" Stalin asked.

Peter Ivanovich nodded.

Stalin gave a little wag of his head. "My driver this evening, how should we put it? He is an imbecile." He laughed and asked for a ride to his quarters in the Kremlin.

Peter did not understand how Stalin could know his name. His hands trembled, but he quickly began driving down the treacherous street, snow still falling, the wonder of the night turning into a new wonder. He slipped his hand inside his coat as if to warm it. He felt the revolver and thought, I am alone with Stalin and I have a gun in my hand. This thought moved through his body, warming it, making him sweat, tingling his arms. The consequential moments of a person's life too often go unnoticed—a casual remark changing one's destiny, a trivial misunderstanding destroying all one's plans. I am alone with Stalin, he thought, and I have a gun in my hand.

Stalin talked distractedly about his driver and the men's responsibility to free the limousine. His voice was high and did not fit him. He said nothing about the woman, nothing at all of importance, but he kept words in the air.

Peter listened and did not listen. He understood that he had the power to change history. He could deposit the body in the snow, cover it, and drive west. The snow and cold weather would hide it. He could reach Poland before anyone realized Stalin was missing, or at least before Peter could be connected to the disappearance. He had crossed into Poland both legally and illegally in the past. He was confident he could make the crossing again. These thoughts flew through his head like so many winter birds, flitting about at first and then finding a pattern, an order.

In years to come, Soviet expatriates would argue about whether he could have escaped. "It doesn't matter," he would say. He had been a young man with confidence in his physical will. He failed to assassinate Stalin, but not because he feared capture.

His mentor believed Stalin had to be stopped, but lacked the courage to act on his beliefs. He held that Stalin would eventually force men like himself and Zinoviev into exile. Driving in the car that night, Peter asked himself whether killing Stalin would be the best thing for this family that had befriended him, for the Soviet Union, for Russia, for the revolution, for humanity. The answer to every question was yes. While Stalin talked, Peter drove down the icy streets contemplating murder.

History, he knew, might not vindicate him. Not everyone would be so certain that Stalin was a traitor to the revolution. The vast majority of Russians thought of him as their great papa. He was loved as no other leader in the party was loved. Only a few knew the truth. Yet Peter believed the authorities might not even pursue him. The assassination would be hushed up. The Politburo would not want it to look like a coup. A natural cause of death would be offered. The veneer of stability would remain untarnished.

Stalin began a story about a trip with Peter's mentor to Finland before the revolution. They went to meet Lenin. "The weather is like this." Stalin waved his thick fingers at the night sky. He described a train station crowded with people. "The automobiles of that time could not navigate the roads in this kind of weather," he said. They found a horse-pulled carriage to take them out in the storm, but after a few blocks the horse refused to continue, despite the driver's whip. Young Lev Kamenev said to young Joseph Stalin, "We'll have to go on foot." They climbed down from the carriage, the blizzard raging through the narrow streets. "We began walking to what should have been our deaths," Stalin said. "What young fools we were." He laughed and eyed Peter, and at this moment Peter thought his passenger knew what he had been contemplating.

"Unlike tonight," Stalin went on, "no one rescued us." They had marched on for close to an hour, finally finding a lighted establishment, which turned out to be an inn. The innkeeper revealed that they had been hiking in the wrong direction. "We were farther from our destination than we had been at the depot." Stalin laughed again. His breath had an odor. He had been eating fish that night, and Peter Ivanovich smelled it. "To top it off, there were no rooms. We slept in the manager's office."

Peter slipped his gloved hand from the gearshift to his coat,

< 1 8 9 >

sliding it in between the buttons, his fingertips traveling over the revolver. He would turn one more corner, then pull out the weapon. He would not hesitate but would fire immediately. The first shot would put a hole in Stalin's throat. Stalin would grasp at it and fall forward, which would permit Peter to fire a second bullet. This one would penetrate the skull. In this fashion, he might keep most of the blood off the windows. He would drive another few blocks, dump the body by the river, and layer it in snow. The upholstery he would clean with Stalin's pants.

Then Stalin said to him, "You know Zhenya."

Peter rolled through the intersection where he had meant to turn. "I was going too fast."

"We're not worried," Stalin said. "We trust you." He touched the damp shoulder of Peter's coat. "All that walk through the bitter weather, and we had been turned in the wrong direction. That's the story of youth. You take reckless chances, thinking you know what you're doing."

Peter Ivanovich drove Joseph Stalin to the Kremlin. Stalin climbed from the car, and Peter waited, studying the man's retreating back, the simple locomotion of the tyrant's legs.

He drove himself home and woke Lev Kamenev, who climbed from bed and put on his glasses to listen. The story Stalin had told was true, he said, but Trotsky had been with them. Stalin had sent Trotsky into exile, and so he had been erased from the story. "You must leave," he said. "You saw him with her. He could have you arrested."

"I was a fool," Peter said, not to his mentor, but to the crowds who came to hear his story. "I had my opportunity and I let it slip away." He lifted his hands. "Can you see it? There's blood on these hands." But this was mere vaudeville, a distraction from the real question of right and wrong.

In the automobile, Stalin's eyes on his, Stalin's words cast into the heated air, the fan blowing hard at their feet, the night sky pressing against the windows, the snow riddling the dark, those thick peasant fingers gesturing, the smell of fish on his breath, the mention of the woman's name: these things saved him.

Near the end of the lecture, Peter would add, "The revolution could have changed the world for the better, but one little man"—by which he meant himself—"failed to do his duty." With this parody of humility, he argued for the magnitude of his failing—one worthy of a place in history.

He would punctuate the story with the procession of deaths, beginning with Stalin's wife, who shot herself with a gun given to her by her brother-in-law—a death officially attributed to appendicitis. Kamenev and Zinoviev were executed in prison, Maxim Gorky poisoned, Kamenev's elder son—who had been Peter's friend—executed, Kamenev's wife executed, and the younger Kamenev boy shot dead without a trial at the age of seventeen. These deaths served as a drum roll in the context of the story, something to quicken the listener's pulse and lend weight to the tale.

Peter could no longer really consider the story. It had become a solid thing, like a souvenir, that he knew how to display. The ethical question that enticed others to argument only made him weary. He understood that he had possessed the opportunity to change the world, and instead his life had changed nobody and nothing. He lived with this belief and no longer felt obliged to examine it.

And yet there were times he did wonder about the darkness of the sky and the whiteness of the snow, about the shimmering beauty of a moon he could not have seen. In his memory, the landscape of his failure was one of extreme and glorious contrast, while the reality, he knew, had the drabness of the ordinary. Why did memory insist on simplifying the snow, erasing the scars and muddy slashes, and painting the earth with such undulating clarity? Why did the night sky turn the black of a satin dress and yet hold a full moon, as perfect as a pearl against the satin? Why had his memory changed history as he himself had failed to change it? He had no answers for these questions, but there were times when he thought they were the more important questions to ask. For what is the world, after all, for anyone, but the accumulation of images that change as we record them and change again as we recall them and change again as we speak them, the words disappearing at the same moment we give them life?

6

Small accomplishments please the preacher, but it takes a big act to wake the minions.

—Peter Ivanovich Kamenev

Designed by a protégé of Frank Lloyd Wright, the university swimming and diving facility had a square base and top, but the top was smaller than the base, creating trapezoid walls. These walls bulged in the middle, an effect referred to as Moorish in university literature and "like something outta Loony Toons" by the students. It was known unofficially as "Little Fatty."

Zhenya walked to Little Fatty from her office, arriving as the first diver ascended the tower. She scanned the scant crowd for Morgan, but it was Petey who spotted her. "Hey, Mom," he called to her. "My mom is diving from that ladder."

"That's not your mom," Morgan said, looking all the while at Zhenya. "That's another diver. She's competing *against* your mom."

"I know that," Petey said.

Morgan pulled Petey into his lap, and Zhenya scooted in next to them. She gave Petey a kiss on the cheek, which he immediately wiped off. When she wagged a finger at him, he said, "I was rubbing it in," and laughed, an old joke. Children loved repetition, Zhenya thought. And adults were turned into somnambulists by it. She passed her father a thermos. "Pour it in the cap. Don't drink straight out of the bottle."

< 191 >

Peter Ivanovich unscrewed the lid and sniffed. He produced a delighted smile.

"I don't guess that's coffee," Morgan said.

"Nope. Neither is this." She showed Morgan her sports bottle. "His is vodka. Mine's gin and tonic. I'm taking liberties."

"You keep liquor in your office now?"

She hated that tone, that superior tone of his. "I shopped earlier," she said. "I think ahead. Women do that." The diver reached the platform and waited for the judges' signal. She had a chunky, overly athletic build and a knobby, unattractive face. Zhenya felt bad for the girl and hoped she was at least a good diver. Zhenya smelled hair spray. The old-fashioned nostril-burning kind. It reminded her of her mother. Old-fashioned hair spray was one of her mother's few anachronisms. Otherwise, she was an extremely progressive woman. Zhenya's nose burned, but to the extent that it recalled her mother, it was a pleasurable pain. "What's the holdup?" she said. "Let's get this show on the road."

Morgan kept his eyes on the platform, where the chunky girl now crossed her arms impatiently. He spoke without facing Zhenya. "I called the bank today."

Zhenya sighed and clutched the metal bleacher she sat on. "I haven't spent a penny of it," she said. "I just didn't want you throwing it away before we talked about it."

"You thought I'd do that?"

She almost said, *No, of course not.* It would be utterly unlike Morgan to do such a thing. Why then had she transferred the money? A voice on the loudspeaker announced technical difficulties. The scoreboard would not light. "I didn't want you tempted." Was that true? It might be. An undeniable truth was that she had tried to spend the money herself, and not just her share of it but the whole amount. She chose not to reveal that. "The board refused to put up the bail?" she asked.

Morgan shrugged. "They can't see the principle involved. I didn't do a good job explaining it."

"No one can see any principle in this but you."

"You thought I'd just go write a check for five thousand dollars without talking to you about it? You really thought I'd do that?"

< 193 >

"I don't know what I thought," she said. That was more or less true, wasn't it?

"Can I have a drink of that?" Petey wanted the sports bottle.

"It's not water," she said. "It's a grown-up drink." She pulled open the lid and let him smell it.

"It smells like something in a car," Petey said.

"Can we talk about this later?" she asked Morgan, but Petey thought she was talking to him.

"Okay," he said, "but I'm *very* thirsty."

Zhenya had attempted to purchase the condominium without Morgan knowing. She had written a check that would have emptied their savings, but the bank had refused her loan. "We need your husband's signature," the banker told her. "And then we can process it."

"I don't want him to know about it," Zhenya had said, and the loan officer, a young black woman wearing green contact lenses that matched her suit, smiled as if Zhenya were joking. She held the smile a long time, well after the amusement lighting her eyes vanished. Then she nodded, somber now. "Once the divorce is final—"

"I make enough money on my own for this mortgage," Zhenya pointed out. "And this check requires only my signature."

The loan officer shook her head. As long as she and Morgan were married, he would be a financial partner in any loan. He had to come in and sign the papers. "Even if a divorce is in the works," the young woman explained, "we can't do anything until the terms of the settlement are final."

"We're *not* divorcing. He'll move in later. After our house is ruined." She had already explained her reasons for wishing to abandon the house on Forest Avenue, and the woman understood the issue completely. However, Zhenya could not make her understand her husband. "He doesn't change. He *can't* change. Unless he has no choice. Unless circumstances force it."

"That would be the time to get the loan," she said, "when he understands that the neighborhood is unlivable."

"The condo will be gone by then. It has to be this specific one. It has to be directly opposite those trees."

The woman reached across the desk and touched Zhenya's hand, which she instinctively withdrew. She would not be condescended to by a twenty-something banker. But the woman surprised her. "Why is it that your husband can't change?" She spoke gently and with concern.

Because our son died, Zhenya thought, but she did not say it. She would not use Philip as an excuse. Instead, she said, "I'll tell him." A lie. Here she was lying to a banker, of all people. "I'll bring him in. It may take a little time . . ."

The woman nodded without her customary smile. She was probably a decent person. She probably had a good heart. She said, "I hope it works out."

The diver was finally given the okay to make her approach. The girl took a deep breath and shook her hands frantically, as if they had fallen asleep while she waited. The platform was longer than the one Morgan had constructed on their deck. The girl started at the rear of it and ran to the end. She leapt off the board beautifully, but her somersaults had a halting quality to them, as if there were three distinct steps to each flip. Her body was vertical as she entered the water, but with a rigidity that lacked grace.

Morgan breathed an audible sigh of relief.

Zhenya said, "She's no competition."

"Fat girls should not be in diving field," her father said, the thermos an inch from his mouth.

"Pour it into the cup," Zhenya said.

"That wasn't my mom," Petey put in.

Morgan held a pocket notebook. His arm was wrapped around Petey, and the hand with the notebook rested on the boy's knee. Along one margin, he had written the judging categories. Zhenya could read only the top one, *APPROACH*. Beside it Morgan wrote 7.2.

"She had no fluency," Zhenya said, "like a sentence that's grammatically correct but boring."

Morgan entered his scores in each category, then he began the math.

"You could see her working," Zhenya said. "That's what amazes me about Emma. It looks like she was born diving. That poor girl looked like a robot—technically okay, but stiff as a corpse."

< 195 >

Morgan turned the notebook to her. He gave the first diver a composite score of 7.3.

Zhenya shook her head. "Lower."

"I rented a video on the Olympics," he said. "This is about right for that kind of dive."

"That's against the best competition in the world," Zhenya said.

"If you don't trust my judgment, then we have a problem."

"Danny Ford is a criminal," she said. "I've researched this. And I don't care that you share a garbage truck with him. And I don't care that you insisted on calling the police. That doesn't make you responsible. He's violent and awful, and we don't owe him one penny of our savings."

Numbers flashed on the official scoreboard, but they were truncated and incoherent—the top half of a seven matched with the bottom half of a five.

"Is Arabic numerals?" Peter Ivanovich asked. But he didn't expect an answer and busied himself with the pouring of a drink. "Is going to spill," he said, annoyed by the bother.

"Did it ever occur to you that I might know him better than you?" Morgan said. "That I could know things about him you can't find in police records?"

"You're soft," she said. "I'm not accusing you of anything. It's just who you are." She drank from the sports bottle. The liquor and tonic water sizzled on her tongue. In her purse, she had a key to the condominium. The real estate agent—Zhenya thought of her as Annelle's mother—had let her borrow it. "I need to measure for blinds," Zhenya had said, "and I want to show the place to my daughter." The loan had already been refused, the check returned, but Zhenya saw no reason to reveal this to Annelle's mother. She had wanted to walk through it one more time.

That was all she had wanted at first, but three days had passed and she still had not returned the key. She was teaching summer school for the first time in her career, and daily she drove to the condominium after her class. She sat on the landing of the stairs in a triangle of sunlight and filled in her grade book with the names of her students, read their chapter responses, memorized their names. She had thought she would need the money from summer school to make the payments on the condo.

Numbers flashed again on the screen, and again they were jumbled, half of one thing and half of another. Annelle's mother had left messages on Zhenya's answering machine in her office. The first message had been sympathetic. "Peggy at the bank explained it all to me. I'm *so* sorry." The first reminder about the key had been likewise friendly. Even the third message was patient. "I suppose you must be awfully busy," it began, but the tone of her voice was less friendly.

Zhenya understood that she could buy the condo only if she divorced Morgan. But if she divorced Morgan, it didn't make sense to purchase a place so large. And if she couldn't have that condo, that specific one, what was the point of divorcing her husband? At times she still fantasized about living on her own, but more often she imagined Morgan finally caving in, agreeing that they had to move, that Forest Avenue was no longer bearable. Her fantasies now were about starting over again.

"They are all wearing same suits?" Peter Ivanovich asked. The second diver had begun climbing the stairs.

"Same team," Morgan began, but he quit speaking in midsentence. The scores for the first diver were finally posted correctly on the board. The judges had awarded the girl an average score of 8.3.

"Emma is going to win this," Zhenya said, shocked by the thought of it. "I don't believe it."

"If she gets off a good dive . . ." Morgan said. "If she doesn't stumble or . . ."

"She's going to win," Zhenya said, studying the next diver now, taking Morgan's hand when he offered it, gripping it firmly, pulling it to her side. "She's going to win," she said. "She's going to win."

Petey fell asleep long before the meet ended, missing all of his mother's optional dives. His warmth against Morgan's chest as he carried the boy through the parking lot felt like an emotional state. Zhenya walked beside them, trying to hold an umbrella high enough to cover them all. Peter Ivanovich waited at the entrance to be

< 197 >

picked up. The pickup would be literal, as he had slumped to the floor and curled up beside a drinking fountain. Two young men who had been there to watch Emma dive had carried the old man out and now stood guard over him in the exit ramp. One was Frank, the former delivery boy. The other was evidently the mysterious Sid. When Zhenya and Morgan left them, Peter Ivanovich was relaying a story involving a dwarf and a black bear, his cheek flat against the concrete ramp.

The rain seemed both light and heavy. Not many drops were falling, but the ones that landed were fat and loud. Raindrops *slapping* the earth, Zhenya thought. She was drunk. She knew she shouldn't drive, but she didn't want to leave her Honda at school. The bottle of gin and tonic had been a good idea, but she had been stingy with the tonic and had eaten almost nothing all day. Now she was unsteady. When they reached the Toyota, she opened the door, raising the umbrella high, while Morgan performed the difficult maneuver of hefting the sleeping boy into his safety seat. "You've certainly gotten your money's worth out of this stinking car," she said.

"Here you go, buddy," Morgan said to the sleeping child.

Emma had not faltered. She hit each dive perfectly, as perfectly as she had dived in their own backyard. Her body had a fluidity that the other divers' lacked, her approach almost feline, her takeoff powerful but understated, and the dive itself—it was almost impossible to separate her moves into their components, so seamlessly did she perform them. With each entry, her body, at the last possible second, straightened, and she entered the water perfectly, with hardly a splash. Her first dive had thrilled them all—Zhenya, Morgan, Peter, and Roy Oberland, who had joined them in his uniform. "Emma invited me," he said apologetically. "I came here directly from work." Since his wife had left him, he seemed at loose ends, and Zhenya was happy to see him. She touched his arm and said, "You're always welcome." He nodded. After Emma's first dive, he leapt to his feet and applauded.

"They're not in the same league with her," Morgan said. "Nobody's even close."

It seemed an eternity before her score was posted. Discarding the high and low marks, Emma Kamenev's first dive received three identical scores from the remaining judges: 7.2.

"Is rigged!" Peter Ivanovich yelled. "Get commissioner!"

Morgan could say nothing, but Zhenya said, "I don't believe it."

They had to wait then for Emma's next turn to see if justice would be done. But it was no better. "The optional dives," Morgan said, meaning that their daughter would find her due there. She scored no higher than 7.5 on any card and never averaged higher than 7.2. Her optional dives were not rated as difficult as those performed by the other divers. She finished far out of the running.

Morgan managed to get Petey strapped in without waking him. The boy's head tilted to the side at an inhuman angle, and Morgan couldn't get it to remain upright. He slid out of the car, almost knocking the umbrella from Zhenya's hand. "I'll give you a ride to yours," he said. "Where you parked?"

"Take me back to the building," Zhenya said. "I'll help you load my father."

They climbed into the front seat. Morgan handed her three framed photographs before turning the key. "What do you think of these?"

Black-and-white photos of people eating. An old man shoveling broccoli into his mouth. A woman with thick glasses, gelatin on her spoon and reflected in her eyeglasses. A man who needed to shave, younger than the others, a bit of corn caught in midair. "As art? They're okay. Almost interesting. Not to my taste," she said. "Who's the photographer?"

Morgan pointed as he approached the entrance. "Sid," he said. "He gave them to Emma."

Zhenya stared at them again. On the one hand, they could have been mistaken for the work of a professional photographer. On the other hand, they seemed derivative and cliché. It embarrassed her to see these before meeting him, and she understood then that embarrassment was what she had felt when Emma's scores were posted. Not over her daughter's low tallies, but over her own loss of perspective.

The two boys, Sid and Frank, lifted Peter Ivanovich by his appendages and began toting him through the rain. The configura-

< 199 >

tion had about it the appearance of emergency. Her father continued to talk while they carried him.

Zhenya slipped as she climbed from the car and almost fell. She was more drunk than she cared to think about. She held the door for the boys, keeping herself dry with the umbrella. "Bear is saying to dwarf, 'Don't you want to know how life is for big animal like bear?' " her father said as they loaded him into the backseat. Sid reached in and buckled the seat belt, pausing to let the old man give his punch line.

"Thank you for the anecdote, Mr. Kamenev," he said before lifting his head out of the car and into the rain.

"See you at the house," Zhenya called to Morgan and shut the door.

Sid and Frank huddled beside her under the umbrella. "I'm Zhenya," she said to Sid as she walked them back to Little Fatty. "Emma's mother."

"Pleased to meet you," he said and introduced himself. "We're joining Emma at the ramp. We have an outing planned."

"An outing," Zhenya said.

"Yes ma'am," Sid said. "You're welcome to join us if you like."

She had heard about Sid's *outings*. Most recently they had done a walking tour of the homes of Sid's friends. At each place, the people had prepared appetizers for them. "He has a weird mix of acquaintances," Emma had said. "Some students, some professors, some people older than you and Dad."

Zhenya declined the opportunity for an outing with Sid. He was dressed in green slacks and a shirt with a button-down collar. Dark wavy hair, nice features. Very straight-looking, clean-cut, not really Emma's taste. But then the only discerning thing about Emma's preferences in boys seemed to be her interest in losers. Frank's hair was not running, despite the rain, she noted. But he needed a trim. "I'll just drop you two off here," she said, and Frank ran to cover, but Sid remained beneath her umbrella.

"May I volunteer to drive you home?" he said. "Emma will take awhile to change. Frank could follow us in my car and drive me back."

Zhenya knew she shouldn't drive, but she thought she had done a better job of hiding it. "I suppose that's a good idea," she said, embarrassed yet again. "I'm in the faculty lot near the library."

Sid ran over to convey the plan to Frank. She was doing the responsible thing, Zhenya told herself. That she had to be escorted by clownish college boys did not make her a clown as well. True, she had stumbled clownishly back at the car, and her appraisal of her daughter's diving was clownishly off. Then she recalled the key to the condo in her purse. Oh, God, she thought, bring on the face paint and big shoes.

"May I carry the umbrella for you?" Sid asked.

She handed it over. What was her daughter doing with a boy who said "May I"? They headed out across the wet commons toward the library. Sid did good work with the umbrella. He kept her dry.

He drove ten miles an hour under the speed limit. Zhenya didn't like other people to drive her car. Morgan had driven it only twice in the year she had owned it. Emma drove it, but only when Zhenya was in the car with her. Sid earned a passing grade. She preferred the slow and cautious type to the hot-rodder or casual speeder.

"What did you think of the diving?" she asked.

Sid nodded as if she had made a statement. "I think I got some terrific photographs," he said. "I'd never seen Emma dive before. I found that pleasurable."

Zhenya reached over and turned up the speed of the windshield wipers. "If I hadn't brought gin, I would have lost my mind." She did not want to explain her disappointment and chagrin at Emma's scores, or the incredible restlessness she felt watching one girl after another perform exactly the same dive. The optional dives had been a little better—more varied, at least—but by that time she understood how completely she had misjudged her daughter's talent, and all she wanted to do was drink. Yet when Emma executed her optional dives, Zhenya repeatedly overestimated them. *Live and don't learn* should be the universal human motto, she thought. "What do you study?" she asked Sid.

"Journalism and philosophy," he said. "I've gone through a num-

< 2 0 1 >

ber of majors. I haven't decided how to spend my life just yet. How do you like political science?"

"I like it well enough. I don't know what else I would have studied. My work involves a lot of history. Sociology."

"Emma is an extraordinary person." He checked the rearview to be certain Frank was still following.

"Is she?" Zhenya turned and spotted Sid's car, an ancient Chevy Nova, red with a white top. Shiny red, she noted, even in the rain. It belonged in a sitcom. "Frank's still with us," she said.

"Yes, he is," Sid said.

"What makes her extraordinary?"

Sid nodded again. "May I have some time for that one?"

A peculiar boy. Another oddball in love with Emma. So neat in his appearance it was spooky. A *wholesome* boy, which in itself made him odd. And he talked as if he had been raised by butlers. "Take all the time you want," she said. "Morgan showed me some photographs you gave Emma."

"They're part of a series," Sid said.

"People eating."

"Yes, they are."

"What are you trying to do with this series?"

"Capture something about expenditure and renewal."

She tried to squelch a laugh but failed. "That's a big subject."

"Thank you," he said. "I think so, too."

"Well," she said.

"Eating is a complex act."

Again she felt the urge to laugh. "That's quite a car you have back there."

"I discovered it in an estate sale. It had eighteen thousand miles on it and a functioning radio. The dash is metal."

"You should get some foam dice to hang from the mirror," she said.

"I'll consider that," he said, "although I'm not fond of dice."

He was damaged, Zhenya suddenly understood. He had some kind of trouble in his past—psychological trouble—and he was working hard to contend with the world. She knew how such a boy could be attractive to her daughter. His vulnerability and his sweetness and his odd attempts at being like everyone else. She would want to protect him. Save him. And she knew in that instant that this boy might well take her daughter's heart.

He pulled into the driveway beside Morgan's Toyota and shifted the Honda into park. "Emma is herself all the time," he said. "When she's frightened, as she often seems to be, she doesn't let on that she's frightened, but that, too, is who she is. She has a dozen different coping mechanisms in order to remain herself and in the world. I admire that."

Zhenya accepted the keys from him. His comments upset her. "What makes you think my daughter's frightened?"

He nodded at the question. "May I have some time on that one?"

The red and white car pulled into the driveway behind them. She reminded herself that this was the boy who had sent flowers without paying for them. "My daughter's not frightened," she said. "She's just complicated. She's a complicated person. We all are."

"Yes, we are," he said.

His eyes had a slight glaze, but they were not the eyes of a lunatic. "Thanks for driving me home," Zhenya said. "You want something to drink before you go? A snack?"

"No, thank you," he said. "We need to get back to Emma." After he had climbed out of the car, he stuck his head back in to say, "I've enjoyed the opportunity to have a conversation with you."

He waved to her as he trotted through the rain to his car. He had a charming smile. The red and white Chevy backed into the street. It occurred to Zhenya that she might not know who her daughter was. She couldn't see her clearly in the world any more than she could on a diving platform. Thinking this made her lonely. She sat in the Honda thinking, watching the rain, listening to it strike the roof, hood, and trunk.

The next idea struck her as forcefully as the fat drops of rain struck her car.

Danny Ford was the father of Emma's child.

Why else would Morgan care so much? Why had the city been willing to hire the thug in the first place? Morgan had pulled strings. Perhaps he had been working all along to rehabilitate the

< 2 0 3 >

boy. *Did it ever occur to you that I might know him better than you?* Morgan had been trying to tell her. To tell her without being explicit. To protect her but let her know. *I know things about him you can't find in police records.*

Where did Danny Ford go to high school? Emma had switched districts to be on a diving team, providing her with friends and acquaintances from all over town. Danny Ford could have been an acquaintance or . . . No, if he had raped her, Morgan would not help him now.

She climbed from the car and ran through the pelting rain. It had been obvious all along. She had behaved like a fool.

When Danny Ford's lawyer revealed that it was Morgan putting up the money, the judge agreed to reduce the bond to thirty thousand dollars. "She had great things to say about you," reported the lawyer. " 'If Mr. Morgan says he won't jump bail, that means something.' "

Morgan shrugged and nodded. He was supposed to be pleased by this, but it did not please him. Instead, when he gave her the check for ten percent of the bond, he was thinking, All of this trouble over three thousand dollars. His wife, he knew, would point out that he drove an artifact from the 1970s; if money didn't mean anything to him, why didn't he buy a new car? That isn't about money, he thought, playing out both sides of the argument in his head. He liked his car. And it still ran fine. What's the point of getting a car built to last forever if you don't hold on to it? How would Zhenya respond to that?

"I'll bring Mr. Ford to you personally," the lawyer said, a sturdy woman with wide, square shoulders.

"I'll be here," Morgan told her. Danny Ford's mother had disowned him and he needed to stay away from his friends, which meant he had nowhere to go but the house on Forest Avenue. Zhenya, when she told Morgan to go ahead and bail him out, had anticipated this. "I suppose he'll wind up staying with us. Can we put a time limit on his visit? I'll make a place for him in the cellar, but I want a time limit on his stay."

Morgan did not know what had caused her turnaround. He

never knew anymore what she would do from one minute to the next. When he asked about it, she simply said, "Just don't make me regret the decision. I'm no longer concerned about the money so much as I am his *influence*. I don't want Danny Ford to have any influence in this house."

The lawyer dropped Danny off later that same day, a Friday when Morgan was not working. She had driven down Forest Avenue despite the flashing warning signs, despite the surface of graded dirt. Her car was as old as Morgan's Toyota and had no ornament or insignia to betray its maker. She threw her leg over the plastic rope that cordoned off the construction. Her wrinkled plaid polyester suit distressed Morgan. Lawyers had to make an impression, didn't they? "He's agreed to a curfew of ten o'clock," she said, eyeing Danny until he nodded. They stood in what had once been the far end of Morgan's front yard, now a scrape of dirt. "If he says one word to any of the boys who were in that car, I will no longer represent him. That includes his brother." Again she eyed Danny, and again he nodded. She was tough. Morgan liked that about her. "See if you can talk some sense into him," she said. "Thinks he's the Sundance Kid and no way is he going to turn in Butch. That kind of nonsense. Honor among jailbirds and all that. The prosecution is confident that one of the boys is going to crack. If Danny talks first, he can cut a deal."

"What do *you* think?" Morgan asked her. "Do you think one of them will confess?"

"I think *all* of them will," she said. "And they'll make it sound like our Mr. Ford did everything and dragged them along." To Danny, she added, "Wise up."

Danny had lost weight in jail but gained another tattoo, this one no more professional than the other. BAD DOG, read the crude blue letters on his forearm. He seemed embarrassed that Morgan was hearing this, and maybe embarrassed that Morgan had done so much to help him.

"I'll do what I can," Morgan promised. He shook her hand, and the lawyer drove off, down the closed street, a plume of dirt trailing her.

"You got a beer anywhere?" Danny said. "No beer in the joint."

< 2 0 5 >

"Follow me." Morgan led him across the abbreviated yard and through the house. They had to step over Prince, who lay in the kitchen doorway. Earlier in the week, Morgan had taken her in to the vet. "If the cancer was in one leg, I could saw it off," he told Morgan. "A three-legged dog can still be a contented, functional animal. I don't recommend saving a dog by amputating two legs."

"You'd save her if she were a person," Morgan said.

"People have rich interior lives," he said. "People doctors have it simple. They always work to save the patient. Sometimes, in my field, we have to make difficult recommendations." He warned Morgan that her death could come quickly. "She's a good pooch," he said. "She won't let you know that she's suffering. You're going to have to pay attention. Don't let her suffer unduly." His expression suggested that she might already be suffering unduly. Morgan had almost asked as much, whether he should just get it over with while he was there. But the vet had a big mustache and an expensive haircut. He was young and so sure of himself that Morgan distrusted him. The dog still took pleasure in things. Even on the ride to the clinic, she had put her head in Morgan's lap while he drove. "I'm sorry, pal," Morgan said to her as they left the vet's office. Her gait was halting, but she looked up at him, happy to be addressed. Happy, too, he guessed, to be leaving. She had always hated the vet's.

The veterinarian's stare haunted Morgan. He imagined him watching while he made a bed for Prince near the door at home, watching while he read the labels on canned dog food in the grocery store. She had pain, but she enjoyed being with her family, Petey especially. Morgan tried to think about it honestly. He didn't want to keep her alive simply because of his own desire not to kill her—what the veterinarian would no doubt call cowardice. It didn't escape Morgan's consideration that she had been Philip's dog. Philip had insisted on naming her Prince even though she was a girl. She had slept in Philip's bed, cut her teeth on his shoes. She was a living link to his son, but Morgan told himself that he would do it once she got to a point where the pain outweighed everything else. He would have her put down.

He took Danny down to the basement. "It isn't much," he conceded. The ceiling was only seven feet high and crisscrossed with pipes and insulated ducts. Paint peeled off the walls, which were concrete block. An old oval rug with a burn at one end covered part of the floor, but the remainder was bare concrete, and the concrete was cracked. A gas furnace took up the far end of the room, while an old stuffed chair, its matching ottoman, and the single bed that had been in Peter Ivanovich's room completed the furnishings. Morgan had hauled the bed down the basement stairs after a new bed had been delivered and set up in the old man's room. The basement smelled of mold and the clothes dryer—contradictory odors. "I don't suppose this is actually even as good as jail," Morgan said.

"No worries," Danny said. "It's fine."

Morgan wasn't certain Danny would fit on the bed. His lawyer had been unwilling to say how long it might be before the trial. Possibly as much as six months. "We're both stalling," she explained. "The prosecutors want to arrest the kids who actually did the shooting. They're trying to force Mr. Ford into cooperating. I, of course, am hoping Mr. Ford will do the same." No one believed Danny was responsible for anything but attempting to hide the gun. But the man who was shot had died, which meant Danny could be sent to prison for decades.

"I won't burn you," he said, touching the striped sheets on the new bed. He took a sip of beer. "Means something to me. You know. Doing this. I won't burn you."

"You can borrow my car to get your stuff from home." Morgan tossed the keys, and Danny snatched them out of the air. Had he been an athlete in school? Had he been in too much trouble to play sports? "Maybe your mother will have a change of heart once she lays eyes on you."

"Doubtful." He shook his head, that little twitch. "I can do the yard. Mowing and like that. Or I can cover for you guys if something comes up. Dishes." He spoke quickly, as if nervous, or maybe he was just excited to be back in the world. "Could wake up that car of yours." He gave the keys a shake. "If you want me to. Tune-up or wash. Even with the kid, you know. Walk him around the park. Pay my way."

< 2 0 7 >

"What you do is up to you," Morgan said. "You don't owe me anything."

"There's got to be stuff." His brows furrowed, the pale flesh wrinkling like the curlicues of tripe in a butcher's window. "Like raking leaves. If you got leaves. And they fall. Early for that, I know. My mom would shit if she saw me doing, you know, *chores*. At least it's cool down here. I'll be gone by the time for raking leaves, I guess. Who knows?" He jerked his head, annoyed with himself. "Look, you got me out of a bad situation. I didn't like it in there. Okay at first, actually, but there's guys in there who don't even—no matter who you are—they don't give a shit. Not clean, either. Crud in the cracks and slimelike stuff."

Morgan said nothing, let him ramble.

"That's not even counting the food and no girls," Danny went on. "Or beer." He raised his beer bottle. "It's funny what you miss. Like work. I miss it."

"I'll clean out a dresser for you while you get your stuff," Morgan said. "You can help me haul it down when you get back. Anything else you need?"

"I was going to," Danny said. "The only chance I see of getting out of it. But I won't run now. I promise you that."

"Your lawyer says you can still make a deal."

He sniffed and jerked his head again. "No can do. They're my friends, they'd kill me." He took a long swallow, emptying the bottle. "You ought to get better beer, man."

"It was on sale."

"*You* wouldn't rat. Don't make like you would."

"If I was looking at prison? When I did nothing and they shot somebody?"

"You wouldn't. I'm the proof of it. Me sitting here in your house instead of on that smelly bed. I hated that the most, the smell of that fucking mattress."

"You can help me with the dog," Morgan said, glancing again at the new tattoo on the boy's forearm. "Maybe a chore here and there. Get settled in. Take a swim if you want. Get your stuff from home."

"Tomorrow my mom works. First day back on the job after

breast surgery. My lawyer told me. So tomorrow I could go and not
have to see her."

This big man was afraid of his mother, Morgan thought. "Okay,"
he said. "Do it your way." He felt no elation at having his partner
out of jail. Relief and maybe something more, something he couldn't
name. Zhenya had done such an abrupt about-face, he didn't know
how to think about that, either.

"Here." Danny threw the keys back to him, but Morgan was not
as quick, and they struck the wall behind him and bounced to the
floor.

He bent to retrieve them. "I can lend you a T-shirt or whatever
you need. Until you get your stuff."

"I could drink another beer," Danny said. "You got it in cans?
I'm more used to cans."

"The dog has cancer. That's why I may need some help with her."

"Right," Danny said. "Dog duty." He sat on the bed, then
stretched out. It was just large enough.

"Okay, then," Morgan said, but he thought there should be
something more, something that would pass between them. "The
cancer is in the dog's legs," he said to Danny. "So you won't need to
walk her. She's not much of a walker anymore. She can't always control her . . . functions. We have to bathe her fairly often."

"She about dead?" Danny asked.

Morgan nodded, slipped the keys into his pocket.

"What do you think happens to dogs when they die?" Danny
said. "Not like there's a dog hell or nothing. That would be a waste.
Just a bunch of cats and rolled-up newspapers or something."

"They just die," Morgan said, heading for the wooden stairs.
"They're just gone."

They tried to work in the kitchen, but neither Zhenya nor her father
cared to be in the same room as Danny Ford, and he could not seem
to stay out of the kitchen. "Isn't it a little early for beer?" Zhenya
asked. It was ten a.m.

Danny lifted the can and looked at it, as if to be certain that it was
indeed beer he was drinking. "Nah," he said. "I'm used to it. Don't

< 2 0 9 >

worry about me." He moved his lips slightly, which was evidently meant to be a smile, then dropped one shoulder a millimeter, which might or might not have been a shrug, and then he drank, leaning against the kitchen wall. If he were Petey's father, wouldn't Petey be gargantuan by now? She knew genetics could play out in odd ways. They were both pale, and there was something about Danny's eyes that she could see in Petey. She hated not knowing.

She was trying to help her father "translate" the final portion of his new essay. The translation was from ungrammatical and poorly written English to the standard fare. She was surprised by the dismal quality of his prose. "Is first time writing even first draft in English," he had explained. Usually, he wrote a draft in Russian, found someone to translate it, and then worked with yet another person to find the style he wanted. The ideas were sound, but the writing was careless, marred by imprecise word choice, poor subject-verb agreement, sentence fragments. At times he didn't even bother to conjugate the verbs. Zhenya imagined that he'd had people—the women who had loved him, no doubt—cleaning up his prose for decades. It seemed his principle that he would learn as little about English as he possibly could.

She had planned to use this time to point out the inaccuracies in his claims, and to reveal her plan to expose them. But the new essay was more speculative and philosophical than his previous work, which meant he made no new outrageous claims. And she couldn't find a way to talk about her obligation to document his lies that didn't sound harsh—and she certainly couldn't do it with Danny Ford hovering over them. He just stood there—*slouched* there—against the wall, idly drinking, watching like a purse snatcher scouting a crowd. Earlier in the week Zhenya had received a phone call from a student at Columbia who was preparing a profile of Peter Ivanovich Kamenev for a history assignment. "I understand you know his stuff really well," she had said.

"Pretty well," Zhenya said and asked her name.

"Gloria, like in that old song? G-L-O-R-I-A!"

"I can spell, thank you."

"I don't know if you feel comfortable talking about him," Gloria said. "None of his other ex-wives have been very cooperative."

Zhenya had laughed at that, but she did not correct the girl. Instead she joked about her father's exaggerations and then spoke about the merits of his insights. It was the closest she had ever come to revealing the dirt on him, and she padded it with talk about his intelligence. "He lectured at my own university not long ago," Zhenya told the girl, "and even I was impressed." The girl was more interested in the dirt, and she was persistent. Zhenya tried to put her off, but when she insisted, Zhenya said, "You have to promise me that this is not for an article. I'm writing my own article." It had sounded definitive once she said it aloud.

"You mean for publication or something? No chance. Scout's honor."

Once Zhenya got started, she found she had a lot to say. It felt good to describe her father's peculiar brand of duplicity, and she went on for a while, repeating certain parts like an accident victim describing a crash. She felt lighter in spirit after she put down the phone, almost high from the experience. That evening, though, she came home to find Danny Ford camping in her basement, and her spirits plummeted. Her father disliked him even more than she. "Is like type of man I see all my life. They surround more worse type of man and do what he says. They are jackbooted gendarmes. Is how you say it?"

Zhenya supposed it might be how someone would say it.

Part of her annoyance was simply at having another body in the house. That he was a thug didn't help. But he played with Petey pretty well, and he didn't mind watching Pokémon. Could that be genetic? His lurking by the table annoyed her, but she did not feel physically threatened by him. She just wished he would go back to the basement. "Do you need something?" she asked him. "Besides the beer, I mean?"

Danny Ford shrugged again. "You don't have to wait on me or nothing. I can pull my own pud, you know."

"What? You can do what?"

"Anything, really," he said. "I just mean you don't have to do nothing for me. I can handle myself."

Communication was impossible. Wasn't that the real message of the ages? She turned back to her father's work. Sprinkled through-

< 2 1 1 >

out the essay, in stark contrast to the remainder of it, new aphorisms appeared, written in perfect English, a dozen or more crossed-out versions preceding the final one. He wormed them in, confident that they would be picked up and passed along. Bartlett's already had a long section devoted to Peter Ivanovich Kamenev—not as long as the ones for William Shakespeare or Oscar Wilde, but very respectable in length. Most of them were genuinely new, but at times he would take an obscure quotation, alter it a bit, and then claim it as his own. As far as she could tell, all the new ones were original, but they didn't really belong in the essay. *The idea of finding satisfaction with one's life is a myth as pernicious as the notion of racial superiority.* A good line, she supposed, but what did it have to do with social class in Tsarist Russia? *Beauty touches on that which we can neither name nor recall. That is what beauty means.* Did that actually convey something? Maybe it did. She couldn't tell. *The human spectacle has a history millions of years long, but on average, only five and one half feet high.* Could that line have any justification for its existence? Yet she didn't confront him about his practices, and she couldn't seem to tell him about her research into his lies. He was her father, and she still desired his approval. In fact, she had shown him the new essay she was working on.

The paper had started out as a collaboration with a colleague in her department, a man in his thirties named Stan Maulner, a nice enough guy who needed the publication for his tenure file. She had gone over to his apartment one afternoon to discuss how they should pursue the topic, but Stan offered wine and Zhenya noticed that he had rented a pile of videos, including *Key Largo.* They meant to discuss the research while the movie provided background entertainment, but they got caught up in the hurricane and the sexual tension between Bogart and Bacall. They wound up talking not at all about the paper, although they did touch on the controversy surrounding the photograph of nudes in Zhenya's office. "I guess I should have defended you," Stan said, "but too many people know about me and my ex." He and his ex-wife still dated. They rented pornographic films and masturbated together. "My support for you might backfire, might seem to prove that the picture is porn." After awhile he added, "It's oddly exciting. Watching the movies together and entertaining ourselves. It's the safest kind of safe sex." It had sounded like an invitation. He had drunk a lot of wine and his shoes were off. Zhenya was not tempted, but the fact of the offer pleased her.

That had been a good day. It spurred her to work that night. In the morning, reviewing her work, she had decided to cut Stan out of it. She had a lot of projects, and she supposed it was selfish to drop him from this one, but he had not made himself indispensable. That had been the advice of her thesis adviser way back when. *Make yourself indispensable.* She had accomplished that by doing the legwork for him on two papers they wrote together. She had fucked him, too, of course. Stan's offer was not all that odd, she supposed. The next day at school, she went to his office to tell him she wanted to write the article on her own. He stood as soon as she entered and rushed to the door, bruising his thigh on the corner of his desk, to push the door shut. "I'm really sorry," he said. "For yesterday. I didn't mean anything by that comment about watching videos with my ex. I wasn't coming on—or maybe I was, but I was loaded."

He was so humiliated that he could not meet her eyes for more than an instant. "I haven't thought twice about it," Zhenya said.

"I have," Stan said. "I couldn't sleep thinking about it. I was drunk."

"So you're saying you wouldn't find me attractive unless you were drinking?"

He did meet her eye then, humiliation replaced by panic, but he could see she was joking. He smiled. "Either way I answer that one, I'm screwed."

"Interesting word choice," she said, and then she told him about all the work she had accomplished after leaving his place. She couldn't cut him out of it now, she understood. It would be cruel. She would give him specific tasks. He would be less than indispensable, but she would not dispense with him. She had relaxed with him while watching *Key Largo.* She did not often let herself do that. Little wonder it had been misunderstood.

The article was aimed at changing the way people thought about the economy. Her long night of writing had led her to an environmental metaphor that made the paper suddenly more cohesive.

< 2 1 3 >

Everyone understood that environmental disasters did not limit themselves to international borders. Acid rain produced by one country could pour down on a dozen others. The hydrology of the world was one system. Zhenya argued that the world economy functioned much the same way. Abuses in one country could rain down on others. She ended the article with three steps the major countries should take:

1. Recognize that inhumane conditions and miserable pay amount to economic slavery.
2. Boycott products made by slaves.
3. Enforce a worldwide minimum wage.

When she showed the first draft of the article to her father, he took the night to read it—which surprised her. He was more the skim-and-make-pronouncements sort of fellow. The following evening he told her that he admired it but did not like it. "I know what means these words, but I don't like how they taste on tongue." He wanted her to cut the academic jargon and pepper it with a few catchy sayings. "This title," he said, shaking his head, pursing his mouth as about to belch. "Is mile long. Nobody but people in same profession understand this 'diminishment of exploitation rates.' Is crap."

"Snappy proverbs are not my thing. It's not the way formal academia works."

"University writing is dry like eating ashes," he said, making a face and smacking his lips. "I never write nozzing like this, and all the academics want for me to visit classrooms, give lectures, write books."

"I have my own style," she said. "My own standards."

"Is your style? Is not your style. Is style of intellectual undertaker. Is person who finds good body of thought but first makes sure language kills all interest in body. Then he sees what he can revive." He waved his hand, dismissive. "You cannot revive corpse, so don't kill it."

"I should do what you do—borrow other people's words and—"

"I don't borrow," her father insisted. "I steal. Is different. Borrower always owes somebody. Thief makes words his own. I give you one sentence, yes? For your essay. I work on sentence for you."

"I don't need that kind of help," Zhenya had said, but now, sitting beside him, explaining her editing marks on his work, hunching under the dark cloud that was Danny Ford, she wondered if he had come up with a sentence for her and what that sentence might be. A sentence was also a prison term, she reminded herself, and that thought reminded her that she still had the key to the condominium. Twice she had gone there late at night and lain on the plush carpet. Annelle's mother had given up calling her to ask for it back. Perhaps she had forgotten. Zhenya had slept briefly on that carpet and wakened wanting to make love. That desire did not endure the drive home. She had climbed into her separate bed without waking Morgan.

"What is all this writing for, anyway?" Danny Ford asked.

"It's what we do," Zhenya said, sighing heavily and with intent. "I'm a political scientist. It means that I study governments and other institutions that control our lives."

"Like sex?" he said.

"I beg your pardon?"

"Controls most of the stiffs I know."

"Could you just let us work in peace?"

"Sure," he said. "No worries." He took another sip of beer and continued leaning against the wall.

"Is like talking to microwave oven," Peter said under his breath. Then he waved his arms about. "Get me drink. Is enough work. I am fixing all the words just like you write. Tonight I do it. Now is time for drink."

"I can get it," Danny Ford said. "My first stepdad was a bartender. He sort of died mixing a drink."

"How did he *sort of* die mixing a drink?" Zhenya asked, while Peter said, "Vodka tonic vis ice."

"This guy shot him in the stomach." Danny knew where the liquor was—Zhenya imagined that it was the first thing about the house he had investigated—and fingered the bottles until he found the vodka. "Don't ever get shot in the stomach," he said. " 'Cause you're gonna die."

< 2 1 5 >

"A robbery?" Zhenya asked.

Danny froze with the vodka bottle in his hand. "What do you mean?"

"Your stepfather was killed during a robbery?"

"Oh. Thought you were accusing me of stealing." He exhaled in a fashion that resembled laughter. He fetched a glass and poured the drink while he talked. "It was this husband who had gotten syphilis from my stepdad through his own wife. Pissed him off. He explained it all in court and got off with ten years. Served five. He's dead now, though."

Zhenya felt a cold chill along her spine. "What happened to him?"

Danny shrugged. "Just turned up dead." He handed Peter the vodka tonic. "Forgot the lime. You have limes?"

"Not necessary," Peter said and guzzled.

Zhenya declined his offer to make her a drink. Was he telling them that he had killed the man who murdered his stepfather? That was what it sounded like. He reclaimed his spot against the wall. He was like the dog, she thought, claiming a spot and staying there, no matter the awkwardness it caused. And yet she could believe that Emma would give herself to a boy like this. Not because of his size or his muscled body, but because he seemed a prisoner of his size and strength. Certainly Emma could have seen it that way when she was fourteen.

"Clouds know no borders," her father said, then drained the glass. "Anozzer, please." He handed Danny his empty glass.

"Are you having a 'senior moment'?" Zhenya asked. "What does 'clouds and no-no borders mean?'"

Her father wrote the sentence out on his notebook. *Clouds know no borders.* "For academic paper. I give to you." He ripped the page out of the notebook and placed it on the table before her. "Start vis this and talk about acid rain. I put it out here for you." He tapped the scrap of paper. "Steal it."

For a while, a kid in Parks and Rec was assigned to Morgan's truck, nice enough, with a freckled, pimpled, sunburned face, and a deep incomprehension of the world. But he had no interest in working trash. Today Morgan was to get Danny's permanent replacement. Last-minute forms were holding him up. Morgan waited for him in the truck. If Danny wasn't convicted, he would get his job back. Did hiring a replacement mean they were certain Danny was going to prison? Did government agencies share information? Could the city manager call a prosecutor to get a report on an employee charged with a serious crime?

The sky this morning carried the faint color of shallow water and seemed itself shallow, a thin covering to disguise what lay beyond. Morgan took his hard hat from the truck's floorboard and slipped it on. According to regulations, he was supposed to wear it, anyway. Why not make a good impression on the new man? They were now thirty minutes late getting started, the summer so entrenched that the dark had almost entirely lifted, revealing this superficial morning sky. His arms seemed weighted down, as if in a coat of armor. He had wakened with the familiar heaviness, but today it refused to go away. The real estate agent who had tried to sell them a condominium had come by the house while Zhenya was out. "Your wife has a key to one of our properties," she said, "the one I showed you."

"I don't think so," Morgan said. "Why would she have a key?"

The woman stared at him for a moment and then at some point far past him and then at her shoes. "Your wife attempted to purchase the condo without your knowing," she said. "I feel awful telling you this, but I will have to rekey the locks if I don't get that key back."

Morgan asked her to explain. She said his wife had wanted the apartment as "a safeguard against what was happening to your neighborhood." She turned then to survey the damage. As if on cue, one of the roadworkers yelled an obscenity at another man. "I'm not supposed to lend keys, but I do sometimes. To people I trust."

"Rekey it or install new locks or whatever," Morgan told her. "Send me the bill."

"Wouldn't it be simpler to—"

"No, it wouldn't. I'm going to let her tell me about this when she decides she ought to."

"I'm going to charge you for my time," the woman told him.

< 2 1 7 >

"Fair enough," Morgan had said.

The new man finally emerged from the office, a lanky fellow with pale skin and a red goatee. "Welcome aboard," Morgan called out. The man nodded but ignored the outstretched hand. This was all he needed, Morgan thought, a fool with an attitude.

"Vic," he said, in response to Morgan's direct question. He didn't ask for Morgan's name and glared out the windshield with his arms crossed, the skin on his face turning a deeper shade of red. After knowing him thirty seconds, Morgan understood that Vic would not get through the probationary period. To his surprise, this made him happy.

"We have the red route today," Morgan told Vic, who turned away and muttered something unintelligible. Morgan attempted to explain their duties.

"Yeah, yeah," Vic said.

Morgan felt the odd pleasure grow. He had no compulsion to have sympathy for Vic. "Maybe you didn't hear me." He started in again, but Vic cut him off.

"It's not fucking brain surgery, is it?" He scowled at Morgan, a stupid angry scowl that made Morgan almost giddy.

"It's a goddamn beautiful day, isn't it?"

Vic's scowl turned to a look of mocking disbelief. "It'll be hot as fuck and you know it." He spoke almost too softly to be heard, and then he clammed up.

Morgan wheeled through the empty streets, upping the truck's speed, rounding corners widely, roaming into the next lane, making driving noises the way Petey would. A breeze lifted the branches of the trees lining the streets, their limbs and leaves waving about as if to wipe clean the air. "Alley number one for this goddamn beautiful day coming up," he crowed, then cut sharply into the gravel lane and braked hard. "Let's go to it."

When Vic slid out of the truck, Morgan burst into a smile. He couldn't guess why having a fool along should make him happy, but it did. In the midst of this happiness, he summoned an image of his son. He recalled an afternoon when he had come home from work and found the house empty. He went from room to room looking for life. Pushing open his son's door, he found Philip on his bed with a book in his hands, his eyes red from crying. "They went to the grocery. I didn't want to go," he said.

"What's wrong?" Morgan asked.

"*Nothing,*" Philip said.

Morgan waited, but the boy refused to say more. "How about some catch?" he offered, and when that failed, he rattled off other games. Philip hadn't liked any of his ideas. "What do you want to do?" Morgan asked.

"Just leave me alone," he said, and Morgan had. In a few minutes, the boy came down the stairs carrying a board game, and they played at the kitchen table. Philip cheered up. When Zhenya and Emma got home with the groceries, they put them away together. Afterward, Philip and Emma ran off to watch television.

Why such a banal memory came to him this morning, he couldn't guess. Philip arrived every day, one way or another. He didn't question it. He understood only the obligation to pursue the moments to memory's end. Maybe even now, the glee he felt watching this idiot Vic, maybe that, too, had something to do with Philip. He thought for another moment—Life. That was what they had played. A tedious game, but they'd had fun.

The alley was lined by crappy fences protecting miserable little yards. Morgan thought he might be the only person in the city who had driven more miles in alleys than on city streets. Meanwhile, Vic handled the garbage cans as if they had insulted him. Morgan could feel his spirits lifting again. The redheaded idiot. The angry young shit. Could there be a worse kind of loser?

Morgan waited until they were on their first trip to the dump to engage Vic again. "You upset about something?" Vic glared. A well-practiced scowl. Morgan imagined Vic in front of a mirror, trimming his Satanesque goatee and rehearsing his evil look. It made him laugh. He couldn't help it. "Well?" Morgan said. "What is it?"

Vic said, "Why are *you* driving?"

"It's my job."

"That's what I'm asking. Why do you have the job of driving while I have to heft all the goddamn cans?"

< 2 1 9 >

"I lifted one or two of those cans."

Vic jerked his head around, furious. "You pick the lightest ones and you know it."

"You can tell by looking at a garbage can how much it weighs?"

"Once you've been doing it for a while you can."

"You've been doing it all of two hours."

"It's not like it's fucking brain surgery."

"I've been doing this more than twenty years," Morgan told him. "I drive because I have the position and the seniority."

"Hah!" Vic crossed his arms dramatically. "If that's what you want me to believe, let's drop it."

"What *is* it that you believe?"

"I have a chauffeur's license. I'm legal to drive this truck. All you have is connections."

Morgan let go a long, honest fall of laughter. He could not remember the last time he laughed so hard for so long. Finally, he said, "You weren't hired to drive, Vic."

"I don't drive because I don't kiss nobody's ass," Vic said. Then his anger shifted inside, and he said nothing but nodded and twitched as his internal arguments proved his every assertion.

On the road to the dump, Morgan recalled a specific sky he had seen long ago from the cab of the very truck he was driving. Back then there had been three men to a crew, but they had dropped off one man at the union store before making the run. The other had slept in the seat beside him. He remembered that he had just maneuvered through the gate and into the landfill. Storm clouds had dropped in among the high branches of the oaks and sycamores that lay just beyond the edge of the dump. The clouds paused there, swirling among the topmost limbs of the distant trees like a child's drawing of leaves. Early-morning light angled beneath the dark clouds, lighting the forest floor, so that the gray trunks seemed to hold up the whole of the sky. Morgan nudged his remaining partner, waking him, and pointed to the gray panorama beyond their windshield. His partner raised his chin from his chest and blinked at the storm. "Rain weather," he said and spread his arms wide, stretching and yawning.

"Rain before seven, fine by eleven," Morgan said.

"You don't know that," his partner replied, sitting up then, a young black man wearing a white undershirt that was ribbed like the flesh of a banana.

"Just something people say," Morgan said. The air was thick with the anticipation of rain. Drops plinked against the windshield before the last of the garbage had slid from the truck into the land-fill. It was pouring by the time they left the dump. But the rain was gone before they pulled into the alley behind the union store to retrieve the third man. A summer squall, here and gone. "Rain before seven, fine by eleven," Morgan repeated. He would think about that later, after coming home to tragedy. If it had rained longer, the children wouldn't have been playing outside. His son would be alive. And what if Morgan hadn't let the one man remain at the store during the dump run? They might have finished a few minutes earlier. Morgan might have been home in time. These possibilities and dozens more, all the random things that could have saved his son, haunted him daily for years, as did the terrible beauty of that tree-tethered sky.

Morgan drove as far as the stand of white pines. He stopped the truck, got out, and circled to the other side. "Scoot over," he said. "Go ahead. Drive the son of a bitch."

"You think I won't?" Vic demanded.

"I just *said* go ahead."

Vic slid in behind the wheel. He barked at Morgan, "Close your door."

Morgan felt the giddy rush return. "Gimme a second, boss man. I'm doing my darnedest to please you. Really, I am."

"Very funny." Vic shoved the idling truck into gear, released the brake, and let out the clutch—too quickly. The truck died. Morgan expected this. He had intentionally pulled off in loose gravel. It took a careful clutch to get the old truck moving from a standstill.

Vic angrily turned the key, staring out the driver's-side window. Morgan said, "It *sure* is a purty day."

Vic stalled the truck again. "I'm not saying I won't have to get the

< 221 >

hang of the truck," he said, furious all over again. "I never said that."

His tone was angry enough that Morgan dropped the stupid voice, but he felt good, as good as he could ever remember feeling. "Slushy gravel," he said. "Let the clutch engage just slightly, then up the gas a tiny bit."

"I know how to drive," Vic insisted.

"Jesus," Morgan said. "You are something else."

Vic followed Morgan's instructions but pressed the accelerator too hard and the truck gave a little jump. He adjusted quickly, though, and kept the truck moving. Vic probably could get the hang of it pretty fast, Morgan thought. They drove past the lush summer growth. Morgan enjoyed the slightly different view from the opposite side of the cab. He spotted a squirrel beyond the pines and saw movement deep within the woods that might have been a deer or might have been merely movement, pure motion.

They passed through the gate and down the road around the teardrop ravine. Vic drove too fast but not unsafely. The sharp angle of the morning sun made shards of glass in the dump glitter. A plastic carton that once had held milk tumbled across the other garbage as if the wind had singled it out. Morgan felt almost as if he were in love. He lowered his window, stuck his hand out, and hammered against the door. He whooped and hollered. Something inside him demanded it.

"Holy fuck," Vic said. "Chill out."

At the marked location for the day's dumping, Morgan said, "Vic, my bud, you want to pull around and back right into—"

"I can see what to do. I don't need my mother."

"There's a procedure—"

"Stuff it."

Morgan reached over and turned the ignition off. He laughed as he removed the key. "I can't let you do this unless you listen to me." He wanted to say more, tell him about the joy in his heart that had arrived as the result of the man's arrogance, anger, and stupidity. Vic didn't let him. His enraged words sent spittle flying. "I don't have to take this shit!" He bolted out of the truck and began stomping back to the entrance.

Morgan stared at his back in the big mirror on the side of the cab. "I think we handled that very nicely," he said aloud, as if there were someone to hear.

On the trunk lid of their blue patrol car, next to the keyhole, someone had used a Magic Marker to write *skank wagon*. Adele was certain it hadn't been there this morning, and it was only noon now. "You want to be a dick, you ought to be able to solve this one," she said to Roy. She licked the cuff of one sleeve and tried to wipe away the lettering, cleaning an oval about the graffiti, making it stand out all the more. "Do we have to call in piddly crap like this?"

Roy nodded. They didn't really have to, but he saw this as a way to steal some time. "You radio it in. I'll get sandwiches." They were parked in the lot of a barbecue joint. The entire neighborhood smelled of barbecue. He knew who had written on the car. Roy had watched it happen without realizing what was going on. That morning they had stopped at an adult bookstore that had been robbed weeks earlier by a man wearing a Halloween mask. The tape of the 911 call made the rounds. "I'm calling from Booty Books and Tapes. I was just robbed at gunpoint by Casper the Friendly Ghost. Looked like a Luger. Got a couple hundred bucks and a Perfect Pussy." The press labeled the robber Casper the Lonely Ghost.

This past weekend a convenience store in Alton was robbed by a man wearing a Scooby-Doo mask. Roy and Adele went to Booty Books to drop off a surveillance photo of the robber. The only connection between the robberies was the cartoon masks. Roy had let Adele handle it. He was afraid to go in. Emma liked dirty pictures and stories. Not videos. She didn't like the bodies to be moving. She was too young to buy the smut herself. He hadn't thought about it before, but there was another crime he had committed— distributing pornography to a minor.

Adele took her time in Booty Books, and Roy climbed out of the cruiser. He leaned on the hood to wait for her. A skinny kid on a bike raced into the parking lot, skidding to a stop at the opposite end of the patrol car—a teenager, black, spaces between his front teeth.

< 2 2 3 >

"They get robbed?" the kid asked. His deep voice made Roy look closer. The bike had misled him. This was a young man.

Roy said, "Not today."

"Just shopping, huh?" the guy said. Roy explained the circumstances. The guy liked the story, especially the part about the theft of the Perfect Pussy. The way the handlebars of the bike moved slightly should have tipped Roy off. The man had written on the car while Roy was staring right at him.

Roy had no interest in conveying this to Adele. He had something else on his mind. It had tormented him now for three days and three nights. That didn't sound like a long time. He recalled reading about a young mother who had shaken her baby senseless because she couldn't take his constant crying. The baby had been one week old. He would never be able to pass judgment on another person, he thought, which would make him a lousy cop. Danny Ford had moved into Emma's house. Morgan had made the bail. A stupid thing to do, but Roy couldn't muster much anger against Morgan. He was who he was. He couldn't help it any more than Roy could help loving Emma. He would judge nobody. He ordered barbecue sandwiches. Adele would eat anything, so he got to choose where they went for lunch. The place was crowded, a local restaurant run by a black couple and their kids. Their order would go to the top of the list. Cops were served fast. He took an empty booth.

In the three days since Ford had moved into Emma's house, Roy had heard nothing from her. She had not called, had not come over. From his window he had watched her dive, imagining Morgan, Zhenya, and Petey watching from the deck, and the old man, that incontinent dog of theirs, and maybe Mrs. East—all of these people able to be with the woman he loved simply by knocking on a door or passing through a gate, and yet he had to stand at the window, his imperfect view limited to her approach and leap. He could not see her splash into the water, although if he opened the window, he could hear it. After attending the diving meet, he could even imagine it. All the others saw it every day, and now among them sat Danny Ford, pasty-faced and drinking Morgan's beer, ogling Emma's wet body, thinking what he would like to do with it, the two of them sleeping under the same roof, eating at the same table, pissing in the same porcelain bowl.

For three days Roy pictured Danny Ford wandering through the house in his underwear, knowing that Morgan left for work before daylight, knowing that the old man was feeble, knowing every contour of Emma's body, the flimsy bathing suit more an invitation than a covering. Why hadn't she called him?

And what was she thinking all this time? Ford was built like Hercules. She was bound to take note of that. Roy spent hours watering his yard, figuring she would come out and speak to him, but no one did. He dialed her number, hoping she would answer, but he never got anything but the machine and hung up. Didn't she hear all those hang-ups? Couldn't she guess who was calling? He could just go over there and be let in. He was their neighbor, after all. For that matter, he was a single man and she a single woman, but between himself and this simple act of knocking on a door lay their long history. His lies. His seduction of one child and fathering of another. All the things that he had not acknowledged—now the only things that had any meaning for him.

Through the greasy window of the restaurant, Roy could see Adele talking into the radio mike. The car's lights were on. She had it idling to run the air conditioner. She didn't like to come inside this place. Too hot. Which was why Roy picked it. To be free of her for a few minutes.

Three days without a phone call or visit did not really mean anything, he told himself in his calmer moments. They often remained separated far longer than that. Even since Diana left him, they had spent four or five days apart. Emma had summer school, Petey to take care of, her unhappy father, her distant mother, her grandfather who expected to be served, and now a dangerous criminal camping in her house. She had her hands full. She needed him. Why didn't she call?

She had said she would marry him if he got Danny Ford off the hook. Maybe she hadn't meant it, maybe she had just been talking. But she had said it, and they were going to be married eventually anyway, weren't they? At times she seemed more resigned to it than anything else, and that bothered Roy, but he knew she would change

< 2 2 5 >

over time. Once they were married, she would love him as she had before. He had lost his wife because of his love for Emma. She would not leave him hanging. So what if she felt more obligation than infatuation this month? They had been together for years. And wasn't he obliged to her as well? It was inevitable, their marriage. Sooner or later. Sooner if he freed Danny Ford. If Roy insisted, Emma would keep her word. And Ford, once he was free, could prance about in his underwear in some other house.

This argument occurred to him the first night that Danny Ford moved in next door. Setting Ford free—really free, and not just out on bail—was an unthinkable act, but there Roy was thinking about it. He put it out of his head until the next morning—four-thirty and he could not sleep. He made himself coffee, took it up to his room, where he stood on his bed and stared out at the diving platform in the faint light of dawn. Even if he was willing to consider somehow helping Ford, it was not a thing he could manage. It could not be done. If he changed his testimony—maybe he could get away with that, claim some kind of confusion, privately point to his wife leaving him. She had, after all, abandoned him the very day that he arrested Ford. Couldn't that account for the confusion? Maybe he could even keep his promotion, the one he knew was coming. But Adele would have to go along, and even then there was the gun with the boy's fingerprints on it. As long as there was the gun, Ford was nailed. One of his pals would rat him out to save his own hide, and the prosecution wouldn't even need Roy's testimony. It was not possible to get Ford off. Any plan would have to include Adele, and he could not let her have that over him. It would be the end of his career as a police officer. He had decided this and felt some peace with the firmness of his resolution as he stood on his bed, drinking his coffee, staring out the window, the mattress springs subtly shifting beneath him.

At the diving meet, he had watched Emma's family and friends wrestle the drunken old man down the stairs and out to the parking lot. There had been two boys, the same ones who had crowded around Emma at the reception. From the very beginning of their long affair, Emma had always dated boys. Roy was married and she dated, but they kept their love for each other separate, pure.

But something had changed. Diana's leaving, yes, but that didn't account for all of it, didn't account for their inability to talk or do anything but fuck. She had feelings for one of those boys, the one with the old Nova, red and white like the flag—he had spied it in front of her house. Of the two boys, it was clearly the neat one—not that he was particularly handsome or well built. Roy would destroy him in a fight. But how did you fight youth? How did you assert your prior claim when neither his face nor hers had a single line? Gray stubble, he recalled. His five o'clock shadow. Usually, he shaved when he got off work. A habit. Diana had called him "sand-paper cheeks," and he had fallen into the habit of shaving twice a day. But he had forgotten one day, and the next morning, in the bathroom mirror, he spotted gray in the faint shadow of his beard. He was fourteen years older than Emma. She had been fourteen years old when he first slept with her. Didn't that mean something?

He had forgotten to shave that day because when he pulled into his driveway, Danny Ford had been outside Emma's house with a can of gasoline. Roy had pounded the brake and leapt from the car. Ford had raised his head, his malevolent eyes zeroing in on Roy. Those eyes so fierce that Roy had not even seen the lawn mower right there, the yard partially mowed, did not see it until he walked in the just-cut grass. Ford glanced at him, then shoved the nozzle of the gas can into the open mouth of the lawn mower. Roy had been on the verge of yelling something, but what would Emma think of him then? It was bad enough he had arrested her father's partner. He stopped at the edge of the grass. Ford screwed the cap back on. As he stood, he calmly flipped Roy off. Then he set the gas can aside and yanked at the cord to the mower. He was a colossal man, a man of great physical strength, a man who could dismember Roy. How could you fight Hercules? Any consideration he had given to going over to the house left him. He would lose control with Ford there. He went inside his own house and had not given a thought to shaving. He dialed Emma's number. The machine. Morgan's sad-sack voice on tape.

Now a woman placed a bag of barbecue sandwiches on his table. She had lovely dark skin and fine features. A lovely woman. "Thank

< 227 >

you," he said, with such emotion that it seemed to allude to something else.

She nodded at him. "Our mother's getting much better," she said.

He realized that she was not really a woman but a girl. "That's good to hear," he said, having no idea what she was referring to. She was a teenager. He glanced past her retreating back and beyond the counter to her father, who also nodded. Had his hair and beard always been white? Roy returned the nod.

"She's going be all right," the girl's father called. "Praise the Redeemer."

Roy nodded again. He opened the sack and pretended to check the contents. He had forgotten to order anything to drink. Adele would gripe about that. It made it worse, he thought, to be right next door to Emma and yet be unable to see her. Distance could provide an excuse. Distance could be a comfort. Coming inside his house after his encounter with Ford, Roy discovered his mail slot filled with letters. He had forgotten to look for a couple of days. He scooped them up and climbed the stairs. Standing on his bed in his uniform, armed with a pistol, a dozen letters in his hands, his shoes making prints on the sheets, he went through the mail, glancing back and forth between the white envelopes and the vacant diving platform. One of the letters was from Diana. He dropped the others to the bed, checked the platform again, then ripped open the envelope.

I have a job. Roy looked at the envelope again. Phoenix address. The chrome arms of the platform rail reflected the sun. *My parents helped me buy a car. A Saturn. My dad owns a Mercury. We're working on a whole solar system.* Emma's head appeared, bobbing as she climbed the ladder, her hair tied back in a ponytail, bathing suit dry—he had not missed a jump. The phone rang. He let it ring. She ran her fingers around the hem of the suit at the back. The climbing made the cheeks of her butt show, and this gesture, this little act of modesty she ritually performed, made his face heat up, his vision blur.

In another moment she was gone. He heard her splash, but the tree in his yard blocked his view. *I feel that I may have been unfair to you. I may have been too harsh. I know my sister told you that I'm seeing someone, but he's just a friend. We go to movies. He has kids my age. He's bald. She just wanted to get back at you. What you did was wrong. I didn't expect to be writing this letter. I miss you.* Emma's head and shoulders, her hair wet and dripping, her face in the sunlight glittering with pool water. He imagined that he could see her nipples through the material. He imagined Ford staring openly at those nipples, Morgan not willing to do a goddamn thing about it. Was Ford down there in a bathing suit himself? Showing off his body? He dropped the letter onto the bed, the pages separating, one remaining on the mattress, one landing on the floor atop the discarded electric bill.

"Did you want something else?" The young black woman— the girl—stood before him again. "My dad said Cokes are on the house." She held out two large cups. They needed the booth. People were waiting to sit. He thanked her and left.

The frigid air inside the cruiser made him shiver. He could see through the big window a family being seated at his booth. Father, mother, son, and a baby. He and Emma could have another child. The world would circle around the baby, and while it did, he would find his bearings again. Adele had been watching him. She had seen him sit there while their sandwiches grew cold. She knew something was up. He could help her, especially after he became a detective. She needed an ally in the department. He had something to offer for her help.

"Eat in the park?" she said.

"No," Roy said. "You drive, I eat. I drive, you eat."

She made no comment, which was not like her. She was waiting for him to come clean, to fess up. And he knew that he would, but he didn't know how to begin.

"I can drive *and* eat," Adele said.

"We'll park then," he said. "Wherever you want."

"The mother die? Is that it?"

"What are you talking about?"

"The barbecue people. Their mother was shot in that holdup. What was it, a month ago?"

< 2 2 9 >

He had forgotten. It seemed like ages ago. It was long before Danny Ford had moved into Emma's house. "They said she's getting better. Or she's fine already—listen, I've got something to talk to you about. Something we need to discuss. Here's the deal," and he began explaining the help he needed.

7

Weakness lingers in the hollow parts of our bodies—the lungs, the arteries, the heart.

—Peter Ivanovich Kamenev

Dr. Gallen was curious about the connection between Emma's memory of the baseball game and her memory of dancing. Emma had visited him weekly as a child, from the time her brother killed himself to the time she became Roy Oberland's lover. Because she could not imagine telling Dr. Gallen about sex with Roy, she had quit going. Now, all these years later, she returned to therapy, and she discovered she couldn't tell Dr. Gallen why she was back.

He had aged in the time she was away. His nose had thickened and lost its shape, and coarse hair grew from his nostrils like the tips of artist's brushes. The skin about his jowls bagged and swayed with the movement of his head. He had never been good-looking, but she had liked watching him, especially when he adjusted his tie or took off his coat. Once he had rolled up his sleeves. Now the dark pockets beneath his eyes reminded her of the boils her brother used to get on his back. Even his breath had grown old and sour.

His office, meanwhile, had become younger. Pastel wallpaper, yellow bordered by gray, had replaced the stolid brown paneling. Instead of a generic flowers-in-a-vase still life, a colorful abstract print hung over a new, fashionable couch. Why had he done this? she wanted to ask him. Had he gone through a midlife crisis? Had he left his wife? Had he taken an interior designer as a lover?

< 2 3 0 >

< 2 3 1 >

The problem she wanted to bring to Dr. Gallen now was t
the man she had loved for years was suddenly free of his wife and
wanted to marry her. It didn't sound so bad when she put it that way.
She couldn't say that she no longer loved him, because that wouldn't
be true. She couldn't say that she loved him like a brother. Having a
dead brother made some things impossible to say.

She couldn't say anything to Dr. Gallen without telling him all
the stuff she had withheld in the past, and that would hurt his feelings. She wasn't certain why she had come again to see Dr. Gallen,
but she knew it wasn't to hurt him. Seeing a new therapist would
require so much explanation, so much history. And she had always
liked Dr. Gallen. Sitting on his new couch, aware of all she could not
say, she decided to tell him about the two memories, how she could
not ever recall one without recalling the other, how—odd as it
seemed—she could barely keep them straight, the memory of the
game and the memory of dancing.

"Attempting to figure out the connection between the memories
may be the wrong strategy," he said. His voice had the flat directness
of the Midwest; that had not changed. If she closed her eyes while
he spoke, she could picture the younger Dr. Gallen. "Maybe you
should simply talk about the memories and permit the connection
between them to inform your understanding of the whole."

He said things like that, things she thought to be smart but not
especially smart. Often barely smart enough. She knew only a few
people who were genuinely smart. Roy Oberland was not among
them. She preferred intelligent people, but she didn't require it. Her
mother was smart in all the traditional ways—quick, shrewd, logical, systematic. Her father was smart in an odd way, a kind of smart
she did not have words for. A useless kind of smart, by most mea-
sures. But many of the most important things could not be measured. She knew that much.

If Roy Oberland had not been standing in his yard on that distant
day, her brother might be alive and she never would have touched
any part of Roy's body—except his hands. They would have run
into each other at the grocery, he with his wife and she with her
brother, and they would have all shaken hands. And he would mean
nothing to her. Everyone you knew was merely a coincidence in your

life—except for your family. Whose blood you shared. Whose story was your story. There was no escaping family.

Then it occurred to her that if her brother were alive and she had never become Roy's lover, there would be no Petey. Would she trade her son to have her brother back? That was a stupid way of thinking. It was inconceivable that she would give up her son. It was inconceivable that she would not save her brother.

She began with the baseball game, which was played in the street, unlike the dance, which had taken place in the living room of their home. She was ten years old at the time of the game. Her brother liked to pitch, kicking his leg high, twisting his body, the hand that held the ball sinking almost to the pavement before whipping forward. He threw hard to the guys, but not to her and not to the little kids they recruited. They never had enough players for two teams. On that afternoon, there were three batters and ten fielders. A batter stayed up until he made an out. The Haney boys started the game at second base, shortstop, and third. Emma batted first, as she always did. Philip insisted on that. One of his rules. He lobbed the ball to her. After a couple of hits, she popped out to King Haney at third base. She took up the position of lookout, which meant she stood beyond the outfielders and watched for cars. It was her favorite position. "We could have played in the park, but the trees made fly balls impossible," she said, hearing, for a moment, the rustling movement of the wind through the giant trees in the park and the mulberry that canopied the street behind home plate.

When the next batter made an out, she was supposed to move to left field. But she had been inside getting a plastic table when the boy flied out, and he had skipped over her to left field. "I didn't care," she said. "I always batted first, and then I didn't care whether I batted again." She dragged a table from her room to the street, putting on it her lamp with the red bulb. The boys interrupted the game to connect extension cords that ran all the way back to their house. Philip made them do that. The light warned approaching cars. It made her position official.

One of the outfielders, a boy a year or so younger than Emma, had worn boots with plastic spurs that flashed in the sun, and a cowboy hat. "Only he said it wasn't a cowboy hat. It was a *ten-gallon hat.*"

< 2 3 3 >

She smiled when she said this, and Dr. Gallen acknowledged the smile with a shifting of his crinkled lips. The boy always wore the boots, spurs, and hat, even to school, she said, although that seemed unlikely, she admitted, now that she thought about it. Maybe she was making that up. But he wore the outfit often, and his mother had dark hair and painted her lips the red of flashing lights, which had also been the color of Emma's tutu the night of the dance. Not the real dance. The real dance had taken place in the cafeteria at school, but it was the rehearsal at home that mattered, in the living room, with her mother, father, and brother watching. This was longer ago. She had been five or six. Prince had watched, too, just a puppy in her brother's arms. She could figure out her exact age at the time if she counted back to the year they got Prince. Her brother named the dog. Emma gave in to him. She could not remember now what name she had wanted. During the daylight hours, she always gave in to her brother. During the night hours, she was in charge— although the routine they followed was still of his making.

A doorway linked their rooms, and the door was propped open at night. From her bed, Emma could see Philip lying in his bed, reading or drawing. The lamp that painted a circle of light over him had a torn shade. Philip would not let their parents replace it. If he liked what he drew, he would hold it up for her approval. She would nod or make a face. Sometimes he drew pictures of grown-up women wearing no clothes at all. Targets for breasts, and nothing between the legs, just a place where one leg met the other. Emma made a face at these, even though she liked them. The naughtiness of them. And her brother knowing she would never tell.

Even all these years later, Emma slept in the same bed on her side of the doorway, but it was now her son who occupied the connecting room. He sometimes called to her in the night, much as Philip had, except that Philip had whispered *Emma*, and Petey called *Mama*, but the urgency was the same, and it was this urgency that cut through her sleep and lifted her to consciousness. Her brother had called for her every night without fail. An hour or two after falling asleep, he would wake and whisper her name. She would rouse immediately, hop to the floor, and go to her brother's bed. She would stand beside it, facing away, and he would sit up, put his hands on her shoulders, and then stand. They would walk together in this fashion, like children in a play pretending to be a four-legged animal. She would lead him to the bathroom and turn on the bathroom light for him, then wait in the hall for him to finish. He would close the door but not all the way. Philip was afraid of the dark, and she was not. She had never been afraid of the dark. From the age of three until the night before his death, she led her big brother nightly down the hallway and then back to his bed.

Roy Oberland wanted to marry her. It felt inevitable, in a way, their marriage. As if they had never had any choice. As if they used up all their choices on the day Philip killed himself. In their ball game on the street, the players kept rotating from position to position. Some would leave for a while to eat or check in with their mothers, and then they would come back. In the real game of baseball, the official games at a ballpark or on television, once a player left, he could not return. If the game went long enough, at some point the ones still on the field would be all the eligible players that remained. No matter how many innings had to be played. "There's no clock in baseball," Philip used to say. "One game can last forever."

When Philip batted, he had a routine, tapping the plate twice, swiveling his front foot once, cocking his arms back and above his head, the motion of his wrists making the head of the bat loop. The dance, Emma's dance, involved toe pointing and arm lifting to the tune of "Give My Regards to Broadway." Ballet outfit and show-tune music—a silly dance, she understood now. She had been a tiny girl wearing a red tutu with sparkles in the ruffles. The boy who dressed like a cowboy had not lived in the neighborhood back then. He had been around only that one summer and fall, and then the family moved away. Forest Avenue had been a different place, full of kids, most of them poor. She and her brother and the Haney boys had seemed rich in comparison. Philip and King Haney were best friends, the most popular kids. King was Emma's age. Later, when she was pregnant, her parents would think King might be the father, which was one reason they never pushed to find out. They feared it was another fourteen-year-old.

Philip always did things, came up with ideas. One year on Easter

< 2 3 5 >

Sunday he told all the kids to bring their hard-boiled eggs out to the street. He showed up with his baseball bat. King lobbed the eggs to him, and they exploded against his swing. It made a thrilling mess on the street and on him, his clothes and face and in his hair. "Explosive power," he had said, describing himself as a baseball announcer might. He had announced the dance as well, Emma's dance in the living room. "The ballerina does a riveting spin," he said. "She's going to try a leap! Both feet off the ground! Can she do it? Can she do it? Yes, ladies and gentlemen, both feet are in the air!" She did not remember the words to the song that she had danced to, but she could hear his voice. He had made a pun about "amazing feat" and "amazing feet."

"I guess I do remember one line of the song," she told Dr. Gallen, "because there was a word we couldn't understand—Philip and I. We played the tape over and over. 'Remember me to—something— Square.' Philip kept changing that one word: Tombstone Square, Roundball Square, Circle Square." Emma wanted Dr. Gallen to understand how funny it was, how funny Philip could be. "He took things hard, though, and he was mean to me—to everybody—when something went wrong."

She had brought out a lawn chair to put beside the table that held the lamp with the red bulb, whose glow could hardly be detected in the brilliant light of the sun. She went in again and found her umbrella. Philip told her that it wasn't an umbrella if it wasn't raining. It was something else then. She couldn't remember what.

She raised the thing that wasn't an umbrella and sat in its shade. Mr. Oberland was in his front yard washing his squad car, which was parked in the grass of his lawn. He'd had a roommate back then, another policeman. One time Mr. Oberland had let her and her brother climb inside the car and check it out. Philip had gone for the microphone and its spiral of cord and begun narrating an arrest; Emma had turned the other way and put her fingers in the wire screen that separated the front seat from the back. "That's the cage," Mr. Oberland had told her. His roommate did not stay in the neighborhood for long. "Roy would have left, too, except for what happened," Emma said. "Except for Philip strangling himself." After that, Roy Oberland was not capable of moving, she thought, but she did not tell Dr. Gallen this. She did not tell him why she had come again to be his patient. He seemed too fragile to hear anything. And it would take a long time, she realized, to explain Roy and her, what they had been together, what they still were. She could say, "I'm not sleeping well, Dr. Gallen." She could say, "Some nights I wake in a panic." But she could not say, "I want to get to choose, to have a choice. But I don't want to turn my back on the life that has chosen me."

What she actually said was "When we chose sides for games, Philip always chose me, and I always chose Philip."

"You were very close," Dr. Gallen said, and she knew that she would not be able to make him understand. She made one more try.

"It was our rule," she said, "and we always followed it. But what it meant was we never really got to choose at all."

He furrowed his brows, nodded thoughtfully, a gesture that meant nothing. Just something to let her know he was listening. He was trying. She wouldn't be mean to him. He was doing his best. She would protect him from all he didn't know. Protecting people seemed to be her job in the world.

After a couple of batters popped up, it was Philip's turn to hit. He was almost impossible to get out. That day he wore a horizontally striped shirt with narrow stripes, alternating black and yellow, like the body of a bee. "Sometimes when I picture the baseball game I see myself in the tutu," she said, "but I had on regular clothes. I sat in the lawn chair beside the table and held an umbrella in my right hand. I had a baseball glove on my left."

Mr. Oberland shouted something to his roommate, who was in the house. He wore cutoff jeans and a T-shirt, rinsing the car with a hose, a nozzle on the end to make the spray intense. His lawn needed mowing, but he had not owned the house back then. Just a renter. Water dribbled from the police car onto the long grass and ran into the gutter, where soap bubbles massed, refracting sunlight into all the visible colors. Mr. Oberland would buy the house eventually. "You might think he'd want to get away. But he didn't." She smiled as she said this, but Dr. Gallen did not understand the smile. Perhaps she liked knowing things she could not tell.

Something had been wrong in young Mr. Oberland's life. Years

< 2 3 7 >

later she would ask him about it. "I was sort of an angry guy," he would say to her. "What was wrong was the whole world." He said this to Emma one afternoon in bed. She had been sixteen. She had been his lover for two years already. She had given birth to his child. She had waited that long to ask. She had been naked, her face in a pillow, Roy mounting her from behind, and she had asked what had been his problem back then. When she heard his answer, she understood that Philip's death had cured him of this anger. It had made him a better person. How could she tell Dr. Gallen this? How could she tell him that she had no longer needed therapy once she started fucking Roy? Not because sex cured her or saved her or even sometimes gave her pleasure. But because it gave her a secret life she could bear.

Could that make sense to anyone in the world but her?

Philip had a beautiful swing. He hit the ball high and deep and right at her. All she had to do was stand to catch it. She did not even drop the umbrella. The ball made a snap hitting her glove. When she remembered this moment, she could hear Philip saying, "He hit it hard but right at her. She caught it dead in her tracks." He never said that, of course. Instead, he yelled, "No fair." He hated making outs. By the time he got to bat again, everyone would be ready to quit. He argued that the lookout could not catch the ball. "That was a home run," he said. The others laughed. They were happy to have him out. The boy in the cowboy boots slapped his own behind and made horse noises as he ran to his new position.

Philip lost it. He screamed and complained. He threatened. When King Haney called him a baby, he chased after King with the bat, swinging it around in circles, windmill-style. He pursued him into the outfield. One of the swings hit the lamp, and it exploded, glass flying up into the air, raining down on Emma's umbrella.

Is it an umbrella when it's raining glass?

Mr. Oberland saw the lamp explode, and he yelled. He commanded Philip to stop. "Hold it right *there*," he said as if apprehending a criminal, holding the nozzle of the hose like it was a gun. "Freeze!"

It wasn't in Philip's nature to stop. Mr. Oberland ran after and grabbed him. Philip tried to wrestle free, but Roy Oberland was a grown man. "Apologize," Mr. Oberland demanded. Philip wouldn't do it. "You're going to apologize to everyone here," he said. "We'll stand out here all day if we have to."

Her brother held out a long time. No one was permitted to leave. The kids who knew Philip thought it would be the grown-up who would grow weary and finally shrug, shake his head, and let Philip go. But Mr. Oberland just held him and waited while the other children stood around and witnessed the final hour of her brother's life.

When Philip finally gave in, Mr. Oberland carried him from one kid to the next, and Philip said he was sorry to each, something inside him twisting up with each apology, until finally . . . she didn't know. What did that do to Philip? *Emma,* he would call into his dark room every night, and every night Emma would go to him. For years after he was gone she would wake to his voice and slip through the dark into his room, knowing he wasn't there but feeling she must look. She would not be disloyal to him.

Mrs. East heard the ruckus in the street. She came out of her house to see what was happening. She was their baby-sitter, and she loved Philip. Emma could tell she liked him best. Mrs. East walked quickly across her yard to the street. To Mr. Oberland, she said, "What seems to be the trouble here?" He made Philip apologize to her, too. Mrs. East had almost taken Philip away from him then. Emma could still see how her body moved to do it, how she knew it was the right thing to do. In the end, though, she could not quite contradict the young policeman. In the end she did nothing.

Finally, Mr. Oberland set her brother down and Philip ran inside. Everyone went home. The boy in the cowboy clothes was crying. Emma remembered that. He had a red bandanna around his neck. The star on his chest had read SHERIFF. Emma entered the house just as Philip left their mother's study and stomped down the hall to his room, slamming the door.

When their father came home, when she heard him cry out and try to make Philip breathe again, Emma was in her room. She pushed open the connecting door and stood in the doorway. When her father ran from the room with Philip limp in his arms, she padded across the floor and felt beneath the mattress for her brother's draw-

< 2 3 9 >

ings of naked women. She hid them from her parents. She didn't want him to get into trouble. She understood that he was dead.

"Emma," Dr. Gallen said, "tell me why you've come to see me."

"I saw King Haney not long ago," she said. "He plays in a band with his brothers." Unlike almost every other kid, King never asked her why Philip killed himself. At the funeral he said, "You know the real reason Egyptians wrap up mummies? So dead people can't get up and run after them." Then he added, "Philip told me that. I have his glove. He left it in the street." When Mr. Oberland in his dark suit and dark sunglasses took a chair near them, King leaned in close to Emma and said, "He shouldn't have made Philip so mad. Everybody knows you don't want to get Philip mad."

Emma thought of being in the police car with Philip. Mr. Oberland had turned a knob, and suddenly Philip's voice was broadcast outside. "We've got trouble," her brother was saying. "Officer in trouble."

The boy in the cowboy outfit was at the funeral, too, but without his hat and boots and spurs. Emma did not recognize him at first. He cried hard and loudly, which meant she and King didn't have to. The cowboy cried for them. And so did Mr. Oberland.

"You were a child," Dr. Gallen said. "Would you hold your own son responsible for a tragedy? You are not responsible for your brother's death."

"I know that," she said. *The therapist swings wildly and misses.* What was the point of telling him anything? Roy Oberland had carried her brother in his arms from one child to the next. He was the last to hold her living brother in his arms. When it was her turn, when Mr. Oberland carried Philip up to Emma, Philip did not look up at her. He kept his head down and spoke softly. "Sorry," he said, and she had thought, Remember this moment, because he'll never say that to you again.

Dr. Gallen would tell her not to marry Roy. Wasn't that what she wanted to hear? But first he would need to watch Roy, as she had watched him. He would have to see how Roy stood and how he moved. He would have to see, as she did, how he still carried her brother. Then what would the doctor say?

Or perhaps she could just ask Dr. Gallen this: "What does the princess do if she doesn't want to live happily ever after?" But she was afraid he would say, "It's all right to be happy. Give yourself permission to be happy."

What did she really want him to say? Weren't she and Roy the perfect couple, really? The one who caught the fly ball and the one who caught the boy. How many married couples had something like that in common?

"You still haven't told, Emma, why you're here."

"Haven't I?"

He shook his head, his jowls' slight sway making her feel sad.

"I'm sorry," she said. "I meant to."

When she had come in from the street, the door between their rooms had been shut, but she heard her brother in there. She could not make out the words he was speaking, but she could hear their familiar rhythm. He was narrating an event, just as he had when she danced for her family, which had been, she believed, the happiest moment in her life.

Peter Ivanovich insisted that Zhenya drive him to the interview with CBS. Mrs. East had offered, but he wanted Zhenya. Yet he preferred Mrs. East's car. "Adriana gives me keys," Peter Ivanovich said, handing them over. "I wait at curb."

Zhenya didn't want to drive Mrs. East's boat. "Emma could do it. She can handle that barge. I'll watch Petey."

"Must be you," Peter Ivanovich said. "And Adriana's car. Must relax before discussion. Little car makes for unfavorable interview."

He didn't need to explain why he didn't want Mrs. East to drive. Zhenya had already heard that the interviewer was a woman. "All right, hell," Zhenya said, "but you can cross the street with me."

"Is unnecessary work," said Peter Ivanovich. "Most important, must concentrate vigor."

Zhenya picked him up in the driveway. Driving Mrs. East's car was like sledding in a king-size bed. They waddled down the street.

"You know what is named this car?" Peter Ivanovich asked.

< 2 4 1 >

"Lincoln. After great liberator of Negroes. Is funny, yes? Martyred president is remembered as elitist car."

"Why did you want to take it if you don't like it?"

"I like Lincoln car very much. Is just ironic name."

The local CBS studio was situated on the east side of downtown in a decaying business district. According to the person who had returned Zhenya's call, the interview would take place by satellite feed. A reporter in New York would ask Peter Ivanovich a few questions, and they would tape his responses. The producer of the CBS special would use the tape to decide whether to send a reporter to Hayden to conduct a more thorough interview. "They're worried he's too old to be of much use," the local newsman confided to Zhenya. "Give him his Geritol. Tell him to ham it up a little."

"Not necessary," Zhenya had said. She directed the Lincoln to a parking spot directly in front of the building that housed the CBS affiliate. The first floor was a pawnshop. So much for the glamour of television, she thought. Peter Ivanovich climbed from the car, then paused to stare through the window. "Hock shop," he said. "Misery of others for sale."

"Morgan bought a guitar at a pawnshop once," Zhenya said. The guitar had been for Philip. For a while he had wanted to be a rock star.

"Misery of others," Peter Ivanovich repeated.

Of course he didn't say "others" but *ozzers*, as if referring to an obscure sea mammal vaguely related to otters. She was not in the mood for this.

She guided him by the elbow through glass doors and down a shabby hall to an elevator. Mrs. East had taken him shopping, and he wore an unsoiled gray suit and new black shoes. He carried a handsome leather briefcase. Mrs. East had to have paid for everything. Her father didn't seem to have any savings. He kept a roll of bills bound by a rubber band between the mattress and box springs of his bed. Zhenya had discovered it changing his sheets. Three hundred eighty-seven dollars. Otherwise, he had nothing. Yet his hair had been cut, and someone besides himself had shaved him. He looked altogether presentable. While they waited for the elevator, he offered the briefcase to Zhenya. "Please to hold like table, please," he said.

Zhenya held the briefcase flat. Peter Ivanovich flicked the latches, and it sprang open. He took a bottle from a Velcro holder and a shot glass from a similar strap. He poured himself a drink. "Cheers," he said, then tipped the glass to his mouth as the elevator doors opened. He shoved the bottle back in its holder and dropped the glass beside it in the briefcase, which held nothing else.

Zhenya put the glass back in its strap to avoid clanking. She noted that the bottle was not capped and had already sloshed against the lining. She was tempted to leave it that way. "I'd say you've found the right woman for you." She capped the vodka bottle and strapped it in. "Seems to know just what you need."

Peter Ivanovich was not listening. "One hundred years is not so much," he said softly.

"What?" Zhenya asked, but realized her father was practicing. When the elevator reached the second floor, she took him again by the elbow, and they ambled down the hallway.

Even in the waiting room Peter understood that he was not in the best state of mind for the audition. The turning blades of the ceiling fan sounded like great wings in flight, and it seemed to him that rather than answer questions and perform for an audience, he should be formulating a question himself, one that only he could answer. Some particular question crowded his mind, and he had to name it before he could be as clever and resourceful as he needed to be for talking on television.

Zhenya sat beside him leafing through a magazine full of color photographs. Faces and bodies of beautiful people, page after page. He tried to concentrate on the things he would say to earn himself a spot on the television special. The old routines would be easy to launch into, and he had three new quotable lines. Wisdom that fit in a lunch box, that was what the public wanted. Here and everywhere. Americans were no more shallow than any other people, just more pampered, so they had come to treasure their shallowness, making

< 2 4 3 >

pop singers and television actors their most revered leaders. Pampered but lovable. He loved America, even though he held it in contempt. Love and contempt were not incompatible. In fact, one was rarely found without the other. Yes, he thought, he should write that down.

He took a deep breath and suddenly found himself again poised on the brink of that question. What was it? Why did he feel that not naming it threatened his performance? The woman behind the ugly desk called his name. Why did Americans put up with such ugly furniture everywhere? He was not in a perfect frame of mind. So what? He would still impress them. He stood, smiled, and waved to the receptionist. She led him to a door that opened into a tiny room no larger than a toilet stall. Four close, padded walls, blank but for the door, which had a square window. A man held the door open for him. He guessed that neither the man nor the receptionist were important. Lackeys made the world go round. The male lackey seated Peter Ivanovich on an uncomfortable stool in the tiny box of a room. A strong smell pervaded the box—goat, he thought, although he knew that was impossible. The odor of goats and the suffocating sense of incarceration put a sour taste on his tongue. He became aware of his breathing, the sound of it, the whistle of air through his nostrils, the heaving of his own bellows. The lackey wore a blue baseball cap and a gray T-shirt that did not cover his stomach when he raised his arms to fit the large earphones to Peter Ivanovich's head. "Is necessary?" Peter asked. "Hides new haircut."

"It's just a run-through thing today," the man in the gray shirt said. "Prelim to the real hickey."

"Hickey?" Peter Ivanovich said. "What is 'hickey'?"

"The whole hickey-do," the man said. "The long banana. The real deal."

"I see," said Peter Ivanovich. "Is nonsense word like 'workaholic.' "

"Nah, that's a guy can't quit working even if it kills him. That's not nonsense, that's the American way."

"But, please, what has to do vis alcohol? Work-aholic. Is nonsense."

The man aimed at him a microphone with a fat puff of foam on the end of it. "You don't get it 'cause you're a foreigner. If you were American like me, you'd get it, capiche?"

"Where is monitor for me?"

"You don't have one," he said. "I'll be back here running the camera. They'll see you in New York, but all we have is an audio feed."

No sooner had the man in the gray shirt closed the door and pulled a shade over its square window than a voice came over the speakers covering his ears. "Mr. Kamenev?" A young woman's voice.

Peter Ivanovich looked around as if befuddled. He could not think of the reporter's name. He had written it down. Jane Something. "Am hearing voices? Russian folk tale vorns about when old men start hearing voice of beautiful girl. End is near."

Jane Something laughed. "It's a pleasure to meet you, even though you're all cockeyed on our screen. Oh, there you go." The man in the gray shirt had seated himself behind the camera and begun adjusting it. "This is just a practice run," Jane went on. "Do we need those earphones?"

The cameraman replied, "If you want him to hear you, you do."

"All right," Jane said. To Peter she said, "I'll ask you a few questions. Just answer naturally. I'll show the tape around, and if there's interest, one of our producers will fly out there and sub for whoever winds up anchoring the show."

"Very good," Peter Ivanovich said. In fact, he hated the situation. He needed an audience to respond to him. Being seen without seeing anyone himself was tricky. He didn't know quite how to play his age, either. He needed to seem old enough to be the age he claimed, yet vital enough to warrant a spot on the show. He said, "May I bring in daughter to sit here? Old Russians like to have *big* audience—at least one person."

She laughed again. "That's fine."

"I'll get her," the cameraman said. "Don't you move."

When Zhenya stepped into the booth, Peter Ivanovich put his hand over the microphone and whispered, "Listen and react!" He pulled back and eyed her. "Yes?"

< 2 4 5 >

Zhenya sighed and shrugged. Peter Ivanovich directed her to place her folding chair beside the eye of the camera. The man in the gray shirt gave Zhenya an earpiece she had to hold up to her ear.

"We're rolling," Jane Something said. "You look good on-screen, Mr. Kamenev."

"Call me please Peter," he said.

Her first question was about the span of his life and the events he had witnessed. It was an easy question, and he made the most of it, talking about his notoriety in Russia and in the United States, emphasizing the actors, singers, writers, scientists, and icons with whom he had associated, leading into a statement about being best known for his famous encounter with Stalin. He ended there, forcing her to ask him about it.

Zhenya was impressed but not surprised. She harbored no doubt that he would seduce the network. He quipped and quoted, dropped names, alluded to a dozen stories while telling one, and at the same time worked his audience, exaggerated his expressions, made fists, waved his arms in an explosive manner, rolled his eyes at the right moment. He was a born actor, storyteller, con man. And there was substance to what he had to say—part of the time, anyway. He controlled the first twenty minutes of the interview with no trouble.

Then the woman interviewing him changed the tone.

"One of my researchers has been talking to experts in . . . well . . . *you,* and she has come up with a few questions." Then her voice sounded distant, as if she had turned her head from the microphone. "Not this. The sheet Gloria prepared."

Zhenya let out a tiny gasp. G-L-O-R-I-A. The first question had to do with his name. She used the term "fraud" in asking it. Had Zhenya talked to Gloria about her father's name? She probably had, but she knew her father had an answer for this one. It would not be simple to undo him.

Peter Ivanovich smiled and let his head shake sadly. "Is question I answer thousand times. Comrade Lev Kamenev, the great man in revolution, is uncle of this man here you are talking to, Peter Ivanovich Kamenev. But how? How is Peter named Kamenev if Comrade Lev Kamenev is not really Kamenev? Answer—neither is

Kamenev. Is Party pseudonym. He takes it. I take it." He went on with his standard rap on this, pointing out that Stalin and Lenin were also pseudonyms, hinting that the man who had first made this accusation had ulterior motives. "As young man perhaps I like one beautiful woman or another too much. This man had for wife beautiful woman." He shrugged. "Once mud gets slinging is hard to stop."

In the pause that followed his response, Zhenya could hear a faint conversation between the interviewer and someone with her. Evidently, Peter Ivanovich could detect it as well. "Am sorry," he said, "but these words I am not hearing."

"Just a moment," the interviewer said.

Peter Ivanovich used the time to make faces of wonderment at the camera. Zhenya forced a smile, and he shot her a quick wink. She hoped desperately not to have the information she provided used against her father. Not like this.

The interviewer said, "Mr. Kamenev, my associate has compiled a list of dates and times that you've given . . . just a sec . . . I don't need all of that . . . Here's one I'm interested in. It has you meeting Tolstoy when you were a boy?"

Zhenya's heart dropped. They had her research, and it would destroy her father's chances.

Peter began the Tolstoy anecdote, but Jane Something did not let him finish. She had another dozen dates and names for him to verify. "Now your first encounter with Carl Jung and your first encounter with Mary Harris Jones: our research—based on your statements and published works—has those things happening the same month and year. It looks like they would have to be the same day. One in New York and one in London."

Peter Ivanovich felt a pressure at his temples, and the animal smell again attacked his nostrils. "Don't ask for exact days or years from old man," he said and mumbled a laugh. He thought he saw something in the little window in the door. It was the face of Comrade Stalin, displaying that grin of his as he had in the car window, the car still smelling of the vanished girl's sex. "Years are many," Peter Ivanovich said, glancing down at Zhenya, who looked worried and sad, and then back at the face in the glass, which of course was

< 2 4 7 >

his own face. He began to think clearly again with the rational, unexcited part of his mind.

"Russians are no good vis dates," he said with sudden enthusiasm, as if this were a treasured fact. "For example, what is most famous event in past one hundred years of Russian history? October Revolution. Now, most important, when does October Revolution take place?" He paused, looking about with bright, wide eyes. "*November!* Is true! Time for Russian people is like water below bridge—what you think is one place, you look again is somewhere else."

Jane Something laughed appreciatively at that, and Peter understood that he had won her over. He had pulled it off despite everything. Her assistant was trying to sabotage him, but he had answered these questions a million times. He had handled men like David Brinkley, who appreciated humor, and Walter Cronkite, who liked stories, and Ed Murrow, who liked to feel he had the inside scoop. He had been grilled by Mike Wallace and Walter Winchell, needled by—what was that man's name with the bad hair on *Nightline?* He had defended Gorbachev to that bow-tie reactionary George Will and put down Castro's jailing of dissidents to that giant bully Eldridge Cleaver. He had been told to gargle with razor blades by the cable zealot Joe Pyne and still managed to turn the sympathies of the audience in his own favor. He had outwitted William F. Buckley in an argument about the CIA and put Spiro Agnew in his place with a barrage of one-liners. Who did this assistant to Jane Nobody think she was talking to?

"Papa," Zhenya said. "She's asking you about McCarthyism."

"Of course," he said. "I am recalling day when Roy Cohn comes to my apartment in New York City. You want to hear, yes?"

"I'd like to," the voice in his headphones said, "but it looks to me like we're all out of time. You certainly have a definite take on the century."

"Most important, I must say this. People argue does history make man, or does man make history? I am here to tell you, is wrong question—"

"I'll make a note of that," she said. "Good-bye."

"One minute, please," he said, but the interview had ended.

Zhenya let her hand drop from her ear. Peter Ivanovich spoke directly to her. "History is like mountain air. You breathe it in and let it out. It tells you nothing, but visout it, you cannot live. Visout it, you lose whole hickey-do." He smiled at his daughter. "Not bad, eh?"

Zhenya leaned forward. There were no shadows in this odd booth, but his daughter's face seemed to come from the shadows anyway. She looked terrible, and he understood that he had made a mess of the interview. "What's a hickey-do?" she asked.

"You are out of center of things," Peter Ivanovich said, and he sounded, even to himself, angry. He softened his voice. "I must educate you now." He felt suddenly that he had failed his daughter in some important way. Something even larger than this miserable show with the television network. He was her father. He had left her mother for another woman. Left her, and then he had been inattentive. Why should that matter now? But what else could it be? He said, "Man must have woman, yes? Visout woman, what are we doing all the time? You understand, daughter? Is nature of man and woman."

Zhenya only stared at him. The door opened and caught her in the shoulder.

"Sorry 'bout that," the man in the gray shirt said. To Peter Ivanovich, he added, "She was one fanged bitch, wasn't she?"

"She tried to resist Russian charm," Peter Ivanovich said. "But no woman can." With the door to the booth open, the animal smell was gone, and he could breathe freely. But when he stood, his legs did not want to support him. He fell back against the stool and might have tumbled to the floor, but Zhenya caught his arm. "Standing too fast," Peter Ivanovich said. "Is nozzing."

He would not take the elevator, not another box. His daughter did not question his decision, although the stairs gave him trouble. He accepted Zhenya's hand and then held on to her arm. "Is good . . ." he began but could not catch his breath to continue and could not think of the word "exercise," although there it was, the word "exercise" appeared in his mind, but he could not get it to his lips.

Outside, he felt better, but the day had grown hot. How long

< 2 4 9 >

had they been in there? Did he leave his briefcase? No, his daughter had it. In the pawnshop, a tarnished silver picture frame dully reflected the sky. Beside it was the round face of a pocket watch that had turned yellow from the light, the numbers impossible to read. What ridiculous people Americans were. How could such an interview be adequate to determine whether he belonged in the small circle of those who understood the century?

"What?" Zhenya said. She squinted in the sun.

"Bastards," Peter Ivanovich said. "Am defeated by stupid cubicle and bad earphones."

Zhenya shook her head but did not speak. She shaded her face with her hand. She seemed about to speak troubled words, but Peter did not want to hear them. He pointed at the pocket watch in the window. "I am like watch in sun's reflection. Visout a face you can see, I am nozzing."

"They could see your face," Zhenya said. "You did okay. You were fine."

"Do not condescend to Peter Ivanovich Kamenev." He tapped the window with his fingernail. "I want this little clock. Is open, pawnshop?"

"Yes, but it's an antique. They want two hundred dollars for it."

"I don't want it, anyway," Peter said and turned from the window. "Hock shop is evil place." He stared at Zhenya. "I am seventy-six years old," he said. "Not one hundred."

She nodded. "Why have you lied about it?"

Peter Ivanovich knew he was actually eighty-three, and in his confusion was not aware which lie Zhenya was referring to. "No reason," Peter said. "Just for spotlight. You don't miss spotlight?"

It was Zhenya's turn to be confused. She was as famous in her field as she had ever been. He was probably referring to the notoriety she and Morgan had had as a couple back when Morgan had been the union president. Then she recalled something else. The reporters at their door, sheepish but wanting a story, and that officious man from social services. Zhenya had almost forgotten about that cruel little man. "No," she said, "I don't miss it."

"I do," Peter Ivanovich said. "What good is being ordinary person?"

"Let's get out of the heat."

"Not yet. Most important, must have clock for pocket. You have money to borrow for me?"

"I didn't bring my checkbook," Zhenya said. Something in her had hardened, and she felt nothing now but ready to go. "And it's not worth the money."

"Eighty-three years," Peter Ivanovich said. "What good has come from any of them?" There it was, the question that had dwelled at the edge of his consciousness. "I've lived too long," he said, slipping into Russian, "with nothing to show."

She could read Russian, but she could not speak it. She tried to tell him this, but he was not listening. "I'm sorry," she said. "I'm sorry they asked those questions."

He took no notice of her and continued speaking in Russian. "I am simply an old creature ready for the worms." He looked into his daughter's eyes and said, "I could have changed history. I could have been one of the most important men of the century. Instead I have nothing to show for my life." He gripped her arm and shook it. "Not one thing."

His daughter guided him into the car and spoke softly in reply, but she could not understand him and he could not hear her.

8

I have watched pots until they boiled. Ferreting out the truth demands boredom.

—Peter Ivanovich Kamenev

The rain began as they boarded the Honda. They each had a bouquet of flowers, but Morgan did not have calla lilies, which upset Zhenya. On this one day of the year, she depended on his constancy.

"They couldn't get any," he explained without being asked. He backed the car slowly out of the drive. On August 12 he always drove her car. She wanted to accuse him of forgetting, of ordering too late, but she knew there were things Morgan never forgot. He must have his reasons. It surprised her that he and she had picked the same flowers, tall blue hyacinths. Emma had her roses, taken from Mrs. East's long bed. Emma began the conversation. Conversation was required. She had a report on Mrs. East and Peter Ivanovich. He had moved out of the house and across the street. "She calls him Peter I., as in 'Now, Peter I., it's not even noon!' "

Zhenya and Morgan laughed. The rain began to fall a little harder.

"She makes him breakfast in bed and serves him on this fancy tray with short legs," Emma continued. "They're like a couple out of a black-and-white movie."

"If he's being treated like that, he'll never come back," Morgan said.

< 251 >

"You don't sound disappointed," Zhenya said. Her father refused to return until Danny Ford was gone. "Vulgar boy," her father had said, as if he wasn't a vulgar man. "Doesn't flush toilet," he told her. "For any bodily function." Zhenya believed the reasons were more complicated than her father could admit, that it had to do with Danny's vitality and strength. You had to envy it or deny the envy by focusing on his poor manners or obvious ignorance. Her father was terrified of Danny Ford. Zhenya didn't like him, but she could tolerate him—at least for a while. She had become increasingly convinced that he was Petey's genetic father, in part because of the interest he showed in Petey, and in part because of his complete absence of interest in Emma. He spent most of his time in the basement. His trial had been scheduled, which meant that before long, one way or the other, he would be gone.

It occurred to her that Morgan's greatest attraction as a young man might have been his vitality, his strong young body. Everyone had wanted to be his friend, and she had been no different. They rode in the Honda through the rain and talked about almost nothing. Petey was staying with Roy Oberland, who had taken the day off. A kind gesture, Zhenya thought. He, as well as anyone in the world, understood the importance of this day to them. They could not bring Petey. Too much would have to be explained, talked about. Outside, the city played its plotless movie on their windows. Another August 12. A kite wrapped around a high wire waved its white tail in the gusting shower. The billboard this year advertised the "Corvette of the 21st Century." The Honda smelled of flowers.

By the time they reached the cemetery, the rain had become a downpour. It was already one of the wettest summers of the century. No other cars were parked in the asphalt lot. They climbed out and stood by the Honda. Morgan held a frayed black umbrella. One of the ties was torn, and the canopy fluttered with each rush of wind. Zhenya's was the red of pomegranates, the canopy a deeper bell and of better material than Morgan's, more narrow and less likely to be inverted by the wind. Emma's was green around the rim and red with black spots in the middle—a watermelon. She'd had the same umbrella for years.

They each had their flowers, Zhenya's and Morgan's wrapped

< 2 5 3 >

in professional green paper. Emma had wrapped the roses in the brown paper of a grocery sack. The sack had red lettering facing the rose stems, but the writing showed through the damp paper. LUCKY'S MEAT, it read, the partial image of a steak just below the letters.

Zhenya had worn heels. If she left the path of round concrete stones, the heels would puncture the spongy ground. The mud would hobble her. The trees, animated by the wind and rain, made noises like those of a huge and impatient crowd. Water gathered about the base of each grassy mound. The back of the cemetery encompassed a small hill, the slope gentle, the grass there patchy. Streams cut through the wet earth. Some of the concrete disks on which they walked were already covered by a muddy film.

The cemetery had elaborate gravestones and small statues or busts, along with more modest marble stones. Many of the oldest graves bore only wooden crosses. The dead dated back to before the Civil War. Zhenya had wandered this yard often enough to know. But there would be no wandering today. The weather would not permit it.

A few of the grave sites had little fences around them and living flowers, like bedding, on either side of the mound. Zhenya forgot each year, until she began this walk, how dedicated some of the living were to the dead—watering, mowing, planting, trimming—as if to do so changed something about the dead or something about those who survived.

The stones that made up the path were large enough for only one foot at a time. Umbrella in one hand, flowers in the other, they walked single file on the concrete dots which followed the meander of graves. *Indian-style,* she had called it as a kid, and then she thought of that fairy tale where the boy and girl leave bread crumbs as a trail to make their way back to safety, only to discover that birds have eaten the crumbs and they are lost in a great wilderness.

When they reached the grave, they stood awkwardly beneath their umbrellas on the concrete circles, one foot on each, their legs spread like cowboys. Morgan was the first to step away, his good shoes sinking in the muck. Emma followed him to the tombstone. Zhenya stood on the two stones directly at the foot of Philip's grave.

Strange plastic flowers already lay upon it. They were painted and had glitter on them.

"They're from Sid." Emma had to yell to be heard over the rain. "I guess I told him about today."

Zhenya did not like hearing a boy's name spoken here. She wanted to begrudge him the flowers as well, but he'd had the sense to come and go without disturbing them. She couldn't be too angry, and it confirmed her suspicion that Emma was falling hard for him.

Morgan squatted before the marker. Chiseled into the stone were three lines:

PHILIP KAMENEV MORGAN
1977–1989
SON AND BROTHER

Zhenya looked up from the plastic flowers just long enough to identify the marker as the correct destination.

Morgan turned to her. "Should we just leave the flowers in the rain?" he called out. "It doesn't feel right." Without waiting for an answer, he knelt and pulled at the tall grass around the base of the grave marker. When he straightened, damp ovals colored the knees of his pants.

A flash of lightning caused their heads to turn. Zhenya felt a strange tingle on her neck that might have come from the electrical charge or might have been her imagination. She could see Morgan's lips twitch as he counted. Thunder rumbled low and then cracked open the air.

"Just around the corner," Morgan called out. He placed his bouquet on the grave. The rain immediately caused the paper to wilt and tear. It would make a mess. He squatted again and unwrapped the flowers with his free hand, picking at the stems to remove the disintegrating paper. Emma pulled the brown paper from her roses and placed them beside the hyacinths. Morgan walked back to Zhenya and extended his hand, offering to put hers next to the others. She shook her head and stepped from the concrete, her heels sinking into the mire. She took a few wobbly paces, then lifted her feet out of her shoes, leaving them where they had planted them-

< 2 5 5 >

selves. She walked in her stocking feet to the grave of her son. She had the wild impulse to leave her umbrella there over the flowers, but she recognized the desire for what it was—a bit of sentimental drama that would undermine the day. She placed her flowers on top of the others and hurried back, in the direction from which they had come.

If Morgan hadn't retrieved her shoes, she would have left them.

Adele Wurtz entered Roy Oberland's house as if she were entering the mansion of a war profiteer. "Any ghosts in this place?" she asked. She didn't own an umbrella. Her hair and shoulders and chest were damp.

Roy shook his head. "Not that I'm aware."

"Nice digs." She whistled through her teeth.

"It's all right, I guess." He had visited her house only once, after it had been vandalized. The desk jockey forwarded the news to them, and they swung by in the cruiser. Adele had not let Roy or the investigating officers inside. "It's nothing," she said of a broken window and a spray-painted cock and balls on a side wall. The house had the squat look of poverty about it, and the stained curtains showing in the front window suggested something worse. Unfair assumptions, Roy supposed, but not without some legitimacy.

"It didn't go as smooth as we'd planned," Adele said. She continued gawking as she spoke, and Roy understood that she was avoiding his eyes. Dread made itself evident in the narrow stems of his body, his wrists and ankles suddenly leaden and weak.

"What happened?" he asked.

"Can I get some water, partner?"

He hadn't often seen her in street clothes. She wore a man's checkered shirt and pants made of some cheap stretch material. Roy led her through the living room, where Petey sat on the floor watching afternoon cartoons. Roy had finally talked with Emma. He had watched from his high window until he saw her go out with the trash, and then he had run to the alley. He knew that about her, that she emptied the trash daily. It had always been her chore. He ran to her, put his arms around her, and told her the plan. "You'll do that?"

she said, and he assured her that he would. "Then I have to marry you?" she said. He didn't like the way she put it, but he said, "That was our agreement," as if they had actually discussed it and negotiated a deal. It did not matter how she felt now. They had years of feeling to fall back upon. Once they were finally together, she would love him as she always had. He was confident of that. It was what he had to believe. She had kissed him there in the alley by the barrels of trash, and he had volunteered to look after Petey on August 12.

The living room was empty except for the portable television and the table it sat upon. Roy had to call the boy's name twice to get his attention away from the set. "This is my partner, Officer Wurtz," he said. "This is Petey. He lives next door."

"I know who he is," Adele said. Roy didn't like the way she said it. He wondered how much she knew. Petey waved to her. "Yeah," she said. Ponderously, she bent over and went to one knee. "Good to meet you, Mr. Petey Boy."

"This is not the real Bugs," he said, pointing at the screen. "It's when he's a baby."

"How 'bout that. Should we let them get away with that?" she asked, but Petey had already turned back to the cartoons. Adele pushed against her knee to get back up. "She didn't leave you much," she said to Roy. "Sitting-down-wise."

"Let's go into the kitchen," Roy said. "There are chairs." Something had gone terribly wrong. Or she was playing him, working to make him uneasy. He had promised to help her, once he was promoted, to be her protector, her friend in the department.

He let the water run awhile to get cool, filled a glass for her, then added ice anyway. "I've got sodas. Beer if you prefer," he said.

She sat at the oak table—a gift from his father and one of the few pieces of furniture Diana hadn't taken. His father had found the top in a used furniture place and built a base to go with it. That made it Roy's.

"Water's a good start," she said, then tipped the glass up and drank.

He hoped the absence of her typical chatter had to do with being out of uniform, with being inside his house. He had changed from denim shorts to slacks in anticipation of her arrival. Every conversa-

< 2 5 7 >

tion with Adele was some kind of battle, and he wanted to have the necessary armor.

"Headcase showed," she said, wiping her mouth. "That's the good news."

Adele had decided that Roy should stay out of it, take the day off. He picked August 12 so it would be him and not Danny Ford looking after Petey. "Danny's competent," Emma had said. To which Roy had replied, "That's hardly the point."

Adele had arrived at the station in the early a.m. Louis Headkin, her old partner, came in under the pretense of checking out a weekend job. The department used retired officers to work traffic at ball games and concerts. He was there too early to see the duty officer, but Headcase was the kind of guy who liked to hang around and talk. It wasn't suspicious. The evidence officer was a pal of his who went by Turk. The plan called for Headcase to engage Turk in a conversation, and Adele would join them under the pretense of gabbing with her old partner. However, Headcase would be in the process of running Adele down, hinting at damning information about her fitness for duty.

Headcase would ask Adele to watch the evidence room for a moment while he and Turk did some business. If Headcase kept trashing her, no one would think they were in it together. Every cop on the force knew he hated Adele. What he would tell Turk—that he had evidence Adele was lesbian—was the kind of rumor he wanted to spread. It deflected the gossip about his having sex with her. She promised to quash the old stories and leave him alone if he helped. She hadn't explained what she was doing, just that she needed a couple of minutes alone in the evidence room. She had planned to take the gun that tied Danny Ford to the shooting and tuck it into her pants. Without the gun, he would be offered a plea bargain. If he had a competent attorney, he would turn it down and walk.

"Headcase did his part," Adele said. "I got the gun. It's in my car. You're going to have to dispose of it. I'm not doing anything else. I've already . . . fuck."

"I know that. We agreed to that."

"I got the gun and was hustling back to the evidence desk, but

I bumped into one of the tables. Knocked shit all over the place. Turk wanted to know what the hell I was doing back there. I had to stay until Lutz showed up and gave me the third degree. Me with the goddamn gun in my pants the whole time. If I could have put it back, I would have." She gave a quick hoarse shout, and Roy thought she might burst into tears. She covered her eyes and worked to control her breathing. "When the gun comes up missing, I'm screwed. They *hate* me. Won't cut me slack, won't give me benefit of the doubt. All I can hope is Turk tries to cover his own ass for letting somebody man his desk—a fucking lesbian at that, according to rumor—and he tries to make it look like he'd already released the gun to somebody else. He could make a paper trail."

Roy leaned back in his chair. The sheer idiocy of what they had attempted suddenly reared up on its hind legs and stared at him. They had behaved like fools. He felt a spiraling in his stomach and a lightness in his head. He recalled the afternoon exactly a decade earlier. Morgan had followed the gurney out of the house and fallen to his knees in the grass. The sound that had come from him had not been a human sound but one like the clanking of metal. Roy could see Morgan attempting to stand and falling again.

"It's my fault," Roy said. It was what he should have said long ago.

"If I wasn't so fucking fat, I'd of been in and out, no trouble."

"Here's what you do," Roy said. "You go in tomorrow and tell them I took the gun, and you were trying to put it back. Tell them you came here and begged me to do it, but I wouldn't. You'll get some crap for not handing it over according to procedure and writing me up. You may even get a suspension, but nothing worse than that. Protecting your partner carries a lot of weight."

"Won't work," she said. "They won't believe me, and if they did, you'd get hammered."

He nodded. "I'll turn in my resignation."

"The fuck you will. What are you thinking?"

"They'll take that as punishment enough. They *do* like me. Evidence gets misplaced sometimes. They'll probably use your bumping the table to account for the fuck-up—send the D.A. some similar gun and then send paperwork to point out the discrepancy in

< 2 5 9 >

the weapons. You'll get written up, probation maybe. And a new partner."

They sat for a while in the kitchen without talking. The rain got harder and the room turned gray. His life was bleaching out, Roy thought, turning a new, fainter color.

"I fucked it up," Adele said.

"I shouldn't have gotten you involved. This is my fault," Roy said. "I did this." He said it again. "I did this."

She raised one of her great arms and pointed. "That boy out there is what it's about, am I right?"

Roy nodded before he could think better of it. "He's a part of it."

"Ford's the boy's father or something?"

"Something like that," Roy said.

"Get rid of the fucking gun," she said. "Do it now. You got any friends? It might be better if you didn't know what happened to it."

He nodded. "I have a plan. It's all worked out."

"You don't need a plan, you just need to do it. Come to my car and get the damn thing." She puffed up her big cheeks and blew, but she didn't get up. "What a goddamn mess. You know it's not just Ford who's going to get off. The kids that did the shooting are going to walk, too."

"I can't help that," Roy said.

"Sooner or later one of them will shoot somebody else. You prepared for that? It doesn't mean shit to me, but—"

"But you've been thinking about it anyway."

"Fuck, partner. Since this morning I've been doing nothing but thinking. And eating. It'd probably help save my ass if I lost some weight. You think?"

Roy knew that it would. "Wouldn't hurt." Neither was ready to get up. Roy checked his watch. The day had only just begun. If he were not a cop, then what would he be? Just some guy with a job. But he didn't feel as bad as he would have expected. He would be the guy married to Emma, he reminded himself. He would be the guy who was the father of Petey. "So, Adele, you want to tell me something?"

"No point in keeping secrets now," she said.

"Why this act?"

"What act?" Her mouth contorted into the shape of a smile, but her face showed neither pleasure nor humor.

"This act," he said. "Your ongoing act."

Adele held the smile awhile, then took another drink of water. "You know what my sister does in Dallas? A cashier at an all-night quickie-mart kinda place. Minimum wage, no benefits. Got a boy been taken away from her and put in a foster home. She may or may not turn tricks. Her ex is on the run in Mexico or some damn place for holding up a clothing store. What kind of idiot holds up a clothing store? His gun went off and a woman took a bullet in the knee. She gets to walk for the rest of her life like a puppet on a string. And there's my brother. Got kicked out of the marines. Something about gambling. Don't know where he is or what he's doing. Dead, for all I know."

"What are you telling me?"

"That you don't know *shit*. I've come a lot further than you, put it that way. If I can keep my badge after this shit, I'm still a step ahead of where I got any right being. And I got here by taking a bite out of the world before it could take a bite out of me. You've had the whole deal handed to you, so you wonder why I'm always trying to swipe a little here and there. *Nothing* was handed to me."

Petey appeared behind Adele. "Can I have a cut-up apple?" he asked.

"Sure," Roy said. "I'll bring it in to you."

"On a silver platter," Adele said to the boy. She shook her head as the child ran back to the television. "No way he's Ford's kid." She kept staring at the empty doorway. "Families never suspect one of their own, do they? Can't ever see the big picture." She gave Roy a knowing look, studied him, then looked down and patted her thighs. Her shoes were police issue. "Come get this weapon," she said softly, and then she pushed herself upright. "The boy can wait for his apple." Lightning flashed outside the window and they both paused, waiting for the crash that had to follow.

The dinner was for eight. Zhenya and Emma fried chicken. Morgan peeled and diced a bag of potatoes, then washed a head of let-

< 261 >

tuce. Petey had come home from next door, and he helped Danny
Ford bathe the dog in the downstairs tub. Zhenya overheard them
talking.

Petey said, "If we were all dogs and we didn't have cars, we could
sleep all day like Prince. I wish we were dogs."

Danny said, "Sleep. Right. What about toys?"

"Dogs have toys. Haven't you ever heard of *dog* toys?"

"Kinda boring, though," Danny said. "Chew stuff."

Zhenya watched the two of them climb the stairs to clean up
afterward. For some reason Danny didn't want to hold Petey's hand,
but he waited for him on each step. They climbed the stairs together.
It was easier to think of them as brothers than father and son, but it
was not hard to think they were related. "Sometimes he doesn't seem
so bad," she said to Morgan.

"Danny?" Morgan said. "He's a good guy. Petey likes him."

Emma had her hands full of raw chicken. "One of the aides at the
Montessori took me aside yesterday when I picked Petey up. She
said Petey wanted to name one of the new turtles 'Motherfucker.' "

"I'll talk to Danny," Morgan said quickly. "He has some bad
habits."

Zhenya wondered again why she had refused to listen to Morgan
when he defended Danny, trusting her impression and Roy Oberland's official story instead of Morgan's long acquaintance. Why
had she been so certain of the boy's guilt and Morgan's mistake?
Even if Danny was not Petey's father, Morgan had acted correctly
in getting him out of jail. "How old is he?" she asked.

"I don't know," Morgan said. "Twenty-two, twenty-three."

"He just turned twenty-three," Emma said.

Perhaps Morgan had needed the distraction, Zhenya thought,
a project, like her research, something to fill the hours and at the
same time at least *feel* meaningful. They had eaten their traditional
lunch at the diner, come home and watched *The Philadelphia Story*.
The morning rain had turned into a classic midwestern storm.
Twice, the electricity went out. It would rain all day and night. Some
of the streets would flood. If it kept raining this hard, one or two
people would die. They would drive a car into a flooded underpass
or try to pass a diesel on the interstate and spin out of control.

Storms like this made demands, and those demands were always met.

Petey came down the stairs a few minutes later in his best clothes—long pants, a shirt, and clip-on tie. He even had on a belt. Danny Ford had dressed him. "You look handsome," Zhenya said.

Petey nodded. "I know." He sounded resigned and world-weary, his beauty a fact he could do nothing but bear.

By the time Danny had dressed himself and emerged from the basement, Petey had been set before the television. Zhenya and Emma had carried the plate of chicken to the table and plopped down in chairs to commiserate about the ventilation in the kitchen. Morgan had already set out the salad and bowl of mashed potatoes. A simple, traditional meal. Morgan went to the front door, thinking he had heard a knock. The doorbell often failed to work, especially during storms. Danny walked into the room with his hands in the rear pockets of his pants—jeans, but clean and with creases where he had attempted to press them. He had showered, and his hair was wet and still showed the rakes of his comb. He wore a white shirt with a collar and buttons. He didn't have a tie, but he had put on a sweater vest. It was too small for him and too hot for anyone this time of year and *ugly*, but Zhenya understood the gesture and it touched her. He took a seat at the far end of the table just as Morgan returned. "False alarm," Morgan said. "Nobody here yet." He seated himself next to Danny. "Any minute now," Morgan said.

The four of them sat at the table. The sun, as it set, peeked through the clouds, illuminating the puffy folds from below, lighting the rain as it fell, casting shadows that stretched across the full length of the dining room floor.

Peter Ivanovich insisted on being driven. He did not really want to go to the dinner. He objected to the ceremony, but he did not want to disappoint Emma. He had come to Hayden to see her, but the stupid CBS interview had soured him on making the effort. And that hoodlum living in the house had just about driven him mad. But Emma needed him today, and he was determined to rise to the occasion.

< 263 >

Adriana had given him an umbrella, but he didn't know what he'd done with it. He pulled a plastic raincoat over his head and walked into her yard and around to the side of the house, where she waited in the idling car. Forest Avenue was now completely torn up. They had to drive around the park to get to his daughter's house.

"Where is your umbrella?" Adriana asked as he climbed in the car.

"I am stupid man," he said. "Is impossible for stupid man to hold on to umbrella."

She pulled into the street and said, "Shape up now."

"I will," he said. "Not to worry." He smiled at her briefly. "See, already charm is starting."

They circled the park and entered Zhenya and Morgan's house through the back. Peter would not let Adriana take her umbrella. "We huddle," he said. "Get me in mood for more charm." They crowded together beneath the plastic raincoat. Peter did not like to walk in the rain as he once had, but he still loved the smell of it, and in this weather he could enjoy its cool release from the long summer. But he worried about falling. A broken hip could be the beginning of the end. They called out as they entered the house. He let his voice sound light and good-natured as he shouted. Hurrying through the rain together had made Adriana giddy, and she patted his elbow. When he turned to her, she kissed him on the lips.

"I am taking you carnally right here," he said, which made her laugh. Yes, he would be able to do this. The interview had been a slip, an exception, a freak occurrence. He wore the same jacket and tie that he had that day and perhaps the same pants, he couldn't tell. They matched, anyway, or close to it. At one time, he had worn clothing this fine all the time. He called out again. When no one answered, he said, "Cars are here. Where are people?"

They began to search the house. It did not take long. They heard the sound of television voices in the living room, and so it surprised them to find all of the adults sitting around the table in the dining room. Peter and Adriana paused, staring at Morgan and Zhenya and Emma and Danny Ford, sitting in the semidark, sitting so quietly that, if they had been a different sort of family, one might have thought they were praying. The odd angle of light made the scene eerie.

"We are late?" Peter asked. He switched on the light, and they came to life, each of them rising from the table as if he had hit a battery switch that made the toys begin their dance.

Roy Oberland appeared at the new doors that Morgan had installed. A crew of men had taken two days to do it. Zhenya could not understand why Morgan had insisted on these doors, but it was so rare for him to want something new, she had not tried to stop him. She opened them now for Roy. He wore a hooded raincoat and seemed comfortable in the shower. Forest Avenue was still closed for paving, and yellow lights blinked through the rain. Zhenya came and went by the rear door, and she had not really taken in the new doors until now, the blinking lights reflecting in the old glass. "My God," she said, realizing that they were beautiful.

Roy took this the wrong way. "Morgan and Emma invited me," he said. "I watched Petey for them—for all of you—this morning."

"No," Zhenya said and patted his arm to apologize. "These doors. I hadn't really looked at them before. They change the way you enter the house, don't they?"

Roy examined them as he stepped inside. "You should add metal security doors. One tap and a burglar's through this glass."

Zhenya merely rocked her head in reply. It would be nice to think he did not always have to be a policeman. Beneath his raincoat, he wore a wide gold tie and short-sleeved shirt. He had a paper sack with him. "You didn't need to bring anything," she said. "Dinner is all ready, and there's plenty of wine."

"This is for later." He wanted to put it someplace out of the way. Zhenya took him into what was once her study and was recently her father's room and now was neither. The bed was unmade and still smelled of her father. Socks and papers lay about the floor. The clutter annoyed her, but she reminded herself that this room no longer had anything to do with her. She opened the closet door, but Roy declined to hand her the package. He stepped past her and stuffed it up high, on the shelf with their winter sweaters. The floor of the closet was layered in her father's dirty clothes. It was hard to believe he had moved out. "This could use some airing," she said, but Roy

< 265 >

pushed the closet door shut. "When do we get to open the sack and see the surprise?" she asked.

Roy put his finger to his lips. "Don't tell anyone, okay? Is Ford at this thing?"

She nodded, whispered, "He's dressed like a schoolboy."

Roy said, "I suppose there was no way around it."

Zhenya did not like the presumption. He had no business commenting on the guest list. "I forget that you arrested him," she said. His eyes had taken on a kind of hardness. "Is it something more than that?"

"I don't like him," he said and looked around the room, as if for a place to tuck himself away. "But I'll be good. I promise."

Emma pushed open the study door. "We're hungry," she said. She looked Roy over and then turned away. "Come on."

Zhenya was happy with the look of the table. The cool rain permitted them to light candles. She didn't like candles on hot nights. It didn't matter that they put out very little heat, they oppressed her. And so she welcomed the rain. While the chicken and mashed potatoes circulated the table, her father raised his wineglass. "First a toast—"

Morgan cut him off. "We don't have toasts today."

"Must have toast," Peter Ivanovich said, making wide eyes at the others.

"No," Morgan said. "There will be no toasts."

Zhenya appreciated Morgan's firmness. There should not be toasts on August 12.

A few moments later Morgan lifted his head and said, "Where's Prince?" The dog could no longer control her bowel movements and could not raise herself up long enough to keep the mess out of her fur.

"The kitchen," Emma told him. "You stepped over him a dozen times."

"Is older than me, Prince dog," Peter Ivanovich said. "And better cared for."

Adriana East swatted his shoulder. She made her own teasing

comment, which permitted Emma to say that she had heard about Peter I. having breakfast in bed. The uneasy banter sparked and then faltered until Peter Ivanovich stepped in to talk about a woman who had taken care of him in Russia during a winter when people were dying of influenza. He would get them through the meal. He had moved out of the house, so there was no reason Zhenya should feel now that she had to stay. She had considered leaving a dozen times, but she had decided not to think about it until after August 12.

"I remember old joke I hear from Winston Churchill," Peter Ivanovich was saying now. Zhenya had missed a transition, or perhaps there had been none. "Was big dinner party in London after war, and many butlers are running in and out. Nozzing on earth like English butler." Even when he paused to drink, he eyed them over his glass and raised his bushy brows to keep their attention. It impressed her. No matter the antagonisms within the group, he could keep the conversation alive. In this small and consequential matter, her father was a genius.

Pain had become the norm, but Prince could still imagine the cessation of pain, which is to say she had an intuition of death. She lay in her favorite place, the doorway to the kitchen, a location she originally favored for its simultaneous view of the kitchen and dining room and, through the French doors, a piece of the yard. When she lay here, people were constantly coming to her, speaking to her, moving their bodies over hers. She no longer recalled or considered the reasons for her attachment to this spot. It was simply hers, and it possessed the comfort of the familiar, and she lay there, her breathing loud and rattling and painful.

Because she could no longer walk, she had dreams of nothing else. Simpler dreams than those she was accustomed to, dreams of walking on a leash and without one, dreams of running, dreams of her legs paddling in cold water—dreams of locomotion. She longed now for such a dream, but she could not yet sleep. Pain, or something like pain, kept her awake.

A door opened and closed, a cue for her to trot down the hall,

< 2 6 7 >

a cue so powerful that she felt the muscles in her legs moving, although her actual legs did nothing. Morgan entered the kitchen. She recognized his smell before she saw him. He knelt beside her. She still longed for touch, and he touched her gently. She never, in all her life, questioned her desire to be stroked and spoken to softly. She lifted her head to him, but she could not hold it aloft. He caught her, held her, then lay her head back on the pad gently. She fell asleep this way and dreamed of her body in motion. No other creature existed in the dream. She did not, anymore, mourn for the boy she had lost. At long last she had been healed of that wound by the only thing that could cure it—the cancer that would kill her.

It was while Morgan and Roy played Candyland with Petey that Morgan asked about their task for the evening. Roy knew the ritual well, knew that the last rite involved doing something for others. A few days earlier, he had told Morgan he had something in mind for them. "That's a relief," Morgan had said, "because I've been drawing blanks."

Roy had taken Petey with him to turn in his resignation. It had been his last chance to show his son the police station. He took the boy on a full tour, introducing him to everybody, letting him wear a hat and hold a nightstick before putting the sealed envelope on the captain's desk. Then he drove to a gas station, filled his tank, and called Danny Ford's lawyer from a pay phone. "It's not important who I am," he said. "But you should know that the police have lost the weapon connecting Danny Ford to any crime." He hung up.

He had not enjoyed the meal and had said nothing the whole time. He didn't like breaking bread with Danny Ford, hated the way they treated him as family. Roy thought he could judge no one, but Danny Ford remained the exception. More than ever now because Roy had ensured his freedom. Ford had done nothing during the meal but eat, his head down. He had not made eye contact with Roy. Perhaps it had been a conscious gesture. Not for Roy, but out of respect for the family who had taken him in.

Ford disappeared after dessert, and Roy began to feel better. It wasn't hard to imagine that the guy was gone for good. He felt the urge to tell them all that he and Emma were getting married, but she didn't want him to. Not on this day. He would respect that.

"So it's about that time," Morgan said, moving his game piece one step less than called for to avoid getting a shortcut that would put him ahead of Petey. "You said you had our project for the night. We always do—"

"I have something for you," Roy said.

Zhenya seemed to understand what they were talking about, although she couldn't have overheard them. She left the couch and settled on the floor beside the game board. "Let me guess," she said. "Emma says your place is barren. We're moving furniture. I hope it's already stacked up inside. This rain is dreadful."

"I have the weapon your partner got caught with." Roy said this softly, but both Morgan and Zhenya turned to be certain Petey had not understood. "It sort of fell into my hands. I'll explain it all some other time. Without the gun, they can't convict Ford."

"What are you saying?" Morgan asked.

"I'm giving it to you. It's up to you to make it disappear." Roy turned over his card and moved his player. Then he said, "Don't let Ford know. He could use it against me somehow. I don't trust him. And I want you to keep Emma out of it. She has to stay here. I know you usually do this with her, but I think it's best if it's just the two of you."

"What are we supposed to do?" Zhenya said.

"There's no going back now," Roy said. "I'm trusting you with this. It has to vanish. You have to make it disappear."

They parked the Honda at the edge of the dump and watched the rain in the headlights. Morgan was wet from unlocking and opening the gate. The rain was not cold and felt good in small doses. The wind had died, just water falling from the sky. It occurred to him that he had never before been to the dump with his wife. It amazed him to realize this.

"What do we do?" she asked.

< 269 >

"Hike out a ways. Dig a hole. Fairly deep one if we can manage it. Bury it. Go home."

The gun was in a backpack on the floorboard at Zhenya's feet, as was a flashlight. The handle of the shovel lay between the bucket seats, the blade rested in the back.

Morgan wrestled the shovel from the car after climbing out. Zhenya stood beneath her umbrella, holding the flashlight, the backpack slung over her shoulder. Morgan declined the umbrella. He was going to get wet. One could not dig a hole and hold on to an umbrella. He pointed, and they began the trek over the uneven ground. Zhenya had thought to borrow running shoes from Emma. They were too big for her, and she wore two pairs of her daughter's white athletic socks to compensate. The umbrella kept her dry. Without wind, the rain was easy enough to keep off her head and body, but the ground was riddled with puddles she could not jump, and the shoes got wet. They had not changed their clothes, and this seemed foolish now. They had felt such an urgency to leave, to get the gun out of the house, but they could have changed their clothes.

Morgan asked for the flashlight. He should have brought one of his own. She didn't want to relinquish it, aiming the beam in the general direction he was facing. "How far out are we going?" she asked him.

"The farther the better," he said. "To be safe." He didn't know what kind of inquiry would follow, but he was certain that he could make the gun disappear. He knew this place as well as anyone possibly could. No one would find it. He was even happy for the rain, which would wash away evidence of digging. He wished he could bury it right where Danny had thrown it that morning. It seemed like a long time ago. He would like to bury it there and pretend he had never retrieved it.

By the light of her narrow beam, Zhenya navigated for them. She did not like stepping on garbage, but she preferred it to sloshing through puddles covering hidden hazards. A scattering of window glass sparkled in her light. Morgan came here a dozen times a week, she thought. This place was to him what the university was to her. What an odd thought. The light revealed a flattened can of soup and the plastic head of Disney's Pinocchio, his long nose smeared with mud. Just beyond it lay a sopping pile of sun-bleached papers. She hated the spongy feel of the terrain, the filthy water, the things projecting up from the ground that could tear into her or rip her clothing. "This is hellish," she said, turning to Morgan, but he was not there. She felt an immediate terror. "Morgan!"

"I'm back here," he said, and she shone the light on him. He lifted the hand with the shovel to block his eyes. His clothes were plastered to his skin. "I can't see what I'm doing by your light." He had to yell to be heard over the rain. "I do better in the dark."

"I'll wait for you," she said. She aimed the light at his feet, then moved it forward as he walked, delineating a path for him. "Watch that metal thing. Don't step on it."

"I see it." It was the fender from a car older than Morgan, shaped like a wing. It had once been a beautiful piece of metal, he thought. It had no business out here. It ought to be in a junkyard, where someday, maybe, someone would come looking for just such a fender. Zhenya seemed to want him to step right through it. He wished she would pay attention to where *he* wanted to go, but it was his own fault for forgetting a flashlight.

"Look at that," Zhenya said. Her light hit a scatter of books. Hardbacks, some opened, some closed, raindrops bouncing off them. "Why would anyone—" she began.

"I can't see," Morgan said. "Either shine it for me or don't."

"Sorry," she said.

He slipped in some kind of muck and threw down the end of the shovel to catch himself. When he tried to pull his foot from the stuff, it didn't want to let him go. He planted the shovel and pushed against it, the sludge making a kissing sound as he tugged his foot free of it. His shoe oozed, but it stayed on. He had been stupid not to change into his work clothes. Here they were dressed for churchgoing and tromping through this crap in the pouring rain, but they had fled the house. Seeing the gun had made them flee. He could not tell what he had stepped in, but bits of white, like eggshell, clung to his shoe. The light moved forward into a mess of wire or fence. He didn't want to step there, but Zhenya steadied the beam upon it, as if insisting.

< 2 7 1 >

"Turn that off, will you? It's not that dark. I can see better without it." The rain had let up a little, and the moon peeked through the clouds.

"I am *not* turning this off," she said.

"Then shine it somewhere else. You've got me walking through barbwire."

"If you'd keep up with me, this wouldn't be a problem."

"Just turn around and scout out a place where we can dig." He had to stand motionless while his eyes adjusted again to the dark. Without the light, the terrain became an uneven field of shapes—simple mounds and complicated geometric figures, stick limbs and partial bodies, junk that flapped with the rain, sharp angles of garbage, voluptuous curves of it. His eyes were not going to adjust. Either it had gotten darker or he had been following the indirect glow of Zhenya's lamp all along.

"I give up," he said. "Shine it around here so I can walk."

"All right," she said. *"Christ."* While her husband plodded toward her, she felt the ocean of trash about her change shape, grow close, approach her in some way. She wanted to check with the light to be certain nothing was moving, but she would not let herself give in to emotional hallucination. It could be resisted by the power of her will, and she set herself to that task, keeping the light steadily scanning the area at her husband's feet. Why would he refuse to take the umbrella from the car? What kind of logic was that? This place felt to her like the lair of an exhibitionist, or the life's work of some quixotic, talentless artist. She guided her husband through a mound of splintered lumber that had once been a cheap couch, over a pile of old windshield wipers, and onto the flat cardboard of a packing box, which sank as he stepped on it and slipped to one knee. He quickly righted himself.

"I'm all right," he said, close to her now.

Between them lay a rusted and bare box spring, the coils dripping rain.

"How'd you get over there?" he asked.

"I don't know," she said.

Morgan tried to pull the bedspring out of his way, but it was partially buried and wouldn't budge. He stepped cautiously onto the wire hatching at the top but shook his head. "I'm going to have to back up. Or can you come around?"

"No," she said. "I don't want to try."

Morgan tugged at the cardboard box he had crossed earlier. He lay the cardboard over the box spring. On his hands and knees, he traversed the bed. When Zhenya offered her hand, he took it. "We're about as stupid as two people can be," he said, coming to his feet. He stood beside her, his very skin seeming to swell with water, his clothing binding him now, having twisted about him as he crawled. He pulled at his pants and shirt to straighten them, while Zhenya watched, still dry herself, except for her feet and the spatters on her stockings and the hem of her dress.

When Morgan finished wrestling with his clothes, she said, "Let's put it here somewhere and leave."

"We're going to bury it," Morgan said.

"Fine, but do it here."

He scouted with his shovel, clanking against metal in one spot, against something as strong as metal elsewhere—he couldn't determine what it was. One of his shoes began to sink in ooze again, so he repositioned himself and planted the shovel there. The first few inches of it was household garbage, then he struck a layer of folded cardboard cartons. Carriers for six-packs of beer. The top ones were soaked. His shovel pierced them easily. The lower ones he had to slide the shovel beneath, a few at a time, then fling out of the way. A layer of mud came next, sediment from the Caterpillar's work. He shoveled through this, appreciative of actual dirt to dig in, widening the hole to give himself room to work. He had been fatigued and laden with dread when he started digging, but the work itself made him energetic. He felt the body's desire to heal itself in exertion. An oil can appeared in the mud and he tossed it out, then a tortured steel filament like the eating utensil of a foreign, giant people.

It was not in anything he uncovered that he became overcome by emotion, not in the specific remains of bottles, cloth, and plastic— none of these things made the digging man cry. It was not the physical act of throwing down the blade into the mire and pulling out its load, not the strain in the gut, the fire in the shoulders—it was no single thing that made him cry, but he began to nonetheless.

< 2 7 3 >

"Stop it," Zhenya said. "That's deep enough. Stop it." The hole was two or three feet deep and large enough for him to stand in. She could see that he was crying, and it infuriated her. "You stop it," she said angrily. "Stop digging." The flashlight lit up the hole, his shovel still moving. "Stop crying," she screamed at him. "I know what you're doing! I'll leave you out here if you don't stop it."

But he would not stop until she flicked off the light and the darkness that had been crowding in on them all along made them still.

Morgan fell to one knee. Grasping at the edge of the hole, he found her ankle. He leaned his head against her legs. She bent down, lifting her skirt and tucking it around her legs to keep it out of the filth. She squatted and pulled his head to her lap. She held the umbrella over them in the dark. "It's deep enough," she said softly. "We've done what we had to do."

Morgan's sobbing slowed and finally stopped. Zhenya flicked on the light and gave him her hand. He climbed from the hole. From her shoulder, she took the backpack that held the gun. It was dry and clean. She unzipped it and held it upside down. The gun slid out and fell into the hole.

Morgan shoveled the dirt and cardboard and glass on top of it. He covered it up. It didn't take long. He took Zhenya's hand. His was grimy, hers had been clean. They hiked back through the sea of discarded things, their clothes a parody of finery now. The rain had saturated Morgan's dress pants and shirt, and the cuffs of his pants had turned brown. His shoes were ruined, the soles separating with every sloshing step, forcing him to raise one foot high to keep the sole from folding backward, giving his gait the look of injury. Zhenya kept the umbrella carefully erect, her arm aching, the black dress bearing the single stain of her husband's grime, a muddy shape against the black fabric, obscenely located, as if it had leaked out of her.

In the driveway, Morgan asked if she wanted to share a shower.

Zhenya hesitated, although she had no interest in sex right now. That was what he was really asking, wasn't it? But she knew, too, that he did not think of it that way. Sex was two steps beyond what he was thinking. He was imagining warm water and being held. "No, I don't think so," she said. Then she said, "Thank you." The high windows in their house were dark, but all of the lights downstairs appeared to be on. "You should take your shoes off before you go in."

"I don't want to," he said. "I'll clean it up later." He got out of the car and walked ahead of her to the house, leaving a trail through the hall and up the stairs. Well, she thought, hanging her umbrella by the back door, it's his house, too. Which reminded her of the doors. She wished they'd had doors like those all along. Doors like those made a difference in a house. Her father stood in the kitchen before the open refrigerator. "I thought you'd be across the street," she said.

"Why you don't keep vodka in freezer?" His head jerked back when he took in her appearance. "You go somewhere? Is car trouble?"

"A walk in the rain," she said.

"Most romantic," Peter said. "Adriana goes home too early. I sleep here tonight. Make your father a drink, yes?"

The vodka bottle was empty. They were out of hard liquor. The refrigerator light revealed aluminum-foiled mounds. Emma was good at putting away leftovers and cleaning. Zhenya noted that the dishes were done as well. She offered her father a beer.

"Open please," he said.

She twisted off the cap and stepped over Prince to go into the dining room and search for wine. Emma had wiped the table clean. Someone had finished off the wine. Television lit the living room, and through the doorway, she saw Petey sleeping on the couch, his head in Emma's lap. Emma was sitting in the shadows, at a funny angle. Zhenya did not disturb them. She returned instead to the kitchen to get herself a beer. She would rather have gin or wine, but beer would have to do.

Her father had seated himself at the kitchen table and appeared to be reading the label on his beer bottle. He pointed at the doorway. "Interesting, yes?"

She had not yet crossed the threshold, and she thought at first that he was pointing at her. She turned, looking again at the dark

< 2 7 5 >

dining room and beyond that to the fragment of dimly lit living room. She could just make out Petey's white socks in the gloom. "What do you mean?"

"I am always meaning to ask," he said, speaking softly. "Who is father of namesake?" He said it as if it had only just occurred to him to wonder.

She again stepped over the dog and into the kitchen. "We don't know," she said. "I've asked, and she has made it clear she doesn't want to talk about it." She had not asked now in a long time. As long as Danny Ford was the prime suspect, she would not ask again. "Where's your beer?"

"Is gone. American beer is invisible. Is nozzing like real beer."

"I'll get you another one." She took a bottle of beer from the refrigerator for her father and one for herself, too. While she was bent over to fetch it, she heard the dog's lungs rattling behind her, and she realized that she had been hearing the dog's tortured breathing all afternoon. It had been so consistent that she had tuned it out, as she did the high electronic sear of appliances, the whir of fans, the ticking of clocks, the fall of rain. She placed the bottles of beer on the kitchen table and knelt beside the dog, who began to pant. It occurred to her that this was something she could do for Morgan. She could have Prince put to sleep. She would do it in the morning. This desire to offer Morgan something had been there, too, for a long time, so long she had learned to ignore it. Her heart rocked a bit inside her chest, as she wondered at all the other things that must be lurking about, patiently awaiting her attention.

While she studied Prince, a sallow pool of liquid appeared beneath the dog, and a stream began to spread across the floor. Zhenya retrieved paper towels. "It's all right, girl," she said softly. "It's almost over." She cleaned up the mess on the floor, but the dog needed to be bathed yet again. She recalled taking Prince into the shower stall one time, the two of them showering together. Prince had been a much smaller dog then, and she had been immeasurably younger herself. The tub would do. She liked the idea of doing this. She would bathe the dog in warm water and dry her with a towel.

Zhenya slid her arms beneath Prince. She weighed so little now. Zhenya carefully stood. Lifting Prince reminded her of something, but she could not immediately say what and did not pursue it. Her father looked up from the table and said, "Where is beer?"

"On the table. Right in front of you. You can have mine, too. I'm going to wash the dog in the tub." The doorway would be difficult. Prince was an awkward bundle to hold. Her father asked her to wait, waving the beer bottle at her, as if she could twist off the cap with a dog in her arms. "Can't you see that my hands are full?"

"Of course," he said, taking a dish towel from its ring and thrusting it into her hand. "Bottle cap tears old man's skin," he said, prodding the toweled hand that held the dog with the beer bottle. Zhenya sighed, ruffling the fur on Prince's back. The dog's anguished breathing paused and then started anew. Zhenya gripped the bottle cap, and her father turned the bottle. "Is nother one," he said and retrieved the other sweating bottle.

"Hurry up, this dog is getting heavy."

He pushed the bottle into her hand and twisted it. Flipping the dish towel at the table and missing, she crossed into the hall. The bathroom under the stairs had only a tiny tub and shower, but it would be plenty for Prince. At the bathroom door, as she shifted the dog to reach for the knob, the lights on the stairway suddenly came on. Facing her at the foot of the stairs stood Roy Oberland. He cradled the sleeping Petey in his arms much as she held the dog, then he shifted the child so that Petey's sleeping face turned. The light fell equally on Roy and Petey, the same fair contours of flesh on each.

The light illuminated Zhenya as well. She stood right beside the stairs, but Roy did not see her. Had Roy been in there with his arms around Emma? Is that why she had appeared to be sitting oddly? *Who is father of namesake?* Her face burned. All this time the truth had been staring her in the face. How could any human be so blind? Roy climbed out of her view. Prince began panting and lifted her head to lay it against Zhenya's chest. It could not be possible that Roy Oberland had sex with her daughter when she was fourteen. It was not possible.

"Daughter." Her father's form stood in the kitchen doorway. He shrugged slightly and opened his ivory hands. He whispered, "Policeman is always the father."

Zhenya turned and hurried down the hall to the back door. She

< 277 >

pushed open the door, but the sound of the insistent rain stopped her. Where was she going? Why was she still carrying the dog? An inch of light showed from beneath the basement door. She should throw Danny Ford out now. If he was not the father, there was no reason to put up with him for another moment. How could she ever have thought Emma would give herself to the likes of Danny Ford? Instead she had been raped by Roy Oberland. How was that any more plausible? Suddenly there were two monsters in her house. She had refused to see one and concocted a story to dress up the other. She kicked at the door with her foot and it flew open onto the stairs. Almost immediately, Danny Ford came running up, taking the steps two at a time. His size and speed frightened her, but she could not drop the dog and run. She could not drop Prince down a flight of stairs.

Danny reached the top step and put out his arms. "She dead finally?" He took the dog from her.

"No," Zhenya said. "No. Not yet."

"He can't have her knocked off," Danny said, his pasty face breaking into a smile. He had gold fillings. "Morgan can't. Too soft, that guy." He pivoted on the stairs and trotted down them carrying the dog, as if it were nothing to navigate stairs with such an armload. She hesitated, then followed him, shutting the door behind her. He set the dog on a rug beside an old armchair. A thin book lay on the chair and several empty beer cans lined the clothes dryer beside it. "I was sort of thinking down here," he said. He sat on the book to conceal it. She thought it must be pornography.

"What is that you're hiding?" she demanded.

His shoulder barely moved, but she recognized it as his shrug. "A play. Nothing." He pointed at the dog. "Should I take care of it?"

"What do you mean?"

"The old lady is suffering, isn't she?"

"What do you mean? How? How would you take care of her?"

The shoulder made its tiny movement again. He stood, placed the book on the arm of the chair, and removed the chair's cushion. He paused, staring at Zhenya, who could not respond to him without acknowledging the turbulent mixture of thoughts and memories demanding her attention. She could not exert the effort it took to ignore them and respond to his look at the same time. She under-stood then what work it was to constantly ignore them, how exhaust-ing it was to be Zhenya Kamenev.

Meanwhile, Danny Ford knelt and fitted the cushion over Prince's head. The dog's front legs made desperate movements, as if digging a hole. Her back legs did not move at all.

She ran up the stairs, shut the basement door, and leaned against it. The sound of television gabble made her flinch. She could not stay up here, either. If Roy Oberland was really Petey's father, she would have him arrested. Even now her daughter was only twenty. The noise of water rushing through the house's old pipes abruptly ended, another sound she had not noticed until it vanished. She did not want to see Morgan. The shower would have revived him. He would be feeling good about burying the gun. He would be happy that Roy was still around. He would want to sit and talk and hold Zhenya's hand. In her purse, she had the key to the condominium. She didn't have to consider it long. She grabbed her umbrella, then hurried back to the kitchen to grab her purse.

"Where you are going?" her father said. "Don't go nowhere. We should talk about truth of boy's pedigree." He looked around then. "Where is dog?"

"I don't want to talk about that, about anything. I don't want to know," Zhenya said, angry, accusing. "I don't want to know." This was the truth. She wished she did not know.

"Daughter, wait," he said. "Is raining. Must have ride to old woman's house. Take me please."

"I thought you were staying here." She did not want him along. The day had demanded enough of her. She needed to make her escape.

"Most important," he said, standing, "must have nightcap. Is nozzing here but this piss-water beer. We drink everything at dinner."

"Come on, then," she said, but he had half a bottle of beer that he would want to guzzle. "I'll start the car," she said, and she was out the door and running beneath her umbrella through the rain.

< 279 >

The driver's seat was a mess. She should have insisted on driving after the dump, but there was nothing to be done about it now. Her dress still held the shape of Morgan's grime and was flecked now with the dog's blond fur. She would throw these clothes away, she decided. Her car was soiled and smelled bad, but it was still utterly reliable. It started with the turn of the key. If Emma and Roy were dating, if they were in love, they might have begun seeing each other only recently. But the man holding the boy on the stairs was the father of that boy. There was no denying it, and there was no end to the ugliness of this world.

Peter Ivanovich came trudging through the rain, holding a plastic coat held over his head. "Turn on heater, please," he said as he climbed in.

"You're not cold, you're just wet." She turned it on anyway and let the car idle until the air grew warm. She switched the vents to defrost. Her father's chin touched his chest. "Are you awake?" she asked.

"Eyes open," he said, raising his head. "Ears to ground. Nose to grindstones."

"Don't joke. It's not a day for joking." She turned on the headlights, shifted into reverse, backed down the drive and into the street. Flashing yellow signs blocked off Forest Avenue. "The road is closed. What am I supposed to do?"

"Drive round park to opposite side. Five minutes tops. No trouble for you."

She shook her head but said nothing, making a U-turn to go up the street. The park was two blocks long but only a half-block deep. If Roy was really the father, how could they have failed to notice all these years? It had not even entered into the realm of possibility. Zhenya made a right at the corner, splashing through a depression near the gutter. The gutter was already full, she thought, and the rain was still coming down. "How can Morgan stand to be in that house with that awful thug?" she said suddenly, as if she did not share the same house, as if that were the most pressing problem in her life.

Her father's cry was a rasp of air. "Is *criminal*, this boy, who wants only to be tough guy. Is all in whole life he wants. He puts on nice act this day, but is just act. I am hating this boy first time I see him."

This afternoon she thought she had grasped Morgan's attachment to Danny Ford. Danny had been sweet to Petey and quiet at their dinner. But her father was right. It had been an act. She turned again after the half-block, a dark street bordered by old brick bungalows that faced the park. A few had newer buildings in the back, cheap apartments made of budget lumber and covered with stucco. The center of the park had already been cleared of trees, the sidewalks poured. It would be scraped and paved in a matter of weeks, and Forest Avenue would never again be the same.

"Is million men like him in old Soviet days," her father went on. "Big brass buttons on their costumes, but are nozzing but criminals. Convicts. Outlaws. Bullies."

The windshield wiper on her side streaked more than cleaned, and Zhenya had to hunch to see the road, but the rain was not as hard as it had been before. The lights at this end of the park didn't work, she realized. Perhaps they hadn't worked in a long time. She never went to the park anymore. Shouldn't she have wandered around it before it was bulldozed and divided? What had she been thinking? She turned again at the end of the block.

"I hate that Morgan brings such bad character into house," her father kept on. Danny Ford was a sore spot with him. He had smothered the dog, she thought. And it meant nothing to him. That must be why she hated him anew. She had stood there like an idiot and watched. Speechless. Her father continued ranting, "Prison should be home to criminal. Am not bleeding heart. People misinterpret Peter Ivanovich about this. Incarceration is only thing for criminals."

Zhenya slowed. The street had become a pond. A crumpled white sack floated on the black water, which splashed against the underside of the Honda. She made the final turn to come full circle and headed toward the opposite side of Forest Avenue. Her father had quit ranting, and she didn't want him to quit. She egged him on. "What does Morgan see in that cretin? That's what I don't get."

"No, you are missing point."

"I am *not* missing the point," she said. Danny Ford was not

< 2 8 1 >

Petey's father. There was no reason to endure him. She had missed every other point, but she was certain about this. "That's the real mystery. So what if they ride in the same stinking garbage truck? He means *nothing* to us. *Nothing*. But Morgan will do anything. House him. Hand over our savings."

Peter shook his big head. "What is mystery? Is simple. Is same age dead boy would be now."

Zhenya hit the brake too hard. The car slid on the wet road, and she and her father rocked in their seats. She spun as she fell back against the headrest, slapping her father's face in the same movement. Hitting him hard. A crack like a tree limb breaking. "You can't talk like that," she said. "Just shut up about that. Just shut up and let me drive."

Peter Ivanovich put his hand to his cheek.

"Just shut up," she said.

The key slid into the lock, but it would not turn. Zhenya rattled the knob, unable to think. She shoved the keys back in her purse and sprinted down the block. The rain had turned to a mist, a shroud for the great sycamores. At the end of the connected row of condos, she cut through the yard and to the back, her purse bouncing against her thigh. Only one of the condos at this end was lit, the one at the very end. An elderly couple sat at the kitchen bar, brightly lit, talking, gesturing with their hands. Zhenya counted the back doors until she reached hers. She tried the key again, but the locks had been changed. She had left the kitchen window open a sliver for just such an emergency. She tugged off the screen and pushed, but the window was latched.

This defeated her. She sat on the concrete stoop and covered her face, her breathing heavy from running. The rain picked up for a moment, like a movement in a symphony, growing louder, more intense. She stood, held her purse by the looping handle, and swung it against the window. It cracked. She swung it again.

When the glass finally shattered, she took her cell phone from her purse and hammered the protruding shards out of the casement. Then she heaved herself through. She climbed out onto the kitchen counter and slid down to the floor. She crunched across the glass to the edge of the carpet, where she kicked off her shoes. She knelt on the carpet and then lay down. The room was unusually bright. A car faced the condo, its lights on. Someone had called the police, she thought. Then she understood that it was her own car. She had left it in the driveway, the high beams shining. It was almost enough to make her cry.

She went to the door that led to the garage. She knew her way around. The garage light came on when she threw the switch. This was still the display condo, and it did not surprise her that the lights worked. She punched a button on the wall, and the garage door began to rise, revealing the headlights, shining now on her. She trotted out into the rain and climbed into the car. The filth appalled her. She would drive down the street to a convenience store and purchase cleaning products. She would return, park in the garage, and clean her car.

This was exactly what she needed. Something to do. A way to stay busy. A plan.

Shopping took no time at all. She parked in the garage and punched the button to make the door shut. Then she took off her dress and left it in a heap on the concrete. She had wound up at an all-night grocery and found gray sweatpants, a T-shirt bearing the image of Michael Jordan, and a plastic bag filled with pairs of white socks. Perfect clothes for cleaning, she told herself. She took out her cell phone and called Morgan. "I'm driving around. I may eat something. I may go to an all-night car wash. Don't wait up."

"You're driving? It doesn't sound like it. There's none of that—"

"I'm stopped at a light."

"Are you all right?" he asked. "What are you doing?"

"I'll talk to you tomorrow," she said and hung up.

The filthy shovel still lay between the bucket seats. Why hadn't they thought to take the Toyota? Why hadn't they changed clothes? Why hadn't the most obvious things been apparent to them? She scrubbed the seats and wondered at the astonishing extent of their stupidity and blindness. They were prepared for nothing. She

< 2 8 3 >

worked a sponge over the dash. She removed the floor mats and sprayed them with cleaning foam. But it did not turn out to be the kind of work that could shut down her mind, regardless of the effort she put into it. After awhile, she quit scrubbing.

The windshield held a brown slash where she had made a muddy swipe with the sponge. She had accomplished little but the soiling of the sweatpants and T-shirt. She stripped off her clothes again and added them to the pile, tossing in her underwear as well. She tramped through the house naked, carrying a tiny bottle of shampoo and a wrapped bar of soap. She had thought ahead. That was one of her talents.

There were no lights upstairs. How could that be? How could the electricity be on in only part of the house? Her father hated this place. He couldn't see what it had to offer. "Is like Soviet apartment. Bigger, but same kind of place." She realized that there were no bulbs in the fixtures upstairs. She felt her way to the bathroom. There was hot water, and that was all she needed. She showered in the dark.

Emma had become pregnant as a freshman in high school. Zhenya had had sex herself when she was fourteen. With a college student. He mispronounced the word "poignant," she recalled, but she couldn't really picture his face, couldn't remember his name. He had thanked her afterwards. She remembered that. She stayed in the shower stall until all the hot water was gone. She had been more mature at that age than Emma had been, and she had not let herself get pregnant. Eddie. That was his name. Eddie Thompson. He had a goatee. He had a little dog. She refused to believe Roy Oberland was capable of fucking a child. There were too many things she had to live with already. Looking back did nothing but keep one from looking forward. Eddie Thompson had been a kid, a college student but still a kid. Five or six years older, but not a grown man.

She had not thought of towels. She wiped water from her body as best she could, then went down the stairs and dressed again in the sweatpants and T-shirt. She lay on the carpet in the living room. The smell of it pleased her, but the powerful restless motion in her chest would not let her sleep. What was going on here? She had not thought of liquor, either. A drink would help. She could go out again, but that would be pushing her luck. Sooner or later someone would notice the break-in and call the police. No, if she left, she would not come back. And she could not yet face going home. She found the cell phone again. Their machine picked up, Morgan's recorded voice. She looked at her watch. It was after one in the morning. "It's me," she said. "Are you there? I've got something to tell you. I think. I don't want anyone else to hear this. I'm not sure what I have to say. Maybe I found out something tonight." She lay back against the carpet. The pants were too small. "Just a second," she said to keep the machine from cutting off. She yanked the sweatpants down, then worked her feet to free them while she spoke. "All this time we were thinking about . . . one thing, there were other things. What I'm trying to say is . . ." What was she trying to say? She kicked the gray pants aside. What was it that coiled in her abdomen and demanded to be spoken for? She had to say something or the machine would cut off. "I don't know how to live, Morgan," she said. "I can't seem to find a way through all of this." And then she said, "Philip would have finished college this year." She hung up.

The click that followed made Morgan call her back immediately, but when he tried, a mechanical voice told him her phone was turned off. He could not remember when he had last heard her speak their son's name. The house was dark and quiet. Everyone was gone or asleep. Morgan had tried to sleep himself, but Zhenya's bed was empty, and he worried about this sudden decision to go driving in the rain on the anniversary of their son's death. He had been outside when the phone rang the second time. He had thought she might have driven her father across the street and then stayed to help him get inside, but there was no Honda at Mrs. East's. The message light was flashing when he came back.

He sat at the kitchen table and waited for her to call again. He would not go to work tomorrow, he thought. He would stay home and talk to her about Philip. Morgan could not imagine Philip in college. He had made himself remember his son every day for ten years, but it was always Philip as he had been, Philip at the age of twelve riding his bike, Philip at ten playing Little League, Philip at six going to his first day of elementary school. Philip would be in

< 2 8 5 >

college, or graduated from college, or maybe he would be working and out on his own. He would be almost as old as Morgan had been when he met Zhenya.

Morgan couldn't picture this Philip, this adult Philip, this man, and even though he willed himself to conjure up the boy, nothing came. He would be tall, Morgan thought, a taller man than Morgan, but the word "man" bothered him, seemed dishonest. Yet it was the truth. Philip would be a man. There would be no boy now, even if Philip had lived.

It was then he realized that Prince was missing. He searched the usual spots, then the remainder of the ground floor. He went out into the side yard, in the rain, with an umbrella and flashlight. Danny could have carried her out and then forgotten about her. He called her name. It felt funny in his mouth. Inside, he climbed the stairs, thinking Emma might have carried her up there, but she was not in Emma's room and not with Petey. A light was on in the basement, and he threw open the door. "Danny?"

Danny came flying up the stairs. "What's wrong, man?"

"I can't find Prince."

He nodded. "You can't?" He turned around, as if checking for her in the basement. "I don't know," he said. He turned back and faced Morgan. "You want help looking?"

Morgan shook his head. "I can do it," he said. "She has to be here somewhere."

"Let me do it," Danny said, but Morgan put his hand against Danny's chest to stop him. He stepped away and shut the door. Cupping his hands about his eyes, he leaned against a window to search the backyard. He could see nothing. He opened the back door and checked by the pool, turning on the underwater lights on the off chance that the dog had drowned. The surface of the pool erupted with the falling rain. Lit from below, it appeared to be boiling.

He went out into the street and called for her. Yellow lights blinked their warnings. Morgan recalled a cat he'd had as a child that had crawled beneath the house to die. He stepped past the lights, yelling for the dog. He had to jump down to the scraped street. Adrenaline, he thought. Maybe adrenaline had given her strength and she made it to the park. He did not believe this, but he could not give himself permission to stop looking.

He marched over the muddy, ruined street to the park. A band of trees had been cleared for the road, and the sidewalks and gutters were poured, but where the street would go was only grass and eruptions of mud where the trees had been. It looked strange. A grass street.

He was fooling himself. The dog could not walk. If she was not in the house, she was dead. Someone had carted off the body. There it was. His wife was trying to spare him. She had taken away Prince's body and could not decide how to dispose of it. She was driving around town in the rain trying to save him from his portion of grief—at least to delay it until another day.

So she did. She loved him. Still. Here, at last, was his proof.

Upon returning home, he searched the first floor of the house again. When he didn't find her, he knew for certain that Prince was dead. The dog had died on the anniversary of Philip's death, and his wife was trying to spare him this sorrow. At least for the night. At least until after the twelfth.

Morgan's pants were soaked around the ankles from the tall grass in the park, and his shirt was damp despite the umbrella. He sat on a kitchen chair, listening to the relentless drizzle. The dog had been Philip's, and now even the dog was gone. Nothing of the boy remained except what they kept alive within themselves. Morgan tried again to call up his son, but he couldn't do it. Philip would be a man now if bad luck had not intervened, and to think of him as a child seemed wrong. Wasn't it the parent's duty to let his child grow up? Was the duty the same even if the child was dead? Morgan tried again to picture Philip as a young man, but the image was too arbitrary. He could not do it. Tomorrow might be different, but this night he could not imagine his son.

Morgan, at last, was alone.

The night of the twelfth confirmed Zhenya's great fear—that one flaw in the armor will ruin it. She lay on the floor, the sweatpants folded beneath her head, the bed of carpet growing harder the

< 2 8 7 >

longer she lay upon it. She remembered that in the year following their son's death, Morgan had wanted the family to go together to see Emma's therapist, Dr. Gallen. Zhenya had emphatically refused. But one night she had secretly attended a support group for parents who had lost children. The people had been kind to her and circumspect, and she had appreciated their willingness to let her merely sit and observe. They sat in a circle in a stuffy room, and they took turns talking.

By the end of the night Zhenya had loathed them.

She came to understand what they were saying—that her pain was like theirs. She knew this was not true, not even possible, for while they had all lost children, none had a child—just a boy, not even a teenager—who had taken his own life. None had sent her child to his room to punish him and then never saw the living child again. None had heard her husband's inarticulate cry quite the way she had. None had rushed up the stairs to find her child with a cord around his neck, his face an inhuman color, his body a slack and useless thing. She had known he was dead the second she saw him, knew Morgan's attempts to revive the boy were worthless, knew even as she dialed for an ambulance, that none was needed. These people wanted her to believe they knew her pain, but none had endured what she had. People died, she knew that. Children died. Every year, a million tragedies. All of human history was a record of losses, and those people sitting in that claustrophobic room needed to lay claim to their rightful share of it. But none of them had known her son. None of them had loved her son. She had loved him more than her husband, more than her daughter. A difficult child and hers. None in that crowd had lost Philip. Sitting in the back of the room on a folding chair, listening to a man describe his adult daughter's overdose, Zhenya recalled the last words she ever spoke to her son, and these old words returned to her as she lay on the floor of that blank, tidy room. She had said, "I'm ashamed of you."

9

Silence is the largest part of music—and love.

—Peter Ivanovich Kamenev

On the morning of the wedding, Zhenya carried a stack of folders into her father's bedroom and dropped it onto his bed. He sat on the opposite end of the mattress, a handwritten letter flattened against his thigh, his fingers tracing the sentences. He had not moved back into Zhenya's house after she had Morgan kick out Danny Ford, but his mail still came there and much of his clothing still littered the floor. The room retained the vinegary smell of his body and the mordant odor of his cologne. Pages from his manuscript flagged the walls. He liked to stand with his nose an inch from the print and read the sentences aloud, a red marker in his hand. Zhenya had watched him do this and wondered if his physical locomotion from page to page helped him concentrate. Entering the final phase of revision, he had become suddenly serious about every word in the text. The red ink penetrated the paper and the adhesive tape stripped plaster from the walls. It did not matter where he slept; this room was undeniably his.

He took off his glasses to peer at her and the pile of manila folders, his face contorting to convey surprise and curiosity. Was he genuinely surprised and curious? Zhenya had no way of knowing. His expressions concealed more than they revealed. Mrs. East had bought him a gray sweatsuit, and he seemed to wear it all the time. Zhenya disliked the outfit. It suggested decline, diminishment, the

< 288 >

< 2 8 9 >

surrender of standards. She hoped he had the sense to put on something presentable for the wedding. If he changed here, she would
volunteer to wash the sweatsuit and then she would destroy it.
Maybe she would replace it with a real suit, conservative and well-
made, as well as slacks appropriate for his age, new white shirts,
dark socks, even a fedora if she could find one. She would spend the
money she earned teaching summer school on him.

"They're about you," she said, gesturing to the folders with a tilt of
her head. "They document your . . . the false stories you've told. I had
my own plans for them, but I've decided I should give them to you."

"False stories," he said. "What are you meaning by this?"

"Look at the files," she said.

He stared at the spreading mound of folders and nodded, as if to
comply with her request. "Do not leave yet," he said softly. "Am
reading letter from old lover." He pressed his hand against the
creased paper and looked up at her. "Your mozzer."

Zhenya was so certain of her mother's estrangement from him,
she did not immediately convert "mozzer" to "mother." Finally she
said, "She wrote *you?*"

"We write. Now and then. We have no bitterness."

Zhenya knew that to be false. If she had kept files on his private
lies, they would dwarf the pile on the bed. She would need a ware-
house to store them all. But perhaps she had it wrong. After all,
there was the letter on his bony thigh. Her mother's precise pen-
manship was unmistakable.

"She is sorry to miss wedding. Is happening too fast for her to
come."

"I've talked to my mother. No one expected her to fly out."

"She is asking should she come later. See what is matter vis
everybody. Asks my opinion should she come."

"Why didn't she ask me?" Zhenya had spoken on the phone with
her mother for more than an hour on the evening Emma and Roy
revealed their plans. "What's the big rush?" her mother had asked,
and Zhenya had been unable to provide a satisfactory answer.
"You're keeping secrets," her mother had said. "I understand that
well enough. Most of the secrets we keep aren't even ours, are they?"
Again, Zhenya had found she could offer no response, except to

acknowledge that she could not talk about it. "All right then," her mother had said. "Tell me things you can talk about. Talk to me for a while anyway."

"I am writing her soon," her father said, stroking the paper once more. "I tell her not to worry. Peter Ivanovich is here to take care of family."

A number of caustic responses came to mind, but Zhenya kept them to herself. She had no intention of fighting with her father on Emma's wedding day. The day had enough conflicts, already. Maybe that was why she had presented him with the files, to diminish her number of battles by one.

"Am joking," he said.

"Oh."

"Your mother likes jokes."

That much was true. Her mother often recast Zhenya's travails as jokes. "Think of it this way," she would say. "A college professor and a garbage man are the only survivors of a shipwreck, and they have to share a life raft . . ." But her mother had not attempted to depict Emma's wedding as a joke. She had known better than to try.

"Zhenya," her father said, and the sound of her name in his voice created an immediate pressure behind her eyes. "What is truth, anyway?"

"She doesn't need to come out here. I don't like the fact that Emma is getting married all of a sudden. I *hate* it. But there's nothing Mother could do about it."

"Every story is false story," he said. "Is only way to get at truth." *Truse,* he said, not "truth." It almost sounded like *truce.* He patted the files. "You would do this to Papa?"

"I thought I would. But evidently I can't." She backed out of the room, clinging to the doorknob. She had substituted a truce for the truth, she thought. So be it. "Read this stuff," she said. "Eventually someone besides me is going to figure all of it out."

He smiled at her and waved an admonishing finger. "Cannot resist love for father," he said. "No Russian girl can do bad to father."

Zhenya shut the door on his words and leaned against it. *A girl and a cop are getting married,* she thought. *They first got together when*

< 2 9 1 >

the cop raped the girl when she was a child. She did not let herself continue. She knew enough about self-torture to quit.

"Your time here is up," Morgan had told Danny Ford. "I need you out of the house before the wedding."

Danny had not seemed at all surprised. "My old lady might let me have my room back once I give her the news." His lawyer had come by to let him know about the lost gun. The prosecutor might stall, she said, but the state would eventually drop the charges.

"Call her," Morgan said. "Pack."

His belongings all fit into three plastic garbage bags. Morgan helped him lug the bags to the driveway and on out to the side street. "I remembered to tell my ride Forest is closed," Danny said. "That's the kind of thing I usually forget. Growing smarter in my old age." The paving of Forest Avenue had begun, and the smell of hot asphalt filled their nostrils. When they set the bags down, Danny said, "You got me out of it. Don't think I don't know."

"No, I didn't," Morgan said, but what was true, his complicity in all of it, must have shown.

"I thought so, man."

"I got you *into* it," Morgan insisted, "not out."

"The other guys will think it was some pals of ours, but I know it was you."

"You're going to be given your job back," Morgan said, "but it won't be on my truck." At this, Danny's face fell. "The new models finally arrived," Morgan continued. "I have a training deal, and then I'll be working alone." Most of the crews would still have two men for the time being, but he had offered to work by himself. The new trucks would change the job, make it easier and less interesting, but he was through with Danny Ford. The next trouble that found him would not touch Morgan.

From Forest Avenue came the steely screech of big machinery. Danny suddenly took his own head in his hands and turned it quickly, cracking his big neck. "Why'd you dump me off the truck? I like that truck."

"It's going to be a new truck."

"You know what I mean."

"Long weekends are bad for you."

"That's it? That's the whole reason?"

Morgan couldn't decide how much to explain. "We've been through enough," he said. "Don't you think?"

Danny considered that a moment. "Yeah, you're no bargain to live with, either," he said. "I owe you some money. Found it. Laying around the house. My first paycheck, I'll get it to you."

"You'd better," Morgan said.

"I guess I owe you something else, likewise."

"What's that?"

Danny started to speak, then pointed. "My ride." A big red car, dusty and new, appeared down the street, moving slowly. Danny stepped out to the sidewalk and waved. The car accelerated, then slowed again to pull up to the curb. The trunk popped open, but the driver made no move to get out. Morgan ducked down to look inside. A girl sat behind the wheel, thin, with mouse-colored hair. Pretty. Morgan nodded at her, and she nodded back.

"My MS babe," Danny said. "She's got a special accelerator right on the column. And a brake, which you got to have." He leaned in close to Morgan. His breath smelled fresh and clean, not of toothpaste or mouthwash but uncontaminated and pure—the simple fragrance of youth. "Hey," he said. "Can I have it back?"

Morgan could not think what he meant, except perhaps the time he had lost in jail. "Have what back?"

"The, you know, gun."

The question stunned him. "That's not possible."

"I was thinking it could be like a memento." Danny indicated the car with his head. "Thought she'd like to check it out." He put his mouth next to Morgan's ear. "Guns turn 'em on."

"I'll see you around," Morgan said, pulling back but not walking away.

Danny lifted the garbage bags of his stuff as if they weighed nothing and tossed them into the trunk. He slammed the lid and stared at Morgan. He leaned against the car with both hands and stared. Then he stepped around the car and came back to him.

"I got to explain this one thing," he said. "That guy had been

< 293 >

threatening my boys. Maybe some genius could've figured out a different plan. I couldn't. There was nothing else I could do."

Morgan waited, unsure what he meant, wanting him to leave.

"He was going to mess them up," Danny said. "It was him or us. Not me, actually. I don't run anymore, you know that. But my little brother and the others."

"*They* shot him," Morgan said. "One of *them*."

Danny shook his head, made his slight shrug. "I had to. You know what I mean? They were pussies about it, and it was going to get them all killed." He shook his head. "Sometimes you got to be a man." He put his arm around Morgan's shoulders. The arm was heavy. "I won't forget what you did for me."

Danny Ford jerked open the front door of the red car and slid inside. The door slammed shut. The car made a three point turn and motored off. Morgan remained standing until it disappeared. Then he sat on his driveway. He covered his mouth with his hands. He screamed into his palms. "This goddamn life."

Almost immediately hands touched his shoulders. Emma had been watching. She knelt and put her arms around him. "You'll still see him," she said. "I made him promise."

She said, "You haven't lost him."

Zhenya invited Sid to come into the house, but he declined. He stood on the stoop, sunlight in his wavy hair. Beneath one arm, he held an awkwardly wrapped package. "These doors are very attractive," he said.

"I like them, too," Zhenya said. Had she told Morgan how much she liked them? She thought she probably had. She would go in and tell him right now, but he was taking a nap. Three hours before his daughter was to marry her rapist and Morgan had decided to nap. Fitting, she thought. Although, the truth was that she had not told him about Roy. Not because she wanted to protect Morgan. The opposite. She feared that he would find a way to forgive Roy, and she could not tolerate that idea. She did not want to hear him say "water under the bridge" or some other inanity.

In the street, a city truck belched blue smoke. Sid glanced over his shoulder at the sound. Two men in yellow hardhats examined an exhaust pipe, one of them sniffing at it like a dog investigating a stranger. The other man reached up and rocked his hat, a gesture so much like scratching his head that Zhenya felt the urge to laugh. Forest Avenue would reopen to traffic in another week.

"I live on a busy street," Sid said. "I find much of the congress interesting."

Congress, Zhenya thought. At some distant point in her life, she had used "congress" as a euphemism for sex. He was an odd boy. "Thank you for saying that," she said. "But it's hard for me to believe there'll be a silver lining. I wish you'd come in. I'm sure Emma would like to see you."

"It's her wedding day," Sid said. He smiled then. "I rehearsed saying that. I wanted to be capable of speaking it."

"It sounded fine," she said.

He nodded. "I used to be a theater major."

A shriek of tires caused them both to turn to the street again. The men had climbed inside the cab of the big truck, and were facing the rear window, eyeing the road they had just screeched across. *Laying rubber,* that was what Zhenya's friends had called it when she was a girl. Everything was about sex, she thought. To Sid, she said, "I was hoping they'd take Saturday off."

"I'm perspiring," he said. "I decided to walk over, and it turned out to be more distant than I thought." He removed the package from beneath his arm and offered it to her. "A gift for the happy couple."

The package was the size of the proverbial breadbox and weighed very little. She guessed it was exactly that, a breadbox. The striped paper that he had wrapped it in was too thick and did not tuck well at the ends. At the edges of the wrapping, some kind of backing showed.

"People will give you the ends of the rolls," he told her. "It comes in handy in any number of ways."

"Oh," she said, figuring it out. The gift was wrapped in wall-paper. "You don't have a single dime, do you, Sid?"

He stared at her blankly for a moment, then reached into his pants' pocket and pulled out a few coins. "Two nickels." He offered them to her.

< 2 9 5 >

She accepted the nickels. "Emma's crazy to do this," she said.

"I'm not comfortable with that word." He pulled his damp shirt free from his skin and flapped the material. He wore the same conservative clothing that she'd seen him in before—slacks, a white shirt, penny loafers. His uniform. She wondered if he had gone through a period of his life when he'd had trouble dressing himself, unable to decide what to wear, daunted by the array of textures and patterns in his closet. Now all his clothes were identical, the problem solved. It seemed like an elegant solution in some ways. "At least come in and cool off," she said. "Have a drink of water."

"I had the lead in a number of plays before I switched majors," he said. "I know all of Romeo's lines. I can't seem to forget them. I have to be careful. It wouldn't be fair to use them. Do you know what I like about your daughter?" He grew suddenly still, his body seeming to seize, his mouth holding the shape of the final syllable. He took a breath. "Do you know what I *love* about your daughter?"

"Tell me."

"She knows I'm not going to be Romeo again. Not ever. My parents, whom I also love, they're waiting for a . . . cure. Emma isn't." He corrected himself. "Wasn't."

"She's not married yet," Zhenya said. "She's upstairs. *Talk* to her."

"It's not so much that the person I used to be is dead, but that this person I am now would have to die for me to be cured. 'Healed' is the word my parents prefer. I didn't have to offer that explanation to Emma. She knew it before I did."

"Please come inside with me," Zhenya said. "I want you to."

When he smiled, she could imagine him on the stage. "You're very kind," he said. "But I can't do that."

"Why not?"

"I think of Emma every day."

"I know you do."

"For forty minutes," he said. "It's very pleasurable." Then he added, "Thank you for having this conversation with me." He bowed, so deeply that she thought his head might knock against his knees. "I bid thee adieu," he said without a trace of irony or humor. He turned and began his hike home. He walked, Zhenya noted, like a prince.

She shut the door and climbed the stairs to her daughter, the gift in one hand, the nickels clutched in the other.

"Here's the bride putting on her gown," Emma said.

Zhenya sat on her daughter's bed, Sid's awkward parcel at her side. She did not want to call attention to it. She preferred that Emma ask about it. "That's not really what we call a gown," she said. Her daughter was getting married in a sleeveless drop waist dress. Off-white. "And it's still hours before the wedding."

"Just checking myself out."

"Do you want a gown? We could buy a gown. Have a real wedding. A big one, I mean. Instead of this thing on the pool deck."

"Here's the mother of the bride nervously gabbing," Emma said, zipping herself up. She was slim, limber, athletic. She could zip the back of her dress effortlessly, and she could throw her life away just as easily.

"I wasn't gabbing," Zhenya said. "I don't *gab.*"

"Should I wear stockings?"

"People with nothing better to do than gossip *gab.*"

"It's too hot for stockings, anyway," Emma said. "I ought to have a hat. Why did people quit wearing hats? Does everybody think I'm pregnant?"

"Not everybody," Zhenya said, "but it's a natural assumption, given the short notice. And your age. And his. Given that you're in love with Sid."

Emma was surprised to hear this. "Am I?" Her eyes slid over to the strange package.

"I think you are," Zhenya said. "I've thought that for a while."

"Maybe I am." Emma lifted the clock on the nightstand to look at the time. "But I love Roy, too. And he and I have something else." She turned to examine her mother's eyes, expecting, it seemed, for Zhenya to supply the explanation for what she and Roy possessed. *Petey* was the obvious answer, but Zhenya was not about to help.

Finally, Emma said, "There's a word for it. I just can't think of it."

"But Sid. I thought he might be the one for you. The right one." Zhenya blushed, saying this. She had not meant to go quite so far.

< 2 9 7 >

But there was no point in turning back. "I'm fairly certain that he loves you." She wanted to delay the ceremony, put it off for a few weeks. Give her daughter time to think. "There was something about the way you acted after you came home from seeing Sid. I've just been certain that he's the one."

"Sometimes I was really seeing Roy. We just kept it secret."

"Secret," Zhenya said and swallowed. "For a long time? Is that what you're telling me? Are there other secrets you should tell me about?"

Emma looked straight at her. "Not a thing."

"There's not something more to this? It's so sudden." She waited, wanting her daughter to step in. She needed her daughter to tell her what she already knew. "What is it?"

Emma shook her head. "I don't know what to think." She said it cavalierly, as if they were discussing dinner or the classes she should take next semester. "Some things get decided for you, don't you think? You can have an idea about your life, or someone else can . . ." Then her expression changed. She smiled, but her smile was unmistakably sad—Zhenya was not the type to make this up. She knew that much about herself. Her daughter's smile was not that of a young bride-to-be, but one colored with sorrow.

Emma said, "A *history*. That's what Roy and I have."

As if *that* were hard to come by, Zhenya thought bitterly. All you needed to do was live and you had a history. For that matter, you didn't even need to do that. The dead had their history, too. Every day they claimed a larger share of it.

"He resigned from the police department," Emma told her.

"He *what?*"

Emma nodded. "He quit."

"So he's not only fourteen years older than you and divorced for all of an hour, he also doesn't have a job?"

"Quite the catch, eh?" Emma offered her smile again, but she would not, on this day, get Zhenya to play along. "He sort of had to resign."

It took her a moment, but only that. "The gun?"

Emma nodded.

"But he hates Danny Ford."

Emma nodded again. "The bride and her mother have a moment of intimacy before the wedding."

"Is that what this is? Are you saying he did it for you? For Morgan? What are you saying?"

Emma turned again to the mirror on the door that connected her room to the next one. "Where's Petey?" she asked.

"He's at Mrs. East's. They're baking your wedding cake."

"I did have a different plan at one time," Emma said, examining her image in the mirror. "I was going to become an explorer and have a big house in Africa that I would share with Philip. He was going to be a race-car driver and a doctor of some sort. There was supposed to be a smaller house in the back where you and Dad would live." She crossed the room and joined her mother on the bed. "And neither one of us were likely ever to get married at all, but if one of us did, it had to be to somebody who would pledge his undying commitment to us both, even if it meant risking his life." She pointed to their reflection. They looked very much like mother and daughter. She spoke to her mother's reflection. "So Roy and I are not moving to Africa. But he fits the rest of the bill."

"You're saying that he risked his life to get that gun?"

"He gave up his job. He'd already given up his wife. She left him because of me. Career and spouse, that's a life, isn't it?" She put her head on Zhenya's shoulder. She spoke more softly now. "And there was another time. Years ago. He risked everything for me then, as well. He risked everything to love me."

Zhenya slid away from her daughter and stood. "It's hard for me to think of it that way," she said. "It isn't the way I think."

"Africa was Philip's idea," Emma said. "He always had ideas."

"Your brother's dead," Zhenya said, and she stopped, waiting, thinking she might be swept away by some powerful force, washed off the face of the earth. But nothing happened, and she said it again. "Philip's dead, and he shouldn't have any influence on this decision. This is your decision."

"I know," Emma said. "I've decided."

"When you're fourteen years old and the man is thirty—"

"He was twenty-eight."

"It's *rape*. And it doesn't matter whether you were willing, or

< 299 >

whether it was your idea. *Nothing* matters. An adult knows better. An adult *knows*."

Emma's gaze did not change. She was not upset. Zhenya had the terrible thought that her daughter was deranged in a way that she had never thought to imagine. That she did not really have a hold on reality. Could that be true? How oblivious had Zhenya been? How distracted? What did she really know?

Then, as if Emma had been reading her mind, she said, "I'm not a very good mother."

"I was just thinking that about myself. I've been careless. I haven't paid attention."

Emma shook her head. "Not you. Me. I've let you and Dad raise Petey."

"That's because you were a child when he was born. That's what I've been saying."

"I'm getting better at it," Emma said. "I can't do anything about what happened before. Petey will just have to forgive me. Roy and I will make it up to him the best we can. Sometimes I think all I want is to make things right, normal, ordinary." She picked up Sid's package. "Petey will have to forgive us. Everyone will have to." She held the package up for Zhenya to see. "Wrapping things is not one of his strengths."

"Open it," Zhenya said.

Emma set the package on her lap and tore open one end. The whole wrap unfolded. A cylindrical plastic jar set in a plastic faux-wood base. "It's a straw dispenser," Emma said. Inside were white plastic straws with vertical red stripes. "I bet we don't get two of these."

Zhenya turned the knob on the side, and a straw tumbled out and fell onto Emma's dress. "It's true," Zhenya said. "We all make mistakes. But you don't have to marry yourself to your mistakes."

Emma said, "Yes, you do. *I* do."

Zhenya could not reply to that. Logic seemed to have no weight in this conversation, and that exhausted her. She wanted out of the room, but she did not want to leave on a gloomy note. It was Emma's wedding day, and if the ceremony was going to take place Zhenya didn't want to ruin it for her daughter. She looked at her watch. She needed to do something. It was too early to dress for the wedding. Petey was already cared for. What was left? "The dress is pretty," she said, "but you should take it off or it will be wrinkled for the ceremony."

"I will," Emma said.

"Do you need help getting out of it?"

Emma shook her head. "Here's the bride examining her straw dispenser."

Zhenya reached for the loose straw, which was about to roll off her daughter's lap and to the floor. When she grasped it, the nickels fell from her grip. She had forgotten she was holding them. They slid to the hem of the wedding dress and stared back at her. "I'm going then," she said. It seemed to her that the nickels watched her walk to the door. She understood that her desire was for companionship. She no longer wanted to be alone. "There are nickels in your lap," she said as she slipped through the door.

Morgan became aware of the other body in his narrow bed before the hand touched his chest. His awareness preceded even his waking, coming to him in his sleep, causing a shift in his dreamless slumber, an accommodation in that dark passage of the body when it is neither awake nor dreaming but in its own particular stillness.

He made room in his sleep for the other body. How could he know what he knew, that someone was joining him in bed, that it was the body of a woman, that the woman was his wife, that she wanted to make love with him? How could he know all this before waking, moving to let her in, to take her in? She was unexpected, his waking mind would say, but his sleeping mind was at the ready and knew before it was possible to know.

Zhenya put her hand on his chest, the warmth of that hand a wonder to him, waking him, taking him to the brink of light, although when he opened his eyes, the curtained room was dim. His wife leaned unsteadily on an elbow, her face just above his, the shapes that were her features reconfiguring the dim light around her. He was still half asleep, and his wife slipping into his bed felt as magical as the entrance in a dream of the dead. He took her in his arms, felt her lips on his brow and the lid of one eye. She tugged at

< 3 0 1 >

his T-shirt and he lifted his back to let her pull it free, consciousness rising in him along with desire.

She sat up and lifted her shirt over her head. She pushed the sheet down with her feet. They lay together, husband and wife, mouth engaged with mouth, one bare hand on the other's bare back, the flesh of her belly against the flesh of his. How true life seemed to him in this moment, how much he believed in love. Her body was the one his body longed for, and she had come to him now, once again. How could he think anything but that this body would be his forever, as they themselves had promised, one unto the other, so many years ago.

Roy's father had built a four-poster bed in his woodworking shop as a wedding present. He assembled it on the pool deck, tying a blue ribbon around one of its posts. Three rows of rented chairs were set out beside the bed. A long table on the opposite side of the chairs held two large vases of roses, a modest swell of brightly wrapped gifts, and a three-layer cake with white frosting. In the center of the cake stood two of Petey's plastic figures—an army man bearing a rifle, and the smiling mermaid from the Disney movie.

During the ceremony the justice of the peace asked Emma and Roy to remain sweethearts. "Can you promise me that?"

"I do," said Roy.

Emma nodded her head in small, rapid movements.

After the ceremony, there was nothing to do but stand around in their good clothes in the heat of the afternoon sun and drink. Roy's father had drunk too much bourbon while assembling the bed and went next door to Roy's house to nap. Adele Wurtz left as soon as the vows were spoken. Guy and Vinnie presented the couple with a bottle of cognac and headed for home. Stan Maulner advised Zhenya that a petition protesting the photograph in her office had been sent to the dean. "I refused to sign it," he told her. He had put away a lot of champagne and was proud of his solidarity. "I've been looking around for a picture of some naked babe to hang in my office as a show of support." When Zhenya didn't laugh, his swagger turned flaccid. "That last part was an attempt at humor."

"I know the dean," Zhenya said. "He'll consider the whole petition a joke. At least, I think he will."

Stan nodded. "I just figured I'd let you know. I didn't mean anything by that crack." He took a cab home.

Adriana East stayed, sitting beside Peter Ivanovich and reading from a picture book to Petey, who had climbed into her lap. " 'If you become a bird and fly away from me,' said the mother, 'I will be a tree that you come home to.' "

"What if I became a dog?" Petey asked her.

"Runaway Rabbit," Zhenya said. "I used to read that to you all the time." As soon as she spoke the words she realized her mistake. She hadn't read the story to Petey but to her own children.

Petey didn't betray her mistake. He said, "Prince ran away, didn't she?"

"Daughter," Peter Ivanovich called, although he was only in the next chair. He waved his empty glass of champagne.

Zhenya put her hand on Petey's head, touched the soft skin of his forehead. "If you became a dog, I'd become a . . . a steak. That'd bring you running, wouldn't it?"

"I guess so," Petey said uncertainly. "Is Prince really dead?"

"Let's get back to the story," Adriana suggested.

"Yes," Zhenya said. "Prince was very old and she hurt inside. And she died."

"I thought so," Petey said, and Adriana resumed reading to him.

Zhenya fetched the champagne and poured her father a drink. He held her wrist after she filled his glass, and she thought he would gulp the champagne and demand an immediate refill. Instead, he said, "Wait, please." He took a sip and added, "I have announcement." He took another drink and repeated himself, speaking loudly this time. He patted Adriana's knee, and she quit reading. He swept his eyes over the group to be certain he had everyone's attention. "They think they destroy Peter Ivanovich Kamenev," he said, "but they only point out mistake."

"Who or what are you talking about?" Zhenya asked.

< 303 >

"Television network," Peter said. "And other persons. They show my mistake. I have been trying to be man of old century." His long white fingers spread open, as if to display the magnitude of his error. "Old century is century of *big* man, so I blow up like floating man in parade. But television network has needle, and pop goes floating man." He clapped his hands together. "Even college professor sees this puffing up I am doing." He did not look at Zhenya but turned to be certain he had the attention of the bride and groom. "Is the end for old Russian?" He wagged a single finger back and forth. "Is not end. Most important, old century is *over*. Few months left only. New century is *baby*." He pointed to Emma. "When is due, baby?"

Emma shook her head. "There's no baby."

"Maybe is born early," Peter said. "First of new century." He raised his bushy brows and made a happy frowning face. "New century is turn for *little* man. Everywhere you look, little man is running everything. So Peter Ivanovich is shrinking. Look, this coat doesn't fit." He tugged at a sleeve and made it flap. "Am writing new book. Already this morning five pages. I talk and Adriana type it down. Very fast. Her fingers like wings on hummingbird. Is little-man book. Peter Ivanovich confesses to everything. Tells all the worst stories. Confess to every lie people say I make." He eyed his daughter. "And some surprises even worst enemy never guesses. Apologies to everybody. This is new way to make person famous." He held up his hand, as if for a karate chop, and waited for silence. His mouth opened wide, and he kept it that way an extra second before saying, "*Contrition.*" He nodded. "Is taking place of courage, wisdom, flattery—everything but money. Now I am on bus. Starting vis own children. Daughter, take from old Russian apology for not being good father."

Zhenya's hands choked the thin neck of a champagne bottle. She shook her head. "I don't accept your apology. I don't particularly need one, but I certainly won't accept one like this."

The old man shook his head. "Was bad father. You are too nice to say—"

"You were a *terrible* father," Zhenya said. "I didn't even know it until I married him." She made a movement of her head to indicate Morgan. "But I'm an adult with no interest in pursuing grudges. I don't blame you for any of this. In fact, I enjoy having you around. However, I will not accept your apology."

"Wait!" Peter Ivanovich yelled, because Zhenya had turned to pour Emma another glass of champagne. "Wait one minute." He glared at Zhenya a moment, then his face softened. "Is true? You don't accept apology from father?"

"You heard me."

Peter Ivanovich patted Adriana East's knee once more, and she covered his hand with her own. He leaned toward her but spoke loudly enough for all to hear. "I write new chapter about crack in father-daughter relationship. Is all book needs. Is perfect." He turned back to Zhenya. "I dedicate whole story to you."

Zhenya sat in the sun beside Morgan in the front row of rented chairs. She had begun thinking again of a girl at fourteen becoming the neighbor's mistress while the mother of the fourteen-year-old knew nothing. She had not paid the right kind of attention. And now that she did know, she needed to forget. How many times would she be taught the same lesson?

She drank from the champagne in her glass. Mrs. East had supplied it—leftovers from her truncated reception for Zhenya's father. Mrs. East—Adriana—had baked the cake, too. She had ordered the flowers, rented the chairs. She had even taken Zhenya's father off their hands. Happily. Zhenya realized she had never given the woman the credit she deserved. Or the gratitude. She recalled then that Mrs. East had gone out to the street on that long-ago day when Philip lost his temper. She had come to the house later and apologized, weeping. She had said, "I saw that Philip needed someone to comfort him, and I failed to offer it. I'm sorry. I can't tell you how sorry I am." Zhenya had barely been able to listen. Her every word had felt like an accusation.

Zhenya drank again from her champagne. What was it now, she wondered. What should she be paying attention to now? How was she supposed to know? The world waited just outside their gate, vicious, voracious, never sated. What future misfortune could be averted if she could only see the world with clarity?

< 3 0 5 >

Morgan shifted in the chair beside her. Someone had fetched a boom box, and music played. She had been so certain that Roy was a good man. He had suffered when Philip died. He was a part of that tragedy. And now he had wedded himself to it. Which meant he understood that it was something he would never get beyond. Instead he embraced it. He dressed it up and called it his love.

Zhenya reached over, found Morgan's hand, and gripped it. She could not forgive Roy Oberland, but she understood that one day she might accept him. It distressed her to realize it, but she knew that much to be true.

She would not let herself evade the truth.

Morgan danced on the deck with his daughter. "Who is this?" he asked.

"I don't know," she said. "It must be my music, but I can't place it."

The four-poster bed limited their movement. Morgan kept his head down to watch his feet. He didn't want to step on her toes, which showed through at the tips of her high-heeled shoes. Were they new? They matched her dress. Morgan hoped they were new. He didn't like the idea of his daughter getting married in old shoes.

They took a turn near the pool. A rawhide bone floated in the water. He had never seen Prince's body. He did not know how Zhenya had disposed of it that rainy night, and he would not ask. She had spared him that knowledge. He was doing the same for her concerning Danny Ford, another resident of the house now gone. Morgan had not told her of Danny's confession. He would never tell her. The knowledge of that travesty would belong to Morgan alone.

Peter Ivanovich had left the house, as well, he thought. And now Emma was moving next door, a married woman, and Petey would go with her. He lost the rhythm of the steps and shuffled his feet to get it back. "It's hard for me to believe that you're married," he said.

"We took pictures," Emma said. "There's hard evidence."

The empty house would be evidence enough, he thought. Prince, Danny, Peter Ivanovich, Emma, and Petey. All of them gone. Only he and Zhenya remained in the big house. It seemed like a waste. Maybe they really should move to a condo. Or take in people. The song ended. Morgan kissed his daughter's cheek. "Thanks for the dance," he said.

"You're a really good dancer, Daddy."

"I don't think so," he said. "I don't know how to lead, and I have trouble keeping up when I follow."

"No," Emma insisted. "You're good. You're Fred Astaire."

Emma's husband stepped in and took her hand as the next song came on. Morgan looked for his wife. She had moved from the chairs to the rail of the bed, where she sat, watching the newlyweds dance. He could not read her face. Morgan and Zhenya, he thought, alone together once again. This would either save their marriage or destroy it.

She had come to his bed this afternoon, and they had made love. Moments ago, while they sat together, she had silently groped for his hand and held it. He knew these small gestures did not really mean anything, and yet he could not help himself. He was optimistic. He sat on the bed rail beside his wife.

"That was sweet," she said. "The dancing. Do you want a drink? I'm getting myself a refill."

"I guess," he said. The bed rail felt solid. Roy's father did good work. Morgan put his elbows on his knees and fit his chin against his fist. Roy knew how to lead and determined the steps, but Emma somehow seemed the point of their traffic, as if he were merely taxiing her. Maybe, Morgan acknowledged, he saw it this way because Emma was his daughter. He realized then that he had not thought, while counting those who abandoned the house, to include his son. What did *that* mean? He pictured Philip in the pool, the halting stroke and wildly thrashing legs. Never was much of a swimmer. Morgan had tried to persuade the boy to take lessons. Philip had not wanted to. He could hack his way from one end of the pool to the other, and he had been content with that. Morgan let himself suffer this specific regret: he had never made his son take swimming lessons.

His wife touched his shoulder, handed him a glass of champagne. He wished he could tell her what he was thinking. But it

< 3 0 7 >

would anger her. Or she would want to be logical about it. Or she wouldn't be willing to sit with him.

"I've had too much to drink," Zhenya said. "And there's nothing else to do but keep drinking." She leaned into him, resting the back of her head against him. "I tried to talk Emma out of this," she said softly.

"Did you?"

She nodded, her head knocking against him. "She didn't say so directly, but Philip is tied up in this."

Their son's name still sounded strange coming from her mouth. Of course, he was tied up in this union. How could anyone possibly think otherwise? Morgan said, "Do you know what I was thinking?" He did not give her time to answer. "This is silly, but I was thinking how I should have forced Philip to take swimming lessons."

Zhenya shifted, but she did not get up, did not walk away.

"It's dumb, I know," he said.

"He had lessons," she said. "That summer. I took him."

"Really?" he said. "I don't remember that."

"He wanted to surprise you. Two mornings a week. The pool in Young Park."

"Well," he said. "I'm glad. I'm glad for that."

"There was never any reason to tell you," she said.

There were a million reasons, he thought, but none of them mattered now. A drop of sweat fell from his nose to the deck. "Thank you," he said, just as Emma and Roy took a turn right in front of them, so close that Roy's jacket brushed Morgan's cheek.

No one but Peter Ivanovich would have asked.

"For good luck," he said. "Most important, must start marriage vis act of diving."

They moved the chairs out of their tidy rows and sat in a scatter. By this time, the jackets had come off and sweat blotched their nice clothes. Liquor made their faces slack.

Everyone had gone home but the ones who mattered—mother, father, grandfather, sister, the neighbors, the child. The bride shed her wedding dress and emerged from the house in her bathing suit.

Her son ran to her and she picked him up, held him on her hip. He whispered something that made her shake her head and kiss his cheek. She handed him off to his father.

Emma climbed the platform. A breeze lifted her hair and touched her shoulders. From this height she could hear the men working on Forest Avenue, and she smelled asphalt and heated oil, scorched rubber and a vaguely sweet odor—like burnt sugar. The men yelled to one another and swore. Their vehicles made scolding cries. But the widening of the street did not change the movement of the sun across the sky, which meant the parallelogram of light shone clearly on the water. She concentrated on that floating, radiant geometry. The window that reflected the light was now her own bedroom window, while on the deck below, all the people she loved waited for her performance. What could she do for them now?

She stopped a few steps shy of the end of the platform, turned around, and began bending over backward, throwing her arms out until they gripped the sides of the platform. She kicked her legs up. She had turned herself on her head. She held the handstand the required seconds and then somersaulted off the ledge.

The people watching her could not resist it. The low hum of their voices started as soon as the splash subsided, those little sounds of astonishment and delight that fail language. The group scooted closer together on the concrete slab, poured themselves new drinks, and watched the bride climb dripping wet from the pool and stride past them to the handmade tower.

Through the remainder of the afternoon and into the evening Emma exhausted herself, leaping time and again into the same water, and those who witnessed it felt changed. The petty resentments lifted. The fatigue of living abated. Even the legitimate, hard-won grief that daily colored their lives vanished. For the moment they were joined together by a shared fascination and an intuition that their lives had meaning and might still one day be redeemed. The wind died and darkness gathered, while they drank and watched and murmured praise, witness to a beauty they could not judge.